Praise for Michael Connelly

'The brilliant Michael Connelly incorporates his favourite themes in this double helix of a plot. A serial killer and a dark political conspiracy are unearthed by the ageing Harry Bosch' *Daily Mirror*

'With *The Fifth Witness* it's beginning to seem that Connelly can do no wrong. This latest novel is as shamelessly entertaining as its predecessors, with the customary skilful plotting even more burnished . . . in the crime fiction stakes Connelly is comfortably in the upper bracket'
Daily Express

'*The Fifth Witness* is the best Haller book so far. It is not only a clever thriller with a brilliant double twist but also a heartfelt examination of the difference between natural justice and the law' *Evening Standard*

'The ensuing Scott Turow-style court drama, starring both of Connelly's favourite characters, is as exciting as anything this formidable writer has ever produced' *Daily Mail*

'Connelly masterfully manages to marry an absorbing courtroom drama with a tense and exciting thriller of detection' *The Times*

'Haller, gunning for the prosecution for the first time, and Bosch, investigating a crime that may have been misread, have their work cut out for them in a tale that skids across Los Angeles's landscape, from canyons to courtroom'
Time Out

'Expect surprises and plenty of dark moments in this punchy legal drama from an ever-reliable writer' *Financial Times*

A former police reporter for the *Los Angeles Times*, Michael Connelly is the author of twenty-five acclaimed and bestselling novels and one non-fiction book. His novels have won an Edgar Award, the Nero Wolfe prize and the Anthony Award. He lives in Florida with his wife and daughter. Visit his website at www.michaelconnelly.co.uk

MICHAEL CONNELLY

The Drop

An Orion paperback

First published in Great Britain in 2011
by Orion
This paperback edition published in 2012
by Orion Books,
an imprint of The Orion Publishing Group Ltd,
Orion House, 5 Upper St Martin's Lane,
London WC2H 9EA

An Hachette UK company

3 5 7 9 10 8 6 4 2

A CIP catalogue record for this book
is available from the British Library.

ISBN 978-1-4091-3630-9

Printed in Great Britain by Clays Ltd, St Ives plc

The Orion Publishing Group's policy is to use papers that
are natural, renewable and recyclable products and
made from wood grown in sustainable forests. The logging
and manufacturing processes are expected to conform to
the environmental regulations of the country of origin.

www.orionbooks.co.uk

This is for Rick, Tim and Jay,
who know what Harry Bosch knows.

The Drop

1

Christmas came once a month in the Open-Unsolved Unit. That was when the lieutenant made her way around the squad room like Santa Claus, parceling out the assignments like presents to the squad's six detective teams. The cold hits were the lifeblood of the unit. The teams didn't wait for callouts and fresh kills in Open-Unsolved. They waited for cold hits.

The Open-Unsolved Unit investigated unsolved murders going back fifty years in Los Angeles. There were twelve detectives, a secretary, a squad room supervisor, known as the whip, and the lieutenant. And there were ten thousand cases. The first five detective teams split up the fifty years, each pair taking ten randomly chosen years. Their task was to pull all the unsolved homicide cases from their assigned years out of archives, evaluate them and submit long-stored and forgotten evidence for reanalysis with contemporary technology. All DNA submissions were handled by the new regional lab out at Cal State. When DNA from an old case was matched to an individual whose genetic profile was carried in any of the nation's DNA databases, it was called a cold hit. The lab put cold hit notices in the mail at the end of every month. They would arrive a day or two later at the Police Administration Building in downtown Los Angeles. Usually by 8 A.M. that day, the

3

lieutenant would open the door of her private office and enter the squad room. She carried the envelopes in her hand. Each hit sheet was mailed individually in a yellow business envelope. Generally, the envelopes were handed to the same detectives who had submitted the DNA evidence to the lab. But sometimes there were too many cold hits for one team to handle at once. Sometimes detectives were in court or on vacation or on leave. And sometimes the cold hits revealed circumstances that required the utmost finesse and experience. That was where the sixth team came in. Detectives Harry Bosch and David Chu were the sixth team. They were floaters. They handled overflow cases and special investigations.

On Monday morning, October 3, Lieutenant Gail Duvall stepped out of her office and into the squad room, carrying only three yellow envelopes. Harry Bosch almost sighed at the sight of such a paltry return on the squad's DNA submissions. He knew that with so few envelopes he would not be getting a new case to work.

Bosch had been back in the unit for almost a year following a two-year reassignment to Homicide Special. But coming back for his second tour of duty in Open-Unsolved, he had quickly fallen into the rhythm of the squad. It wasn't a fly squad. There was no dashing out the door to get to a crime scene. In fact, there were no crime scenes. There were only files and archive boxes. It was primarily an eight-to-four gig with an asterisk, that asterisk meaning that there was more travel than with other detective squads. People who got away with murder, or at least thought they had, tended not to stick around. They moved elsewhere and often the OU detectives had to travel to retrieve them.

A big part of the rhythm was the monthly cycle of waiting for the yellow envelopes to come out. Sometimes Bosch found it hard to sleep during the nights leading up to Christmas. He never took time off during the first week of the month and never came to work late if there was a chance that the yellow envelopes were in. Even his teenage daughter noticed his monthly cycle of antici-pation and agitation, and had likened it to a menstrual cycle. Bosch didn't see the humor in this and was embar-rassed whenever she brought it up.

Now his disappointment at the sight of so few envel-opes in the lieutenant's hand was something palpable in his throat. He wanted a new case. He *needed* a new case. He needed to see the look on the killer's face when he knocked on the door and showed his badge, the embodiment of unexpected justice come calling after so many years. It was addictive and Bosch was craving it now.

The lieutenant handed the first envelope to Rick Jackson. He and his partner, Rich Bengtson, were solid investigators who had been with the unit since its incep-tion. Bosch had no complaint there. The next envelope was placed on an empty desk belonging to Teddy Baker. She and her partner, Greg Kehoe, were on their way back from a pickup in Tampa – an airline pilot who had been connected through fingerprints to the 1991 strangulation of a flight attendant in Marina del Rey.

Bosch was about to suggest to the lieutenant that Baker and Kehoe might have their hands full with the Marina case and that the envelope should be given to another team, namely his, when the lieutenant looked at him and used the last remaining envelope to beckon him to her office.

'Can you guys step in for a minute? You, too, Tim.'

Tim Marcia was the squad whip, the detective three who handled mostly supervisory and fill-in duties in the squad. He mentored the young detectives and made sure the old ones didn't get lazy. With Jackson and Bosch being the only two investigators in that latter classification, Marcia had very little to worry about there. Both Jackson and Bosch were in the unit because they carried a drive to clear cases.

Bosch was up out of his seat before the lieutenant had finished her question. He headed toward the lieutenant's office with Chu and Marcia trailing behind.

'Close the door,' Duvall said. 'Sit down.'

Duvall had a corner office with windows that looked across Spring Street at the Los Angeles Times Building. Paranoid that reporters were watching from the newsroom across the way, Duvall kept her shades permanently lowered. It made the office dim and cavelike. Bosch and Chu took the two seats positioned in front of the lieutenant's desk. Marcia followed them in, moved to the side of Duvall's desk and leaned against an old evidence safe.

'I want you two to handle this hit,' she said, proffering the yellow envelope to Bosch. 'There's something wrong there and I want you to keep quiet about it until you find out what it is. Keep Tim in the loop but keep it low-key.'

The envelope had already been opened. Chu leaned over to look as Harry lifted the flap and pulled out the hit sheet. It listed the case number for which DNA evidence had been submitted, plus the name, age, last known address and criminal history of the person whose genetic profile matched it. Bosch first noticed that the case number had an 89 prefix, meaning it was a case from 1989. There were no details about the crime, just the year. But Bosch knew that 1989 cases belonged to the team of Ross Shuler and Adriana Dolan. He knew this because 1989 had been a busy year for him working murders for the Homicide Special team, and he had recently checked on one of his own unsolved cases and learned that jurisdiction over cases from that year belonged to Shuler and Dolan. They were known in the unit as 'the kids.' They were young, passionate and very skillful investigators, but between them they had fewer than eight years' experience working homicides. If there was something unusual about this cold hit, it was not surprising that the lieutenant wanted Bosch on it. Bosch had worked more killings than everybody in the unit combined. That is, if you took out Jackson. He had been around forever.

Bosch next studied the name on the hit sheet. Clayton S. Pell. It meant nothing to him. But Pell's record included numerous arrests and three separate convictions for indecent exposure, false imprisonment and forcible rape. He had spent six years in prison for the rape before being released eighteen months earlier. He had a four-year parole tail and his last known address came from the state probation and parole board. He was living in a halfway house for sexual offenders in Panorama City.

Based on Pell's record, Bosch believed the 1989 case was likely a sex-related murder. He could feel his insides beginning to tighten. He was going to go out and grab Clayton Pell and bring him to justice.

'Do you see it?' Duvall asked.

'See what?' Bosch asked. 'Was this a sex killing? This guy has the classic pred—'

'The birth date,' Duvall said.

Bosch looked back down at the hit sheet as Chu leaned over farther.

'Yeah, right here,' Bosch said. 'November nine, nineteen eighty-one. What's that got—'

'He's too young,' Chu said.

Bosch glanced at him and then back at the sheet. He suddenly got it. Clayton Pell was born in 1981. He was only eight years old at the time of the murder on the hit sheet.

'Exactly,' Duvall said. 'So I want you to get the book and box from Shuler and Dolan and very quietly figure out what we have here. I'm hoping to God they didn't get two cases mixed up.'

Bosch knew that if Shuler and Dolan had somehow sent in genetic material from the old case labeled under a more recent case, then both cases would be tainted beyond any hope of eventual prosecution.

'Like you were about to say,' Duvall continued, 'this guy on the hit sheet is no doubt a predator, but I don't think he got away with a killing when he was only eight years old. So something doesn't fit. Find it and come back to me before you do anything. If they screwed up and we can correct it, then we won't need to worry about IAD or anybody else. We'll just keep it right here.'

She may have appeared to be trying to protect Shuler and Dolan from Internal Affairs, but she was also

8

protecting herself, and Bosch knew it. There would not be much vertical movement in the department for a lieutenant who had presided over an evidence-handling scandal in her own unit.

'What other years are assigned to Shuler and Dolan?' Bosch asked.

'On the recent side, they've got 'ninety-seven and two thousand,' Marcia said. 'This could have come from a case they were working from one of those two years.'

Bosch nodded. He could see the scenario. The reckless handling of genetic evidence from one case cross-pollinates with another. The end result would be two tainted cases and scandal that would taint anybody near it.

'What do we say to Shuler and Dolan?' Chu asked. 'What's the reason we're taking the case off them?'

Duvall looked up at Marcia for an answer.

'They've got a trial coming up,' he offered. 'Jury selection starts Thursday.'

Duvall nodded.

'I'll tell them I want them clear for that.'

'And what if they say they still want the case?' Chu asked. 'What if they say they can handle it?'

'I'll put them straight,' Duvall said. 'Anything else, Detectives?'

Bosch looked up at her.

'We'll work the case, Lieutenant, and see what's what. But I don't investigate other cops.'

'That's fine. I'm not asking you to. Work the case and tell me how the DNA came back to an eight-year-old kid, okay?'

9

Bosch nodded and started to stand up.

'Just remember,' Duvall added, 'you talk to me before you do anything with what you learn.'

'You got it,' Bosch said.

They were about to leave the room.

'Harry,' the lieutenant said. 'Hang back a second.'

Bosch looked at Chu and raised his eyebrows. He didn't know what this was about. The lieutenant came around from behind her desk and closed the door after Chu and Marcia had left. She stayed standing and businesslike.

'I just wanted you to know that your application for an extension on your DROP came through. They gave you four years retroactive.'

Bosch looked at her, doing the math. He nodded. He had asked for the maximum – five years nonretroactive – but he'd take what they gave. It wouldn't keep him much past high school but it was better than nothing.

'Well, I'm glad,' Duvall said. 'It gives you thirty-nine more months with us.'

Her tone indicated that she had read disappointment in his face.

'No,' he said quickly. 'I'm glad. I was just thinking about where that would put me with my daughter. It's good. I'm happy.'

'Good, then.'

That was her way of saying the meeting was over. Bosch thanked her and left the office. As he stepped back into the squad room, he looked across the vast expanse of desks and dividers and file cabinets. He knew it was home and that he would get to stay – for now.

2

The Open-Unsolved Unit shared access to the two fifth-floor conference rooms with all other units in the Robbery-Homicide Division. Usually detectives had to reserve time in one of the rooms, signing on the clipboard hooked on the door. But this early on a Monday, they both were open and Bosch, Chu, Shuler and Dolan commandeered the smaller of the two rooms without making a reservation.

They brought with them the murder book and the small archival evidence box from the 1989 case.

'Okay,' Bosch said when everyone was seated. 'So you are cool with us running with this case? If you're not, we can go back to the lieutenant and say you really want to work it.'

'No, it's okay,' Shuler said. 'We both are involved in the trial, so it's better this way. It's our first case in the unit and we want to see it through to that guilty verdict.'

Bosch nodded as he casually opened the murder book.

'You want to give us the rundown on this one, then?'

Shuler gave Dolan a nod and she began to summarize the 1989 case as Bosch flipped through the pages of the binder.

'We have a nineteen-year-old victim named Lily Price. She was snatched off the street while walking home from the beach in Venice on a Sunday afternoon. At the time, they narrowed the grab point down to the vicinity of Speedway and Voyage. Price lived on Voyage with three roommates. One was with her on the beach and two were in the apartment. She disappeared between those two points. She said she was going back to use the bathroom and she never made it.'

'She left her towel and a Walkman on the beach,' Shuler said. 'Sunscreen. So it was clear she was intending to come back. She never did.'

'Her body was found the next morning on the rocks down at the cut,' Dolan said. 'She was naked and had been raped and strangled. Her clothes were never found. The ligature was removed.'

Bosch flipped through several plastic pages containing faded Polaroid shots of the crime scene. Looking at the victim, he couldn't help but think of his own daughter, who at fifteen had a full life in front of her. There had been a time when looking at photos like this fueled him, gave him the fire he needed to be relentless. But since Maddie had come to live with him, it was increasingly more difficult for him to look at victims.

It didn't stop him from building the fire, however.

'Where did the DNA come from?' he asked. 'Semen?'

'No, the killer used a condom or didn't ejaculate,' Dolan said. 'No semen.'

'It came from a small smear of blood,' Shuler said. 'It was found on her neck, right below the right ear. She had no wounds in that area. It was assumed that it had come from the killer, that he had been cut in the struggle or maybe was already bleeding. It was just a drop. A smear, really. She was strangled with a ligature. If she was strangled from behind, then his hand could have been against her neck there. If there was a cut on his hand ...'

'Transfer deposit,' Chu said.

'Exactly.'

Bosch found the Polaroid that showed the victim's neck and the smear of blood. The photo was washed out by time and he could barely see the blood. A ruler had been placed on the young woman's neck so that the blood smear could be measured in the photo. It was less than an inch long.

'So this blood was collected and stored,' he said, a statement meant to draw further explanation.

'Yes,' Shuler said. 'Because it was a smear it was swabbed. Back then, they typed it. O positive. The swab was stored in a tube and we found it still in Property when we pulled the case. The blood had turned to powder.'

He tapped the top of the archive box with a pen.

Bosch's phone started to vibrate in his pocket. Normally, he would let the call go to message, but his daughter was home sick from school and alone. He needed to make sure she wasn't calling. He pulled the phone out of his pocket and glanced at the screen. It wasn't his daughter. It was a former partner, Kizmin Rider, now a lieutenant assigned to the OCP – Office of the Chief of Police. He decided he would return her call after the meeting. They had lunch together about once a month and he assumed she was free today, or calling because she'd heard about him getting approved for another four years on the DROP. He shoved the phone back into his pocket.

'Did you open the tube?' he asked.

'Of course not,' Shuler said.

'Okay, so four months ago you sent the tube containing the swab and what was left of the blood out to the regional lab, right?' he asked.

'That's right,' Shuler said.

Bosch flipped through the murder book to the autopsy report. He was acting like he was more interested in what he was seeing than what he was saying.

'And at that time, did you submit anything else to the lab?'

'From the Price case?' Dolan asked. 'No, that was the only biological evidence they came up with back at the time.'

Bosch nodded, hoping she would keep talking.

'But back then it didn't lead to anything,' she said. 'They never came up with a suspect. Who'd they come up with on the cold hit?'

'We'll get to that in a second,' Bosch said. 'What I meant was, did you submit to the lab from any other cases you were working? Or was this all you had going?'

'No, that was it,' Shuler said, his eyes squinting in suspicion. 'What's going on here, Harry?'

Bosch reached into his inside coat pocket and pulled out the hit sheet. He slid it across the table to Shuler.

'The hit comes back to a sexual predator who would look real good for this except for one thing.'

Shuler unfolded the sheet and he and Dolan leaned together to read it, just as Bosch and Chu had earlier.

'What's that?' Dolan said, not picking up on the significance of the birth date yet. 'This guy looks perfect.'

'He's perfect now,' Bosch said. 'But back then he was only eight years old.'

'You're kidding,' Dolan said.

'What the fuck?' Shuler added.

Dolan pulled the sheet away from her partner as if to see it clearer and to double-check the birth date. Shuler leaned back and looked at Bosch with those suspicious eyes.

'So you think we fucked up and mixed up cases,' he said.

'Nope,' Bosch said. 'The lieutenant asked us to check out the possibility but I don't see any fuckup on this end.'

'So it happened at the lab,' Shuler said. 'Do you realize that if they screwed things up at regional, every defense lawyer in the county is going to be able to raise doubt about DNA matches that come out of there?'

'Yeah, I kind of figured that,' Bosch said. 'Which is why you should keep this under your hats until we know what happened. There are other possibilities.'

Dolan held up the hit sheet.

'Yeah, what if there is no fuckup anywhere in the line? What if it's really this kid's blood on that dead girl?'

'An eight-year-old boy snatches a nineteen-year-old girl off the street, rapes and strangles her and dumps the body four blocks away?' Chu asked. 'Never happened.'

'Well, maybe he was there,' Dolan said. 'Maybe this was how he got his start as a predator. You see his record. This guy fits – except for his age.'

Bosch nodded.

'Maybe,' he said. 'Like I said, there are other possibilities. No reason to panic yet.'

His phone started to vibrate again. He pulled it and

saw it was Kiz Rider again. Two calls in five minutes, he decided he'd better take it. This wasn't about lunch.

'I have to step out for a second.'

He got up and answered the call as he stepped out of the conference room into the hallway.

'Kiz?'

'Harry, I've been trying to get to you with a heads-up.'

'I'm in a meeting. What heads-up?'

'You are about to get a forthwith from the OCP.'

'You want me to come up to ten?'

In the new PAB, the chief's suite of offices was on the tenth floor, complete with a private courtyard balcony that looked out across the civic center.

'No, Sunset Strip. You're going to be told to go to a scene and take over a case. And you're not going to like it.'

'Look, Lieutenant, I just got a case this morning. I don't need another one.'

He thought that using her formal title would communicate his wariness. Forthwiths and assignments out of the OCP always carried high jingo – political overtones. It was sometimes hard to navigate your way through it.

'He's not going to give you a choice here, Harry.'

'He' being the chief of police.

'What's the case?'

'A jumper at the Chateau Marmont.'

'Who was it?'

'Harry, I think you should wait for the chief to call you. I just wanted to—'

'Who was it, Kiz? If you know anything about me,

I think you know I can keep a secret until it's no longer a secret.'

She paused before answering.

'From what I understand, there is not a lot that is recognizable – he came down seven floors onto concrete. But the initial ID is George Thomas Irving. Age forty-six of eight—'

'Irving as in Irvin Irving? As in Councilman Irvin Irving?'

'Scourge of the LAPD in general and one Detective Harry Bosch in particular. Yes, one and the same. It's his son, and Councilman Irving has insisted to the chief that you take over the investigation. The chief said no problem.'

Bosch paused with his mouth open for a moment before responding.

'Why does Irving want me? He's spent most of his careers in police and politics trying to end mine.'

'This I don't know, Harry. I only know that he wants you.'

'When did this come in?'

'The call came in at about five forty-five this morning. My understanding is that it is unclear when it actually happened.'

Bosch checked his watch. The case was more than three hours old. That was quite late to be coming into a death investigation. He'd be starting out at a disadvantage.

'What's to investigate?' he asked. 'You said it was a jumper.'

'Hollywood originally responded and they were going to wrap it up as a suicide. The councilman arrived and is not ready to sign off on that. That's why he wants you.'

'And does the chief understand that I have a history with Irving that—'

'Yes, he does. He also understands that he needs every vote he can get on the council if we ever want to get overtime flowing to the department again.'

Bosch saw his boss, Lieutenant Duvall, enter the hallway from the Open-Unsolved Unit's door. She made a *There you are!* gesture and started toward him.

'Looks like I'm about to get the official word,' Bosch said into the phone. 'Thanks for the heads-up, Kiz. Doesn't make any sense to me, but thanks. If you hear anything else, let me know.'

'Harry, you be careful with this. Irving's old but he's still got teeth.'

'I know that.'

Bosch closed his phone just as Duvall got to him, holding out a piece of paper.

'Sorry, Harry, change of plans. You and Chu need to go to this address and take a live case.'

'What are you talking about?'

Bosch looked at the address. It was the Chateau Marmont.

'Orders from the chief's office. You and Chu are to proceed code three and take over a case. That's all I know. That and that the chief himself is there, waiting.'

'What about the case you just gave us?'

'Move it to the back burner for now. I want you on it, but just get to it when you can.'

She pointed to the piece of paper in his hand.

'That's the priority.'

'You sure about this, Lieutenant?'

'Of course I'm sure. The chief called me directly and he's going to call you. So grab Chu and get going.'

3

As expected, Chu was full of questions while they were driving out of downtown on the 101 freeway. They had been partnered for nearly two years and by now Bosch was more than used to the manifestation of Chu's insecurities in a nonstop verbal outpouring of questions, comments and observations. He usually spoke about one thing while his real concern was something else. Sometimes Bosch took it easy on him and told him what he wanted to know. Sometimes he let things play out till they became excruciating to his young partner.

'Harry, what the hell is going on? We got one case this morning and now they say we have another?'

'The LAPD is a paramilitary organization, Chu. That means when someone of higher rank tells you to do something, you do it. The order came down from the chief and we're following it. That's what's going on. We'll eventually get back to the cold hit. But for now we have a live one and it's the priority.'

'Sounds like bullshit politics.'

'High jingo.'

'What's that?'

'The confluence of police and politics. We are investigating the death of Councilman Irvin Irving's son. You know about Irving, right?'

'Yeah, he was a deputy chief when I came on. Then he quit and ran for the council.'

'Well, he didn't voluntarily quit. He was forced out and ran for the council so he could seek his revenge on the department. Pure and simple, he lives for one thing – putting the boot to the LAPD. You should also know that back in the day, he had a particular dislike for me. We had a few collisions, you could say.'

'Then why would he want you on his son's case?'

'We'll be finding that out pretty soon.'

'What did the lieutenant tell you about this case? Is it suicide?'

'She didn't tell me anything. She just gave me the address.'

He decided not to reveal anything else he knew about the case. To do so might also reveal that he had a source inside the OCP. He didn't want to share that with Chu yet and had always kept his monthly lunches with Kiz Rider private.

'This all sounds a little spooky.'

Bosch's phone buzzed and he checked the screen. The ID was blocked but he took the call. It was the chief of police. Bosch had known him for years and had even worked cases with him. He had come up through the ranks, including a long stint in RHD as both an investigator and supervisor. He had been chief for only a couple years and still had the support of the rank and file.

'Harry, it's Marty. What's your location?'

'We're on the one-oh-one. We left as soon as I got the word.'

'I need to clear before the media gets wind of this,

which won't be long now. No need to turn this from a one-ring to a three-ring circus. As you no doubt have been told, the victim is the son of Councilman Irving. The councilman insisted that I bring you into this.'

'Why?'

'He hasn't really expressed his reasons to me. I know you two have a history.'

'But not a good one. What can you tell me about the case?'

'Not a lot.'

He gave Bosch the same summary as Rider had with few additional details.

'Who's there from Hollywood?'

'Glanville and Solomon.'

Bosch was familiar with them from prior cases and task forces. Both investigators were known for their wide bodies and tall egos. They were called Crate and Barrel and enjoyed it. They were flashy dressers with big pinkie rings. And as far as Bosch knew, they were competent detectives. If they were about to wrap the investigation as a suicide, then they most likely had it right.

'They will continue under your direction,' the chief said. 'I told them personally.'

'Okay, Chief.'

'Harry, I need your best work on this. I don't care about your history. Put it aside. We can't have the councilman go off and say we laid down on this.'

'Understood.'

Bosch was silent for a moment as he thought about what else to ask.

'Chief, where is the councilman?'

'We've got him down in the lobby.'

'Did he go into the room?'

'He insisted. I let him look around without touching anything and then we walked him out.'

'You shouldn't have done that, Marty.'

Bosch knew he was taking a risk telling the chief of police he had done something wrong. It didn't matter that they used to roll bodies over together.

'I guess you had no choice,' Bosch added.

'Just get here as soon as you can and keep me apprised. If you can't get directly to me, use Lieutenant Rider as a go-between.'

But he didn't offer his cell phone's blocked number, so the message was clear to Bosch. He would no longer be talking directly with his old pal the chief. What wasn't clear was what the chief was telling Bosch to do about the investigation.

'Chief,' he said, going formal to make sure it was clear he wasn't calling on old loyalties. 'If I get up there and it's a suicide, I'm going to call it a suicide. If you want something else, get somebody else.'

'It's okay, Harry. Just let the chips fall. It is what it is.'

'You sure about that? Is that what Irving wants?'

'It's what I want.'

'Got it.'

'By the way, did Duvall give you the news about the DROP?'

'Yeah, she told me.'

'I pushed for the whole five but you got a couple of people on the commission who didn't like everything in your file. We got what we could, Harry.'

'I appreciate that.'

'Good.'

The chief closed the connection. Bosch barely had time to close his phone before Chu was on him with questions about what had been said. Harry relayed the conversation as he pulled off the freeway onto Sunset Boulevard and headed west.

Chu parlayed the report on the chief's call into a question about what really had been bothering him all morning.

'What about the lieutenant?' he said. 'Are you ever going to tell me what that was about?'

Bosch played dumb.

'What what was about?'

'Don't play dumb, Harry. When she held you back in the office, what was she saying? She wants me out of the unit, doesn't she? I never liked her either.'

Bosch couldn't help himself. His partner's glass was always half empty and an opportunity to needle him about it was not to be missed.

'She said she wanted to move you laterally – keep you in homicide. She said there were some slots coming up in South Bureau and she's talking to them about a switch.'

'Jesus Christ!'

Chu had recently moved out to Pasadena. The commute to South Bureau would be a nightmare.

'Well, what did you tell her?' he demanded. 'Did you stick up for me?'

'South is a good gig, man. I told her you'd get seasoned down there in two years. It would take five anywhere else.'

'Harry!'

Bosch started laughing. It was a good release. The impending meeting with Irving was weighing on him. It was coming and he wasn't sure yet how to play it.

'Are you shitting me?' Chu cried, fully turned in his seat now. 'Are you fucking shitting me?'

'Yes, I'm fucking shitting you, Chu. So chill out. All she told me was that my DROP came through. You're going to have to put up with me for another three years and three months, okay?'

'Oh . . . well, that's good, right?'

'Yes, that's good.'

Chu was too young to worry about things like the DROP. Almost ten years before, Bosch had taken a full pension and retired from the department in an ill-advised decision. After two years as a citizen he came back under the department's Deferred Retirement Option Plan, which was designed to keep experienced detectives in the department and doing the work they did best. For Bosch that was homicide. He was a retread with a seven-year contract. Not everybody in the department was happy with the program, especially divisional detectives hoping for a shot at some of the prestige slots in the downtown Robbery-Homicide Division.

Department policy allowed for one extension of the DROP of three to five years. After that, retirement was mandated. Bosch had applied for his second contract the year before and, bureaucracy being what it was in the department, waited more than a year for the news the lieutenant gave him, going well past his original DROP date. He had been anxious while waiting, knowing that he could be dismissed from the department immediately if the police commission decided not to extend his stay. It was certainly good news to finally get but he now saw a defined limit on his time carrying a badge. So the good news was tinged with a certain melancholy. When he got the formal notification from the commission, it would have an exact date on it that would be his last day as a cop. He couldn't help but focus on that. His future had limitations. Maybe he was a half-empty kind of guy himself.

Chu gave him a break on the questions after that and Harry tried to avoid thinking about the DROP. Instead he thought about Irvin Irving as he drove west. The councilman had spent more than forty years in the police department but had never gotten to the top floor. After a career spent grooming and positioning himself for the chief's job, it had been snatched from him in a political windstorm. A few years after that, he was engineered out of the department – with Bosch's help. A man scorned, he ran for the city council, won the election, and made it his business to exact retribution on the department where he had toiled for so many decades. He had gone so far as to vote against every proposed raise in salaries for police officers and expansion of the department. He was always first to call for an independent review or investigation of any perceived impropriety or alleged transgression committed by officers. His sharpest poke, however, had come the year before when he had whole-heartedly joined the cost-cutting charge that slashed a hundred million in overtime out of the department budget. That hurt every officer up and down the ladder.

Bosch had no doubt that the current chief of police had made some sort of deal with Irving. A quid pro quo. Bosch would be delivered to take over the case in exchange for something else. While Harry had never considered himself very politically astute, he was confident he would figure things out soon enough.

4

The Chateau Marmont sat at the east end of the Sunset Strip, an iconic structure set against the Hollywood Hills that had enticed movie stars, writers, rock and rollers and their entourages for decades. Several times during his career Bosch had been to the hotel as he had followed cases and sought witnesses and suspects. He knew its beamed lobby and hedged courtyard and the layout of its spacious suites. Other hotels offered amazing levels of comfort and personal service. The Chateau offered Old World charm and a lack of interest in your personal business. Most hotels had security cameras, hidden or not, in all public spaces. The Chateau had few. The one thing the Chateau offered that no other hotel on the strip could touch was privacy. Behind its walls and tall hedges was a world without intrusion, where those who didn't want to be watched were not. That is, until things went wrong, or private behavior became public.

Just past Laurel Canyon Boulevard the hotel rose behind the profusion of billboards that lined Sunset. By night the hotel was marked with a simple neon-lit sign, modest by Sunset Strip standards, and even more so by day, when the light was off. The hotel was technically located on Marmont Lane, which split off from Sunset and wound around the hotel and up into the hills. As they approached, Bosch saw that Marmont Lane was

28

blocked by temporary barricades. Two patrol cars and two media trucks were parked along the hedge line at the front of the hotel. This told him that the death scene was on the west side or rear of the hotel. He pulled in behind one of the black-and-whites.

'The vultures are already here,' Chu said, nodding toward the media vans.

It was impossible to keep a secret in this town, especially a secret like this. A neighbor would call, a hotel guest or a patrol officer, maybe somebody down at the coroner's office trying to impress a blond TV reporter. News traveled fast.

They got out of the car and approached the barricades. Bosch signaled one of the uniformed officers away from the two camera crews so they could speak without the media hearing.

'Where is it?' Bosch asked.

The cop looked like he had at least ten years on the job. His shirt plate said RAMPONE.

'We have two scenes,' he said. 'We've got the splat around back here on the side. And then the room the guy was using. That's the top floor, room seventy-nine.'

It was the routine way of police officers to dehumanize the daily horrors that came with the job. Jumpers were called splats.

Bosch had left his rover in the car. He nodded to the mike on Rampone's shoulder.

'Find out where Glanville and Solomon are.'

Rampone cocked his head toward his shoulder and pressed the transmit button. He quickly located the initial investigative team in room seventy-nine.

'Okay, tell them to stay put. We're going to check out the lower scene and then head up.'

Bosch went back to his car to grab the rover out of the charging dock and then walked with Chu around the barricade and up the sidewalk.

'Harry, you want me to go up and talk to those guys?' Chu asked.

'No, it always starts with the body and goes from there. Always.'

Chu was used to working cold cases, where there was never a crime scene. Only reports. Also, he had issues with seeing dead bodies. It was the reason he'd opted for the cold case squad. No fresh kills, no murder scenes, no autopsies. This time things would be different.

Marmont Lane was a steep and narrow road. They came to the death scene at the northwestern corner of the hotel. The forensics team had put up a canopy over the scene to guard against visual intrusion from media choppers and the houses that terraced the hills behind the hotel.

Before stepping under the canopy, Bosch looked up the side of the hotel. He saw a man in a suit leaning over the parapet, looking down from a balcony on the top floor. He guessed it was Glanville or Solomon.

Bosch went under the canopy and found a bustle of activities involving forensic techs, coroner's investigators and police photographers. At the center of it all was Gabriel Van Atta, whom Bosch had known for years. Van Atta had spent twenty-five years working for the LAPD as a crime scene tech and supervisor before retiring and taking a job with the coroner. Now he got a salary and a pension and still worked crime scenes. That counted as a break for Bosch. He knew that Van Atta wouldn't be cagey about anything. He would tell Harry exactly what he thought.

Bosch and Chu stood under the canopy but stayed on the periphery. The scene belonged to the techs at the moment. Bosch could tell that the body had been turned over from the impact point and that they were far along. The body would soon be removed and transported to the medical examiner's office. This bothered him but it was the cost of coming into a case so late.

The gruesome extent of the injuries from seven floors of gravity was on full display. Bosch could almost feel his partner's revulsion at the sight. Harry decided to give him a break.

'Tell you what, I'll handle this and meet you upstairs.'

'Really?'

'Really. But you're not getting out of the autopsy.'

'That's a deal, Harry.'

The conversation had drawn Van Atta's attention.

'Harry B.,' he said. 'I thought you were still working cold cases.'

'This one's a special, Gabe. All right if I step in?'

Meaning the inner circle of the death scene. Van Atta waved him in. As Chu ducked out from under the canopy, Bosch grabbed a pair of paper booties from a dispenser and put them on over his shoes. He then put on rubber gloves and worked his way as best he could around the coagulated blood on the sidewalk and squatted down next to what was left of George Thomas Irving.

Death takes everything, including one's dignity. George's naked and battered body was surrounded on all sides by technicians who viewed it as a piece of work.

His earthly vessel had been reduced to a ripped bag of skin containing shattered bones and organs and blood vessels. His body had bled out through every natural orifice and many new ones created by his impact on the sidewalk. His skull was shattered, leaving his head and face grossly misshapen like it would be in a fun house mirror. His left eye had broken free of its orbit and hung loosely on his cheek. His chest had been crushed by the impact and several sheared bones from the ribs and clavicle protruded through the skin.

Unblinking, Bosch studied the body carefully, looking for the unusual on a canvas that was anything but usual. He searched the inside of the arms for needle tracks, the fingernails for foreign debris.

'I got here late,' he said. 'Anything I should know?'

'I'm thinking the guy hit face-first which is very unusual, even for a suicide,' Van Atta said. 'And I want to draw your attention to something here.'

He pointed to the victim's right arm and then the left, which were spread in the blood puddle.

'Every bone in both arms is broken, Harry. Shattered, actually. But we have no compound injuries, no breaking of the skin.'

'Which tells us what?'

'It means one of two extremes. One, he was really serious about taking a high dive and didn't even put his hands out to break the fall. If he had, we would've had shearing and compound fractures. We don't.'

'And the other extreme?'

'That the reason he didn't put his arms out to break the fall was that he wasn't conscious when he hit the ground.'

'Meaning he was thrown.'

'Yeah, or more likely dropped. We'll have to do some distance modeling but this looks like he came straight down. If he was pushed or thrown, as you say, I think he would have been a couple feet farther out from the structure.'

'Got it. What about time of death?'

'We took the liver temperature and did the math. This isn't official, as you know, but we think between four and five.'

'So he was here on the sidewalk for an hour or more before somebody saw him.'

'It could happen. We'll try to narrow the TOD at autopsy. Can we get him rolling now?'

'If that's all the wisdom you have for me today, yes, you can get him out of here.'

A few minutes later Bosch headed up the entrance drive to the hotel's garage. A black Lincoln Town Car with city plates was idling on the cobblestones. Councilman Irving's car. As he walked past, Bosch saw a young driver behind the wheel and an older man in a suit in the front passenger seat. The back seat appeared to be empty but it was hard to determine through the smoked glass.

Bosch took the stairs up to the next level, where the front desk and lobby were located.

Most people who stayed at the Chateau were night creatures. The lobby was deserted except for Irvin Irving, who was sitting by himself on a couch with a cell phone pressed to his ear. When he saw Bosch coming, he quickly ended the call and pointed toward a couch directly opposite his. Harry had hoped to stay standing and to keep momentum but it was one of those times when he took direction. As he sat down he pulled a notebook out of his back pocket.

'Detective Bosch,' Irving said. 'Thank you for coming.'

'I didn't have the choice, Councilman.'

'I guess not.'

'First, I'd like to express my sympathy for the loss of your son. Second, I'd like to know why you want me here.'

Irving nodded and glanced out one of the lobby's tall windows. There was an outdoor restaurant beneath palm trees and umbrellas and space heaters. It was empty, too, except for the wait staff.

'I guess nobody gets up around here till noon,' he said.

Bosch didn't reply. He waited for the answer to his question. Irving's signature physical trait had always been the shaved and polished scalp. He had the look going long before it was fashionable. In the department, he had been known as Mr Clean because he had the look and he was the guy brought in to clean up the political and social messes that routinely arose in a heavily armed and political bureaucracy.

But now Irving's look was shopworn. His skin was gray and loose and he looked older than he actually was.

'I always heard that losing a child was the most difficult pain,' Irving said. 'Now I know it's true. It doesn't matter what age or what circumstances ... it's just not supposed to happen. It's not the natural order of things.'

There was nothing Bosch could say to that. He had sat with enough parents of dead children to know there was no debating what the councilman had said. Irving had his head down, eyes on the ornate pattern of the rug in front of him.

'I've worked for this city in one capacity or another for over fifty years,' he continued. 'And here I am and I can't trust a soul in it. So I reach out to a man I've tried to destroy in the past. Why? I'm not even sure myself. I suppose it's because there was an integrity to our skirmishes. An integrity to you. I didn't like you or your methods but I respected you.'

He looked up at Bosch now.

'I want you to tell me what happened to my son, Detective Bosch. I want the truth and I think I can trust you to give it to me.'

'No matter how it falls?'

'No matter how it falls.'

Bosch nodded.

'I can do that.'

He started to get up but paused when Irving continued.

'You said once that everybody counts or nobody counts. I remember that. This would put that to the test. Does the son of your enemy count? Will you give your best effort for him? Will you be relentless for him?'

Bosch just stared at him. *Everybody counts or nobody counts.* It was his code as a man. But it was never spoken. It was only followed. He was sure he had never said it to Irving.

'When?'

'Excuse me?'

'When did I say that?'

Realizing he may have misspoken, Irving shrugged and adopted the pose of a confused old man even though his eyes were as sharp as black marbles in snow.

'I don't remember, actually. It's just something I know about you.'

Bosch stood up.

'I'll find out what happened to your son. Is there anything you can tell me about what he was doing here?'

'No, nothing.'

'How did you find out this morning?'

'I was called by the chief of police. Personally. I came right away. But they wouldn't let me see him.'

'They were right. Did he have a family? I mean besides you.'

'A wife and son – the boy just went away to college. I was just on the phone with Deborah. I told her the news.'

'If you call her back, tell her I'll be coming to see her.'

'Of course.'

'What did your son do for a living?'

'He was a lawyer specializing in corporate relations.'

Bosch waited for more but that was all that was offered.

'"Corporate relations"? What does that mean?'

'It means he got things done. People came to him when they wanted things done in this city. He had worked for the city. First as a cop, then for the City Attorney.'

'And he had an office?'

'He had a small place downtown, but mostly he had a cell phone. That was how he worked.'

'What did he call his company?'

'It was a law firm. Irving and Associates – only there weren't any associates. Just a one-man shop.'

Bosch knew he would have to come back to this. But it wasn't useful to spar with Irving when he had so little basic knowledge through which to filter the councilman's answers. He would wait until he knew more.

'I'll be in touch,' he said.

Irving raised his hand and flipped two fingers out with a business card between them.

'This is my private cell number. I'll expect to hear something from you by the end of the day.'

Or you'll take another ten million out of the overtime budget? Bosch didn't like this. But he took the card and headed to the elevators.

On the way up to seven he thought about the stilted conversation with Irving. What bothered him most was that Irving knew his code, and Harry had a pretty good idea how he had come by the information. It was something he would have to deal with later.

5

The upper floors of the hotel followed an L pattern. Bosch got off the elevator on seven and took a left to go around a corner and down to room 79 at the end of the hallway. There was a uniformed officer on the door. It made Bosch think of something and he pulled his phone. He called Kiz Rider's cell and she answered right away.

'Did you know what he did for a living?' he asked.

'Who are you talking about, Harry?' she responded.

'Who else, George Irving. Did you know he was some sort of fixer?'

'I heard that he was a lobbyist.'

'A lawyer lobbyist. Listen, I need you to flex the muscles of the chief's office and put a cop on his office door until I can get there. Nobody in or out.'

'Not a problem. Is what he did as a lobbyist in play here?'

'You never know. I'd just feel better if there was somebody on the door.'

'You got it, Harry.'

'I'll talk to you later.'

Bosch put his phone away and approached the cop posted in front of room 79. He signed his clipboard, noting the time, and went in. He stepped into a living room with open French doors that led to the balcony and a western exposure. The wind was billowing the curtains and Bosch saw Chu out there on the balcony. He was looking down.

Standing in the room were Solomon and Glanville. Crate and Barrel. They didn't look happy. When Jerry Solomon saw Bosch, he stretched his hands out in a *what gives?* gesture. Actually, Bosch realized, it was more of a *what the fuck?* gesture.

'What can I tell you?' Bosch said. 'High jingo. We do what we're told.'

'You aren't going to find anything here we didn't find. We have it right, the guy took the dive.'

'And that's what I told the chief and the councilman, but here I am.'

Now Bosch spread his hands in a *what can I do?* gesture.

'So you want to stand around complaining about it or you want to tell me what you've got?'

Solomon nodded to Glanville, the junior of the two partners, and he pulled a notebook out of his back pocket. He flipped through a few pages and then started telling the story. Meantime, Chu came in from the balcony to listen as well.

'Last night at eight fifty the front desk gets a call from a man identifying himself as George Irving. He reserves a room for the night and says he's on the way. He specifically asks what rooms with balconies they've got on the top floor. They give him a choice and he takes seventy-nine. He gives an American Express number to hold the room and it checks out to the card in his wallet, which is in the bedroom in the safe.'

Glanville pointed down a hallway to Bosch's left. Harry saw an open doorway at the end and a bed.

'Okay, so he shows up at nine forty,' Glanville continued. 'He valets his car in the garage, uses the AmEx to register and then goes up to his room. Nobody ever sees him again.'

'Until they find him on the sidewalk down below,' Solomon said.

'When?' Bosch asked.

'At five fifty one of the kitchen guys reports for work. He's heading up the sidewalk to get to the rear entrance where the time-card rack is located. He finds the body. Patrol comes out first, then we get called when they make a tentative ID.'

Bosch nodded and looked around the room. There was a writing table next to the balcony door.

'No note?'

'Not that we've found in here.'

Bosch noticed a digital clock on the floor. It was plugged into a wall outlet near the desk.

'Is that how that was found? Is it supposed to be on the desk?'

'It's where we found it,' Solomon said. 'We don't know where it is supposed to be.'

Bosch walked over and squatted down next to the clock while he put on a fresh set of gloves. He carefully picked up the clock and studied it. It had a dock for connecting an iPod or an iPhone.

'Do we know what kind of phone Irving had?'

'Yeah, iPhone,' Glanville said. 'It's in the safe in the bedroom.'

Bosch checked the alarm on the clock. It was switched off. He pushed the set button to see what time it had previously been set for. The red digits shifted. The last time the alarm was used it was set for 4 A.M.

Bosch put the clock back on the floor and stood up, his knee joints popping with the effort. He left the main room behind and stepped through the French doors onto the balcony. There was a small table and two chairs. A white terry cloth robe had been left lying across one of the chairs. Bosch looked down over the edge. The first thing he noticed was that the balustrade came up only to the top of his thighs. It seemed low to him, and while he had no idea how tall Irving had been, he immediately had to consider the possibility of an accidental fall. He wondered whether that was what he was here for. Nobody wants a suicide on the family ledger. An accidental tumble over a low balustrade was far more acceptable.

He looked directly down and saw the canopy the forensic team had put up. He also saw the body, on a gurney and covered in a blue blanket, being loaded into the coroner's van.

'I know what you're thinking,' Solomon said from behind him.

'Yeah, what am I thinking?'

'That he didn't jump. That it was an accident.'

Bosch didn't respond.

'But there are things to consider.'

'What are they?'

'The guy's naked. The bed isn't slept in and he didn't check in with any luggage. He just checked into a hotel room in his own city without a suitcase. He asked for the top floor and a room with a balcony. He then goes up to his room, takes off his clothes, puts on the bathrobe they give you in a place like this and goes out on the balcony to contemplate the stars or something. He then takes off the bathrobe and falls face-fucking-first off the balcony by accident?'

'And no scream,' Glanville added. 'Nobody reported a scream – that's why they didn't find him till this morning. You don't accidentally fall off a freakin' balcony and not scream your lungs out.'

'So maybe he wasn't conscious,' Bosch suggested. 'Maybe he wasn't alone up here. Maybe it wasn't an accident.'

'Oh, man, is that what this is about?' Solomon said. 'The councilman wants a murder investigation and you're sent out to make sure he gets it.'

Bosch gave Solomon a look that let him know he was making a mistake suggesting Harry was carrying out Irving's bidding.

'Look, nothing personal,' Solomon said quickly. 'I'm just saying we don't see that angle at all here. Suicide note or not, this scene adds up to only one thing. A high dive.'

Bosch didn't respond. He noticed the fire escape ladder at the other end of the balcony. It led up to the roof and down to the balcony below on the sixth floor.

'Anybody go up on the roof?'

'Not yet,' Solomon said. 'We were awaiting further instructions.'

'What about the rest of the hotel? Did you knock on any doors?'

'Same thing. Further instructions.'

Solomon was being an ass but Bosch ignored it.

'How did you confirm ID on the body? The facial damage was extensive.'

'Yeah, this one's going to be closed casket,' Glanville said. 'That's for sure.'

'We got the name off the hotel registration and the plate on the car in valet,' Solomon said. 'This was before we got the room safe open and found the wallet. We figured we better be sure and we better be quick. I had patrol send over the division's MPR and got it off the guy's thumb.'

Each of the department's divisions had a mobile print reader that took a digital thumbprint and instantly compared it to the Department of Motor Vehicles database. It was primarily used in the station house jails to confirm IDs, as there had been several incidents in which felons sought on warrants had given false IDs upon arrest and were able to bail out before the jailers knew they'd had a wanted individual in custody. But the department was always looking for other applications of the equipment and this had been a smart use of the new technology by Crate and Barrel.

'Good going,' Bosch said.

He turned and looked at the bathrobe.

'Anybody check that?'

Solomon and Glanville looked at each other and Bosch saw the exchange. Neither had checked, thinking the other had.

Solomon went to the robe and Bosch stepped back into the suite. As he did so he spotted a small object next to a leg of the coffee table in front of the couch. He squatted down to see what it was without touching it. It was a small black button that had blended in with the dark pattern of the carpet.

Bosch picked the button up so he could look closely

at it. He guessed that it had come off a men's dress shirt. He put the button back in the place he had found it. He could tell one of the detectives had come in from the balcony and was behind him.

'Where are his clothes?'

'Folded and hung nice and neat in the closet,' Glanville said. 'What's that?'

'A button, probably nothing. But get the photographer back up here to shoot it before we collect it. Anything in the bathrobe?'

'The room key. That's it.'

Bosch headed down the hallway. The first room on the right was a small kitchen with a table for two against one wall. On the counter opposite was a display of alcoholic beverages and snacks available for purchase by the suite's guest. Bosch checked the waste can in the corner. It was empty. He opened the refrigerator and found it stocked with more beverages – beer, champagne, sodas and fruit drinks. None of it looked disturbed.

Harry moved on down the hall, checking out the bathroom before finally entering the bedroom.

Solomon had been right about the bed. The spread was neat and pulled tight at the corners. No one had even sat on the bed since it had been made. There was a closet with a mirrored door. As Bosch approached it he could see Glanville in the room's doorway behind him, watching.

In the closet, Irving's clothes were on hangers – shirt, pants and jacket – and his underwear, socks and shoes were on a side shelf next to a room safe with a partially opened door. Inside the safe were a wallet and a wedding ring along with an iPhone and a watch.

The safe had a four-digit combination lock. Solomon had said it was found closed and locked. Bosch knew that the hotel management most likely had an electronic reader that was used to unlock the room safes. People forget combinations or check out, forgetting they've locked the safe. The device quickly goes through the ten thousand possible combinations until it hits the winner.

'What was the combination?'

'To the safe? I don't know. Maybe Jerry got it from her.'

'Her?'

'The assistant manager who opened it for us. Her name's Tamara.'

Bosch removed the phone from the safe. He had the same model himself. But when he tried to access it he found it was password-protected.

'What do you want to bet that the password he keyed into the safe is the same password on the phone?'

Glanville didn't answer. Bosch put the phone back into the safe.

'We need to get somebody up here to bag this stuff.'

'We?'

Bosch smiled, though Glanville couldn't see it. He slid the hangers apart and checked the pockets on the clothing. They were empty. He then started looking at the buttons on the shirt. It was a dark blue dress shirt with black buttons. He checked the rest of the shirt and found that the right cuff was missing a button.

He felt Glanville come up and look over his shoulder.

'I think it's a match to the one out there on the floor,' Bosch said.

'Yeah, what's it mean?' Glanville said.

Bosch turned around and looked at him.

'I don't know.'

Before leaving the room, Bosch noticed that one of the bed's side tables was askew. One corner had been pulled away from the wall and Bosch guessed it had been done when Irving unplugged the clock.

'What do you think, that he took the clock out there to listen to music from his iPhone?' he asked without looking back at Glanville.

'Could be but there's another dock out there under the TV for that. Maybe he just didn't see it.'

'Maybe.'

Bosch moved back out to the suite's living room and Glanville followed. Chu was on his phone and Bosch gave him the *cut it off* sign. Chu put his hand over the phone and said, 'I'm getting good stuff here.'

'Yeah, well, get it later,' Bosch said. 'We have things to do.'

Chu got off the phone and the four detectives stood in a circle in the middle of the room.

'Okay, this is how I want to do this,' Bosch began. 'We're going to knock on every door in this building. We ask what people heard, what they saw. We cover—'

'Jesus Christ, what a waste of time,' Solomon said, turning from the circle and looking out one of the windows.

'We can leave no stone unturned,' Bosch said. 'That way, if and when we call it suicide, nobody can second-guess us. Not the councilman, not the chief, not even the press. So the three of you split up the floors and start knocking on doors.'

'People in here are all night crawlers,' Glanville said. 'They're still going to be sleeping.'

'That's good. That means we'll get to them before they get out of the building.'

'Okay, so *we* get to wake everybody up,' Solomon said. 'What are *you* going to be doing?'

'I'm going down to see the manager. I want a copy of the registration and the combination used to lock the room safe. I'll see about cameras and after that I'll check Irving's car in the garage. You never know, maybe he left a notè in the car. You two never checked it.'

'We would've gotten to it,' Glanville said defensively.

'Well, I'll get to it now,' Bosch said.

'The safe combo, Harry?' Chu asked. 'What for?'

'Because it might tell us whether it was Irving who punched it in.'

Chu had a confused look on his face. Bosch decided he would explain it all later.

'Chu, I also want you to climb that ladder out there and check the roof. Do that first, before you start knocking on doors.'

'Got it.'

'Thank you.'

It was refreshing not to get a complaint. Bosch turned back to Crate and Barrel.

'Now, here's the part you two aren't going to like.'

'Oh, really?' Solomon said. 'Imagine that.'

Bosch walked over to the balcony doors, signaling them over. They stepped back out and Bosch pointed a finger and swept it across the vista of homes that terraced the hillside. Though on the seventh floor, he was level with numerous homes with windows facing the Chateau.

47

'I want all of them canvassed,' he said. 'Use patrol if they can spare the bodies, but I want all those doors knocked on. Somebody might have seen something.'

'Don't you think we would've heard from them?' Glanville said. 'You see a guy jump off a balcony and I think you're going to call it in.'

Bosch glanced from the view to Glanville and then back out to the view.

'Maybe they saw something before the drop. Maybe they saw him out here alone. Maybe he wasn't alone. And maybe they saw him get thrown and they're too scared to get involved. Too many *maybes* to let it go, Crate. It has to be done.'

'He's Crate. I'm Barrel.'

'Sorry. I couldn't tell the difference.'

The disdain in Bosch's voice was unmistakable.

6

After finally clearing the scene, they took Laurel Canyon Boulevard over the hill to the San Fernando Valley. Along the way, Bosch and Chu traded reports on their efforts of the previous two hours, starting with the fact that the knocking on doors in the hotel had produced not a single guest who had heard or seen anything in regard to Irving's death. Bosch found this surprising. He was sure that the sound of the impact of the body landing would have been loud, and yet no one in the hotel had reported hearing even that.

'A waste of time,' Chu said.

Which, of course, Bosch knew, was not the case. There was value in knowing that Irving had not shouted as he came down. This fact lent itself to the two scenarios Van Atta had mentioned; Irving had intentionally jumped or was unconscious when he was dropped.

'It's never a waste of time,' he said. 'Did any of you knock on the doors of the pool bungalows?'

'Not me. They're all the way over on the other side of the building. I didn't figure it was—'

'What about Crate and Barrel?'

'I don't think so.'

Bosch pulled his phone. He called Solomon.

'What's your location?' he asked.

'We're on Marmont Lane, knocking on doors. Like we were told.'

'Did you get anything out of the hotel?'

'Nope, nobody heard nothing.'

'Did you hit any of the bungalows?'

There was a hesitation before Solomon answered.

'Nope, we weren't told to hit the bungalows, remember?'

Bosch was annoyed.

'I need you to go back and talk to a guest named Thomas Rapport in bungalow two.'

'Who's he?'

'He's supposedly some kind of famous writer. He checked in right after Irving and might've talked to him.'

'Let's see, that's about six hours or so before our guy jumped. And you want us to talk to a guy who was next in line to check in?'

'That's right. I'd do it myself but I need to get to Irving's wife.'

'Bungalow two, got it.'

'Today. You can e-mail me the report.'

Bosch closed the phone, annoyed with Solomon's tone during the entire call. Chu immediately hit him with a question.

'How'd you know about this guy Rapport?'

Bosch reached into the side pocket of his suit coat and pulled free a clear plastic sleeve containing a DVD.

'There are not a lot of cameras in that hotel. But there is one over the front desk. It's got Irving checking in and the rest of the night right up until the body's discovered. Rapport came in right after Irving. He might've even ridden up in the elevator from the garage with him.'

'Did you look at the disc?'

'Just the part with him checking in. I'll watch the rest later.'

'Anything else from the manager?'

'The hotel call logs and the combination that was entered on the room safe.'

Bosch told him the combination on the room safe was 1492 and that it was not a default number. Whoever had locked Irving's possessions in the safe had keyed the number in either randomly or intentionally.

'Christopher Columbus,' Chu said.

'What do you mean?'

'Harry, I'm the foreigner. Don't you know your history lessons? "In fourteen hundred ninety-two Columbus sailed the ocean blue" – remember?'

'Yeah, sure. Columbus. But what's it have to do with this?'

It seemed like a stretch to Bosch that the discovery of America was the inspiration for the combination.

'And that's not even the oldest date connected to this thing,' Chu added excitedly.

'What are you talking about?'

'The hotel, Harry. The Chateau Marmont is a duplicate of a French chateau built in the thirteenth century in the Loire Valley.'

'Okay, so?'

'I looked it up on Google. That's what I was doing on my phone. Turns out that back then, the average height of Western Europeans was five foot three. So if they copied that place, that would explain why the balcony walls are so short.'

'The balustrades. But what's that got to—'

'Accidental death, Harry. The guy comes out on the balcony to get some fresh air or something and goes right over the balcony. Do you know that Jim Morrison, that guy from the Doors, fell off a balcony there like that in nineteen seventy?'

'That's great. What about a little more recently, Chu? Are you saying they have a—'

'No, there's no history there. I'm just saying ... you know.'

'No, I don't know. What are you saying?'

'I'm saying that if we have to make this an accident so the chief and the powers that be are happy, then there's our way to it.'

They had just crested the mountain and crossed Mulholland. They were now dropping down into Studio City, where George Irving had lived with his family. At the next street, Bosch jerked the wheel and pulled into Dona Pegita and stopped. He slammed the car into park and turned in his seat to confront his partner.

'What gave you the idea that we're looking to appease the powers that be?'

Chu immediately became flustered.

'Well ... I don't ... I'm just saying if we want – look, Harry, I'm not saying what happened. It's just a possibility.'

'Possibility, my ass. He either checked in because he wanted to check out, or somebody drew him there, knocked him out and then dropped him. There was no accident and I'm not looking for anything but what really happened. If this guy offed himself, then he offed himself and the councilman has to live with it.'

'Okay, Harry.'

'I don't want to hear about the Loire Valley or the Doors or anything else that is a distraction. There's a good chance it wasn't this guy's idea to end up on the sidewalk at the Chateau Marmont. Right now it could go either way. And all politics aside, I'm going to find out.'

'I hear you, Harry. I didn't mean anything, okay? I was just trying to help. Casting a big net. Remember, you told me that's how it's done.'

'Sure.'

Bosch turned forward again and dropped the car into drive. He made a U-turn and headed back to Laurel Canyon Boulevard. Chu desperately tried to change the subject.

'Was there anything on the call logs worth looking at?'

'No calls coming in. Irving called down to the garage about midnight and that was it.'

'What was that about?'

'We have to talk to the midnight man – he got out of there before we could hold him. They keep a log in the office down there and it says Irving called to ask him to see if he left his phone in his car. We found the phone in the safe, so either Irving was mistaken or the phone was left in the car and brought up to his room.'

They were silent for a moment as they considered the call to the garage. Finally, Chu spoke.

'Did you check out the car?'

'I did. There was nothing there.'

'Damn. I guess that would have made it easier, if there had been a note or something.'

'Yeah. But there wasn't.'

'Too bad.'

'Yeah, too bad.'

They rode the rest of the way to George Irving's home in silence.

When they got to the address that was on their victim's driver's license, Bosch saw a familiar Lincoln Town Car parked at the curb. The same two men were in the front. It meant Councilman Irving was on the premises. Bosch got ready for another face-to-face with the enemy.

7

Councilman Irving answered the door of his son's home. He opened it just as wide as his own body, and it was clear before he said anything that he did not want to allow Bosch and Chu admittance.

'Councilman,' Bosch said, 'we'd like to ask your son's wife a few questions.'

'Deborah's taken this very hard, Detective. It would be better if you could come back at another time.'

Bosch looked around on the doorstep, even glanced behind him and down at Chu on the lower step, before turning back to Irving and answering.

'We're conducting an investigation, Councilman. Her interview is important and we can't put it off.'

They stared at each other, neither yielding.

'You asked for me and you told me to proceed with urgency,' Bosch finally said. 'This is what I'm doing. Are you going to let us come in or not?'

Irving relented and stepped back, opening the door wider. Bosch and Chu entered a vestibule with a table for dropping off keys and packages.

'What did you learn from the crime scene?' Irving said quickly.

Bosch hesitated, not sure whether to discuss the case with him this soon.

'So far not a lot. A case like this, a lot will ride on the autopsy.'

'When will that be?'

'It hasn't been scheduled.'

Bosch checked his watch.

'Your son's body only got to the morgue a couple hours ago.'

'Well, I hope you insisted that they schedule it quickly.'

Bosch tried to smile but it didn't work out that way.

'Can you take us to your daughter-in-law now?'

'So that means you did not insist on any urgency.'

Bosch looked over Irving's shoulder and saw the room opened into a larger room with a winding staircase. There was no sign of anyone else in the house.

'Councilman, don't tell me how to run the investigation. If you want to take me off it, then fine, call the chief and have me pulled. But as long as I'm on the case, then I'm going to run the investigation the way I see best.'

Irving backed off.

'Of course,' he said. 'I'll go get Deborah. Why don't you and your partner wait in the living room.'

He led them into the house and directed them to the living room. He then disappeared. Bosch looked at Chu and shook his head at the same moment Chu was about to ask a question that Harry knew was going to be about Irving's meddling in the investigation.

Chu held his tongue and just then Irving returned, leading a stunningly beautiful blond woman into the room. Bosch guessed she was in her midforties. She was tall and thin but not too tall and thin. She looked grief-stricken but that didn't take much away from the beauty of a woman who was aging as gracefully as a fine wine. Irving led her by the arm to a seat across a coffee table from a couch. Bosch moved into the seating arrangement but did not sit down. He waited to see what move Irving made, and when it became clear the councilman planned on staying for the interview, Harry objected.

'We're here to talk to Mrs Irving and we need to do that alone,' he said.

'My daughter-in-law wants me to be with her at this time,' Irving responded. 'I'm not going anywhere.'

'That's fine. If you can be here somewhere in the house in case she needs you, that will be most helpful. But I need you to allow us to talk with Mrs Irving alone.'

'Dad, it's okay,' Deborah Irving said, defusing the situation. 'I'll be fine. Why don't you make yourself something to eat in the kitchen?'

Irving looked at Bosch for a long moment, probably second-guessing his demand that Harry be put on the case.

'Just call if you need me,' he said.

Irving then left the room and Bosch and Chu sat down, Harry making their introductions.

'Mrs Irving, I want—'

'You can call me Deborah.'

'Deborah, then. We want you to know that you have our condolences for the loss of your husband. We also appreciate your willingness to talk to us at this difficult time.'

'Thank you, Detective. I am more than willing to talk. It's just that I don't think I have any answers for you and the shock of this is more than ...'

She looked around and Bosch knew what she was

looking for. The tears were coming again. Harry signaled to Chu.

'Find her some tissues. Check the bathroom.'

Chu got up. Bosch intently watched the woman across from him, looking for signs of genuine emotion and loss.

'I don't know why he would have done this,' she said.

'Why don't we start with the easy questions? The ones where there are answers. Why don't you tell me when you last saw your husband?'

'Last night. He left the house after dinner and didn't come back.'

'Did he say where he was going?'

'No, he said he needed air, that he was going to put the top down and take a drive up on Mulholland. He told me not to wait up for him. I didn't.'

Bosch waited but nothing else came.

'Was that unusual, him going out for a drive like that?'

'He had been doing it a lot lately. I didn't think he was really out driving, though.'

'You mean he was doing something else?'

'Connect the dots, Lieutenant.'

'I'm a detective, not a lieutenant. Why don't you connect the dots for me, Deborah. Do you know what your husband was doing?'

'No, I don't. I'm just telling you that I didn't think he was just riding around on Mulholland. I thought he was probably meeting someone.'

'Did you ask him about it?'

'No. I was going to but I was waiting.'

'For what?'

'I don't know exactly. I was just waiting.'

Chu came back with a box of tissues and handed it to

her. But the moment had passed and her eyes looked cold and hard now. Even so, she was beautiful, and Bosch found it hard to believe a husband would take to late-night drives when the woman waiting at home was Deborah Irving.

'Let's go back a second. You said he left after you two had dinner. Was that at home or had you been out?'

'We were home. Neither of us was very hungry. We just had sandwiches.'

'Do you remember what time dinner was?'

'It would've been about seven thirty. He left at eight thirty.'

Bosch took out his notebook and wrote a few things down about what had been said so far. He remembered that Solomon and Glanville had reported that someone – presumably George Irving – had made the reservation at the Chateau at eight fifty, twenty minutes after Deborah said her husband had left their home.

'One-four-nine-two.'

'Excuse me?'

'Do those numbers mean anything to you? One-four-nine-two – fourteen ninety-two?'

'I don't understand what you mean.'

She seemed genuinely confused. Bosch had meant to keep her off balance by asking questions in a non-sequential manner.

'Your husband's property – his wallet and phone and wedding ring – were in the hotel safe. That was the combination that was entered to lock it. Is there any significance to those numbers to your husband or you?'

'I can't think of any.'

'Okay. Did your husband have a familiarity with the

59

Chateau Marmont? Had he stayed there before?'

'We had been there before together, but like I said, I didn't really know where he went when he went on his drives. He could've been going there. I don't know.'

Bosch nodded.

'How would you describe your husband's state of mind when you last saw him?'

She thought for a long moment before shrugging and saying that her husband seemed normal, not burdened or upset as far as she could tell.

'How would you describe the state of your marriage?'

She dropped her eyes to the floor for a moment before bringing them up to his.

'We would have reached our twentieth anniversary in January. Twenty years is a long time. A lot of highs and lows but many more highs than lows.'

Bosch noted that she did not answer the question he had asked.

'What about right now? Were you in a high or a low?'

She paused a long moment before answering.

'Our son – our only child – left in August for college. It has been a difficult adjustment.'

'Empty nest syndrome,' Chu said.

Both Bosch and Deborah Irving looked at him but he added nothing else and looked a little foolish for interrupting.

'What day in January was your anniversary?' Bosch asked.

'The fourth.'

'So you were married on January fourth, nineteen ninety-two?'

'Oh, my god!'

She brought her hands to her mouth in embarrassment over not recognizing the hotel room safe combination. Tears rolled out of her eyes and she pulled tissues from the box.

'How stupid of me! You must think I'm a complete—'

'It's okay,' Bosch offered. 'I said it like a year, not a full date. Do you know if he used that number as a combination or password before?'

She shook her head.

'I don't know.'

'ATM password?'

'No we used our son's birthday – five-two-ninety-three.'

'What about on his cell phone?'

'That's Chad's birthday, too. I've used George's phone.'

Bosch wrote the new date down in his notebook. The cell phone had been logged into evidence by the SID team and was on its way downtown. He would be able to unlock it and access its call records at the PAB. He had to consider what this meant. On the one hand, use of the Irving's anniversary date tended to indicate that it had been George Irving who had set the combination on the room safe. But a wedding date could be found in court records with a computer. Once again it was information that did not exclude either suicide or murder.

He decided to move in a new direction again.

'Deborah, what exactly did your husband do for a living?'

She responded with a more detailed version of what Irvin Irving had already told him. George had followed in his father's footsteps, joining the LAPD at twenty-one. But after five years in patrol he left the department for law school. After earning his JD, he went to work for the City Attorney's Office in the contracts department. That was where he stayed until his father ran for city council and won. George quit working for the city and opened up shop as a consultant for hire, using his experience and connections to his father and others in local government and bureaucracy to give his clients access to the halls of power.

George Irving had a wide range of clients, including towing firms, taxi licensees, concrete suppliers, building contractors, city office cleaners and code-enforcement litigators. He was a man who could plant the request in the right ear at the right time. If you wanted to do business with the city of Los Angeles, a man like George Irving was the one to see. He had an office in the shadow of City Hall, but the office was not where the work was done. Irving roamed the administrative wings and council offices of City Hall. That was where his work was done.

The widow Irving reported that her husband's work brought them a very nice living. The house in which they sat was valued at more than $1 million, even factoring in the downturn in the economy. The work also had the propensity to bring him enemies. Unhappy clients, or those competing for the same contracts as his clients – George Irving didn't operate in a world above contention.

'Did he ever speak about any business or person in particular being upset with him or holding a grudge?'

'No one that he spoke to me about. He has an office manager, though. I guess I should say he did have an office manager. She would probably know more about this area than I would. George didn't share a lot of that with me. He didn't want me to worry about it.'

'What is her name?'

'Dana Rosen. She's been with him a long time – going back to the City Attorney's Office.'

'Have you spoken with her today?'

'Yes, but not since I learned ...'

'You spoke with her before learning your husband was deceased?'

'Yes, when I got up I realized he had not come home last night. He wasn't answering his cell, so at eight o'clock I called the office and talked to Dana to see if she had seen him yet. She said no.'

'Did you call her back after you learned of your husband's death?'

'No, I didn't.'

Bosch wondered if there was a problem or jealousy between the two women. Could Dana Rosen be the woman Deborah thought her husband took drives at night to meet?

He wrote the name down and then closed his notebook. He thought he had plenty to start with. He hadn't covered all the details but this was not the time for a long Q&A session. He was confident that he would be coming back to Deborah Irving. He stood up and Chu followed suit.

'I think this is enough for now, Deborah. We know it is a difficult time and you want to be with family. Have you told your son?'

'No, Dad did. He called him. Chad's flying down tonight.'

'Where's he going to school?'

'USF – the University of San Francisco.'

Bosch nodded. He had been hearing about the school because his daughter was already thinking about the next level of education and had mentioned it as a possibility. He also remembered that it was where Bill Russell had played college ball.

Harry knew he would want to talk to the son but didn't mention it to Deborah. There was no need to have her thinking about it.

'What about friends?' he asked. 'Was he close to anyone?'

'Not really. He really only had one close friend and they hadn't seen much of each other lately.'

'Who was that?'

'His name is Bobby Mason. They knew each other since the police academy.'

'Is Bobby Mason still a cop?'

'Yes.'

'Why hadn't they seen each other lately?'

'I don't know. They just hadn't, I guess. I'm sure it was just a temporary lull in the relationship. I assume that's the way men are.'

Bosch wasn't sure what her last words were meant to convey about men. He didn't have anyone in his life he would consider a best friend but he always thought he was different. That most men had male friends, even best friends. He wrote Mason's name down, then gave Deborah Irving a business card with his cell phone number on it and invited her to call anytime. He said he would be in touch as the investigation progressed.

Bosch wished her good luck and then he and Chu left.

Before they reached the car, Irvin Irving came out the front door and called to them.

'You were just going to leave without checking with me?'

Bosch handed the keys to Chu and told him to back the car out of the driveway. He waited until he and Irving were alone before speaking.

'Councilman, we need to get something straight here. I'm going to keep you informed but I don't report to you. There's a difference. This is a police investigation, not a city hall investigation. You were a cop but you're not anymore. You'll hear from me when I have something to report to you.'

He turned and started walking toward the street.

'Remember, I want an update by the end of the day,' Irving called after him.

Bosch didn't respond. He kept on walking like he didn't hear.

8

Bosch told Chu to drive north toward Panorama City.

'We're up here,' he said. 'We might as well go get a look at Clayton Pell. If he's where he's supposed to be.'

'I thought the Irving case was the priority,' Chu said.

'It is.'

Bosch offered no further explanation. Chu nodded but had something else on his mind.

'What about something to eat?' he asked. 'We worked right through lunch and I'm starving, Harry.'

Bosch realized he was hungry, too. He checked his watch and saw it was almost three.

'The halfway house is way up Woodman,' he said. 'There used to be a pretty good taco truck that parked on Woodman at Nordhoff. I had a trial a few years ago at the San Fernando Courthouse and my partner and I used to hit that truck every day at lunch. It's kind of late but if we're lucky he'll still be there.'

Chu was a semi-vegetarian but usually liked the idea of Mexican food.

'Think they'll have a bean burrito on that truck?'

'Most likely. If not, they've got shrimp tacos. I've had them.'

'Sounds like a plan.'

He goosed the car's accelerator.

'Was that Ignacio?' Chu eventually asked. 'The partner, I mean.'

'Yeah, Ignacio,' Bosch said.

Bosch contemplated the fate of his last partner, who was murdered in the back room of a food market two years earlier while working the case that introduced Harry to Chu. The two current partners maintained silence the rest of the way.

The halfway house that Clayton Pell was assigned to was in Panorama City, which was the expansive neighborhood at the geographic center of the San Fernando Valley. Spawned by post–World War II prosperity and enthusiasm, it was the first planned community of Los Angeles, replacing miles of orange groves and dairy lands with the seemingly unending sprawl of inexpensive and prefabricated tract housing and low-rise apartments that soon defined the look of the Valley. Anchored by the nearby industries of the General Motors plant and the Schlitz brewery, the development represented the epoch of Los Angeles autotopia. Every man with a job and a commute. Every home with a garage. Every view a panorama of the surrounding mountains. Only American-born white people need apply.

At least that was the way they were spinning it in 1947 when the grid work was set and the lots went up for sale. However, over the decades since the glorious ribbon cutting on the community of tomorrow, both GM and Schlitz pulled out and the views of the mountains grew hazy with smog. The streets got crowded with people and traffic, the crime rate went up at a steady pace and people started living in a lot of those garages. Iron bars went over bedroom windows and the courtyard apartment buildings put security gates across the once wide and welcoming entrances. Graffiti marked gang turf and, finally, whereas once the name Panorama City represented a future as wide and unlimited as its 360-degree views, it was now more of a cruel irony. A place with a name that reflected very little of what was actually there. Residents in parts of the once proud suburban nirvana routinely organized to try to break away to the adjoining neighborhoods of Mission Hills, North Hills and even Van Nuys so as not to be associated with Panorama City.

Bosch and Chu were in luck. The Tacos La Familia truck was still parked at the curb on Woodman and Nordhoff. Chu found a space at the curb just two cars behind it and they got out. The *taquero* was cleaning up inside and putting stuff away but he still waited on them. There were no burritos, so Chu took shrimp tacos while Bosch went with carne asada. The man handed a squeeze bottle filled with salsa through the window. They each took a bottle of Jarritos Pineapple to wash it down, and lunch for both of them was eight bucks total. Bosch gave the man a ten and told him to keep the change.

There were no other customers about, so Bosch took the bottle of salsa with him back to the car. He knew that when it came to truck tacos it was all about the salsa. They ate on either side of the front hood, leaning over it so as not to drip salsa or juice on their clothes.

'Not bad, Harry,' Chu said, nodding as he ate.

Bosch nodded back. His mouth was full. Finally he swallowed and squeezed more salsa onto his second taco and then handed the bottle across the hood to his partner.

'Good salsa,' Harry said. 'You ever been to the El Matador truck in East Hollywood?'

'No, where's it at?'

'Western and Lex. This is good but El Matador, I think they're the best. He's only there at night, though, and everything tastes better at night, anyway.'

'Isn't it weird how Western Avenue is in *East* Hollywood?'

'I never thought about it. The point is, next time you're over there after work, try El Matador and tell me what you think.'

Bosch realized he had not been down to the El Matador truck since his daughter had come to live with him. At the time, he didn't think eating in or on cars and getting food from trucks had been right for her. Now maybe things were different. He thought she might enjoy it.

'What are we going to do with Pell?' Chu asked.

Brought back to the reality of the present, Bosch told his partner that he did not want to reveal their true interest in Clayton Pell yet. There were too many unknowns in the case. He wanted to first establish that Pell was where he was supposed to be, get a look at him and maybe engage him in conversation if possible without raising the sex offender's suspicions.

'Hard to do,' Chu said, his mouth full with his last bite.

'I have an idea.'

Bosch outlined the plan, then balled up all the foil and napkins and took them to the trash can by the back of the taco truck. He put the squeeze bottle of salsa on the window counter and waved to the *taquero*.

'*Muy sabroso.*'

'*Gracias.*'

Chu was behind the wheel when he got back to the car. They made a U-turn and started down Woodman. Bosch's phone buzzed and he checked the screen. It was a number out of the PAB but he didn't recognize it. He took the call. It was Marshall Collins, the commander of the media relations unit.

'Detective Bosch, I'm holding them at bay, but we're going to need to put something out on Irving today.'

'There's nothing yet to put out.'

'Can you give me anything? I've gotten twenty-six calls here. What can I tell them?'

Bosch thought for a moment, wondering if there was a way to use the media to help the investigation.

'Tell them that cause of death is under investigation. Mr Irving dropped from the seventh-floor balcony of his room at the Chateau Marmont. It is unknown at this time whether it was accident, suicide or homicide. Anyone with information about Mr Irving's last hours at the hotel or before should contact the Robbery-Homicide Division. Et cetera, et cetera, you know how to put it.'

'So, no suspect at this time.'

'Don't put that out. That implies I am looking for suspects. We aren't even to that point yet. We don't know what happened and we're going to have to wait on autopsy results as well as the ongoing gathering of information.'

'Okay, got it. We'll get it out there.'

Bosch closed the phone and relayed details of the conversation to Chu. In five minutes they came to the

Buena Vista apartments. It was a two-story courtyard complex with major-league security gating and signage warning those without business to stay away. Not only were solicitors not welcome but children were on the no-go list as well. There was a public notice locked in a case mounted on the gate that gave warning that the facility was used to house sexual offenders on probation and parole and undergoing continuing treatment. The case's thick plastic window was scratched and marred from many efforts to shatter it and paint it with graffiti.

To push the door buzzer Bosch had to reach his arm up to his elbow through a small opening in the gate. He then waited and a female voice eventually responded.

'What is it?'

'LAPD. We need to speak to whoever's in charge.'

'She's not here.'

'Then I guess we need to speak to you. Open up.'

There was a camera on the other side of the gate, located far enough back to make it difficult to be vandalized. Bosch reached his hand through the opening again with his badge and held it up. A few more moments went by and the door lock buzzed. He and Chu pushed through.

The gate led to a tunnel-like entrance which took them to the center courtyard. As Bosch reached daylight again he saw several men sitting on chairs in a circle. A counseling and rehab session. He had never put much stock in the idea of rehabilitating sexual predators. He didn't think there was a cure beyond castration – surgical preferred over chemical. But he was smart enough to keep such thoughts to himself, depending on the company he was with.

Bosch scanned the men in the circle, hoping to recognize Clayton Pell, but to no avail. Several men had their backs to the entrance, and others were hunched over and hiding their faces below baseball hats or with hands over their mouths in poses of deep thought. Many of them were checking out Bosch and Chu. They would be easily made as cops by the men in the circle.

A few seconds later they were approached by a woman with a name tag on the breast of her hospital scrubs. It said Dr Hannah Stone. She was attractive with reddish-blond hair tied back in a no-nonsense manner. She was midforties and Bosch noticed that her watch was on her right wrist and it partially covered a tattoo.

'I'm Dr Stone. Can I see your identification, gentlemen?'

Bosch and Chu opened their wallets. Their police IDs were checked and then quickly handed back to them.

'Come with me, please. It will be better if the men don't see you out here.'

'Might be too late for that,' Bosch said.

She didn't answer. They were led into an apartment on the front of the building that had been converted into offices and private therapy rooms. Dr Stone told them that she was the rehabilitation program director. Her boss, the facility manager and director, was downtown at a budget meeting all day. She was very curt and to the point.

'What can I do for you, Detectives?'

There was a defensive tone in every word she had spoken so far, even the words about the budget meeting. She knew that cops didn't appreciate what was done here and she was ready to defend it. She didn't appear to be a woman who would back down on anything.

'We're investigating a crime,' Bosch said. 'A rape and murder. We have a description of a suspect we think might be in here. White male, twenty-eight to thirty-two years old. He's got dark hair and his first or last name might begin with the letter C. That letter was tattooed on the suspect's neck.'

So far, Bosch had not told a lie. The rape and murder actually happened. He just left out the part about its being twenty-two years ago. His description matched Clayton Pell to a T because Bosch had gotten the ex-convict's descriptors off the state parole board's computer records. And the DNA hit made Pell a suspect, no matter how unlikely it was that he was involved in the Venice Beach slaying.

'So, anybody here that meets that description?' he asked.

Stone hesitated before speaking. Bosch was hoping she wasn't going to come to the defense of the men in her program. It didn't matter how successful programs claimed to be, any recidivism among sexual offenders was too high.

'There is someone here,' she finally said. 'But he's made tremendous progress in the last five months. I find it hard to—'

'What's his name?' Bosch asked, cutting her off.

'Clayton Pell. He's out there in the circle right now.'

'How often is he allowed to leave this facility?'

'Four hours a day. He has a job.'

'A job?' Chu asked. 'You just let these people loose?'

'Detective, this is not a lockdown facility. Every man here is here voluntarily. They are paroled from prison

73

and have to register with the county and then find a place to live where they are not in violation of rules for sex offenders. We contract with the county to run a living facility that fits within those requirements. But no one has to live here. They do so because they want to assimilate back into society. They want to be productive. They don't want to hurt anyone. If they come here, we provide counseling and job placement. We feed them and give them a bed. But the only way they can stay is if they follow our rules. We work closely with the Department of Probation and Parole and our recidivism rate is lower than the national average.'

'Which means it's not perfect,' Bosch said. 'For many of them, once a predator always a predator.'

'For some that is true. But what choice do we have but to try? When people have completed their sentences, they must be released into society. This program may be one of the best last chances of preventing future crimes.'

Bosch realized that Stone was insulted by their questions. They had made their first false move. He didn't want this woman working against them. He wanted her cooperation.

'Sorry,' he said. 'I am sure the program is worthwhile. I was just thinking about the details of the crime we're investigating.'

Bosch stepped over to the front window and looked out into the courtyard.

'Which one is Clayton Pell?'

Stone came up next to him and pointed.

'The man with the shaved head, on the right. That's him.'

'When did he shave his head?'

'A few weeks ago. When was the attack you're investigating?'

Bosch turned and looked at her.

'Before that.'

She looked at him and nodded. She got the message. He was here to ask questions, not be asked.

'You said he has a job. Doing what?'

'He works for the Grande Mercado up near Roscoe. He works in the parking lot, collecting the shopping carts and emptying trash cans, that sort of thing. They pay him twenty-five dollars a day. It keeps him in cigarettes and potato chips. He's addicted to both.'

'What are the hours he works?'

'They vary by the day. His schedule is posted at the market. Today he went to work early and just got back.'

It was good to know about the schedule being available at the market. It would help if they later wanted to pick up Pell away from the Buena Vista facility.

'Dr Stone, is Pell one of your patients?'

She nodded.

'I have sessions with him four times a week. He works with other therapists here, too.'

'What can you tell me about him?'

'I can't tell you anything about our sessions. The doctor–patient confidentiality bond exists even in this sort of situation.'

'Yeah, I get that but the evidence in our case indicates he abducted, raped and then strangled a nineteen-year-old girl. I need to know what makes the man sitting out there in that circle tick. I need—'

'Wait a minute. Just wait.'

She put up her hand in a *stop* gesture.

'You said a nineteen-year-old *girl?*'

'That's right and his DNA was found on her.'

Again, not a lie, but not the whole truth.

'That's impossible.'

'Don't tell me it's impossible. The science isn't wrong. His—'

'Well, it is this time. Clayton Pell didn't rape a nineteen-year-old girl. First of all, he is a homosexual. And he's a pedophile. Almost all of the men here are. They are predators convicted of crimes against children. Second, two years ago he was assaulted in prison by a group of men and he was castrated. So there is no way that Clayton Pell is your suspect.'

Bosch heard a sharp intake of breath from his partner. He, like Chu, was shocked by the doctor's revelation as well as how it echoed the thoughts he'd had as he entered the facility.

'Clayton's sickness is that he is obsessed with pre-pubescent boys,' Stone continued. 'I would have thought you'd do a little homework before you came here.'

Bosch stared at her for a long moment as the burn of embarrassment colored his face. Not only had the ruse he had planned been disastrously wrong but there was now even further evidence that something was seriously amiss in the Lily Price case.

Struggling to move away from his gaffe, he blurted out a question.

'Prepubescent . . . you're talking about eight-year-olds? Ten-year-olds? Why that age?'

'I can't go into it,' Stone said. 'You're crossing into confidential territory.'

Bosch walked back to the window and looked out at

Clayton Pell in the circle session. He was sitting up straight in his chair and looked to be closely following the conversation. He wasn't one of those who hid his face, and there was no outward show of the trauma he had suffered.

'Does everybody in the circle know?'

'Only I know, and I made a serious breach telling you. The group sessions are of great therapeutic value to most of our residents. That's why they come here. That's why they stay.'

Bosch could have argued that they stayed because of the shelter and food. But he raised his hands in surrender and apology.

'Doctor, do us a favor,' he said. 'Don't tell Pell that we were here asking about him.'

'I wouldn't. It would only upset him. If I'm asked, I will simply say you two were here to investigate the latest vandalism.'

'Sounds good. What was the latest vandalism?'

'My car. Someone spray-painted "I love baby rapers" on the side. They'd like to get us out of the neighborhood, if they could. You see the man opposite Clayton in the circle? The one with the patch over his eye?'

Bosch looked and nodded.

'He was caught walking from the bus stop back to the center after coming from his job. Caught by the local gang – the T-Dub Boyz. They put his eye out with a broken bottle.'

Bosch turned back to her. He knew she was referring to a Latino gang from up around the Tujunga Wash. Latin gangbangers were notorious for their intolerance and violence toward sexual deviants.

'Anyone get arrested for it?'

She laughed derisively.

'To make an arrest, there would have to be an investigation. But you see, none of the vandalism or violence around here ever gets investigated by your department or anyone else.'

Bosch nodded without looking at her. He knew the score.

'Now, if there are no other questions, I need to get back to work.'

'No, no more questions,' Bosch said. 'Go back to your good work, Doctor, and we'll go back to ours.'

9

Bosch had just gotten back to the PAB from the Hall of Records with a stack of files under his arm. It was after five, so the squad room was almost deserted. Chu had gone home, which was fine with Bosch. He planned to leave himself and to start reviewing files and the disc from the Chateau Marmont at home. He was loading the files into a briefcase when he saw Kiz Rider enter the squad room and make a beeline in his direction. He quickly snapped the briefcase closed. He didn't want Rider asking about the files and learning that they were not from the Irving case.

'Harry, I thought we were going to keep in touch,' she said by way of greeting.

'We are going to, when I have something to keep in touch about. Hello to you, too, Kiz.'

'Look, Harry, I don't really have time for niceties. I'm under pressure from the chief, who is under pressure from Irving and the rest of the city council members he has managed to get behind this.'

'Get behind what?'

'Wanting to know what happened to his son.'

'Well, I'm glad you're there to shoulder that burden and keep it off the investigators so we can do our work.'

She let out a deep breath in frustration. Bosch could see the jagged edge of a scar on her neck just under the

79

collar of her blouse. It reminded him of the day she got shot. Her last day as his partner.

He stood up and lifted the briefcase off the desk.

'You're leaving already?' she exclaimed.

Bosch pointed to the clock on the far wall.

'Almost five thirty and I punched in at seven thirty. I ate lunch for ten minutes on the hood of my car. No matter how you cut it, I got in about two hours of overtime that the city doesn't pay anymore. So, yeah, I'm going home to where I have a sick kid waiting for me to bring her some soup. That is, unless you want to call up the city council and see if they'll authorize.'

'Harry, it's me, Kiz. Why are you acting like this?'

'Like what? Like I'm fed up with the political intrusion on my case? Tell you what, I've got another one working – a nineteen-year-old girl raped and left dead on the rocks at the Marina. The crabs got to her body. It's funny but nobody on the city council has called me up about that one.'

Kiz nodded to his point.

'I know, Harry, it's not fair. With you everybody counts or nobody counts. That doesn't work with politics.'

Bosch stared at her for a long moment. She quickly grew uncomfortable.

'What?'

'It was you, wasn't it?'

'It was me what?'

'"Everybody counts or nobody counts." You turned it into a slogan and you told it to Irving. Then he tried to act like he'd known it all along.'

Rider shook her head in frustration.

'Jesus Christ, Harry, what's the big deal? His front

man called up and said, Who is the best investigator in RHD? I said you but then he came back and said Irving didn't want you because of your shared history. I said you would put the history aside because with you everybody counts or nobody counts. That's all. If that's too political for you, then I offer my resignation as your friend.'

Bosch looked at her for a few moments. She was half smiling, not taking his upset seriously.

'I'll think about it and let you know.'

He stepped out of his pod and headed down the aisle.

'Wait a minute, would you?'

He turned back to her.

'What?'

'If you are not willing to talk to me as a friend, then talk to me as a detective. I am a lieutenant and you are a detective. What is the update on the Irving case?'

Now the humor in her face and words was gone. Now she was annoyed.

'The update is that we're waiting on the autopsy. There was nothing about the physical scene that leads us to any final conclusion. We have pretty much eliminated accidental death. It's going to go suicide or murder, and my money at the moment is on suicide.'

She put her hands on her hips.

'How has accidental already been eliminated?'

Bosch's briefcase was heavy with files. He switched it to his other hand because his shoulder was beginning to ache. Almost twenty years before, he had been hit by a bullet during a shootout in a tunnel and it had taken three surgeries to repair the rotator cuff. He had gone almost fifteen years without its bothering him. But not anymore.

'His son checked in without luggage. He took off his clothes and hung them neatly in the closet. A bathrobe was draped over a chair on the balcony. He went down face-first but didn't scream because no one in the hotel heard a thing. He did not put his arms out to break his fall. For these and other reasons it doesn't look like an accident to me. If you are telling me that you need it to be an accident, then come out and say it, Kiz, and then get yourself another boy.'

Her face showed the pain of his betrayal.

'Harry, how can you say that to me? I was your partner. You saved my life once and you think I would repay you by putting you into something that would compromise you?'

'I don't know, Kiz. I'm just trying to do my job here and it seems like there's a lot of high jingo on it.'

'There is, but that doesn't mean I haven't been watching out for you. The chief told you he wasn't looking to cook the book on this. I'm not either. All I wanted was an update and now all of this ... bile comes out.'

Bosch realized his anger and frustrations were misdirected.

'Kiz, if that's the way it is, then I believe you. And I'm sorry to take it out on you. I should've known anything with Irving attached was going to go this way. Just keep him off me until we get an autopsy. After that, we'll be able to draw some conclusions and you and the chief will be the first to know.'

'Okay, Harry. I'm sorry, too.'

'Talk to you tomorrow.'

Bosch was about to step away when he changed direction and came back to her. He gave her a one-armed hug.

'Are we okay?' she asked.

'Sure,' he said.

'How's your shoulder? I saw you switch hands with your case.'

'It's fine.'

'What's wrong with Maddie?'

'She's got a bug, that's all.'

'Tell her I said hi.'

'I will. See you, Kiz.'

He left her then and headed home. As he moved in slow traffic on the 101, he wasn't feeling good about either of the cases he was working. And he was upset that those feelings had made him act poorly with Rider. Most cops would cherish having an inside source in the OCP. At times he certainly had. But he had just treated her badly and had no legitimate excuse. He would have to make it up to her.

He was also bothered by Dr Stone and the way he had arrogantly dismissed her cause. In many ways, she was doing more than he was. Trying to stop crimes before they happened. Trying to save people from becoming victims. He had treated her like a sympathizer of the predators and he knew that was not the case. It was a city where not enough people cared about making it a better and safer place to live. She did and he had dismissed her. Shame on me, he thought.

He pulled his phone and called his daughter's cell.

'You doing okay?'

'Yeah. I'm feeling better.'

'Did Ashlyn's mom check on you?'

'Yes, they both came by after school and brought me a cupcake.'

That morning Bosch had e-mailed her best friend's mother to ask for the favor.

'Did they bring you your homework?'

'Yes, but I'm not feeling that much better. Did you get a case? You never called today, so I'm thinking you did.'

'Sorry about that. Actually, I got two cases.'

He noted her skill in changing the subject from homework.

'Wow.'

'Yeah, so I'm going to be a little late. I've got one more stop and then I'll be home. You want soup from Jerry's Deli? I'm going to be up in the Valley.'

'Chicken noodle.'

'You got it. Make a sandwich if you get hungry before I get back. And make sure the door's locked.'

'I know, Dad.'

'And you know where the Glock is.'

'Yes, I know where it is and I know how to use it.'

'Okay, that's my girl.'

He closed the phone.

10

It took him forty-five minutes in rush-hour traffic to get back to Panorama City. He cruised by the Buena Vista apartments and saw lights on behind the shaded windows he believed belonged to the office he had been in earlier. He also saw a driveway on the side of the building that led to a fenced parking area in the rear. There was a no trespassing sign on the gate and it was topped with barbed wire.

At the next corner he turned left and soon came to an alley that would take him behind the row of apartment buildings that fronted Woodman. He came to the fenced parking lot behind the Buena Vista and pulled to the side of the alley next to a green trash bin. He surveyed the well-lit lot and noted the eight-foot security fence that surrounded it. It was topped with three strands of barbed wire. There was a walk-through gate for accessing the trash bin but it was padlocked and also topped with barbed wire. It appeared to be a fully secured compound.

There were only three cars in the lot. One of them was a white four-door with what looked like paint damage on its side. He studied the car and soon realized the damage was actually fresh paint. A bad match of flat white paint had been sprayed on the driver's side doors to cover the graffiti. He knew it was Dr Stone's car and that she was still at work inside. He noted that graffiti had also been white-washed along the back wall of the building. A ladder was leaning against the wall next to a door marked with the same sort of warning signs he had seen up front earlier in the day.

Bosch turned off his car and got out.

Twenty minutes later he was leaning on the back of the white car in the lot when the rear door of the apartment building opened and Dr Stone emerged. She was escorted by a man and they both stopped short when they saw Bosch. The man took a protective step in front of Stone but then she put her hand on his arm.

'It's okay, Rico. He's the detective who was here earlier.'

She continued walking toward her car. Bosch stood up straight.

'I didn't mean to scare you. I just wanted to talk to you.'

This last part slowed her down as she considered it. She then turned to her escort.

'Thank you, Rico. I'll be all right with Detective Bosch. I'll see you tomorrow.'

'You sure?'

'Yes, thank you.'

'See you tomorrow.'

Rico headed back to the door and used a key to open it. Stone waited until he was back in the building before addressing Bosch.

'Detective, what are you doing? How did you get back here?'

'I got back here the same way the gangbangers with the paint did. You have a security problem.'

He pointed through the fence to the green trash bin.

'Kind of defeats the purpose of the fence when you have a Dumpster pushed up against it like that. Gives them a climbing platform. If I could get over at my age, it would be a piece of cake for those fifteen-year-olds.'

Her mouth opened slightly as she looked at the fence line, and the obvious dawned on her. She then looked at Bosch.

'You came back just to check the security of our parking lot?'

'No, I came back to apologize.'

'For what?'

'The attitude. You're trying to do a good thing here and I acted as though you were part of the problem. I'm sorry for that.'

She was clearly taken aback.

'I still can't tell you about Clayton Pell.'

'I know. That's not why I'm here. I'm already punched out for the day.'

She pointed to the Mustang on the other side of the fence.

'Is that your car? How are you going to get back to it?'

'It's mine. Now, if I were a TW boy I'd take that ladder you've conveniently provided and climb back over. But climbing in was enough for me. I'm hoping you'll just unlock the padlock on that gate and let me out.'

She smiled and it was disarming. A few strands of her carefully pulled-back hair had come loose and were framing her face.

'Unfortunately, I don't have a key to that gate.

I wouldn't mind seeing you make that climb but why don't I just drive you around?'

'Sounds good.'

He got into the passenger side of her car and they drove out through the gate and onto Woodman.

'Who is Rico?' Bosch asked.

'He's our overnight orderly,' Stone said. 'Works six to six.'

'Is he from the neighborhood?'

'Yes, but he's a good kid. We trust him. Anything happens or anybody acts up, he calls me or the director right away.'

'Good.'

They came down the alley and she stopped behind his car.

'The problem is, the trash bin is on wheels,' she said. 'We can push it away from the fence but they can push it right back.'

'Can't you expand that gate and keep it inside the compound?'

'If we put that in the budget, we'll probably get it approved in about three years.'

Bosch nodded. Every bureaucracy was in budget crisis.

'Have Rico take the lid off the Dumpster. Then they'll have nothing to stand on. It might make a difference.'

She nodded.

'Might be worth a try.'

'And keep having Rico walk you out.'

'Oh, I do. Every night.'

He nodded and put his hand on the door handle. He decided to go with his instincts. He had seen no ring on her finger.

'Where's home from here, north or south?'

'Oh, south. I live in North Hollywood.'

'Well, I'm heading to Jerry's Deli to pick up some chicken noodle soup for my daughter. You want to meet me there and maybe get something to eat?'

She hesitated. He could see her eyes in the dim light from the dash.

'Um, Detective . . .'

'You can call me Harry.'

'Harry, I don't think that would be such a good idea.'

'Really? Why? I'm talking about a quick sandwich. I have to bring soup home.'

'Well, because . . .'

She paused and then started laughing.

'What?'

'I don't know. Never mind. Yes, I'll meet you there.'

'Good. Then I'll see you in a few minutes.'

He got out of the car and headed to his own. The whole way to Jerry's he kept checking the rearview mirror. She was following him and he half expected her to suddenly take a screaming turn to the left or right when she changed her mind.

But she never did and soon they were sitting across from each other in a booth. In the well-lit deli he noticed her eyes for the first time. There was a sadness in them he had not noticed before. Maybe it was from the work. She dealt with the lowest form of human life. The predators. Those who took advantage of the smaller and the weaker. Those the rest of society couldn't stand to look at.

'How old is your daughter?'

'Fifteen going on thirty.'

She smiled.

'She's home sick from school today and I barely got the chance to check in on her. It's been a busy day.'

'It's just you and her?'

'Yes. Her mother – my ex – died a couple years ago. I went from living alone to trying to raise a thirteen-year-old. It's been . . . interesting.'

'I bet.'

He smiled.

'The truth is, I've loved every minute of it. It's changed my life for the better. I just don't know if she's better off.'

'But there's no other choice, is there?'

'No, that's the thing. She's stuck with me.'

'I'm sure she's happy, even if she doesn't express it. It's hard to read teenage girls.'

'Yeah.'

He checked his watch. He felt guilty now that he had put himself first. He wouldn't get home till at least eight thirty with the soup. The waiter came and asked for their drink order and Bosch told him that they needed to order everything to save time. Stone ordered half a turkey sandwich. Bosch ordered a whole turkey sandwich and the soup to go.

'What about you?' he asked when they were left alone.

Stone told him she had been divorced for over ten years and had had only one serious relationship in the time since. She had a grown son who lived up in the San Francisco area and she rarely saw him. She was pretty much dedicated to her job at the Buena Vista, where she had worked for four years after a midlife change in direction. She went from being a therapist who specialized in treating narcissistic professionals to retooling for a year in school before treating sex offenders.

Bosch got the idea that her decision to change her professional life and work with the most hated members of society was some sort of penance but he didn't know her well enough to go further with his suspicion. It was a mystery he would have to wait to solve, if he got the chance.

'Thank you for what you said back in the parking lot,' she said. 'Most cops, they just think these people should be taken out and shot.'

'Well ... not without a trial.'

He smiled but she didn't see the humor in it.

'Every one of these men is a mystery. I'm a detective like you. I try to find out what happened to them. People aren't natural-born predators. Please don't tell me you believe that.'

Bosch hesitated.

'I don't know. I sort of come in after the fact to clean things up. All I know is that there is evil out there in the world. I've seen it. I'm just not sure where it comes from.'

'Well, my job is to find that out. Find out what happened to these people that put them on this path. If I can find it out, I can help them. If I help them, then I am helping the cause of society. Most police don't get that. But you, what you said tonight, I think maybe you do.'

Bosch nodded but felt guilty about what he was hiding from her. She read it right away.

'What aren't you telling me?'

He shook his head, embarrassed at the easy read.

'Listen, I want to level with you about today.'

Her stare turned hard. It was as though she realized the dinner invitation had been some sort of a setup.

'Wait, it's not what you're thinking. I didn't lie to you today but I didn't tell you the whole story about Pell. You know the case I'm working? With Pell's DNA on the victim? It's twenty-two years old.'

The suspicion on her face was quickly replaced with bewilderment.

'I know,' he said. 'Doesn't make sense. But it is what it is. His blood was found on a girl murdered twenty-two years ago.'

'That would've made him eight years old. That's impossible.'

'I know. We're looking at a possible screwup in the pipeline – the lab work. I'm checking that out tomorrow but I also had to get a look at Pell because until I learned from you he was a homosexual predator, he made the perfect suspect – if he had access to a time machine or something.'

The waiter came with their food and the soup in a container in a bag. Bosch said he'd take the check right away so he could pay and they'd be able to go as soon as they were finished eating.

'What do you want from me?' Stone asked when they were alone again.

'Nothing. What do you mean?'

'Are you hoping I'll reveal privileged information in exchange for half a turkey sandwich?'

Bosch couldn't tell if she was kidding or not.

'No. I just thought . . . there was just something I liked about you. I was out of line today. That's all.'

She was quiet for a long moment while she ate. He

didn't push things. Bringing up his case seemed to put a freeze on everything.

'There's something there,' she said. 'That's all I can tell you.'

'Look, don't compromise yourself. I pulled his files from Probation and Parole today. All his psychologicals will be in there.'

She smirked with her mouth full.

'You're talking about PSIs and parole evaluations. They only go skin-deep.'

Bosch put his hand up to stop her.

'Look, Doc, this isn't about getting you to break a confidence. Let's talk about something else.'

'Don't call me Doc.'

'Sorry. Doctor.'

'No, I mean just call me Hannah.'

'Okay. Hannah. Hannah, let's talk about something else.'

'Okay, what?'

Bosch was silent as he tried to think of something to go with. Soon they both started laughing.

But they didn't mention Clayton Pell again.

11

It was nine o'clock when Bosch came through the front door. He hurried down the hall and looked in the open door of his daughter's bedroom. She was in bed under the covers with her laptop open next to her.

'I'm so sorry, Maddie. I'll heat this up and bring it in.'

Standing in the doorway, he held up the bag from Jerry's.

'It's all right, Dad. I already ate.'

'What did you eat?'

'PB and J.'

Bosch felt the crushing guilt of selfishness. He came into the room and sat on the edge of the bed. Before he could apologize further, she once again let him off the hook.

'It's *okay*. You got two new cases and it was a busy day.'

He shook his head.

'No, for the last hour I was just with somebody. I met her today on the case but then she met me at Jerry's for a sandwich and I stayed too long. Mads, I'm so—'

'God, that's even better! You actually met someone. Who is she?'

'Just somebody – she's a shrink who deals with criminals.'

'Cool. Is she pretty?'

He noticed that she had her Facebook page up on her computer screen.

'We're just friends. Did you do any homework?'

'No, I didn't feel good.'

'I thought you said you were better.'

'Relapse city.'

'Look, you gotta go to school tomorrow. You don't want to fall behind.'

'I *know!*'

He didn't want to get into an argument.

'Hey, if you're not doing your homework, can I use your laptop for a little bit? I have to look at a disc.'

'Sure.'

She reached over and closed out the screen. He went around the bed to where there was more room. He pulled the disc from the Chateau Marmont's front-desk security camera out of his pocket and handed it to her. He wasn't sure how to get it to play.

Maddie put the disc into a side slot and went through the commands to make it play. There was a time stamp in the lower corner of the screen and Bosch told her to fast-forward until she got to the time George Irving checked in. The image was clear but was angled from an overhead camera, so Irving's face was not fully visible. Bosch had only watched the check-in part once and wanted to see it again.

'So, what is this?' Maddie asked.

Bosch pointed at the screen.

'The Chateau Marmont. This guy checking in, he goes up to his room on the seventh floor last night and this morning he's found on the sidewalk below. I have to figure out if he jumped or if he got dropped.'

She stopped the playback.

'If he *was* dropped, Dad. *Please*. You sound like a palooka when you talk like that.'

'Sorry. How do you know what a "palooka" is, anyway?'

'Tennessee Williams. I read. A palooka is an old fighter who's like a lout. You don't want to be like that.'

'You're right. But since you know so much about words, what do you call one of those names that is spelled the same going front and back?'

'What do you mean?'

'You know, like Otto. Or Hannah.'

'It's a palindrome. Is that your girlfriend's name?'

'She's not my girlfriend. I had a turkey sandwich with her.'

'Yeah, while your sick daughter was starving at home.'

'Come on. You had peanut butter and jelly, the best sandwich ever invented.'

He gently elbowed her side.

'I just hope being with Otto was worth it.'

He burst out laughing and reached over and pulled her into a hug.

'Don't worry about Otto. You'll always be my girl.'

'Well, I do like the name Hannah,' she conceded.

'Good. Can we watch now?'

She hit the play button and they watched the computer screen silently as Irving began the check-in process with the night deskman named Alberto Galvin. Soon the second guest appeared behind him, waiting to check in.

Irving wore the same clothes Bosch had seen in the closet in the suite. He slid a credit card across the desk and Galvin printed out the room contract. Irving quickly initialed and signed the document and slid it back in exchange for a key. He then left the camera's view in the direction of the elevators and Galvin began the process all over again with the next guest in line.

The video confirmed that Irving had checked in without luggage.

'He jumped.'

Bosch looked from the screen to his daughter.

'Why do you say that?'

Manipulating the controls, she backed the video up to the point where Galvin slid the contract across the desk to Irving. She then hit play.

'Watch,' she said. 'He doesn't even look at it. He just signs where the guy tells him to sign.'

'Yeah, so?'

'This is when people check to see if they're getting ripped off. You know, they check what they are getting charged, but he doesn't even look. He doesn't care because he knows he'll never pay that bill.'

Bosch watched the video. She was right about what she saw. But it wasn't conclusive. Still, he was proud of her read. He had noticed that her powers of observation were increasingly impressive. He often quizzed her on what she could remember from different places they had been and scenes they had encountered. She always picked up and retained more than he expected.

She had told him a year earlier that she wanted to be a cop when she grew up. A detective like him. He didn't know if it was just a passing idea, but he rolled with it and began passing on what he knew. One of their favorite things to do was to go to a restaurant like Du-par's and watch the other patrons and pull reads off their faces

97

and mannerisms. Bosch was teaching her to look for tells.

'That's a good read,' he said. 'Play it again.'

They watched the video for the third time and this time Bosch picked up something new.

'You see that. He looks at his watch real quick there after he signs.'

'So?'

'It just seems a little off to me. I mean, what's time to a dead man? If he was going to jump, why would he wonder what time it was? It just seems like more of a businessman's move. It makes me think he was going to meet somebody. Or someone was going to call. But no one did.'

Bosch had already checked with the hotel and no call had come in or gone out of room 79 after Irving checked in. Bosch also had a report from forensics which examined Irving's cell phone after Bosch had given the password his widow had provided. Irving had made no calls after a 5 P.M. call to his son Chad. It had lasted eight minutes. He had received three calls from his wife the following morning – after he was dead. By that time Deborah Irving was looking for him. She left messages each time telling her husband to call back.

Bosch took over the controls of the video and played the check-in sequence once again. He then continued on, using the fast-forward control to move quickly through the chunks of time during the night when there was nothing happening at the front desk. His daughter eventually got bored and turned on her side to go to sleep.

'I might need to go out,' he said to her. 'You'll be okay?'

'Going back to see Hannah?'

'No, I might go back to the hotel. You'll be okay?'

'Sure. I've got the Glock.'

'Right.'

The summer before, she had trained on a range and Bosch considered her proficient in weapon safety and marksmanship – in fact, she was scheduled to compete for the first time the following weekend. More important than her skills with the gun was her understanding of the responsibility of the weapon. He hoped she would never use the weapon outside of a range. But if the time came, she'd be ready.

He stayed on the bed next to her and continued to watch the video. He saw nothing on it that intrigued him or that he felt he had to follow up on. He decided not to leave the house.

Finished with the disc, he got up quietly, turned out the light and went out to the dining room. He was going to jump from the Irving case back to the Lily Price investigation. He opened his briefcase and spread out the files he had pulled that afternoon from the state's Department of Probation and Parole.

Clayton Pell had three convictions on his record as an adult. They were sexually motivated crimes that escalated over the ten years of his continued interaction with the justice system. He started at age twenty with indecent exposure, moved up to false imprisonment and indecent exposure at age twenty-one, and then three years later hit the big time with the abduction and forcible rape of a minor below the age of twelve. He got probation and county jail time for the first two convictions but served six years out of a ten-year sentence at Corcoran State

Prison for the third fall. It was there that a barbaric justice was carried out by his fellow inmates.

Bosch read through the details of the crimes. In each case the victim was a boy aged eight to ten years old. The first victim was a neighbor's child. The second was a boy Pell had taken by the hand on a playground and led into a nearby restroom. The third crime involved lying in wait and more strategic planning. The victim was a boy who had gotten off a school bus and was walking home – a stretch of only three blocks – when Pell pulled up in his van and stopped. He told the boy he was with school security and showed him a badge. He said he needed to take the boy home because there had been an incident at school he had to inform his parents about. The boy complied and got in the van. Pell drove to a clearing and committed several sex acts upon the child in the van before releasing him and driving away.

He did not leave DNA on the victim and was caught only because he blew through a red light after pulling out of the neighborhood. A camera took a picture of his van's license plate in the intersection just minutes before the boy was found wandering in a daze a few blocks away. Because of his past record he became a suspect. The victim made an identification at a lineup and the case was filed. But the ID – as with any made by a nine-year-old – was shaky and Pell was offered a deal. He pleaded guilty and got a ten-year sentence. He probably felt he had gotten the better side of things until the day he was cornered in the laundry at Corcoran, held down and castrated with a shank.

With each conviction Pell was psychologically

evaluated as part of the PSI, or pre-sentence investigation. Bosch knew from experience that these tended to piggyback on each other. The evaluators were busy with a crushing caseload and often relied on the evaluation performed the first time. So Bosch paid careful attention to the PSI report from the first conviction for indecent exposure.

The evaluation detailed a truly horrible and traumatic childhood. Pell was the son of a heroin-addicted mother who dragged the boy with her to dealer dens and shooting galleries, often paying for her drugs by performing sex acts on drug dealers right in front of her son. The child did not attend school with any regularity and had no real home that he could remember. He and his mother moved about constantly, living in hotels and motels and with men who put up with them for short periods of time.

Bosch keyed in on a long paragraph that described one particular stretch of time when Pell was eight years old. He described for the evaluator an apartment where he lived for what he believed was the longest period of time he'd ever spent under one roof. His mother had hooked up with a man named Johnny who used her for sex and to buy drugs for him. Often, the boy was left in Johnny's care while his mother went out to sell sex in order to buy drugs. Sometimes she was gone for days and Johnny became angry and frustrated. He alternately left the boy locked in a closet for long periods of time or beat him brutally, often whipping him with a belt. The report noted that Pell still had the scars on his back and buttocks that supported the story. The beatings were horrible enough but the man also took to sexually abusing the boy, forcing him to perform oral sex and threatening him with harsher beatings if he dared tell his mother or anyone else.

Soon after, that situation ended when his mother moved on from Johnny. But the horrors of Pell's childhood veered in a new direction when he was thirteen years old and his mother overdosed on a motel bed while he was sleeping right next to her. He was taken into the custody of the Department of Children and Family Services and placed in a series of foster homes. But he never stayed in one place for long, choosing to run away whenever the opportunity presented itself. He told the evaluator that he had been living on his own since he was seventeen. When asked if he had ever held a job, he said the only thing he had ever been paid for was sex with older men.

It was a gruesome story and Bosch knew that a version of it was shared by many of the denizens of the streets and the prisons, the traumas and depravities of childhood manifesting themselves in adulthood, often in repetitive behavior. It was the mystery Hannah Stone said she investigated on a regular basis.

Bosch checked the two other PSI reports and found variations of the same story, though some of Pell's recollections of the dates and ages shifted slightly. Still, it was largely the same story and its repeated nature was either a testament to the laziness of the evaluators or to Pell's telling the truth. Bosch guessed that it was somewhere in the middle. The evaluators only reported what they had been told or they copied it off a prior report. No effort had been made to confirm Pell's story or even to find the people who had abused him.

Bosch took out his notebook and wrote down a summary of the story about the man named Johnny. He was now sure that there had been no screwup in the handling of evidence. In the morning, he and Chu had an appointment at the regional lab and Chu at least would keep it – if only to eventually be able to testify that they had exhaustively investigated all possibilities.

But Bosch had no doubt that the lab was in the clear. He could feel the trickle of adrenaline dripping into his bloodstream. He knew it would soon become a relentless torrent and he would move with its flow. He believed he now knew who had killed Lily Price.

12

In the morning Bosch called Chu from his car and told him to handle the visit to the crime lab without him.

'But what are you doing?' his partner asked.

'I have to go back to Panorama City. I'm checking out a lead.'

'What lead, Harry?'

'It involves Pell. I read his file last night and came up with something. I need to check it. I don't think there's a problem at the lab but we have to check it out in case it ever came up at trial – if there ever *is* a trial. One of us has to be able to testify that we checked out the lab.'

'So what do I tell them when I get there?'

'We have an appointment with the deputy director. Just tell her you need to double-check how the evidence from the case was handled. You interview the lab rat that ran the case and that will be it. Twenty minutes, tops. Take notes.'

'And what will you be doing?'

'Hopefully talking to Clayton Pell about a man named Johnny.'

'What?'

'I'll tell you when I get back to the PAB. I gotta go.'

'Har—'

Bosch disconnected. He didn't want to get bogged

down with explanations. That slowed things down. He wanted to keep his momentum.

Twenty minutes later he was cruising Woodman looking for a parking slot near the Buena Vista apartments. There was nothing and he ended up parking on a red curb and walking a block back to the halfway house. He reached through the gate to buzz the office. He identified himself and asked for Dr Stone. The gate was unlocked and he entered.

Hannah Stone was waiting for him with a smile in the office suite's lobby area. He asked if she had her own office or a place where they could speak privately and she took him into one of the interview rooms.

'This will have to do,' she said. 'I share an office with two other therapists. What's going on, Harry? I wasn't expecting to see you again so soon.'

Bosch nodded, agreeing that he had thought the same thing.

'I want to talk to Clayton Pell.'

She frowned as though he was putting her in a difficult position.

'Well, Harry, if Clayton is a suspect, then you've put me in a very—'

'He's not. Look, can we sit down for a second?'

She pointed him to what he assumed was the client/patient chair while she took a chair facing it.

'Okay,' Bosch started. 'First, I have to tell you that what I say here will probably sound too coincidental to be coincidence – in fact, I don't even believe in coincidence. But what we talked about last night at dinner hooked into what I did after dinner and here I am. I need your help. I need to talk to Pell.'

'And it's not because he's a suspect?'

'No, he was too young. We know he's not the killer. But he's a witness.'

She shook her head.

'I've been talking to him four times a week for nearly six months. I think if he had witnessed this girl's murder, it would have come up on some level, subconscious or not.'

Bosch held up his hands to stop her.

'Not an eyewitness. He wasn't there and probably doesn't even know a thing about her. But I think he knew the killer. He can help me. Here, just take a look at this.'

He opened his briefcase on the floor between his feet. He pulled out the original Lily Price murder book and quickly opened it to the plastic sleeves containing the faded Polaroid photos of the crime scene. Stone got up and came around to the side of his chair so she could look.

'Okay, these are really old and faded but if you look at the victim's neck, you can make out the pattern left by the ligature. She was strangled.'

Bosch heard her sharp intake of breath.

'Oh, my god,' she said.

He closed the binder quickly and looked up at her. She had brought one hand to her mouth.

'I'm sorry. I thought you were used to seeing stuff like—'

'I am, I am. It's just that you never get used to it. My specialty is sexual deviancy and dysfunction. To see the ultimate . . .'

She pointed to the closed binder.

'That's what I try to stop. It's awful to see it.'

Bosch nodded and she told him to go back to the photos. He reopened the binder and returned to the plastic sleeves. He chose a close-up of the victim's neck and pointed out the vague indentation on Lily Price's skin.

'You see what I'm talking about?'

'Yes,' Stone said. 'Poor girl.'

'Okay, now look at this one.'

He switched to a different Polaroid on the next sleeve and told her once again to look at the ligature pattern. There was a noticeable indentation in the skin.

'I see it but what does it mean?'

'The angle is different on this photo and it shows the top line of the ligature. The first shot shows the lower line.'

He flipped the sleeve back and used his finger to outline the differences between the two shots.

'You see it?'

'Yes. But I'm not following. You have two lines. What do they mean?'

'Well, the lines don't match. They're on different levels of her neck. So it means that they are the top and bottom edges of the ligature. Take them together and we get an idea of how wide the ligature was and, more important, what it was.'

Spacing his thumb and forefinger he traced two lines on one of the photos, outlining a ligature that would have been almost two inches wide.

'It's all we have after so long,' he said. 'The autopsy photos weren't in the archives file. So these photos are it, and they show that the ligature was at least an inch and a half wide on the neck.'

'Like a belt?'

'Exactly. And then look at this. Right under the ear we have another indentation, another pattern.'

He went to another photo in the second sleeve.

'It looks like a square.'

'Right. Like a square belt buckle. Now let's go to the blood.'

He flipped to the first sleeve and zeroed in on the first three Polaroids. They all showed shots of the blood smear on the victim's neck.

'Just one drop of blood that was smeared on her neck. It's right in the middle of the ligature pattern, meaning it could have been transferred from the ligature. Twenty-two years ago their theory was that the guy was cut and was bleeding and a drop fell on her. He wiped it away but left the smear.'

'But you think it was a transfer.'

'Right. And that's where Pell comes in. It was his blood – his eight-year-old blood on her. How did it get there? Well, if we go with the transfer theory, it came off the belt. So the real question is not how did it get on Lily, it's how did it get on the belt?'

Bosch closed the binder and returned it to his briefcase. He pulled out the thick file from the Department of Probation and Parole. He held it up with two hands and shook it.

'Right here. I told you last night when you said you could not reveal client confidences that I already had his PSI evaluations. Well, I read them last night after I got home and there's something here and it ties in with your whole thing about repetitive behavior and—'

'He was whipped with a belt.'

Bosch smiled.

'Careful, Doctor, you don't want to be revealing confidences. Especially because you don't have to. It's all right here. Every time Pell got a psych evaluation, he told the same story. When he was eight years old, he and his mother lived with a guy who abused him physically and eventually sexually. It was probably what sent him down the path he's been on. But the physical abuse included being whipped with a belt.'

Bosch opened the file and handed her the first evaluation report.

'He was whipped so hard he must've bled,' he said. 'That report says he had scars on his backside from the abuse. To leave a scar you have to break the skin. You break the skin and you get blood.'

He watched her as she scanned the report, her eyes fixed in concentration. He felt his phone vibrate but ignored it. He knew it was probably his partner reporting that he had completed the DNA lab visit.

'Johnny,' she said as she handed the report back.

Bosch nodded.

'I think he's our man and I need to talk to Pell to get a line on him. Has he ever told you his full name? In the PSIs he only calls him Johnny.'

'No, he just called him Johnny in our sessions, too.'

'That's why I need to talk to him.'

She paused as she considered something Bosch apparently hadn't thought of. He thought she would be as excited about the lead as he was.

'What?'

'Harry, I have to consider what this will do to him, dredging all of this up. I'm sorry but I have to consider his well-being before the well-being of your investigation.'

Bosch wished she hadn't said that.

'Wait a minute,' he said. 'What do you mean "dredging it up"? It's in all three of his psych reports here. He has to have talked to you about this guy. I'm not asking you to break that confidence. I want to talk directly to him.'

'I know and I can't stop you from talking to him. It's really his option. He'll talk to you or he won't. But my only worry is that he's quite fragile as you can—'

'You can get him to talk to me, Hannah. You can tell him it will help him.'

'You mean lie to him? I won't do that.'

Bosch stood up, since she had not returned to her seat.

'I don't mean lie. I mean tell the truth. This will help him get this guy out of the shadows of the past. Like an exorcism. Maybe he even knows that this guy was killing girls.'

'You mean there's more than one?'

'I don't know but you saw the photos. It doesn't look like a onetime thing, like, oh, I got that out of my system and it's back to being a good citizen again. This was a predator's crime and predators don't stop. You know that as well as I do. It doesn't matter if this happened twenty-two years ago. If this guy Johnny is still out there, I have to find him. And Clayton Pell is the key.'

13

Clayton Pell agreed to talk to Bosch but only if Dr Stone remained present. Harry had no problem with that and thought that having Stone on hand might be helpful during the interview. He only advised her that Pell might become a witness in an eventual trial and as such Bosch would conduct the interview in a methodical and linear fashion.

An orderly walked Pell into the interview room, where three chairs had been set up, one facing the other two. Bosch introduced himself and shook Pell's hand without hesitation. Pell was a small man no more than five foot two and a hundred ten pounds, and Bosch knew that victims of sexual abuse during childhood often suffered from stunted growth. Disrupted psychological growth affected physical growth.

Bosch pointed Pell to his seat and cordially asked if he needed anything.

'I could use a smoke,' Pell said.

When he sat, he brought his legs up and crossed them on the seat. It seemed like a childlike thing to do.

'I could use one, too, but we're not going to break the rules today,' Bosch said.

'That's too bad, then.'

Stone had suggested that they set the three seats up around a table to make it less formal but Bosch had said no. He also choreographed the seating arrangement so that both he and Stone would be left and right of Pell's center view line, which meant he would have to constantly look back and forth between them. Observing eye movement would be a good way for Bosch to measure sincerity and veracity. Pell had become a tragic figure in Stone's estimation but Bosch held no such sympathy. Pell's traumatic history and childlike dimensions didn't matter. He was now a predator. Just ask the nine-year-old boy he had pulled into his van. Bosch planned to constantly remind himself that predators hid themselves and that they lied and waited for their opponents to reveal weaknesses. He wouldn't make a mistake with Pell.

'Why don't we get started here,' Bosch said. 'If you don't mind I will take written notes as we talk.'

'A'right by me,' Pell said.

Bosch pulled out his notebook. It had an LAPD detective's badge embossed on its leather cover. It had been a gift from his daughter, who had had it custom-made through a friend in Hong Kong whose father was in the leather business. The embossing was complete with his badge number – 2997. She'd given it to him at Christmas. It was one of his most treasured possessions because it had come from her, but also because he knew it served a valuable purpose. Every time he flipped it open to jot down a note, he was showing the badge to his interview subjects and reminding them that the power and might of the state was before them.

'So what's this about?' Pell asked in a high, nasal voice. 'Doc didn't tell me nothin' about nothin'.'

Stone did not tell him not to call her Doc.

'It's about a murder, Clayton,' Bosch said. 'From way back when you were just a boy of eight years old.'

'I don't know nothin' about no murder, sir.'

The voice was grating and Bosch wondered if it had always been that way or if it was the by-product of the prison attack.

'I know that. And you should know that you are not suspected in this crime in any way.'

'Then why come to me?'

'Good question, and I'm going to just answer it straight, Clayton. You are in this room because your blood and your DNA were found on the victim's body.'

Pell shot straight up out of his chair.

'Okay, I'm out of here.'

He turned to head toward the door.

'Clay!' Stone called out. 'Hear him out! You are not a suspect! You were eight years old. He just wants to know what you know. Please!'

He looked down at her but pointed at Bosch.

'You can trust this guy but I don't. The cops don't do anybody any favors. Only themselves.'

Stone stood up to make her pitch.

'Clayton, please. Give it a chance.'

Pell reluctantly sat back down. Stone followed and he stared at her while refusing to look at Bosch.

'We think the killer had your blood on him,' Bosch said. 'And it somehow got transferred to the victim. We don't think you had anything to do with the crime.'

'Why don't you just get it over with,' he replied, holding his wrists out together for cuffing.

'Clay, please,' Stone said.

He waved both hands in an *enough already* gesture.

He was small enough that he could completely turn his body in his seat and put both legs over the chair's left arm, giving Bosch the cold shoulder like a child ignoring his parent. He folded his arms across his chest and Bosch could see the top edge of a tattoo peeking out of his collar on the back of his neck.

'Clayton,' Stone said sternly. 'Don't you remember where you were when you were eight? Don't you remember what you've told me over and over?'

Pell tucked his chin down toward his chest and then relented.

'Of course I do.'

'Then answer Detective Bosch's questions.'

He milked it for ten seconds and then nodded.

'Okay. What?'

Just as Bosch was about to ask a question, his phone buzzed in his pocket. Pell heard it.

'If you answer that, I am fucking walking out of here.'

'Don't worry, I hate cell phones.'

Bosch waited for the buzzing to stop and then proceeded.

'Tell me about where you were and how you were living when you were eight years old, Clayton.'

Pell turned back straight in his chair to face Bosch.

'I was living with a monster. A guy who liked to beat the shit out of me whenever my mother wasn't around.'

He paused. Bosch waited and then prompted.

'What else, Clayton?'

'He decided that just beatin' me up wasn't good enough. He decided he liked for me to suck him off, too. A couple times a week. So that's how I was living, Detective.'

'And this man was named Johnny?'

'Where did you get that?'

Pell looked at Stone, assuming she had betrayed his confidence.

'The name's in your PSI reports,' Bosch said quickly. 'I read them. You mention a guy named Johnny in them. Is that who we're talking about here?'

'I just call him that. Now, I mean. He reminded me of Jack Nicholson in that Stephen King movie. The "Here's Johnny" guy, chasing after the boy with an ax all the time. That was what it was like for me, only no ax. He didn't need no ax.'

'What about his real name? Did you know it?'

'Nope, never did.'

'Are you sure?'

'Course I'm sure. The guy fucked me up for life. If I knew his name, I'd remember it. The only thing I remember was his nickname, what everybody called him.'

'What was it?'

A small, thin smile played on Pell's lips. He had something everyone wanted and he was going to work it to his advantage. Bosch could tell. All those years in prison, he had learned to play the angles.

'What do I get for it?' he asked.

Bosch was ready.

'You might get to put the guy who tortured you away for good.'

'What makes you think he's even still alive?'

Bosch shrugged.

'Just a guess. The reports say your mother had you when she was seventeen. So she was about twenty-five when she took up with this guy. My guess is that he wasn't too much older than her. Twenty-two years ago . . . he's probably in his fifties and he's probably still out there doing what he does.'

Pell stared down at the floor and Bosch wondered if he was seeing a memory from the time he was in the man's control.

Stone cleared her voice and spoke.

'Clay, remember how we've talked about evil and whether people are born that way or if it is given to them? About how acts can be evil but the person committing them is not?'

Pell nodded.

'This man is evil. Look what he did to you. And Detective Bosch believes he committed other evil acts on other victims.'

Pell nodded again.

'That fucking belt had letters on the buckle. He used to hit me with that buckle. The fucker. After a while I just didn't want to get hit anymore. It was easier just to give him what he wanted . . .'

Bosch waited. There was no need to ask another question. Stone seemed to sense it as well. After a long moment Pell nodded a third time and spoke.

'Everybody called him Chill. Including my mother.'

Bosch wrote it down.

'You said the belt buckle had letters on it. You mean like initials? What were they?'

'C. H.'

Bosch wrote it down. His adrenaline started to kick in. He might not have a full name but he was getting close. For a split second an image came to him. His fist raised and knocking on a door. No, pounding on a door. A door that would be opened by the man known as Chill.

Pell continued to talk unbidden.

'I thought of Chill last year when I saw all that stuff on the news about the Grim Sleeper. Chill had photos like that guy, too.'

The Grim Sleeper was the name given to a serial killer suspect and the task force investigation that sought him. A single killer was suspected in multiple murders of women, but there were large spaces of time between killings and it was as though he had gone to sleep and was hibernating. When a suspect was identified and captured the year before, investigators found hundreds of photos of women in his possession. Most of the women were naked and in sexually suggestive poses in the shots. The investigation was ongoing as to who the women were and what had happened to them.

'He had photos of women?' Bosch asked.

'Yeah, the women he'd fucked. Naked pictures. His trophies. He took pictures of my mother. I saw 'em. He had one of those cameras where the picture just came right out so he didn't have to worry about taking film to the drugstore and getting found out. Back before they had digital.'

'A Polaroid.'

'Yeah, right. Polaroid.'

'It is not unusual,' Stone said. 'For men who physically hurt women or not. It's a form of control. Ownership. Skins on the wall, keeping score. A symptom of a very controlling personality. In today's world of digital cameras and Internet porn, you see this more and more.'

'Yeah, well then, I guess Chill was a pioneer,' Pell said. 'He didn't have no computer. He kept his pictures in a shoe box. That's how we moved away from him.'

'What do you mean?' Bosch asked.

Pell tightened his lips for a moment before answering.

'He took a picture of me with his dick in my mouth. And he put it in his shoebox. One day I stole it and left it where my mom would see it. We moved out that day.'

'Were there other photos of boys or men in that shoe-box?' Bosch asked.

'I remember seeing one other. It was a kid like me but I didn't know who it was.'

Bosch wrote down a few more notes. Pell's information that Chill was apparently a pansexual predator was a key part of the emerging profile. He then asked if Pell could remember where they lived when he and his mother were with the man called Chill. He could only remember that they were close to Travel Town at Griffith Park, because his mother used to take him there to ride on the trains.

'Could you walk there or did you drive?'

'We took a taxi and I remember it was close. We went there a lot. I liked being on those little trains.'

It was a good note. Bosch knew Travel Town was on the north side of the park and it probably meant Pell had lived with Chill in North Hollywood or Burbank. It would help narrow things.

He then asked for a description of Chill, and Pell only described him as being white, tall and muscular.

'Did he have a job?'

'Not really. I think he was like a handyman or some-thing. He had a lot of tools he kept in his truck.'

'What kind of truck?'

'Van, actually. Ford Econoline. That was where he made me do things to him.'

And a van would be the kind of vehicle Pell would use later to commit the same sort of crime. Bosch didn't mention this, of course.

'How old would you say Chill was back then?' he asked.

'No idea. You're probably right about what you said before. About five years older than my mother.'

'You don't happen to have a photo of him with your things or in storage or something?'

Pell laughed and looked at Bosch like he thought he was an imbecile.

'You think I'd keep his picture around? I don't even have a picture of my mother, man.'

'Sorry, had to ask. Did you ever see this guy with any women other than your mother?'

'You mean like to have sex with?'

'Yes.'

'No.'

'Clayton, what else do you remember about him?'

'I just remember I tried to stay away from him.'

'Do you think you could identify him?'

'What, now? After all these years?'

Bosch nodded.

'I don't know. But I won't ever forget the way he looked back then.'

'Do you remember anything else about the place where you lived with him? Anything that might help me find him?'

Pell thought about it and then shook his head.

'No, man, just what I said.'

'Did he have pets?'

'No, but he beat me like a dog. I guess I was his pet.'

Bosch glanced over at Stone to see if she had anything.

'What about hobbies?' she asked.

'I think his hobby was filling up that shoebox,' Pell said.

'But you never saw any of the other women from the pictures, right?' Bosch asked.

'But that didn't mean anything. You could tell most of the pictures were taken in the van. He had an old mattress back there. He wasn't bringing any of them home, you know?'

It was good information. Bosch wrote it all down.

'You said you saw one photo of a boy. Was that taken in the van, too?'

Pell didn't respond at first. He had committed his own evil acts in a van and the connection was obvious.

'I don't remember,' he finally said.

Bosch moved on.

'Tell me something, Clayton. If I catch this guy and he goes on trial, would you be willing to testify to the things you've told me today?'

Pell considered the question.

'What would I get?' he asked.

'I told you,' Bosch said. 'You'd get satisfaction. You'd help put this guy away for the rest of his life.'

'That's nothing.'

'Well, I can't prom—'

'*Look what he did to me! Everything is because of him!*'

He pointed to his chest as he yelled it. The raw emotion

in his outburst was full of an animal ferocity that belied his diminutive frame. And it got through to Bosch. He realized how powerful it might be if it was put on exhibit in a trial. If he yelled out the same way and the same thing in front of a jury, it would be devastating for the defense.

'Clayton, I'm going to find this guy,' he said. 'And you'll get the chance to tell him that to his face. It may help you with the rest of your life.'

'The rest of my life? Well, that's great. Thanks for that.'

The sarcasm was unmistakable. Bosch was about to offer a comeback when there was a sharp knock on the interview room door. Stone got up to open it, and another therapist stood there. She whispered to Stone and then Stone turned to Bosch.

'There are two police officers at the front gate, asking for you.'

Bosch thanked Pell for his time and said he would be in touch about the investigation. He headed out to the gate, pulling his phone as he went. He saw that he had ignored four calls, one from his partner, two from a 213 number he didn't recognize and the last from Kiz Rider.

The two uniformed cops were from Van Nuys Division. They said they had been sent by the OCP.

'You're not answering your phone or the radio in your car,' the older one said. 'You're supposed to contact a Lieutenant Rider in the chief's office. She says it's urgent.'

Bosch thanked them and explained that he was in an important interview with his phone turned off. As soon as they walked away he called Rider and she answered right away.

'Harry, why aren't you answering your phone?'

'Because I was in the middle of an interview. I usually don't stop to take calls. How'd you find me?'

'Through your partner, who *is* answering his phone. What does that halfway house have to do with the Irving case?'

There was no getting around the answer.

'Nothing. It's another case.'

There was silence while she worked to contain her frustration and fury with him.

'Harry, the chief of police told you to work the Irving matter as a priority. Why would you—'

'Look, I'm waiting on the autopsy. There's nothing I can do about Irving until I get the autopsy and get going from there.'

'Well, guess what?'

Bosch now understood where those two 213 calls he missed had come from.

'What?'

'The autopsy started a half hour ago. If you leave now, you might catch the end of it.'

'Is Chu there?'

'As far as I know he is. He's supposed to be.'

'I'm on my way.'

Embarrassed, he disconnected with no further discussion.

14

By the time Bosch was gowned and gloved and had entered the autopsy suite, George Irving's body was already being sewn closed with thick waxed twine.

'Sorry I'm late,' he announced.

Dr Borja Toron Antons pointed to the microphone hanging from the ceiling over the autopsy table, and Bosch realized his mistake. The details of the autopsy were being recorded and now it would be formally noted that Bosch had all but missed the postmortem medical examination. If the case ever came to a point that there was a trial, a defense attorney would be able to insinuate much from that to the jury. It didn't matter that Chu was in attendance. The fact that the lead investigator was not where he was supposed to be could take on a sinister, even corrupt, connotation in the hands of the right attorney.

Bosch took a position next to Chu, who had his arms folded and was leaning against a worktable across from the foot of the autopsy table. It was about as far from the autopsy as you could get and still say you were there. Even through the plastic germ guard Bosch could tell Chu was not happy. He had once confided to Bosch that he wanted to be in the Open-Unsolved Unit because he wanted to investigate murders but had trouble viewing autopsies. He couldn't stand the sight of the human body being mutilated. That made working cold cases a perfect assignment. He reviewed autopsy reports but didn't actually attend them, and he still got to work murders.

Harry wanted to ask him if anything of interest had come up during the cut but decided to wait to ask Antons directly, and off the tape. Instead, he checked the worktable at the pathologist's back and counted the vials in the tox rack. He saw that Antons had filled five tubes with Irving's blood, meaning he was requesting a full toxicological screening. On a routine autopsy, blood is screened for twelve baseline drug groups. When the county is sparing no expense or there is suspicion of a drug involvement that is off the usual trail, then a full screen widens the net to twenty-six groups. And that takes five vials of blood.

Antons ended the autopsy by describing his closing of the Y incision and then took one of his gloves off to turn off the microphone.

'Glad you could make it, Detective,' he said. 'How were you hitting 'em?'

Off the tape his Spanish accent seemed to grow thicker with his sarcasm.

'I was two under at the turn,' Bosch said, rolling with it. 'But hey, I knew my partner could handle things here. Right, partner?'

He gave Chu a rough clap on the shoulder. By referring to him directly as *partner,* Bosch was sending a coded message to Chu. They had agreed when they first became a team that if ever a play was on or one of them was running a bluff, the tip-off would be to call the other one *partner.* The code word meant that the receiver should play along.

But this time Chu ignored the routine.

'Yeah, right,' he said. 'I tried calling you, man. You didn't answer.'

'I guess you didn't try hard enough.'

Bosch gave Chu a look that almost melted his plastic face guard. He then turned his attention back to Antons.

'I see you're doing the full scan, Doc. Good call. Anything else I should know about?'

'It wasn't my call. I was told to run a full scan by the powers that be. I did, however, point out to your partner an issue that bears further scrutiny.'

Bosch looked at Chu and then at the body on the table.

'An issue? Further scrutiny? Is he talking about detective work?'

'The body's got like a scratch or a bruise or something on the back of the right shoulder,' Chu said. 'It didn't come from the fall because he landed facedown.'

'Antemortem injury,' Antons added.

Bosch stepped closer to the table. He realized that because he had arrived late to the death scene, he had never seen the victim's back. Irving had already been turned over by Van Atta and the crime scene team by the time Bosch had arrived. No one from Van Atta to Crate and Barrel had mentioned anything about an antemortem injury on the shoulder.

'Can I see it?' he asked.

'If you must,' Antons said grumpily. 'If you had been here on time you would have already seen it.'

He reached over a worktable to a shelf and pulled a new set of gloves out of a box.

Bosch helped turn the body over on the table. The

125

back was coated in bloody fluid that had accumulated on the table, which had raised sides like a tray. Antons pulled down an overhead nozzle and sprayed the fluid off the body. Bosch saw the injury immediately. It was about five inches long and included minor surface scratching and slight bruising. There was a discernible pattern that was almost circular. It looked like a series of four crescent moons, repeating about an inch apart, scratched onto the shoulder above the scapula line. Each crescent was about two inches high.

The dread of recognition came over Bosch. He knew Chu was too young and new to the job to be familiar with the pattern. And Antons wouldn't recognize it either. He had only been around a decade or so after coming from Madrid to attend UCLA's med school and never going back.

'Did you check for petechial hemorrhaging?' Bosch asked.

'Of course,' Antons said. 'There was none.'

Petechial hemorrhaging occurred in the blood vessels around the eyes during suffocation.

'Why do you ask about petechial hemorrhaging after seeing this abrasion on the back of the shoulder?' Antons asked.

Bosch shrugged.

'Just covering all the bases.'

Antons and Chu were both staring at him, expecting more. But he didn't give it. They stood there silently for a long moment before Bosch moved on. He pointed to the abrasion on the body's back.

'You said antemortem. How close to death are we talking about?'

'You see that the skin is broken. I took a culture. The histamine levels in the wounds indicate the injury occurred very close to death. I was telling Detective Chu, you need to go back to the hotel. He may have scratched his back on something while climbing over the balcony. You can see there is a pattern to the wound.'

Bosch knew the pattern already but wasn't going to say anything yet.

'Climbing over the balcony? So you're calling this a suicide?'

'Of course not. Not yet. It could be suicide. It could be accidental. There is follow-up needed. We'll do the full toxicological scan, and this injury needs to be explained. You see the pattern. That should help you narrow it down at the hotel.'

'Did you check the hyoid?' Bosch asked.

Antons put his hands on his hips.

'Why would I check the hyoid on a jumper?'

'I thought you just said you weren't ready to call him a jumper.'

Antons didn't answer. He grabbed a scalpel from a rack.

'Help me turn him back over.'

'Wait,' Bosch said. 'Can I get a picture of this first?'

'I took photos. They should be in the printer by now. You can pick them up on the way out.'

Bosch helped him turn the body back over. Antons used the scalpel to open the neck and remove the small U-shaped bone that guarded the windpipe. He carefully cleaned it in a sink and then studied it for fractures under a lighted magnifying lens on the counter.

'Hyoid's intact,' he said.

Bosch nodded. It didn't prove anything one way or the other. An expert could have choked Irving out without cracking the bone or causing bleeding in the eyes. It didn't prove anything at all.

But the marks on the back of the shoulder were something. Bosch felt things changing about the case. Changing rapidly. And it was bringing new meaning to *high jingo*.

15

Chu waited until they were halfway through the parking lot before erupting.

'Okay, Harry, what's going on? What was that all about in there?'

Bosch pulled his phone. He had to make a call.

'I'll tell you when I can tell you. I want you to go back to—'

'That's not good enough, Harry! We're partners, man, and you're constantly doing the lone wolf number on me. You can't do that anymore.'

Chu had stopped and turned to him, his arms spread. Bosch stopped as well.

'Look, I'm trying to protect you. I need to talk to somebody first. Let me do that and then we'll talk.'

Unsatisfied, Chu shook his head.

'You're killing me with this shit, man. What do you want me to do, go back to the office and just sit on my thumbs?'

'No, there's a lot I want you to do. I want you to go to Property and pull out Irving's shirt. Have somebody in SID check the inside shoulder for blood. It's a dark shirt and nobody noticed anything on it yesterday.'

'So if there's blood, we'll know he got those marks while wearing the shirt.'

'That's right.'

'And what will that tell us?'

Bosch didn't answer. He was thinking about the shirt button found on the floor in the hotel suite. There could have been a struggle with Irving being choked out and the button being pulled loose.

'When you're finished with the shirt, get the search warrant going.'

'The search warrant for what?'

'Irving's office. I want to have a warrant before we go in and start looking at files.'

'They're his files and he's dead. What do we need a warrant for?'

'Because the guy was a lawyer and I don't want to trip over any attorney–client privilege bullshit when we go in there. I want everything clean on this.'

'You know, it's going to be hard for me to write up a warrant with you keeping me in the dark about shit.'

'No, it's going to be easy. You say you are conducting an open-ended investigation into this man's death. You say that there were signs of a possible struggle – the button torn from the shirt, the antemortem wound on the back – and you want access to his business papers and product so you can determine if there was any bad blood involving clients or adversaries. Simple. If you can't do it, I'll write it up when I get back.'

'No, I can do it. I'm the writer.'

It was true. In their usual division of labor and respon- sibilities, Chu always did the warrant work.

'Okay, then go do it and stop moping about it.'

'Hey, Harry, fuck you. I'm not moping. You wouldn't like it if this was how I was treating you.'

'I'll tell you what, Chu. If I had a partner who had a

lot more years and experience than me and who said trust me on this until the time is right, then I think I would. And I would thank him for watching out for me.'

Bosch let that sink in for a moment before dismissing Chu.

'I'll see you back there. I gotta go.'

They started walking to their separate cars. Bosch glanced back at his partner and saw him walking with his head down, a hangdog expression on his face. Chu didn't understand the complexities of high jingo. But Bosch did.

By the time he was behind the wheel, Harry had Kiz Rider on the phone.

'Meet me at the academy in fifteen minutes. In the video room.'

'Harry, there's no way. I'm about to go into a budget meeting.'

'Then don't complain to me about not knowing what's going on with the Irving case.'

'Can't you just tell me?'

'No, you have to be shown. When can you meet?'

There was a long pause before she responded.

'Not before one. Go get yourself something to eat and I'll meet you then.'

Bosch was reluctant to slow things down but it was important that Rider know the direction the case was heading.

'See you then. By the way, did you put somebody on Irving's office like I asked you yesterday?'

'Yes, I did. Why?'

'Just wanted to be sure.'

He disconnected before she rebuked him for his lack of confidence in her.

It took Bosch fifteen minutes to get over to Elysian Park and the police academy complex. He stopped in at the café in the Revolver and Athletic Club and took a stool at the counter. He ordered a coffee and a Bratton Burger, named after the prior chief of police, and spent the next hour going over his notes and adding to them.

After paying the tab and checking out some of the police memorabilia hanging on the café wall, he walked through the old gymnasium, the place where he had received his badge on a rainy day more than thirty years before, and into the video room. There was a library here that contained all the training videos used by the department for as long as there had been video. He told the civilian custodian what he was looking for and waited while the man searched for the old tape.

Rider arrived a few minutes later and right on time.

'Okay, Harry, I'm here. As much as I hate daylong budget meetings, I really need to get back as soon as I can. What are we doing here?'

'We're going to look at a training tape, Kiz.'

'And what does it have to do with Irving's son?'

'Maybe everything.'

The custodian brought Bosch the tape. He and Rider went over to a viewing cubicle. Bosch put the video in the machine and started the playback.

'This is one of the old training tapes for the controlled bar hold,' he said. 'More commonly known in the world as the LAPD choke hold.'

'The infamous choke hold,' she said. 'It's been banned since before I even got here.'

'Technically, the bar hold is banned. The controlled carotid hold is still approved in use of deadly force situations. But good luck with that.'

'So like I said, what are we doing here, Harry?'

Bosch gestured toward the screen.

'They used to use these tapes to teach what to do. Now they're used to teach what not to do. This is the bar hold.'

At one time the controlled bar hold was standard in the LAPD's use-of-force progression but it had been outlawed after so many deaths were attributed to it.

The video showed the hold being applied by an instructor on an academy recruit volunteer. From behind the recruit, the instructor brought his left arm across the front of his volunteer's neck. He then cinched the vise closed by gripping the recruit's shoulder. The recruit struggled but within seconds passed out. The instructor gently lowered him to the ground and started patting his cheeks. The volunteer woke immediately and seemed puzzled by what had just happened. He was ushered off camera and another volunteer took his place. This time the instructor moved more slowly and explained the steps of the hold. He then offered tips on how to deal with struggling subjects. The second tip was what Bosch was waiting for.

'There,' he said.

He backed the tape up and played the section again. The instructor called the move the hand creep. The left arm was locked across the volunteer's neck, the hand up at his right shoulder. To guard against the arm being pulled away by the struggling volunteer, the instructor gripped his hands together like hooks at the top of the shoulder and extended his right forearm down the volunteer's back. Then little by little he tightened the vise on the volunteer's neck. The second volunteer passed out.

'I can't believe they actually choked these guys out like that,' Rider said.

'They probably didn't have a choice when it came to volunteering,' Bosch said. 'It's like the Tasers now.'

Every officer who carried a Taser had to be trained in the use of the device and this included being Tased himself.

'So what are you showing me here, Harry?'

'Back when they outlawed the hold, I was put on the task force investigating all the deaths. It was an assignment. I didn't volunteer.'

'And what's it got to do with George Irving?'

'It basically came down to the fact that people were using the hold too often and for too long. The carotid is supposed to open up immediately after you stop the pressure. But sometimes the pressure was held too long and people died. And sometimes the pressure cracked the hyoid bone, crushing the windpipe. Again people died. The bar hold was banned and the carotid hold was relegated to use in deadly force situations only. And deadly force is a whole separate set of criteria. The bottom line was, you could no longer choke somebody out in a basic street scuffle. Okay?'

'Got it.'

'My part was the autopsies. I was coordinator of that. Gathering all the cases going back twenty years and then looking for similarities. There was an anomaly in some of the cases. It didn't really mean anything but it was there. We found a wound pattern on the shoulder. Showed up in maybe a third of the cases. A repeating crescent-moon pattern on the shoulder blade of the victim.'

'What was it?'

Bosch gestured to the video screen. The training tape was frozen on the hand creep move.

'It was the hand creep. A lot of cops wore military watches with the big chrono bezels. During the choke hold, if they made that move and walked the wrist lock up the shoulder, the watch bezel cut the skin or left a bruise. It didn't really have to do with anything other than to help prove there had been a struggle. But I remembered it today.'

'At the autopsy?'

From his inside pocket he pulled out an autopsy photo of George Irving's shoulder.

'That's Irving's shoulder.'

'Could this have happened in the fall?'

'He hit the ground face-first. There shouldn't be an injury like that on his back. The ME confirmed it was antemortem.'

Rider's eyes darkened as she studied the photo.

'So we have a homicide?'

'It's looking that way. He was choked out and then dropped from the balcony.'

'You're sure about this?'

'No, nothing's for sure. But it's the direction I'm now taking it.'

She nodded in acceptance.

'And you think a cop or a former cop did it?'

Bosch shook his head.

'No, I don't think that. It's true that cops of a certain age were trained to use the hold. But they're not the only ones. Military, mixed martial-arts fighters. Any kid who watches YouTube can learn how it's done. There's one thing that's sort of a coincidence, though.'

'Coincidence? You always said there was no such thing as coincidence.'

Bosch shrugged.

'What's the coincidence, Harry?'

'The choke hold task force I was on back then? Deputy Chief Irvin Irving was in command. We worked it out of Central Division. It was the first time Irving and I directly crossed paths.'

'Well, as coincidences go, that's kind of weak.'

'Probably so. But it means Irving will recognize the significance of the crescent marks on his son's back if he is told about them or shown a photo. And I don't want the councilman to know about this yet.'

Rider looked at him sharply.

'Harry, he's all over the chief about this. He's all over me. He's already called three times today about the autopsy. And you want to withhold this from him?'

'I don't want it out there in the open. I want whoever did this to think they're in the clear. That way they won't see me coming.'

'Harry, I don't know about this.'

'Look, who knows what Irving will do with it if he knows? He might end up talking about it with the wrong person or having a press conference and then it gets out and we've lost our edge on it.'

'But you are going to have to go to him with it to conduct your homicide investigation. He'll know then.'

'Eventually he'll have to know. But for now we tell him the jury is still out. We're waiting on the tox results from autopsy. Even with a high-jingo rush, that will take two weeks. Meantime, we are simply leaving no stone unturned, conducting a thorough investigation into all the possibilities. He doesn't need to know about this, Kiz. Not right now.'

Bosch held up the photo. Rider rubbed her mouth as she considered his request.

'I don't think you should even tell the chief,' Bosch added.

'I'm not going there,' she responded immediately. 'The day I start withholding from him is the day I don't deserve the job.'

Bosch shrugged.

'Suit yourself. Just keep it from leaving the building.'

She nodded, having come to a decision.

'I'll give you forty-eight hours and then we reevaluate. Thursday morning I want to know where you are on this and we decide again then.'

It was what Bosch was hoping to get. Just a head start.

'Fine. Thursday.'

'That doesn't mean I don't want to hear from you till Thursday. I want to be kept up-to-date. If something else breaks, you call me.'

'Got it.'

'Where do you go from here on it?'

'We're working on a warrant for Irving's office. He had an office manager who probably knew a lot of the secrets. And the enemies. We need to sit down with her but I want to do that in the office so she can show us through the files and whatever else is there.'

Rider nodded in approval.

'Good. Where's your partner?'

'He's writing up the warrant. We're making sure we're clean, every step of the way.'

'That's smart. Does he know about the choke hold?'

'Not yet. I wanted to talk to you first. But he'll know by the end of the day.'

'I appreciate that, Harry. I have to get back to my budget meeting and figuring out how to do more with less.'

'Yeah, good luck with that.'

'And you be careful. This could lead to some dark places.'

Bosch ejected the tape.

'Don't I know it,' he said.

16

Because George Irving had maintained his legal practice and license with the California bar, getting a search warrant allowing the investigators access to his office and files took most of Tuesday afternoon and evening. The legal document was finally signed and issued by superior court judge Stephen Fluharty after a special master was appointed to review any documents that were viewed or seized by the police. The *special master* was an attorney himself and as such was not governed by the need for speed that homicide investigators working an active case were accustomed to. He set the time of the search for a leisurely 10 A.M. start on Wednesday.

Irving and Associates was housed in a two-room office on Spring Street across from the Los Angeles Times parking garage. That put George Irving just two blocks from City Hall. It also put his office even closer to the Police Administration Building. Bosch and Chu walked over Wednesday morning, arriving to find no police officer on the door and someone inside.

They entered and found a woman in her seventies in the front room, boxing files. She identified herself as Dana Rosen, George Irving's office manager. Bosch had called her the evening before to make sure she would be on hand for the office search.

'Was there a police officer on the door when you arrived?' Bosch asked.

Rosen looked confused.

'No, there was no one.'

'Well, we weren't supposed to start until the special master got here. Mr Hadlow. He's got to look at everything before we put it in boxes.'

'Oh, dear. These are my own files. Does that mean I can't take them?'

'No, it means we just have to wait. Let's put all of that down and step back outside. Mr Hadlow should be here any minute.'

They moved out to the sidewalk and Bosch pulled the door closed. He asked Rosen to lock it with her key. He then pulled his phone and called Kiz Rider. He didn't bother with a greeting.

'I thought you put a uniform on the door at Irving's office.'

'I did.'

'Nobody's here.'

'I'll call you back.'

Bosch closed his phone and appraised Dana Rosen. She was not what he had expected. She was a small and attractive woman but because of her age he dismissed her as a possible mistress of George Irving. Bosch had read that totally wrong with the widow. Dana Rosen could have been Irving's mother.

'How long did you work for George Irving?' Bosch asked.

'Oh, a long time. I was with him at the City Attorney's

Office. Then when he left he offered me a job and I—'

She stopped when Bosch's phone began to buzz. It was Rider.

'The watch commander at Central Division took it upon himself to redeploy the unit on the post at day watch roll call today. He thought that you had already been through the place.'

Bosch knew that meant the office was unguarded for nearly three hours, plenty of time for someone to get in ahead of them and remove files. His suspicions and anger rose in equal increments.

'Who is this guy?' he asked. 'Is he connected to the councilman?'

Irvin Irving had been out of the department for years but still had connections to many officers he mentored or rewarded with promotions during his years in command staff.

'It's a she,' Rider said. 'Captain Grace Reddecker. As far as I can tell, it was a simple mistake. She's not political – in that way.'

Meaning of course Reddecker was politically connected in the department – she would have to be to score a division command – but she didn't play politics on a larger scale.

'She's not one of Irving's disciples?'

'No. Her rise came after he was gone.'

Bosch saw a man in a suit approaching them. He guessed it was the special master.

'I have to go,' he said to Rider. 'I'll deal with this later. I hope it's like you said, just a mistake.'

'I think there's nothing else to it, Harry.'

Bosch disconnected as the man on the sidewalk joined them. He was tall with reddish-brown hair and a golfer's tan.

'Richard Hadlow?' Bosch asked.

'That would be me.'

Bosch made introductions and Rosen unlocked the office so they could enter. Hadlow was from one of the silk-stocking firms on Bunker Hill. The evening before, Judge Fluharty had enlisted him as a special master on a pro bono basis. No pay meant no delay. Hadlow had been leisurely about scheduling the search but now that they were there, he would be interested in getting it done quickly so he could get back to his paying clients. And that was fine with Bosch.

They moved into the offices and set a plan in motion. Hadlow would go to work on the office files, making sure there was no privileged content before turning them over to Chu for review. Meantime, Bosch would continue his discussion with Dana Rosen to determine what was important and timely in terms of Irving's work.

Files and documentation were always valuable in an investigation but Bosch was smart enough to know that the most valuable thing in the office was Rosen. She could tell them the inside story.

While Hadlow and Chu went to work in the rear office, Bosch pulled the seat from the reception desk into position in front of a couch in the front room and asked Rosen to have a seat. He then locked the front door and the formal interview began.

'Is it *Mrs* Rosen?' he asked.

'No, never been married. You can just call me Dana, anyway.'

'Well, Dana, why don't we continue our conversation from the sidewalk. You were telling me that you had been with Mr Irving since the City Attorney's Office?'

'Yes, I was his secretary there before coming with him when he started Irving and Associates. So if you include that, it has been sixteen years.'

'And when he left the City Attorney's Office you came with him right away?'

She nodded.

'We left the same day. It was a good deal. I was vested with the city so I got a pension when I retired, and then I came here. It was thirty hours a week. Nice and easy.'

'How involved were you in Mr Irving's work?'

'Not too much. He wasn't here too much. I sort of just kept the files organized and everything neat and orderly. Answered the phone and took messages. He never took meetings here. Almost never.'

'Did he have a lot of clients?'

'He had a select few, actually. He charged a lot and people expected results. He worked hard for them.'

Bosch had his notebook out but so far had not jotted down a note.

'Who was he concentrating on lately?'

For the first time Rosen was not quick with her response. She had a confused look on her face.

'Am I to assume because of all these questions that George didn't kill himself?'

'All I can tell you is that we are not assuming anything. It's an open investigation and we haven't made a finding in regard to his death. Until we do, we are trying to conduct a thorough investigation of all possibilities. Now, can you answer the question? Who was Mr Irving concentrating his time on most recently?'

'Well, he had two clients that he was working with intensively. One was Western Block and Concrete and the other was Tolson Towing. But both those went to council vote last week. George got what he wanted in both cases and was now just coming up for air.'

Bosch wrote the names down.

'What did his work for those companies involve?' he asked.

'Western was bidding on the contract for the new parking garage at Parker Center. They got it. And Tolson was reapplying as OPG designee for Hollywood and Wilshire Divisions.'

The Official Police Garage designation would mean Tolson would continue to handle all towing called for by the LAPD in those two police divisions. A lucrative deal, just as he assumed the concrete pour on a parking garage would be. Bosch had heard or read that the new city garage would be six levels and was designed to service the overflow from all municipal buildings in the civic center.

'So these were his main clients as of late?' he asked.

'That's right.'

'And they would have been happy with the results they got.'

'Absolutely. Western wasn't even the low bidder and Tolson had strong competition this time. Plus a two-inch-thick complaint file to overcome. George had his work cut out for him but he came through.'

'And how did it work with his father being on the

council? Wasn't that a conflict of interest?'

Rosen nodded emphatically.

'Of course it was. That was why the councilman abstained from voting whenever one of George's clients had business before the council.'

This seemed odd to Bosch. Having a father on the council seemed to give George Irving the inside edge. But if his father excused himself from voting on such matters, the edge disappeared.

Or did it?

Bosch assumed that even if the older Irving made a show of abstaining from voting, the other council members knew they could curry his favor for their own pet projects if they supported his son's.

'What about clients who were unhappy with the work George did?' he asked Rosen.

She said she could not think of a client who was ever upset with George Irving's efforts. Conversely, the companies competing with his clients for city contracts would be upset.

'Anything that you remember from these situations that Mr Irving considered to be a threat?'

'Offhand, not that I know of.'

'You said Western Block and Concrete was not the low bidder on the garage. Who was?'

'A company called Consolidated Block Incorporated. They underbid just to try to get the contract. It happens a lot. But the city planners usually see through that. In this case, George helped them. The planning division recommended Western to the council.'

'And no threat came out of it? No bad blood?'

'Well, I doubt they were happy about it over at CBI

but as far as I know, we didn't hear anything. It was just business.'

Bosch knew that he and Chu would have to review both contracts and Irving's work on them. But he decided to move on.

'What did Mr Irving have coming up next on his work schedule?'

'There wasn't a lot. He had been talking about slowing down a little bit. His son went away to college and George and his wife were going through the empty nest phase. I know George really missed his son. He was depressed about it.'

'So he had no active clients?'

'He was talking to people but he only had one under contract. That was Regent Taxi. They're going to try to get the Hollywood franchise next year and they hired us back in May to work with them.'

Under Bosch's questioning, Rosen explained that the city awarded geographic franchises for taxi service. The city was divided into six taxi zones. Each zone had two or three lease or franchise holders, depending on the population of the district. The franchising controlled where in the city a company could pick up fares. Of course, a taxi with a fare onboard could go anywhere instructed.

The designation allowed them to sit on taxi stands and at hotels or cruise for fares and take phone requests within their franchise zone only. Competition on the streets for fares was sometimes fierce. Competition for a franchise designation was equally so. Rosen explained that Regent Taxi already had a franchise in South L.A.

but was seeking a more lucrative assignment in Hollywood.

'When was that going to come up?' Bosch asked.

'Not till after the new year,' Rosen said. 'George was just getting started on the application.'

'How many franchises are given in Hollywood?'

'There are only two and they are two-year terms. They stagger them, so one comes up for renewal or reassignment every year. Regent has been waiting for this upcoming year because the current franchise holder coming up for renewal has problems and is vulnerable. George told the clients that their best shot was in the coming year.'

'What's the name of the company that's vulnerable?'

'Black and White. Better known as B and W.'

Bosch knew that there had been an issue a decade or so ago with B&W Taxi painting its cars so that they looked a little too much like police cars. The LAPD had complained and the company changed their design to a black and white checkerboard scheme. But he didn't think this was what Rosen meant by the company's being vulnerable.

'You said it has problems. What problems?'

'Well, for starters, they've had three DUIs in the last four months alone.'

'You mean cabdrivers driving drunk?'

'Exactly, and that's the ultimate no-no. That doesn't go over well with the city franchise board or the city council, as you can imagine. Who wants to vote for a company with that record? So George was pretty confident that Regent could get the franchise. They've got a clean record, plus they're minority-owned.'

And he had a father who was a powerful member of the city council, which appointed the members of the franchise board. Bosch was intrigued by this information because it all came down to money. Somebody making it and somebody losing it. That often played into the motivations for murder. He got up and stuck his head into the back room, telling Hadlow and Chu that he would want to take any files relating to the taxi franchise matter.

He then came back to Rosen and moved the interview back toward the personal side of things.

'Did George keep any personal files here?'

'Yes, he did. But they're locked in the desk and I don't have the key.'

From his pocket Bosch pulled the keys that had been taken from the Chateau's valet and impounded along with Irving's car.

'Show me.'

Bosch and Chu emerged from the office at noon and headed back to the PAB. Chu carried the box containing the files and other materials they had seized with Hadlow's approval under the authority of the search warrant. This included the records pertaining to the most recent projects George Irving had been working on or planning, as well as his personal files, which contained a number of insurance policies and a copy of a will that was dated only two months earlier.

As they walked, they discussed their next moves. They agreed that the rest of the day would be worked inside the PAB. They had several records to study concerning Irving's projects and will. Reports were also overdue from Glanville and Solomon concerning their interview of the guest who checked in behind Irving at the Chateau Marmont and the canvasses conducted in the hotel and on the hillside neighborhood behind it.

'It's time to start the murder book,' Bosch said.

It was one of his favorite things to do.

17

The world might have gone digital but Harry Bosch had not gone along with it. He had become proficient with a cell phone and a laptop computer. He listened to music on an iPod and every now and then read the newspaper on his daughter's iPad. But when it came to a murder book he was still, and always would be, a plastic and paper man. He was a dinosaur. It didn't matter that the department was moving to digital archiving and there was no space in the new PAB for shelves to hold the thick blue binders. Bosch was a man who kept traditions, especially when he believed those traditions helped catch killers.

To Bosch, a murder book was a key part of an investigation, as important as any piece of evidence. It was the anchor of the case, a compendium of every move made, interview taken, piece of evidence or potential evidence gathered. It was a physical component with weight and depth and substance. Sure, it could be reduced to a digital computer file and put on a thumb drive, but somehow that made it less real to him, more hidden, and this felt disrespectful to the dead.

Bosch needed to see his work product. He had to be constantly reminded of the burden he carried. He had to see the pages grow as the investigation proceeded. He knew without a doubt that it didn't matter if he had thirty-nine months or thirty-nine years left on the job, he would not change the way he went after killers.

When they got back to the Open-Unsolved Unit Bosch went to the storage cabinets that ran along the back wall of the room. Each detective in OU had one cabinet. It was not much bigger than a half locker because the PAB was built for the digital world, not the stalwarts of the old ways. Bosch used his storage space primarily to hold old blue binders from solved murder cases past. Those cases had been pulled from archives and digitized in an effort to create space. The documents were scanned and shredded and the empty binders destined for the city dump. But Bosch had rescued a dozen and hidden them away in his storage locker so that he would never have to go without.

He now took one of the precious binders, its blue plastic faded by time, from the locker and went to the work cubicle he shared with Chu. His partner was removing Irving's files from the box and stacking them on top of the file cabinet that adjoined their two desks.

'Harry, Harry, Harry,' Chu said when he saw the binder. 'When are you going to change? When are you going to let me join the digital world?'

'In about thirty-nine months,' Bosch said. 'After that you can put your murder files on the head of a pin, for all I'll care. But until then, I'm—'

'—going to do it the way you've always done it. Right, yeah, I get it.'

'You know it.'

Bosch sat down at his desk and opened the binder. He then opened his laptop. He had already prepared several reports for inclusion in the book. He started sending them to the unit's communal printer. He thought of reports due from Solomon and Glanville and scanned the cubicle for an interoffice envelope.

'You get anything from Hollywood?' he asked.

'Nope,' Chu said. 'Check your e-mail.'

Of course. Bosch went online and found that he had two e-mails from Jerry Solomon at Hollywood Division. Each contained an attachment that he downloaded and sent to the printer. The first was a summary of the canvass of the hotel conducted by Solomon and Glanville. The second summarized the canvass of the nearby neighborhood.

Bosch went over to the printer and grabbed his pages out of the tray. On his way back he saw Lieutenant Duvall standing outside his cubicle. Chu was nowhere in sight. Bosch knew that Duvall wanted an update on the Irving case. In the past twenty-four hours she had left him two messages and an e-mail, all of which he had failed to return.

'Harry, have you gotten my messages?' she asked as he approached.

'I got them but every time I was going to call, somebody called me first and I got distracted. Sorry, Lieutenant.'

'Why don't we go into my office so you won't get any more of these distractions.'

It wasn't spoken like a question. Bosch dropped the printouts on his desk and followed the lieutenant to her office. She told him to close the door.

'Is that a murder book you are putting together?' she asked before even sitting down.

'Yes.'

'Are you saying George Irving was a homicide?'

'It's looking that way. But not for public consumption.'

Bosch spent the next twenty minutes giving her the shorthand. She agreed with the plan to keep the new focus of the investigation quiet until more evidence was turned up or it became a strategic advantage to have the information out in the world.

'Keep me posted, Harry. Start returning my calls and e-mails.'

'Right. Will do.'

'And start using the magnets so I know where my people are.'

The lieutenant had put a squad room attendance board up with magnets that could be moved to illustrate whether a detective was in or out of the office. It was greeted by most in the unit as a waste of time. The whip usually knew where everyone was, and the lieutenant would as well if she ever came out of her office or at least opened the blinds.

'Sure,' Bosch said.

Chu was back in the cubicle when Bosch returned.

'Where were you?' he asked.

'In with the lieutenant. Where were you?'

'Uh, I went across the street. I never got breakfast.'

Chu changed the subject, pointing to a document that was on his computer screen.

'Did you read Crate and Barrel's report on the canvass?'

'Not yet.'

'They found a guy who saw somebody on the fire escape. The timing's off but, man, what are the chances?'

Bosch turned back to his desk and found the printout

of the report on the hillside canvass. It was essentially a list of consecutive addresses on Marmont Lane. After each address it said whether the door was answered and a resident interviewed. They used abbreviations Bosch had read in LAPD canvass reports for more than two decades. There were a lot of NBHs, meaning nobody home, and a lot of D-SATs, meaning the residents didn't see a thing, but one entry was several sentences long.

Resident Earl Mitchell (WM, DOB 4/13/61) had insomnia and went to the kitchen to get a bottle of water. The residence's rear windows face rear and side of Chateau Marmont head-on. Resident said he noticed a man descending the fire escape ladder. Resident went to telescope in living room and looked at the hotel. The man on the fire escape was no longer in view. Resident did not call PD. Resident stated that this sighting occurred at approximately 12:40 A.M., which was the time on the bedroom clock when he decided to get up to get water. To the best of his memory, resident believes the figure on the fire escape was between the fifth and sixth floor and descending when seen.

Bosch didn't know whether it was Crate or Barrel who had written the report. Whoever it was, he had employed short sentences in a staccato fashion, but he was no Hemingway. He had simply employed the policeman's KISS rule – Keep It Simple, Sherlock. The fewer words in a report meant the fewer chances and angles of attack from critics and lawyers.

Bosch pulled his phone and called Jerry Solomon.

When Solomon answered, it sounded like he was in a car with the windows open.

'It's Bosch. I'm looking at your canvass report here and have a couple questions.'

'Can it wait ten minutes? I'm in the car and I'm with people. Civilians.'

'Is your partner with you or can I just call him?'

'No, he's here with me.'

'That's nice. You guys go out for a late lunch?'

'Look, Bosch, we haven't—'

'One of you call me as soon as you get back to the squad.'

Harry closed the phone and focused his attention on the second report. This one dealt with the questioning of hotel guests and was set up in the same fashion as the other, only with room numbers instead of addresses. Again there were lots of NBHs and D-SATs. They did, however, manage to interview the man who checked into the hotel right after Irving.

Thomas Rapport (WM, 7/21/56, NYC resident) arrived at the hotel from the airport at 9:40 P.M. Remembers seeing George Irving at check-in. They did not speak to each other and Rapport never saw Irving again. Rapport is a writer in town for script conferences at Archway Studios. Confirmed.

Another completely incomplete report. Bosch checked his watch. It had been twenty minutes since Solomon said he needed ten minutes. Harry opened his phone and called him back.

'I thought you were supposed to call me in ten minutes,' he said by way of a greeting.

'I thought you said you were calling me,' Solomon countered in a phony confused tone.

Bosch closed his eyes for a moment and let the frustration pass. It wasn't worth getting into it with an old bull like Solomon.

'I have questions about the reports you sent me.'

'Ask away. You're the boss.'

As the conversation continued, Bosch opened a drawer and took out a three-hole punch. He started punching holes in the reports he had printed and sliding them onto the prongs of the blue binder. There was something calming about putting the murder book together while dealing with Solomon.

'Okay, first of all, on this guy Mitchell who saw the man on the fire escape, did he give a good reason why the guy just disappeared? I mean, he sees him between the fifth and sixth floors and then when he goes to the telescope, the guy is gone. What happened to floors one through four?'

'That's simple. He said by the time he swung the scope around and got it in focus, the guy was gone. He could've gone all the way down or he could've gone inside on one of the landings.'

Bosch almost asked him why that wasn't in the report but he knew why, just as he knew that George Irving's death would have been written off as a suicide with Crate and Barrel in charge.

'How do we know it wasn't Irving?' Bosch asked.

It was a curve ball and it took Solomon a moment to respond.

'I guess we don't. But what would Irving be doing out there on the ladder?'

'I don't know. Was there any description? Clothes, hair, race?'

'He was too far away to be sure about any of that. He thought it was a white guy and his impression was that it might've been a maintenance man. You know, working for the hotel.'

'At midnight? What made him think that?'

'He said his pants and shirt matched color. You know, like a uniform.'

'What color?'

'Light gray.'

'Did you check at the hotel?'

'Check what at the hotel?'

That false tone of confusion was back in his voice.

'Come on, Solomon, drop the stupid act. Did you check if there was any reason for someone in the hotel or working in the hotel to be on that fire escape? Did you ask them what color uniform their maintenance men wear?'

'No, I didn't, Bosch. There was no need to. The guy was going down the fire escape a good two to four hours before our guy took the high dive. They are unrelated matters. You sending us up that street was a complete waste of our time. That was what was stupid.'

Bosch knew that if he lost his temper with Solomon, the detective would be completely useless for the rest of the investigation. He wasn't ready to lose him yet. Once again, he moved on.

'Okay, on the other report, your interview with this writer, Thomas Rapport. You have any more details on why he's in L.A.?'

'I don't know, he's some kind of a big screenwriter. The studio put him up in one of those bungalows in the back where Belushi died. That's two grand a night and he said he was in town for the whole week. He said he's doing rewrites on a script.'

At least that answered one question before Bosch had to ask it. How long would they have local access to Rapport if they needed him?

'So did the studio pop for a limo? How'd he get to the hotel?'

'Uh ... no, he took a cab in from the airport. His plane landed early and the studio car wasn't there yet, so he grabbed a cab. He said that's why Irving got in front of him at the check-in. They arrived at the same time but Rapport had to wait for the cab driver to print out a receipt and it took forever. He was sort of pissed about that. He was on East Coast time and dead tired. He wanted to get into his bungalow.'

Bosch felt a brief stirring in his gut. It was a mixture of instinct and knowing that there was an order of things in the world. The truth was revealed to the righteous. He often felt it at the moment things started to tumble together on a case.

'Jerry,' he said, 'did Rapport tell you which cab company brought him to the hotel?'

'You mean what kind?'

'Yeah, you know, Valley Cab, Yellow Cab, which company? It says it on the door of the taxi.'

'He didn't say but what's that got to do with anything?'

'Maybe nothing. Did you get a cell phone for this guy?'

'No, but he's there at the hotel for a week.'

'Right. I got that. I tell you what, Jerry, I want you and your partner to go back over to the hotel and ask about the man on the fire escape. Find out if they had anybody working that night who could have been the man on the ladder. And find out about the uniforms they wear.'

'Come on, Bosch. It was at least two hours before Irving went down. Most likely longer.'

'I don't care if it was two days, I want you out there asking the questions. Send me the report when you're done. By tonight.'

Bosch closed the phone. He turned and looked at Chu.

'Let me see the file on Irving's taxi franchise client.'

Chu looked through the stack of files and handed one to Bosch.

'What's going on?' Chu asked.

'Nothing yet. What are you working on?'

'The insurance. So far, it's all legit. But I have to make a call.'

'Me, too.'

Bosch picked up his desk phone and called the Chateau Marmont. He was in luck. When he was transferred to Thomas Rapport's bungalow the writer answered.

'Mr Rapport, this is Detective Bosch with the LAPD. I have a few follow-up questions regarding the interview you gave my colleagues earlier. Would this be a good time to talk?'

'Uh, not really. I'm in the middle of a scene right at the moment.'

'A scene?'

'A movie scene. I'm writing a movie scene.'

'I see and I understand, but this will only take a few

minutes of your time and this is very important to the investigation.'

'Did the guy jump or was he pushed?'

'We can't say for sure, sir, but if you answer a couple questions, we will be closer to knowing.'

'Go ahead, Detective. I'm all yours. From your voice, I'm picturing you as sort of a Columbo-looking guy.'

'That's fine, sir. Can I start?'

'Yes, Detective.'

'You arrived at the hotel on Sunday evening by taxi, is that correct?'

'Yes, it is. Direct from LAX. Archway was supposed to send a car but I got in early and there was no car. I didn't want to wait, so I just took a cab.'

'Do you happen to remember the name of the cab company you used?'

'The company? You mean like Checker Cab or something?'

'Yes, sir. We have several companies that are licensed to operate in the city. I'm looking for the name that was on the door of your cab.'

'I'm sorry. I don't know it. There was just a line of taxis and I jumped in one.'

'You remember what color it was?'

'No. I just remember it was dirty inside. I should've waited for the studio car.'

'You told Detectives Solomon and Glanville that you were delayed a bit on your arrival at the hotel while waiting for the cab driver to print out a receipt. Do you have that receipt handy?'

'Hold on.'

While Bosch waited, he opened the file for Irving's

taxi franchise project and started looking through the documents. He found the contract Irving had signed with Regent five months earlier, then came to a letter that was addressed to the city's franchise board. It informed the board that Regent Taxi would be competing for the Hollywood franchise when it came up for renewal in the coming year. The letter also listed the 'performance and trust' issues facing the current franchise holder, Black & White Taxi. Before Bosch finished reading the letter, Rapport came back on the phone.

'I have it here, Detective. It was Black and White. That was the name of the company.'

'Thank you, Mr Rapport. I have one last question. Does it say on the receipt who the driver was?'

'Uh … hmm … uh, no, it just gives his number. It says driver twenty-six. Does that help?'

'It does, sir. It helps a lot. Now, that's a pretty nice place you're staying in, right?'

'Very nice, and I think you know who died here.'

'Yes, I do. But the reason I ask is, do you know if that room is equipped with a fax machine?'

'I don't have to look. I know it is because I faxed pages to the set an hour ago. You want me to fax you this receipt?'

'Exactly, sir.'

Bosch gave him the number to the fax in the lieutenant's office. No one would be able to look at the receipt except Duvall.

'It will be on its way as soon as I hang up, Lieutenant,' Rapport said.

'That's Detective.'

'I keep forgetting you're not Columbo.'

'No, sir, I'm not. But I am going to hit you with just one more question.'

Rapport laughed.

'Go ahead.'

'It's a tight space in the garage area where you come in. Did your taxi pull in ahead of Mr Irving's car or was it the other way around?'

'Other way. We pulled in right behind him.'

'So when Irving got out of his car, did you see him?'

'Yeah, he stood there and gave his keys to the valet guy. The valet then wrote his name on a receipt and tore off the bottom half and gave it to him. The usual thing.'

'Did your driver see this?'

'I don't know but he had a better view through the windshield than I did in the back.'

'Thank you, Mr Rapport, and good luck with the scene you're writing.'

'I hope I've helped.'

'You have.'

Bosch hung up and while he waited for the receipt to arrive via fax, he called George Irving's office manager, Dana Rosen, and asked her about the letter to the city's franchise board that was in the Regent Taxi file.

'Is this a copy or the original that was not yet sent out?' he asked.

'Oh, no, that was sent out. We sent it individually to every member of the board. That was the first step in announcing the plans to go for the Hollywood franchise.'

Bosch was looking at the letter as they spoke. It was dated two Mondays earlier.

'Was there any response to this?' he asked.

'Not yet. It would have been in the file if there was.'

'Thank you, Dana.'

Bosch hung up and went back to looking through the Regent file. He found a paper-clipped batch of printouts that must have been the backup Irving used for the allegations contained in the letter. There was a copy of a story that had been in the *Times* which reported that the third Black & White driver in four months had been arrested for driving drunk while operating a taxi. The story also reported that a B&W driver was determined to have been at fault in an accident involving serious injuries to the couple in the cab's backseat earlier in the year. The stack also contained copies of the arrest reports on the DUI stops and a batch of moving violations that had been written against B&W drivers. Everything from running red lights to double-parking, the moving violations were probably just routine and collateral to the DUI arrests.

The records made it easy for Bosch to see why Irving thought B&W was vulnerable. Snatching the Hollywood franchise was probably going to be the easiest piece of business he had ever done.

Bosch quickly scanned the arrest reports but was snagged by a curiosity. He noticed that in each of the reports, the same badge number had been entered in the block identifying the arresting officer. Three arrests spread over four months. It seemed beyond coincidence that the same cop would have made all three arrests. He knew that it was conceivable that the badge number simply belonged to the jail officer who had administered the Breathalyzer tests at Hollywood Division after the cab drivers were taken into custody by other officers.

But even that would have been unusual and out of procedure.

He picked up the phone and called the department's personnel office. He gave his own name and badge number and said he needed to get an ID off a badge. He was transferred to a midlevel bureaucrat who looked it up on the computer and gave Bosch the name, rank and assignment.

'Robert Mason, P-three, Hollywood.'

As in Bobby Mason. George Irving's longtime friend – until recently.

Bosch thanked her and hung up. He wrote down the information he had just assembled and then studied it. He could not dismiss as happenstance the fact that Mason had made three DUI arrests of B&W drivers at a time he was apparently still friends with a man representing a rival to B&W's Hollywood franchise.

He circled Mason's name in his notes. The patrol officer was definitely someone Bosch wanted to talk to. But not yet. Bosch needed to know far more than he knew now before he could make the approach.

He moved on and next studied the arrest summaries, which contained the probable cause for detaining the drivers. In each case the driver had been observed driving erratically. In one of the cases, the summary noted that a half-empty bottle of Jack Daniel's whiskey had been found under the driver's seat of the taxi.

Bosch noted that the report did not mention the size of the bottle and for a moment he mused over the choice of the words *half empty* over *half full* and the different interpretations the descriptions might bring.

But then Chu rolled his chair over and leaned against his desk.

'Harry, it sounds like you have something going.'

'Yeah, maybe. You want to take a ride?'

18

Black & White Taxi was located on Gower south of Sunset. It was an industrial neighborhood full of businesses that catered to the movie industry. Costume warehouses, camera houses, prop houses. B&W was in one of two side-by-side soundstages that looked old and worn-out. The cab company operated out of one, and the other was a storage and rental facility for movie cars. Bosch had been in the car storage facility before on a case. He had taken his time walking through. It was like a museum with every car that had ever caught his eye as a teenager.

The two hangar doors of B&W were wide open. Bosch and Chu walked in. In the moment of blindness when their eyes adjusted from the transition of sunlight to shadows, they were almost hit by a taxi heading out to the street. They jumped back and let the black-and-white-checked Impala go between them.

'Asshole,' Chu said.

There were cars sitting dormant and cars up on jacks being worked on by mechanics in greasy coveralls. At the far end of the large space, two picnic tables sat next to a couple of snack and beverage machines. A handful of drivers were hanging out there, waiting for their chariots to pass muster with the mechanics.

To their right was a small office with windows that

were so dirty they were opaque. But behind them Harry could see shapes and movement. He led Chu that way.

Bosch knocked once on the door and went in without waiting for a response. They stepped into an office with three desks pushed up against three of the walls and overflowing with paperwork. Two of them were occupied by men who had not turned to see who had entered. Both of them were wearing headsets. The man on the right was dispatching a car to a pickup at the Roosevelt Hotel. Bosch waited for him to finish.

'Excuse me,' he said.

Both men turned to look at the intruders. Bosch was ready with his badge out.

'I need to ask a couple questions.'

'Well, we're running a business here and don't—'

A phone rang and the man on the left punched a button on his desk to activate his headset.

'Black and White. . . . Yes, ma'am, that will be five to ten minutes. Would you like us to call upon arrival?'

He wrote something down on a yellow Post-it, then tore it off the pad and handed it to the dispatcher so he could send a car to the address.

'Car's on the way, ma'am,' he said, then punched the desk button to disconnect the call.

He swiveled in his seat to face Bosch and Chu.

'You see?' he said. 'We don't have any time for your bullshit.'

'What bullshit is that?'

'I don't know, whatever you're spinning today. We know what you're doing.'

Another call came in, and the info was taken and moved to the dispatcher. Bosch stepped into the space between the two desks. If the call taker wanted to pass a Post-it to the dispatcher now, he'd have to go through Bosch.

'I don't know what you're talking about,' Bosch said.

'Good, then neither do I,' the call taker said. 'We can just never mind this whole thing. Have a good day.'

'Except I still need to ask a couple questions.'

The phone buzzed again but this time when the man reached for the desk button, Bosch was quicker. He pushed it once to connect the call, then again to disconnect it.

'What the fuck you doing, man? This is our business here.'

'It's my business being here, too. They'll just call somebody else. Maybe Regent Cab will get their business.'

Bosch checked him for a reaction and saw his tight-lipped response.

'Now, who is driver twenty-six?'

'We don't give drivers numbers. We give cars numbers.'

His tone was meant to convey that he thought this was the dumbest pair of cops going.

'Then tell me who was driving car twenty-six about nine thirty Sunday night.'

The call taker leaned back so he could look around Bosch at the dispatcher and they exchanged a silent message.

'You got a warrant for that?' the dispatcher asked. 'We're not just going to give you a guy's name so you can go out and trump up another bullshit arrest on us.'

'I don't need a warrant,' Bosch said.

'The hell you don't!' cried the dispatcher.

'What I need is your cooperation, and if I don't get it, those deuces you're worried about are going to be the least of your problems. And at the end of the day, I'm still going to get what I want. So decide right now how you want to play it.'

The two B&W men looked at each other again. Bosch looked at Chu. If the bluff didn't work, they might have to amp up the situation. Bosch checked Chu's face for any sign of retreat. There was none.

The dispatcher opened a binder that was to the side of his desk. From Bosch's angle he could see it was some sort of schedule. He turned back three pages to Sunday.

'All right, Hooch Rollins had that car Sunday night. Now leave, the both of you.'

'Hooch Rollins? What's his real name?'

'How the fuck should we know?'

It was the dispatcher. Bosch was getting pretty annoyed with him. He stepped over closer and looked down at him. The phone rang.

'Don't answer that,' Bosch said.

'You're killing us here, man!'

'They'll call back.'

Bosch locked in on the dispatcher.

'Is Hooch Rollins working right now?'

'Yeah, he's working a double today.'

'Well, dispatcher, get on the radio and call him back here.'

'Yeah, what do I say to get him to do that?'

'You tell him you need to switch out his car. Tell him you've got a better one for him. It just came in on the truck.'

'He won't believe that. We got no truck coming. We're

about to go out of business thanks to you people.'

'Make him believe it.'

Bosch gave the dispatcher a hard look and the man turned to his microphone and called Hooch Rollins in.

Bosch and Chu stepped out of the office and conferred about what to do when Rollins showed up. They decided that they would wait until he was out of the car before making an approach to him.

A few minutes later a beat-up taxi that was a year past needing a wash pulled into the bay area. It was driven by a man in a straw hat. He jumped out and said to no one in particular, 'Where's my new wheels?'

Bosch and Chu approached from two sides. When they got close enough to contain Rollins, Bosch spoke.

'Mr Rollins? We're with the LAPD and we need to ask you some questions.'

Rollins looked confused. Then the fight-or-flight look entered his eyes.

'What?'

'I said we need to ask you a few questions.'

Bosch badged him then so he'd know that it was formal and official. There was no running from the law.

'What'd I do?'

'As far as we know, nothing, Mr Rollins. We want to talk to you about something you may have seen.'

'You're not going to jack me up like the other fellas, are you?'

'We don't know anything about that. Will you please accompany us to the Hollywood police station so we can sit in a quiet room and talk?'

'Am I under arrest?'

'Not now, no. We were counting on you wanting to

cooperate and just answer some questions. We'll get you back here right after.'

'Man, if I'm with you, then I ain't making no money out there.'

Bosch was about to lose his patience.

'We won't take long, Mr Rollins. Please cooperate with us.'

Rollins seemed to read Bosch's tone and realized that it didn't matter whether he went the hard or easy way, he was going nonetheless. The street pragmatist in him made him choose the easy way.

'Okay, let's get it over with. You don't have to cuff me or anything, do you?'

'No cuffs,' Bosch said. 'Just nice and easy.'

On the way, Chu sat in the back with the uncuffed Rollins and Bosch called ahead to the nearby Hollywood Division and reserved an interrogation room in the detective bureau. It was a five-minute ride over and soon they were walking Rollins into a nine-by-nine with a table and three chairs. Bosch made him sit on the side with only one chair.

'Can we get you something before we start?' Bosch asked.

'How about a Coke, a smoke and a poke?'

He started to laugh. The detectives didn't.

'How about just a Coke?' Bosch said.

Bosch reached into his pocket for his change and then picked four quarters off his palm. He handed them to Chu. Since Chu was the junior partner here, he would go out to the machines in the back hallway.

'So, Hooch, why don't we start with you telling me your real full name?'

'Richard Alvin Rollins.'

'How did you get the name Hooch?'

'I don't know, man, I just always had it.'

'What did you mean back at the shop when you said you didn't want to get jacked like the other fellas?'

'That wasn't anythin', man.'

'Sure it was. You said it. So tell me who's getting jacked up. You tell me and it doesn't leave this room.'

'Ah, man, you know. It just looks to us like they coming after us all a sudden with the DUIs and everything.'

'And you think those were setups?'

'Come on, man, its pol-o-tics. What do you expect? I mean, look at what they did to that Armenian bastard.'

Bosch remembered one of the drivers arrested was named Hratch Tartarian. He assumed Rollins was referring to him.

'What about him?'

'He was just sitting on the stand and they pull up and pull 'im outta the car. He refuses to blow but then they find the bottle under the seat and he's toast. That bottle, man, is always under there. It stays in that car and nobody be driving drunk. You take a couple sips a night to make yourself right. But everybody wants to know how those officers knew about that bottle, you know?'

Bosch sat back in his chair and tried to follow and decipher what had been said. Chu came back in and put a can of Coke down in front of Rollins. He then took a seat at the corner of the table and to Bosch's right.

'This conspiracy to set you guys up, who's behind it? Who's running it?'

Rollins raised his hands in a gesture meant to say *Isn't it obvious?*

'It's the councilman and he just lets his son do the dirty work and run things. I mean, he did. Now he's dead.'

'How do you know that?'

'I seen it in the paper. E'rybody knows that.'

'Did you ever see the son before? In person?'

Rollins didn't speak for a long moment. His mind was probably working, dancing around the trap being set for him. He decided not to lie.

'For like ten seconds. I was on a drop Sunday at the Chateau and saw him going in. That was it.'

Bosch nodded.

'How did you know who he was?'

'Because I seen a picture of him.'

'Where? The newspaper?'

'No, somebody had a picture of him after we got the letter.'

'What letter?'

'B and W, man. We got a copy of a letter from the Irving guy telling the city people that they were coming after our ticket. They were going to shut us down. Somebody Googled the motherfucker in the office. They got his picture and showed it around. It was on the bulletin board with the letter. They wanted us drivers to know what was up and what was at stake. That this guy was leading the charge against us and we better shape up and fly straight.'

Bosch understood the strategy.

'So you recognized him when you pulled into the Chateau Marmont on Sunday night.'

'Damn right. I knew he was the asshole tryin' to run us out of business.'

'Have some Coke.'

Bosch needed to break momentum to think about this. While Rollins opened the can and started to drink, Harry thought of the next set of questions. There were a number of things going on here that he had not seen coming.

Rollins took a long drink and put the can down.

'When did you get off shift Sunday night?' Bosch asked.

'I didn't. I need doubles on account of my girl's about to drop a kid without no insurance. I took a second shift just like I'm doing today and worked on through to the light a day. That would be Monday.'

'What were you wearing that night?'

'What is this shit, man? You said I'm not a suspect.'

'You're not as long as you keep answering questions. What were you wearing, Hooch?'

'My usual thing. Tommy Bahama and my cargoes. You sit in a car sixteen hours and you want to be comfortable.'

'What color was the shirt?'

He gestured to his chest.

'This is the shirt.'

It was bright yellow with a surfboard design on it. Bosch was pretty sure of one thing. It was a Tommy Bahama knockoff, not the real thing. Either way, it seemed to him to be a stretch to consider the shirt gray. Unless Rollins had changed clothes, he wasn't the man on the fire escape ladder.

'So who did you tell that you had seen Irving at the hotel?' Bosch asked.

'No one.'

'Are you sure about that, Hooch? You don't want to start lying to us. That would make it tough for us to let you go.'

'Nobody, man.'

Bosch could tell by the sudden lack of eye contact that Rollins was lying.

'That's too bad, Hooch. I figured you were smart enough to know we wouldn't ask a question we didn't already know the answer to.'

Bosch stood up. He reached under his jacket and pulled his handcuffs off his belt.

'I only told my shift supervisor,' Rollins said quickly. 'Just like in passing. On the radio. I said, Guess who I just saw. Like that.'

'Yeah, and did he guess it was Irving?'

'No, I had to tell him. But that was it.'

'Did your shift supervisor ask where you just saw Irving?'

'No, he knew 'cause I had called in my twenty on the drop-off. He knew where I was.'

'What else did you tell him?'

'That was it. Just that, like conversation.'

Bosch paused to see if anything else would come out. Rollins was silent, his eyes holding on the cuffs in Bosch's hand.

'Okay, Hooch, what's the name of the shift supervisor you had Sunday night?'

'Mark McQuillen. He's on the stick at night.'

'The stick?'

'He's the dispatcher. But they call him the stick 'cause in the old days there was like a microphone or something on the desk. The stick. You know, somebody told me he's an ex-cop.'

Bosch looked at Rollins for a long moment as he fit the name McQuillen into the picture. Rollins was right about his being an ex-cop. And the feeling Bosch had had earlier about things tumbling together now returned. Only things weren't tumbling anymore. They were cascading. Mark McQuillen was a name out of the past. Both Bosch's and the department's.

Bosch finally came away from his thoughts and looked at Rollins.

'What did McQuillen say when you told him you saw Irving?'

'Nothing. I think he asked if the guy was checking in.'

'And what did you tell him?'

'That I thought he was. I mean, he was dumping his car at the garage. That garage is too small; they only let hotel guests park there. If you're just going to the bar or something, you have to use the outside valet.'

Bosch nodded. Rollins was right about that.

'Okay, we're going to take you back now, Hooch. If you tell anybody what we talked about here, I'm going to know. And I promise you if that happens, it's not going to turn out good for you.'

Rollins raised his hands in surrender.

'I'm straight with that,' he said.

19

After they dropped Rollins off they headed back toward downtown and the PAB.

'So, McQuillen,' Chu said, as Bosch knew he would. 'Who is he? I could tell the name meant something to you.'

'Like Hooch said, a former cop.'

'But you know him? Or knew him?'

'I knew of him. I never met him.'

'Well, what's the story?'

'He was a cop who was sacrificed to the gods of appeasement. He lost his job for doing it just the way they taught him.'

'Stop talking in circles, Harry. What's going on?'

'What's going on is that I have to go up to the tenth floor and talk to somebody.'

'The chief?'

'No, not the chief.'

'And this is one of those times again where you're not going to tell your partner what's going on until you feel like it.'

Bosch didn't answer. He was grinding things down.

'*Harry!* I'm talking to you.'

'Chu, when we get back, I want you to start a moniker search.'

'Who?'

'Somebody who went by the name Chill in the North Hollywood–Burbank area about twenty-five years ago.'

'What the fuck? Are you talking about the other case now?'

'I want you to find this guy. His initials are C. H. and people called him Chill. It's got to be a variation on his first name.'

Chu shook his head.

'That's it, man, I'm done after this. I can't work this way. I'll tell the lieutenant.'

Bosch just nodded.

'"After this"? Does that mean you'll do the moniker search first?'

Bosch didn't call ahead to Kiz Rider. He just took the elevator up to the tenth floor and entered the OCP suite without invitation or appointment. He was met by twin desks with twin adjutants behind them. He went to his left.

'Detective Harry Bosch. I need to see Lieutenant Rider.'

The adjutant was a young officer in a crisp uniform with the name RIVERA on his nameplate. He picked up a clipboard from the side of his desk and studied it for a moment.

'I don't have anything here. Is the lieutenant expecting you? She's in a meeting.'

'Yes.'

Rivera seemed surprised by the answer. He had to check the clipboard again.

'Why don't you have a seat, Detective, and I'll check on availability.'

'You do that.'

Rivera didn't move. He waited for Bosch to go away. Harry walked over to some chairs arranged near a set of windows that looked out upon the civic center – the signature spire of City Hall took up most of the view. He stayed standing. When Harry was a safe distance from the desk, Rivera picked up his phone and made a call, cupping his hand over the mouthpiece when he spoke to someone on the other end. Soon he hung up but did not even glance in Bosch's direction.

Bosch turned back to the window and looked down. He saw a television camera crew set up on the steps of City Hall, waiting for a sound bite from some politician with something to sell. Bosch wondered if it would be Irving who would come out and descend the marble steps.

'Harry?'

He turned. It was Rider.

'Walk with me.'

He wished she hadn't said that line. But he followed when she turned and walked out the double doors to the hallway. Once they were alone she turned on him.

'What's going on? I have people in my office.'

'We need to talk. Now.'

'So talk.'

'No, not here like this. Things are breaking. It's going the way I warned you. The chief should know. Who's in your office? Is it Irving?'

'No, stop being paranoid.'

'Then why are we talking out here?'

'Because the office is busy and because it was *you* who demanded complete confidentiality on this. Give me ten minutes and meet me by Charlie Chaplin.'

Bosch walked over and pushed the elevator button. There was only a down button.

'I'll be there.'

It was a block's walk to the Bradbury Building. Bosch went in the side door on Third and into the dimly lit stairwell vestibule. There was a bench there and next to it was a sculpture of Charlie Chaplin as his signature character, the Tramp. Bosch took a seat in the shadows next to Charlie and waited. The Bradbury was the oldest and most beautiful building in downtown. It housed private offices as well as LAPD offices, including the board of rights hearing rooms used by Internal Affairs. It was an odd choice for a surreptitious meeting, but it was the spot Bosch and Rider had used in the past. No discussion or direction was needed once Kiz had said meet me at Charlie Chaplin.

Rider was almost ten minutes past the first ten minutes but that was okay with Bosch. He had used the time to construct the story he would tell her. It was complicated and still emerging, even improvisational.

He had just finished walking himself through it when he felt the buzz of an incoming text on his phone. He pulled it from his pocket, half expecting the message to be a cancellation of the meeting from Rider. But it was from his daughter.

Having dinner and study hall at Ash's. Her mom makes goooood pizza. K?

He felt a slight pang of guilt because he welcomed the message. With his daughter taken care of for the evening, he had more time to work his cases. It also meant he could see Hannah Stone again if he could come up with a viable investigative reason. He sent back his approval but told his daughter she had to be home by ten. He told her to call if she needed a ride.

Bosch was pocketing his phone when Rider came in, hesitated a moment while her eyes adjusted to the shadows and then sat down next to him.

'Hi,' she said.

'Hi,' he said.

He waited a moment for her to settle but she wasn't interested in wasting time.

'Well?'

'You ready?'

'Of course. I'm here. Tell me the story.'

'Well, it goes like this. George Irving has a consulting firm that is really an influence firm. He sells his influence, his connection to his father and the faction his father is part of on the city council. He—'

'Do you have documentary evidence of this?'

'Right now it's just a story, Kiz, and it's just you and me here. Let me tell it and then you can ask your questions when I'm done.'

'Go ahead, then.'

The door on Third opened and a uniformed officer walked in, took off his sunglasses and looked around, blindly at first and then focusing on Bosch and Rider and correctly sizing them up as cops.

'Is this where the BORs are heard?' he asked.

'Third floor,' Rider said.

'Thank you.'

'Good luck.'

'Yeah.'

Bosch waited until the cop left the vestibule and rounded the corner into the main lobby where the elevators were located.

'Okay. So George sells influence with the council and by extension with all the different boards the council appoints. In some cases he can do even more than that. He can tilt the game.'

'I don't get it. How so?'

'Do you know how taxi franchises are awarded in this city?'

'Not a clue.'

'By geographic zones and on two-year contracts. You come up for review every two years.'

'All right.'

'So I don't know if George goes to them or they come to George, but there's a franchise holder in South L.A. called Regent Taxi and they hire George to help them get a more lucrative franchise up in Hollywood, where there are highline hotels and tourists on the streets and lots more money to be made. The current franchise holder is Black and White Taxi.'

'I think I know where this is going. But wouldn't Councilman Irving have to be transparent on this? He'd have a conflict of interest voting for any company repped by his son.'

'Of course he would. But the first vote is with the Taxi Franchise Board, and who puts the people on that board? The council. And when it next comes before the council for ratification, sure, Irving nobly cites conflict of interest and steps out on the vote and it all looks completely aboveboard. But what about the backroom trade-offs?

"You vote for me when I step out and next time I'll vote for you." You know what goes on, Kiz. But what George offers is even more of a sure thing. He offers a fuller service, shall we say. Regent says, yes, we'll take the full package, and a month after he's hired by Regent, things start going sideways for the current holder of the franchise, B and W.'

'What do you mean "sideways"?'

'I'm trying to tell you. Less than a month after George Irving is hired by Regent, B and W drivers start getting popped on deuce raps and traffic citations and suddenly the company's not looking so good.'

'How many arrests?'

'Three, the first coming a month after Irving signed on. And then there's an auto accident where the B and W driver is held at fault. There are several traffic violations – all moving violations that give the appearance of reckless driving. Speeding, running traffic lights and stop signs.'

'I think the *Times* wrote about this. The DUIs, anyway.'

'Yeah, I have the story and I'm pretty sure George Irving's the one who tipped them to it. It was all part of an organized plan to get the Hollywood taxi franchise.'

'So you're saying that the son went to the father and said put some pressure on B and W? The father then in turn reached into the department?'

'I am not exactly sure how it worked yet. But both of them – father and son – still have connections in the department. The councilman has sympathizers and his son was a cop for five years. A guy who was a close friend of his works patrol in Hollywood. I have all the

B and W arrest reports and the traffic citations. The same cop – George Irving's friend – made all three DUI arrests and wrote two of the moving violations. A guy named Robert Mason. What are the chances of that? That he'd get all three deuces.'

'It could happen. You make one arrest and then you know what to look for after that.'

'Sure, Kiz, whatever you say. One of these guys wasn't even pulled over. He was parked at a cab stand on La Brea when Mason rolled up on him.'

'Well, were these legit busts or not? Did they blow?'

'They blew and the busts were legit as far as I know. But three busts starting a month after Irving was hired. The DUIs, the moving violations and the accident report then become the centerpiece of Regent's application to the franchise board to take Hollywood away from B and W. He had it completely greased and it just doesn't smell right, Kiz.'

She finally nodded, a tacit agreement with Bosch's point of view.

'Okay, even if I agree with you, there's still the question: How does all of this get George Irving killed? And why?'

'I'm not sure why but let me move to the—'

Bosch stopped when there was a loud explosion of voices from the lobby. After a few seconds they were gone.

'Okay, let me move to the night Irving took the high dive. He arrives by car at nine-forty, gives his keys to the valet and goes upstairs to the lobby to check in. Also arriving at that time is a writer from the East Coast named Thomas Rapport. He comes by cab from the airport and pulls in right behind Irving.'

'Don't tell me. He was in a Black and White cab.'

'You know, Lieutenant, you really ought to be a detective.'

'I tried it, but my partner was an asshole.'

'I heard about that. Anyway, yes, it was a B and W cab and the driver actually recognized Irving as he was turning his car over to the valet. His picture had been shown around the garage when the application letter to the franchise board got copied to B and W. This driver, a guy named Rollins, recognizes Irving and gets on his radio and says, "What do you know, I just saw public enemy number one," or words to that effect. And on the other end of that radio call is the shift supervisor. The night man. A guy named Mark McQuillen.'

Bosch stopped there and waited for her to recognize the name. She didn't.

'McQuillen as in "McKillin,"' he said. 'That ring a bell?'

It still didn't break through. Rider shook her head.

'Before your time,' Bosch said.

'Who is he?'

'A former cop. Maybe ten years younger than me. Back in the day, he became the poster boy for the whole choke hold thing. The controversy. And he got sacrificed to the mob.'

'I don't understand, Harry. What mob? What sacrifice?'

'I told you, I was on the task force. The task force was formed to appease the citizenry of South L.A. who claimed that the choke hold was legalized murder. Cops used it and an inordinate number of people in the south end died. The truth was, they didn't need a task force to change policy. They could've just changed it. But instead they go with a task force so they could feed the media the story about how the department was serious in its effort to respond to the public outcry.'

'All right, so how does this lead to McQuillen?'

'I was just a grunt on the task force. A gatherer. I handled the autopsies. I know this, though. The statistics matched up across racial and geographic lines. Sure, there were more choke hold deaths in the south end. Far more African Americans died than other races. But the ratios were even. There were far more incidents involving use of force in the south end. The more confrontations, scuffles, fights, resisting arrests you get, the more uses of the choke hold. The more you use the choke hold, the more deaths you will have. It was simple math. But nothing is simple when racial politics are involved.'

Rider was black and had grown up in South L.A. But Bosch was speaking to her cop to cop and there was no awkwardness in his telling the story. They had been partners and had operated as a team under extreme pressures. Rider knew Bosch as well as anyone could. They were brother and sister and there was no holdback between them.

'McQuillen worked P.M. watch in Seventy-seventh,' he said. 'He liked action and he got it almost every night. I don't remember the exact number but he'd had something like sixty-plus use-of-force incidents in four years. And as you know, those are only the ones they write reports on. In those incidents, he used the choke hold a lot and he ended up killing two people in a three-year span. Of all the choke hold deaths over all the years, there was nobody involved in more than one. Only him, because he had used it more than anybody else. So when the task force came along ...'

'He got special attention.'

'Right. Now, every one of his use-of-force incidents came back clean on review at the time of occurrence. Including the two deaths. It was determined by a review board that both times he used the hold within policy. But one time and it's an unlucky thing. Two times and there is a pattern. Somebody leaked his name and history to the *Times*, which was hovering over the task force like the smog over downtown. They ran a story and McQuillen became the face of what was wrong in the department. Didn't matter that he was never found to have acted out of policy. He was the guy. A killer cop. The head of the ministers' coalition at the time held a press conference it seemed every other day. He started calling him McKillin and it stuck.'

Bosch got up from the bench so he could pace a little bit as he continued.

'The task force recommended that the bar hold be dropped from the use-of-force progression and it was. Funny thing is, the department then told officers to rely more on their batons – in fact, you could be disciplined if you got out of a patrol car without carrying your baton in your hand or on your belt. Added to that, Tasers were coming into use just as the choke hold went out. And what did we get? Rodney King. A video that changed the world. A video of a guy being Tased and whaled on with batons when a proper choke hold would've just put him to sleep.'

'Huh,' Rider said. 'I never looked at it that way.'

Bosch nodded.

'Anyway, dropping the choke hold wasn't enough. There had to be an offering to the angry mob and it was McQuillen. He was suspended on what I always thought were trumped-up, politically motivated charges. The review of the deaths determined that in the second case he had been out of policy in the escalation of the use-of-force sequence. In other words, the choke hold that killed the guy was okay but everything he did up until he used it was wrong. He was brought up on a board of rights and fired. The case was referred to the DA and the DA took a pass. At the time, I remember thinking McQuillen was lucky they didn't ride the wave and prosecute him. He sued to get his job back but that was a nonstarter. He was done.'

Bosch ended it there for the moment to see if Rider had a response. She had folded her arms across her chest and was staring into the shadows. Bosch knew she was grinding it down. Seeing how all of this played out in the present.

'So,' she finally said. 'Twenty-five years ago a task force headed by Irvin Irving results in McQuillen losing his job and career in a process that, at least in his view, was unfounded and unfair. Now we have what appears to be an attempt by Irving's son and possibly the councilman himself to grab the franchise from the business where McQuillen now works as ... what, a night dispatcher?'

'Shift supervisor. Which I guess really means dispatcher.'

'And this adds up to him murdering George Irving.

I can connect the dots but am having trouble with the motive, Harry.'

'Well, we don't know anything about McQuillen, do we? We don't know if he's been carrying this grudge around like a festering wound and the opportunity simply presented itself. A driver calls in and says, "Guess who I just saw." We have the abrasion pattern on the shoulder – it's unmistakable evidence of the choke hold. We also have a witness who saw somebody on the fire escape.'

'What witness? You didn't tell me you had a witness.'

'I just found out today. The hillside behind the hotel was canvassed and they came up with a resident who saw a man on the fire escape ladder Sunday night. But he says it was twelve-forty A.M. and the coroner puts TOD no earlier than two and as late as four. So we have about a two-hour discrepancy. The guy on the ladder was going down at twelve-forty, not up. There is this, though. The witness described the guy on the ladder as wearing some sort of uniform. Gray top and gray pants. I was in B and W's taxi barn today. It's where the dispatch office is. The mechanics who work on the fleet wear gray coveralls. McQuillen could've put on coveralls before going up the ladder.'

Bosch flipped his hands out at his sides as if to say that was it. That was all he had. Rider was silent for a long moment before asking what Bosch knew she would ask.

'You always taught me to ask where the holes were. "Look at your case and find the holes. Because if you don't find them, a defense attorney will do it for you." So, Harry, where are the holes?'

Bosch shrugged.

'The time discrepancy is a hole. And we don't have anything that would put McQuillen in Irving's room. All prints found in there and on the fire escape ladder were run through the computer. McQuillen's would've come up.'

'How do you deal with the time discrepancy?'

'He was casing the place. That's when the witness saw him. He didn't see when McQuillen came back.'

Rider nodded.

'What about the marks on Irving's shoulder? Can they be matched to McQuillen's watch?'

'It's possible but it won't be conclusive. We might get lucky and even find DNA on the watch. But I think the big hole here is Irving. Why was he at the hotel in the first place? The McQuillen angle relies upon chance. Taxi driver sees Irving. He tells McQuillen. McQuillen's deep-seated anger and bitterness take over. At the end of shift, he grabs a set of mechanic's coveralls and goes to the hotel. He climbs up the side, somehow gets into Irving's suite, and chokes him out. He strips the body and folds the clothes nice and neat but misses the button on the floor. He then drops him off the balcony and it looks like suicide. It works well enough in theory, but what was Irving doing there? Was he meeting someone? Waiting for someone? And why did he put his stuff – his wallet and phone and everything – in the room safe? If we can't answer those questions, we've got a hole big enough to drive a getaway car through.'

She nodded in agreement.

'So what are you proposing we do now?'

'*We* do nothing. *I* continue to work this. But you have

to know and the chief has to know that as this goes forward it's going to get close to the councilman. If I squeeze Robert Mason to find out why he started pulling over B and W drivers, it might come back directly to Irvin Irving himself. The chief should know that.'

'He will. Is that your next move?'

'I'm not sure yet. But I want to know as much as there is to know before I take on McQuillen.'

Rider stood up. She was impatient to go.

'Are you going back now?' she asked. 'You want to walk?'

'No, you go ahead,' Bosch said. 'I think I'm going to make a few phone calls.'

'All right, Harry. Good luck. Be careful out there.'

'Yeah, you, too. Be careful up there.'

She looked at him. She knew he meant on the tenth floor of the PAB. She smiled and he smiled back.

20

Bosch sat back down on the bench and composed himself. He then pulled his phone and called Hannah Stone's cell number. She had given it to him when they parted ways Monday evening.

She answered right away, even though Bosch's number was blocked.

'It's Harry Bosch.'

'I thought it might be you. Is there anything new?'

'No, I'm working on something else today. But my partner is trying to run down the guy Chill.'

'Okay.'

'Anything new on your end?'

'No, just doing the same good work we always do.'

'That's good.'

There was an awkward pause and then Bosch plowed ahead.

'My daughter is studying at a friend's house tonight, so I'm free. And I was wondering – I mean, I know it's pretty soon – but I wanted to see if you wanted to have dinner again tonight.'

'Uh …'

'It's no big deal. It's short notice. I'll—'

'No, no, it's not that. It's just that we have sessions on Wednesday and Thursday nights and I'm supposed to work tonight.'

'Don't you get a dinner break?'

'Yes, but it's too short. Tell you what, can I call you back?'

'Yes, but you don't have to jump through any—'

'I want to, but I have to see if somebody will switch with me. I take tomorrow night if they take tonight. Can I call you back?'

'Sure.'

Bosch gave her his number and they disconnected. He got up, patted Charlie Chaplin on the shoulder and headed out the door.

When Bosch got back to the unit, Chu was working on his laptop and didn't look up as Harry entered the cubicle.

'You find my guy yet?'

'Not yet.'

'How's it looking?'

'Not very good. There are nine hundred eleven variations of Chill in the moniker files. And that's just in California. So don't hold your breath.'

'Is that total or is that just in the time frame I asked for?'

'The time frame doesn't matter. Your guy from 'eighty-eight could easily have been put into the database in any year before or since. It would depend on whether he was arrested, was the subject of a field interview, or was a victim. There are a lot of possibilities. I have to look at all of them.'

Chu was speaking in a clipped tone. Bosch knew he was still angry about being shut out of the Irving investigation.

'All of that might be true but let's prioritize by narrowing the focus to ... let's say pre-'ninety-two. My hunch is that if he's in the box, he went in before then.'

'Fine.'

Chu started typing. He still had not looked up or acknowledged Bosch with his eyes.

'When I came in, I saw that the lieutenant's alone in her office. You could go talk to her about the transfer.'

'I want to get this done.'

Bosch was calling Chu's bluff and they both knew it.

'Good.'

Bosch's cell buzzed and he saw it was an 818 call – the Valley. As he answered, he left the cubicle and headed out to the hallway so he could talk privately. It was Hannah Stone calling from one of her work lines.

'I won't be able to meet you till about eight because of some things here at work. Will that be all right?'

'Sure, that works.'

It would only give him about ninety minutes with her, unless he changed his daughter's curfew.

'Are you sure? You sound—'

'No, it will work. I could work late, too. I've got stuff here. Where do you want to meet?'

'How about somewhere in the middle this time? Do you like sushi?'

'Uh, not really. But I guess I could try it.'

'You mean you've never even tried sushi?'

'Uh ... I sort of have a problem with raw fish.'

He didn't want to mention that it related to his experience in Vietnam. The rancid fish they would come across in the tunnels. The overpowering smell.

'Okay, then scratch sushi. How about Italian?'

'Italian's good. Let's do Italian.'

'You know where Ca' Del Sole is in North Hollywood?'

'I can find it.'

'Eight o'clock?'

'I'll be there.'

'See you soon, Harry.'

'See you soon.'

Bosch ended the call and then made another he wanted to keep private as well. Heath Witcomb had been a smoking pal from Harry's days in Hollywood Division. They had shared the ash can behind the station countless times until Bosch gave up the habit. Witcomb was a patrol sergeant and as such he was in a position to know Robert Mason, the patrol cop credited with all three of the B&W drunk driving arrests. He also still smoked.

'Busy, Harry,' Witcomb said as he answered. 'What do you need?'

'Just call me next time you go out back.'

Bosch disconnected. As he pushed through the door back into the unit, Chu was pushing out.

'Harry, where have you been?'

'I went for a smoke.'

'Harry, you don't smoke.'

'Yeah, so what's up?'

'Chilton Hardy.'

'You found him?'

'I think so. It fits.'

They entered the cubicle and Chu slid into his seat in front of his computer. Bosch leaned over his shoulder to see the screen. Chu hit the space bar to rouse the computer from sleep. The screen lit, and on display was a mug shot of a white man of about thirty with spiky dark hair and acne scars. He cast a sullen look at the camera, staring with cold blue eyes.

'Chilton Aaron Hardy,' Chu said. 'Known as Chill.'

'How old is this?' Bosch asked. 'And where was it?'

'Nineteen eighty-five. North Hollywood Division. Battery on a police officer. He was twenty-eight at the time and lived in an apartment on Cahuenga in Toluca Lake.'

Toluca Lake was at the edge of Burbank and Griffith Park. Bosch knew it was very close to Travel Town, the place where Clayton Pell said he rode the trains when he was living with Chill.

Bosch next did the math. Chilton Hardy would be fifty-four years old if he was still alive.

'Did you put it through DMV?'

Chu had not. He switched screens and plugged Hardy's name into the state database containing the identities of the twenty-four million licensed drivers in California. Chu hit enter to begin the search and they waited to see if Hardy was one of those drivers. Seconds ticked by and Bosch expected a no-match return. As a general rule, people who get away with murder don't stick around.

'Bingo,' Chu said.

Bosch leaned down and closer in toward the screen. There were two matches. Chilton Aaron Hardy, age seventy-seven and still licensed with an address down in Los Alamitos. And Chilton Aaron Hardy Jr., age fifty-four, of Woodland Hills, a suburb of Los Angeles.

'Topanga Canyon Boulevard,' Bosch said, reading the address of the younger Hardy. 'He didn't go too far.'

Chu nodded.

'West Valley.'

'Seems a little too easy. Why'd this guy hang around?'

Chu didn't answer because he knew Bosch was just thinking out loud.

'Let's see the photo,' Bosch said.

Chu pulled up the driver's license photo of Chilton Hardy Jr. In the twenty-six years since his arrest in North Hollywood, he had lost most of his hair, and his skin had turned sallow. His face was lined by years of hard living. But the eyes were still the same. Cold and unforgiving. Bosch looked at the photo for a long moment before speaking.

'All right, good work. Print it.'

'We going up to see Mr Hardy?'

'Not yet. We go slow and deliberate on this one. Hardy's felt safe enough to stay in town all these years. We need to prepare and approach with caution. Print out both the old and new photos and make two six-packs.'

'We're going up to show Pell?'

'Yeah, and maybe take him for a little ride.'

While Chu got busy pulling mug shots and building the photo lineups, Bosch moved back to his desk. He was about to call Hannah Stone to inform her of their plan when a text came in from his daughter.

I told Ashlyn's mom that you're on a hot case. She says I can stay over. Cool?

Bosch thought for a long moment before responding. It was a school night but Maddie had stayed with

Ashlyn before on occasions when Bosch was traveling on cases. Ashlyn's mother was very accommodating and believed she was in some way helping the cause of justice by taking care of Maddie while Bosch pursued murderers.

But he had to wonder if there wasn't something else at work here. Was his daughter clearing the way for him to be with Hannah?

He almost called her but stuck with the texting conversation because he didn't want Chu overhearing.

Are you sure? I won't be that late. I could pick you up on my way home.

She quickly answered that she was sure and wanted to stay over. She said they had gone by the house after school to pick up clothes. Bosch finally sent her back his approval.

He then called Hannah to tell her she would be seeing him before eight o'clock. She said that Bosch and Chu could use one of the counseling rooms to show Pell the photo lineups.

'What if we want to take Pell for a ride? Are there any rules about that?'

'Where would you take him?'

'We have an address. We think it's where he lived with his mother and this guy. I want to see if he recognizes the place. It's an apartment building.'

She was quiet for a moment, probably considering whether it was a good or bad thing for Pell to see the place where he was abused as a child.

'There are no rules,' she finally said. 'He can leave the

facility. But I think I should go, too. He could have a bad reaction. Maybe I should be there.'

'I thought you had meetings. You have work till eight.'

'I just need to get my hours in. I came in late today because I thought I would have sessions tonight. We get audited on our hours. I don't want there ever to be an issue about my working a six-hour day.'

'Got it. Well, we should be there in about an hour. Will Pell be back from work?'

'He's already back. We'll be ready for you. Does this change our dinner plans?'

'Not on my end. I was looking forward to it.'

'Good. Me, too.'

21

Bosch and Chu drove separately out to the Valley so that they would not have to fight their way back downtown in rush-hour traffic after the excursion. Chu could simply head east on the 134 freeway to his home in Pasadena and Bosch could remain in the Valley until his dinner with Hannah Stone.

On the way up on the 101 freeway, Bosch finally heard back from Witcomb of Hollywood Division patrol.

'Sorry, Harry. I was in the middle of something, and then I just sort of forgot to call you back. What can I do you for?'

'You know a P-three in the station named Robert Mason?'

'Bobby Mason, yeah. But he's nights and I'm days, so I don't know him that well. What's up with him?'

'I'm looking at some arrests he's made that have something to do with something I'm working and need to talk to him about it.'

'You're working the Chateau case with Irvin Irving's kid, right?'

It sounded odd to Bosch to call George Irving a kid.

'That's right.'

'What kind of arrests are we talking about?'

'Three deuces.'

'What do three deuces have to do with the Chateau?'

Bosch was silent for a moment, hoping the hesitation would send a message to Witcomb that he was seeking information, not looking to distribute it.

'It's just an angle,' he finally said. 'What have you heard about Mason? Is he doing okay?'

Bosch was largely talking in code, trying to find out if Mason had a reputation one way or the other in terms of being bent or corrupt in any way.

'What I heard was that he was upset yesterday,' Witcomb said.

'About what?'

'About the Chateau. I guess he was old pals with the councilman's son. I heard they were in the same academy class, even.'

Bosch moved his car into the exit lane for Lankershim Boulevard. The plan was to pick up Chu in the commuter lot next to the Metrolink station in Studio City.

He played it cool with Witcomb, not wanting to reveal the importance of things.

'Yeah, I heard they knew each other back then,' he said.

'Looks that way,' Witcomb said. 'But that's all I know, Harry. Like I said, Mason's nights and I'm days. Speaking of which, I'm just about out of here. You got anything else?'

This was Witcomb's way of saying he didn't want to get further involved in discussions about a fellow cop. Bosch didn't really blame him.

'Yeah, you know which basic Mason usually works?'

Hollywood Division was geographically broken into eight basic car areas or patrol zones.

'I can look it up here pretty quick. I'm in the watch office.'

Bosch waited and Witcomb quickly came back.

'This deployment he's in six-Adam-sixty-five so I'd say that's where he usually works.'

A deployment period was twenty-eight days. The first 'six' was for the Hollywood Division designation. 'Adam' referred to his patrol unit and 'sixty-five' was his zone. Bosch couldn't remember the geographic delineations in Hollywood Division but he took a flyer.

'Sixty-five, is that the La Brea corridor?'

'You got it, Harry.'

Bosch asked Witcomb to keep their conversation private, thanked him and ended the call.

Harry considered things and saw that Irvin Irving had an out. If Mason was pulling over B&W drivers in an effort to help tilt the franchise toward Regent, then he could have been doing it solely at the request of his former friend and academy classmate, George Irving. It would be hard to prove that Councilman Irvin Irving had anything to do with it.

Bosch pulled into the commuter lot and circled, looking for his partner. When it became apparent that he had arrived ahead of Chu, he pulled to a stop in the main lane and waited. Palm on the wheel, he drummed his fingers on the dashboard and realized he was disappointed by the acknowledgment that Irvin Irving's actions might not have precipitated his son's death. If the councilman were ever accused of selling his influence on the taxi franchise decision, Bosch had already found the makings of reasonable doubt. Irving could argue that the whole scheme was cooked up and carried out by his dead son, and Bosch didn't think he would be above doing that.

He lowered the car window to let in some fresh air. To rid himself of his unease he jumped over to the other case and started thinking about Clayton Pell and how they were going to handle him. He then thought about Chilton Hardy and realized that he did not want to put off possibly getting a look at the man who was the ultimate target of the Lily Price investigation.

The passenger door opened and Chu slipped into the seat. Bosch had been so absorbed in his thoughts that he had not seen him enter the lot in his Miata and park.

'Okay, Harry.'

'Okay. Hey, I changed my mind about going to Woodland Hills. I want to ski Hardy's place, maybe even get a look at him if we're lucky.'

'"Ski"?'

'As in *schematic*. I want to see the lay of the land for when we do come back for real. We'll do that and then go see Pell. That all right with you?'

'I'm good.'

Bosch left the lot and drove back to the 101. Traffic was heavy going west to Woodland Hills. Twenty minutes later he exited on Topanga Canyon Boulevard and headed north.

The DMV address for Chilton Hardy was a two-story apartment building a half mile north of the big mall that anchored the West Valley. The apartment complex was large, running from sidewalk to back alley with an under-ground parking garage. After driving by it front and back, Bosch parked at the curb out front and he and Chu got out. Assessing the address, Bosch was struck by a familiarity he couldn't place. The complex had gray siding and white trim for a Cape Cod look, with navy-and-white-striped awnings over the windows on the front side.

'You recognize this place?' Bosch asked.

Chu studied the building for a moment.

'No. Should I?'

Bosch didn't answer. He walked to the security gate, where there was a call box. The names of the building's forty-eight tenants were listed along with their apart-ment numbers. Bosch scanned the list and didn't see Chilton Hardy's name. According to the DMV computer, Hardy was supposed to be living in apart-ment 23. The name next to 23 was Phillips. Again, Bosch was hit with a feeling of déjà vu. Had he been here before?

'What do you think?' Chu asked.

'When was the driver's license issued?'

'Two years ago. He could've been here then. He could've come and gone.'

'Or never been here.'

'Yeah, he picks a random address to hide his trail.'

'Maybe not so random.'

Bosch turned around and looked about as he con-sidered whether to risk exploring this further and pos-sibly alerting Hardy – if he was here – that he had drawn the attention of the police. He saw the sign planted near the curb.

Bosch decided he would not call apartment 23 yet. Instead, he punched the number 1 into the call box. It was listed as Manager.

'Yes?'

'We're here to look at the apartment for rent.'

'You must have appointment.'

Bosch looked at the call box and for the first time saw the camera lens next to the speaker. He realized the manager was probably looking at him and didn't like the vibe he was getting.

'We're here now. Do you want to rent it or not?'

'Must have appointment. Sorry.'

Fuck it, Bosch thought.

'Open up. It's the police.'

He pulled his badge and held it up to the camera. A moment later the security gate buzzed and Bosch pushed through.

The gate led to a central area where there was a bank of mailboxes and a bulletin board with notices about the complex. Almost immediately they were approached by a small, dark man of what appeared to be South Asian descent.

'Police,' he said. 'How can I do for you?'

Bosch identified himself and Chu, and the man introduced himself as Irfan Khan and said he was the manager. Bosch told him they were conducting an investigation in the area and were looking for a man who may have been the victim of a crime.

'What crime?' Khan asked.

'We can't tell you that at the moment,' Bosch said. 'We need to simply know if this is where the man lives.'

'What is name?'

'Chilton Hardy. He may use the name Chill.'

'No, not here.'

'You sure, Mr Khan?'

'Yes, sure. I manage building. He not here.'

'Take a look at a picture of him.'

'Okay, you show it.'

Chu pulled out a photo from Hardy's current driver's license and showed Khan. He looked at it for a good five seconds and then shook his head.

'See, I tell you. This man not here.'

'Yeah, I got it. This man not here. How about you, Mr Khan? How long have you been here?'

'I work here three years now. I do very good job.'

'And this guy never lived here? What about two years ago?'

'No, I remember him if he live.'

Bosch nodded.

'Okay, Mr Khan. Thank you for your cooperation.'

'I cooperate fully.'

'Yes, sir.'

Bosch turned and headed back toward the gate. Chu followed. When they got to the car, Bosch looked over the car roof at the building for a long moment before ducking into the driver's seat.

'Do you believe him?' Chu asked.

'Yeah,' Bosch said. 'I guess I do.'

'So then, what do you think?'

'I think we're missing something. Let's go see Clayton Pell.'

He turned the car on and pulled away from the curb. As he steered back toward the freeway, he had the navy-and-white-striped awnings in his mind's eye.

22

It was one of the few times he let Chu drive. Bosch was in the backseat with Clayton Pell. He wanted to be close to him in case of a violent reaction. When Pell had seen the photo lineups earlier and picked Chilton Hardy's photo out each time, he had disappeared behind a wall of controlled rage. Bosch could sense it and he wanted to be close in case he had to do something about it.

Hannah Stone rode in the front passenger seat and from his position Bosch could watch both Pell and her. Stone had a concerned look on her face. The reopening of Pell's old wounds was clearly weighing on her.

Bosch and Chu had choreographed the drive before arriving at the Buena Vista to pick up Pell. From the halfway center they first drove to Travel Town in Griffith Park so that they could begin the tour with Pell seeing what appeared to be one of the places of good memories of his young life. Pell wanted to get out and watch the trains, but Bosch said no, they were on a schedule. The truth was, he didn't want to allow Pell to watch the children on the train rides.

Now Chu turned right onto Cahuenga and started heading north toward the address they had traced Chilton Hardy to during the time period Pell lived with him. By the prearranged plan, they would not point out the apartment building to Pell. They would simply see if he recognized it on his own.

When they were two blocks away Pell showed the first stirring of recognition.

'Yes, this is where we lived. I thought that place was a school and I wanted to go there.'

He pointed out the window at a private day-care center that had a swing set in front behind a wire fence. Bosch could understand how an eight-year-old might think it was a school.

They were coming up to the apartment building now. It was on Pell's side. Chu took his foot off the gas pedal and started to coast, which Bosch thought was a giveaway, but they went right by the address without a word from Pell.

It wasn't a case catastrophe but Bosch was disappointed. He was thinking in terms of a prosecution. If he was able to testify that Pell pointed out the apartment building without any help, that would bolster Pell's story. If they had to specifically point the place out to Pell, a defense attorney would be able to contend that Pell was manipulating the police and creating his testimony out of a revenge fantasy.

'Anything yet?' Bosch asked.

'Yeah, I think we might've just passed it but I'm not sure.'

'You want us to turn around?'

'Is that all right?'

'Sure. Which side were you looking at?'

'My side.'

Bosch nodded. Now things were looking good.

'Detective Chu,' he said. 'Rather than turn around

let's go right and go around so it's on Clayton's side again.'

'Got it.'

Chu turned right at the next block, then took his first right and drove three blocks down. He then turned right and came back to Cahuenga at the corner where the day-care center was. He turned right again and they were only a block and a half from the address.

'Yeah, right up here,' Pell said.

Chu drove well below the speed limit. A car blasted its horn from behind and then passed them. Everyone in the police car ignored it.

'This is it,' Pell said. 'I think.'

Chu pulled to the curb. It was the right address. Every-one was silent while Pell looked out the window at the Camelot Apartments. It was a two-story stucco affair with rounded faux turrets at the two front corners. It was typical of the urban-blight apartments that sprouted in the city in the boom times of the fifties. They were designed and built to last thirty years and were going on twice that now. The stucco was cracked and discolored, the roof line was no longer straight and the flap of a blue plastic tarp was tied over the top of one of the turrets as a makeshift remedy for a leaking roof.

'It was nicer back then,' Pell said.

'Are you sure it's the right place?' Bosch asked.

'Yeah, this is it. I remember it sort of looking like a castle and I was excited about living here. Except I didn't know . . .'

His voice trailed off and he just looked at the building. He had turned halfway in his seat so his back was to Bosch. Harry saw Pell lean his forehead against the window. His shoulders then began to shake and there was a low sound almost like a whistle as he began to cry.

Bosch raised a hand and reached over to Pell's shoulder, but then he stopped. He hesitated and pulled his hand back. Stone had been turning in her seat and she saw the move. In that split second, Bosch saw her disgust with him.

'Clayton,' she said. 'It's all right. It's good to see this, to confront the past head-on.'

She reached over the seat and put her hand on Pell's shoulder, doing what Bosch could not. She didn't look at Bosch again.

'It's all right,' she said again.

'I hope you catch the fucking bastard,' Pell said, his voice strangled with emotion.

'Don't worry,' Bosch said. 'We will.'

'I hope he dies. I hope he puts up a fight and you kill his ass.'

'Come on, Clayton,' Stone said. 'Let's not think about those kinds of—'

He slapped her hand off his shoulder.

'I want him to die!'

'No, Clayton.'

'Yes! Look at me! At what I am! It's all because of him.'

Stone turned back in her seat and sat down.

'I think Clayton has been through enough here,' she said in a clipped tone. 'Can we go back now?'

Bosch reached forward and tapped Chu on the shoulder.

'Let's go,' he said.

Chu pulled away from the curb and headed north. The car was silent the whole way back and it was dark by the time they got back to the Buena Vista. Chu stayed in the car while Bosch walked Pell and Stone to the front gate.

'Clayton, thank you,' Bosch said as Stone used her key to open the passage. 'I know that was tough on you. I appreciate your willingness to do it. It's going to help the case.'

'Doesn't matter if you have a case. Are you going to catch him?'

Bosch hesitated and then nodded.

'I think so. We still have some work to do but we'll get it done and then we'll go find him. I promise you that.'

Pell walked through the open gate without another word.

'Clayton, you should go to the kitchen and see if there's dinner,' Stone instructed.

Pell raised a hand and waved, indicating he had heard her, as he walked off into the center courtyard. Stone turned to close the gate but Bosch was standing there. She looked up at him and Harry could read the disappointment.

'I guess we're not having dinner,' he said.

'Why not? Your daughter?'

'No, she's at her friend's. But I just thought . . . I mean, I'm fine to have dinner. I just need to take my partner to his car in Studio City. You still want to meet at the restaurant?'

'Sure, but let's not wait till eight. After that ride . . . I think I'm finished for the day.'

'All right. I'll drop Chu off and then head over there and meet you. That okay or do you want me to come back here?'

'No, I'll meet you there. Perfect.'

23

They got into the restaurant more than a half hour before their reservation time and were given a quiet booth in a back room near a fireplace. They ordered pastas and a Chianti Hannah chose. Through the dinner the food was good and the talk small – until Stone put Bosch directly on the spot.

'Harry, why couldn't you comfort Clayton in the car today? I saw you. You couldn't touch him.'

Bosch took a long drink of wine before attempting an answer.

'I just didn't think he wanted to be touched. He was upset.'

She shook her head.

'No, Harry, I saw. And I need to know why a man like you could not have any sympathy for a man like him. I need to know that before I could ... before anything could move forward between you and me.'

Bosch looked down at his plate. He put his fork down. He felt tense. He had met this woman only two days ago yet he couldn't deny his attraction to her or that some sort of connection had been established. He didn't want to spoil this chance but he didn't know what to say.

'Life is too short, Harry,' she said. 'I can't waste my time and I can't be with someone who doesn't understand what I do and have a basic human compassion for people who are victims.'

He finally found his voice.

'I have compassion. My job is to speak for victims like Lily Price. But what about Pell's victims? He's damaged people as badly as he has been damaged. Am I supposed to pat him on the back and say, There, there, it's going to be okay? It's not okay now and it's never going to be okay. And the thing is, he knows it.'

He made an open-palms gesture, as if to say, This is me, this is the truth.

'Harry, do you believe there is evil in the world?'

'Of course. I wouldn't have a job if there wasn't.'

'Where does it come from?'

'What are you talking about?'

'Your job. You confront evil almost every day. Where does it come from? How do people become evil? Is it in the air? Do you catch it like you catch a cold?'

'Don't patronize me. It's a little more complicated than that. You know that.'

'I'm not patronizing you. I am trying to figure out how you think so that I can make a decision. I like you, Harry. A lot. Everything I've seen I like except what you did in the backseat of that car today. I don't want to start something only to find out I was wrong about you.'

'So what's this, like a job interview?'

'No. It's me trying to get to know you.'

'It's too much like those speed-dating things they have. You want to know everything before anything even happens. There's something else here you're not telling me.'

She didn't respond right away and that told Bosch he had hit on something.

'Hannah, what is it?'

She ignored his question and insisted on her own.

'Harry, where does evil come from?'

Bosch laughed and shook his head.

'This is not what people talk about when they are trying to get to know each other. Why do you care what I think about that?'

'Because I just do. What's your answer?'

He could see the seriousness in her eyes. This was important to her.

'Look, all I can tell you is that nobody knows where it comes from, okay? It's just out there and it is responsible for truly awful things. And my job is to find it and take it out of the world. I don't need to know where it comes from to do that.'

She composed her thoughts before responding.

'Well said, Harry, but not good enough. You've been at this for a long time. From time to time you must have thought about where the darkness in people comes from. How does the heart turn black?'

'Is this the nature-versus-nurture discussion? Because I—'

'Yes, it is. How do you vote?'

Bosch wanted to smile but somehow knew it would not be received well.

'I don't vote because it doesn't—'

'No, you have to vote. You really do. I want to know.'

She was leaning across the table, talking to him in an urgent whisper. She leaned back as the waiter came to the table and started to clear their plates. Bosch welcomed the interruption because it gave him time to think. They ordered coffee but no dessert. Once the waiter was gone, it was time.

'Okay, what I think is that certainly evil can be nurtured. No doubt that is what happened with Clayton Pell. But for every Pell who acts out and damages somebody, there is someone who has had the exact same childhood who never acts out and never hurts anybody. So there is something else. Another part to the equation. Are people born with something that lies dormant and comes to the surface only under certain circumstances? I don't know, Hannah. I really don't. And I don't think anybody else does either. Not for sure. We only have theories, and none of it really matters in the long run because it is not going to stop the damage.'

'You mean my work is useless?'

'No, but your work – like mine – comes into play after the damage is done. Sure, your efforts will hopefully prevent a lot of these people from going out and doing it again. I do believe that and I told you so the other night. But how is it going to identify and stop the individual who has never acted out or broken a law or done anything before that warns of what's to come? Why are we even talking about this, Hannah? Tell me what you're not telling me.'

The waiter came back with the coffee. Hannah told him to bring their check. Bosch took this as a bad sign. She wanted to get away from him. She wanted to go.

'So that's it. We get the check and you run away without answering the question?'

'No, Harry, that's not it. I asked for the check because

I want you to take me home with you now. But there is something you need to know about me first.'

'Then tell me.'

'I have a son, Harry.'

'I know. You said he's up in the Bay Area.'

'Yes, I go up there to visit him in prison. He's in San Quentin.'

Bosch couldn't say he hadn't expected a secret like this. But he hadn't expected it to be her son. Maybe a former husband or partner. But not her son.

'I'm sorry, Hannah.'

It was all he could think to say. She shook her head as if to ward off his sympathy.

'He did something terrible,' she said. 'Something evil. And to this day I can't fathom where it came from or why.'

Holding the bottle of wine under his arm, Bosch unlocked the front door and held it open for her. He was acting calm but he wasn't. They had talked about her son for almost another hour. Bosch had mostly listened. But in the end all he could do was once more offer her sympathy. Are parents responsible for the sins of their children? Often yes but not always. She was the therapist. She knew that better than he.

He hit the light switch next to the door.

'Why don't we have a glass on the back deck?' he said.

'That sounds lovely,' she said.

He walked her through the living room to the sliding door to the deck.

'This is a great place, Harry. How long have you lived here?'

'I guess it's almost twenty-five years. It just hasn't seemed that long. I rebuilt it once. After the earthquake in 'ninety-four.'

They were greeted by the hissing sound of the freeway from down at the bottom of the pass. In their exposed position on the deck, the wind was crisp. Hannah walked right out to the rail and took in the view.

'Wow.'

She made a full turn, her eyes toward the sky.

'Where's the moon?'

Bosch pointed toward Mount Lee.

'It must be behind the mountain.'

'I hope it comes out.'

Bosch held the bottle up by its neck. It was what was left from the restaurant, brought along because he knew he had nothing at home. He had stopped drinking at home since Maddie had started living with him, and he rarely imbibed when out.

'I'm going to turn on some music and get a couple glasses. I'll be right back.'

Back inside, he turned on the DVD player but wasn't sure what was in the slot. Soon he heard Frank Morgan's saxophone and he knew all was good. He quickly moved down the hallway and did a quick cleanup of his bedroom and bathroom, grabbing fresh sheets from the closet and making the bed. He then went into the kitchen and grabbed two wineglasses before returning to the deck.

'I was wondering what happened to you,' Hannah said.

'I had to straighten up at least a little bit,' he said.

Bosch poured the wine. They touched glasses and

sipped and then Hannah moved close to him and they kissed for the first time. They held it until Hannah broke away from him.

'I'm sorry to have put you through all of that, Harry. My soap opera.'

Bosch shook his head.

'It's not a soap opera. He's your son. Our children are our hearts.'

'"Our children are our hearts." That's nice. Who said that?'

'I don't know. Me, I guess.'

She smiled.

'It doesn't sound like something a hard-boiled detective would say.'

Bosch shrugged.

'Maybe I'm not one. I live with a fifteen-year-old girl. I think she keeps me soft.'

'Have I put you off by being so forward tonight?'

Bosch smiled and shook his head.

'I like what you said about not wasting time. We both felt the connection the other night. So here we are. If it's right, then I don't want to waste time either.'

She put her glass down on the railing and moved closer to him.

'Yes, here we are.'

Bosch put his glass down next to hers. He then stepped into her and put his hand on the back of her neck. He moved even closer and kissed her, using his other hand to hold her body tightly against his.

Eventually, she slipped her lips off his and they stood cheek to cheek. He felt her hand go inside his jacket and up his side.

'Forget about the moon and the wine,' she whispered. 'I want to go inside now.'

'Me, too,' he said.

24

At 10:30 P.M. Bosch walked Hannah Stone out to her car. She had followed him up the hill from the restaurant earlier. She had told him she could not spend the night and he was okay about that. At the car, they held each other in a long embrace. Bosch felt good. The time with her in his bedroom had been wonderful. He had waited a long time for someone like Hannah.

'Call me when you get home, okay?'

'I'll be all right.'

'I know but call me anyway. I want to know you're home safe.'

'Okay.'

They looked at each other for a long moment.

'I had a nice time, Harry. I hope you did, too.'

'You know it.'

'Good. I want to do it again.'

He smiled.

'Yeah, me, too.'

She broke away and opened the door to her car.

'Soon,' she said as she got in.

He nodded. They smiled. She started the car and drove off. Harry watched her taillights disappear around a bend in the road and then he went to his own car.

*

Bosch pulled into the rear lot of Hollywood Division and parked in the first slot he found open. He hoped he was not too late. He got out and walked toward the back door of the station. His phone buzzed and he pulled it from his pocket. It was Hannah.

'You're home?'

'Made it. Where are you?'

'Hollywood Division. I need to see somebody on P.M. watch.'

'So that's why you pushed me out the door.'

'Uh, actually, I think you were the one who said you needed to go.'

'Oh. Well, then, okay. Have fun.'

'It's work. I'll call you tomorrow.'

Bosch walked through the double doors and down the hall to the watch office. There were two custodies cuffed to the bench that ran down the middle of the hall. They were waiting to be processed into the jail. They looked like a couple of Hollywood hustlers who came up short on the hustle.

'Hey, man, you help me out?' one of them asked as Bosch went by.

'Not tonight,' Bosch replied.

Bosch ducked his head into the watch office. There were two sergeants standing side by side, looking at the deployment chart for A.M. watch. No lieutenant. This told Bosch that the next shift was still upstairs in roll call and he hadn't missed the shift change. He knocked on the glass window next to the door. Both sergeants turned to him.

'Bosch, RHD. Can you call Adam-sixty-five in? I need ten minutes with him.'

'He's already on the way. He's first in.'

They staggered the shift change – one car at a time – so the division would not be left with no one on patrol. Usually the first in was the car containing the most senior officer or the patrol team that had had the toughest night.

'You think you can send him over to detectives? I'll wait over there.'

'You got it.'

Bosch walked back past the custodies and then took a left down the back hallway, past the kit room and into the detective squad room. He had worked in Hollywood Division for many years before his RHD assignment and knew the station well. As expected, the D bureau was deserted. At most Bosch thought he might find a patrol officer writing up his reports but there wasn't anyone in the room at all.

There were wooden signs hanging from the ceiling above the pods for the different crime units. Bosch went over to the homicide pod and looked for his old partner Jerry Edgar's desk. He identified it because of a photo taped to the back of the cubicle of Edgar with Tommy Lasorda, the former manager of the Dodgers. Bosch sat down and tried the pen drawer but found it locked. This gave him an idea and he quickly stood back up and scanned all the desks and counters in the squad room until he saw a stack of newspapers on a break table near the front of the room. He walked over and looked through the stack until he found the sports section. He then leafed through it until he found one of the ubiquitous advertisements for pharmaceutical treatment of erectile dysfunction. He tore the ad out and then went back to Edgar's desk.

Bosch had just finished slipping the ad through the crack above Edgar's locked desk drawer when a voice surprised him from behind.

'RHD?'

Bosch swiveled around on Edgar's chair. A uniformed cop was standing by the entrance from the back hallway. He had gray close-cropped hair and a muscular build. He was in his midforties but looked younger, even with the gray hair.

'Yeah, that's me. Robert Mason?'

'That's me. What is—'

'Come on over here so we can talk, Officer Mason.'

Mason came over. Bosch noticed that his short sleeves were tight on his biceps. He was the breed of cop who wanted any potential challengers to see the guns and know what they would be up against.

'Have a seat,' Bosch said.

'No, thanks,' Mason said. 'What's going on? I'm EOW and I want to get out of here.'

'Three deuces.'

'What?'

'You heard me. Three deuces.'

Bosch was watching his eyes, looking for any sort of tell.

'Okay, three deuces. You got me. What does it mean?'

'It means there are no coincidences, Mason. And you writing up three deuces last summer on three different B and W taxi drivers, all in Adam-sixty-five, stretches the limits of possible coincidence. My name isn't RHD. It's Bosch and I'm investigating the murder of your buddy George Irving.'

Now he saw the tell. But it came and went. Mason was about to make a bad choice. But when he did, Bosch was still surprised.

'George Irving was a suicide.'

Bosch looked at him for a moment.

'Really? You know that?'

'I know it's the only way it could've happened. Him going there, to that hotel. He killed himself and it had nothing to do with Black and White. You're barking up the wrong tree, dog.'

Bosch started to get annoyed with this arrogant asshole.

'Let's cut the bullshit, Mason. You've got a choice here. You can take a seat and tell me what you did and who told you to do it and maybe you'll get out of this okay. Or you can stand there and keep spinning bullshit and then I won't really care what happens to you.'

Mason folded his arms across his thick chest. He was going to turn this into a mano a mano battle of who backs down first, and it wasn't a game where big biceps gave you the edge. He was ultimately going to lose.

'I don't want to sit down. I have no involvement in this case other than that I knew the guy who jumped. That's it.'

'Then tell me about the three deuces.'

'I don't have to tell you shit.'

Bosch nodded.

'You're right. You don't.'

He stood up and glanced back at Edgar's desk to make sure he hadn't left anything out of place. He then took a step toward Mason and pointed at his chest.

'Remember this moment. Because this was the

moment you blew it, *dog*. This was the moment you could have saved your job but instead you gave it away. You're not EOW. You just put the P in front of it – permanent end of watch.'

Bosch headed toward the back hallway. He knew he was a walking contradiction. A guy who on Monday morning said he wouldn't investigate cops, and now here he was. He was going to burn this cop in order to get to the truth of George Irving.

'Hey, wait.'

Bosch stopped and turned back. Mason lowered his arms and Bosch read it as a dropping of his guard.

'I did nothing wrong. I responded to a direct request from a member of the city council. It was not a request involving specific action. It was no more than an alert and we get them passed on to us in roll call every day, every shift. Requests from council – RFCs, we call them. I did nothing wrong and if you burn me, you are burning the wrong guy.'

Bosch waited without moving but that was it. He moved back toward Mason. He pointed to a chair.

'Sit down.'

This time Mason did take a seat, pulling one away from the Robbery module. Bosch returned to Edgar's chair and they sat facing each other in the aisle between Robbery and Homicide.

'So tell me about this request from council.'

'I knew George Irving a long time. The academy, we were rookies together. Even after he left for law school we stayed close. I was best man at his wedding. Hell, I was the one who rented the honeymoon suite for them.'

He reached out and gestured behind him in the

direction of the squad lieutenant's office, as if that were the honeymoon suite.

'We did birthdays, Fourth of Julys ... and I knew his father through him and saw him at a lot of these things over the years.'

'Okay.'

'So last summer in June – I forget the exact date – I went to a party for George's kid. He—'

'Chad.'

'Yeah, Chad. Chad had just graduated from high school and was valedictorian and was going on a full ride up to USF, so they had a party for him and I went with Sandy, my wife. The councilman was there and we talked, mostly bullshit about the department and him trying to justify to me why the council fucked us on OT and things like that. Then at the end he told me sort of oh-by-the-way that he got a complaint from a constituent who said she got in a cab outside a restaurant in Hollywood and the driver was drunk. She said the car stank like a brewery and he was clearly impaired. He said that after a few blocks the lady had to tell the guy to pull over and she got out. She said it was a Black and White taxi and so he told me to keep an eye on the taxi drivers, that there could be a problem. He knew I worked P.M. watch and I might see something. And that was it. No conspiracy, no bullshit. I reacted to that when I was on patrol and there was nothing wrong with it at that time. And every case I made on those drivers was righteous.'

Bosch nodded. If it was a true story, Mason had done nothing wrong. But his story brought Irvin Irving solidly back into the picture. The question for the district attorney or even a grand jury would be about the councilman. Was he subtly using his influence to help benefit his son's client, or was he motivated by concerns for public safety? There was a fine line and Bosch doubted the question would ever get so far as a grand jury. Irving was too smart. Still, Bosch was intrigued by what Mason had tagged to the end of his story. There was nothing wrong with the chain of events 'at that time.'

'Did the councilman tell you when this complaint came in or how exactly it got to him?'

'No, he did not.'

'Did this sort of alert ever come up in a roll call over the summer?'

'Not that I remember but I probably wouldn't know, to tell you the truth. I've been around. I've got years and I'm allowed certain indulgences, I guess you might call it. I usually roll in first on shift change. I get priority vacation dibs, shit like that. I miss a lot of roll calls. I've been to too many and I can't stand sitting up there in that little room and listening to the same thing night after night. But my partner, who's a rookie, never misses and he tells me what I need to know. So this RFC could've come up. I just wasn't there.'

'But your partner never told you it came up, right?'

'No, but we were already on it, so he wouldn't have to. First deployment after that party, I started pulling over taxis. So he wouldn't have to tell me if it came up in roll call. See what I mean?'

'I do.'

Bosch pulled out his notebook and flipped it open. There was nothing written on the pages concerning Mason but he wanted time to collect his thoughts and consider what to ask next. He started flipping through his pages of notes.

'Nice,' Mason said. 'That your number on the badge?'

He pointed to the notebook.

'Yeah.'

'Where do you get something like that?'

'Hong Kong. Did you know that your friend George Irving was repping a taxi company that was hoping to take the franchise away from Black and White? Did you know that the DUIs you put on the company's record were going to help George succeed?'

'Like I said, not at the time. Not last summer.'

Mason rubbed his palms up and down his thighs. They were now moving toward something that was uncomfortable for him.

'So at some point you did come to know this?'

He nodded but didn't speak.

'When?' Bosch prompted.

'Uh, that would have been about six weeks ago.'

'Tell me.'

'One night I pulled over a taxi. Saw the guy roll a stop sign and pulled him over. It was a Black and White, and right away the guy starts giving me shit about collusion and all this and I'm thinking, Yeah, yeah, yeah, just touch your nose with your forefinger, asshole. But then he says, "You and Irving Junior are doing this to us" and I'm like, What the hell? So I get in his face and tell him to tell me exactly what he means by that. And that's when I found out my friend Georgie was repping another cab company putting the move on Black and White.'

Bosch leaned forward, closer to Mason, and put his

elbows on his knees. They were getting to the center of it now.

'What did you do?'

'I confronted him. I went to George and gave him every way out, but at the end of the day, there was no way out. I felt he and his father had used me and I told him that. I told him we weren't friends anymore and that was the last time I saw him.'

Bosch nodded.

'And this is why you think he killed himself.'

Mason scoffed.

'No, man. If he used me like that, then I wasn't really that important in his life. I think he killed himself for other reasons. I think Chad leaving was a big thing … and maybe there were other things. The family had secrets, you know what I mean?'

Mason didn't know about McQuillen or the marks on George Irving's back. Bosch decided that this wasn't the time for him to find out.

'Okay, Mason, you have anything else for me?'

Mason shook his head.

'You didn't confront the councilman about all of this, did you?'

'Not yet.'

Bosch thought about that.

'You going to the funeral tomorrow?'

'I haven't decided yet. Tomorrow morning, right?'

'Yeah.'

'I'll guess I'll decide then. We were friends a long time. Things just sort of went wrong at the end.'

'Well, maybe I'll see you there. You can go now. I appreciate you telling the story.'

'Yeah.'

Mason stood up and headed toward the back hallway, his head down. Bosch watched him go and wondered about the vagaries of relationships and investigations. He had come to the division expecting to confront a cop who was bent, who had crossed the line. Instead, he now viewed Mason as another victim of Irvin Irving.

And at the top of the list of Irving's victims was his own son. Mason might not have to worry about confronting the councilman. Bosch might get there first.

25

George Irving's Thursday morning funeral was crowded. But it was hard for Bosch to tell if all the people were there to mourn the loss of George Irving or to buttress their ties to his father, the city councilman. Many of the city's political elite were there, along with the command staff of the police department. Even Councilman Irving's opponent in the upcoming election – the guy who didn't have a chance – was present. It was as if a truce in politics had been called so respect could be shown for the dead.

Bosch stood on the periphery of the graveside gathering and watched the parade of who's who make their way to Irvin Irving and the rest of the dead man's family to offer condolences. It was Bosch's first look at Chad Irving, the third generation of the family. He clearly favored his mother in his looks. He stood next to her with his head down, barely looking up whenever someone offered a hand or a grip of the upper arm. He seemed bereft, whereas his mother was tearless and stoic, possibly operating behind a pharmaceutical haze.

Bosch was so intent on studying the family and political permutations of the scene that he didn't notice Kiz Rider slip away from the police chief's side. She came up on Harry's left as silent as an assassin.

'Harry?'

Bosch turned.

'Lieutenant Rider. I'm surprised to see you here.'

'I came with the chief.'

'Yeah, I saw that. Big mistake.'

'Why's that?'

'I wouldn't be showing support for Irvin Irving right about now. That's all.'

'Have things advanced since our discussion yesterday?'

'Yeah, you could say that.'

Bosch summarized his interview of Robert Mason and the clear implication that the councilman was complicit in the effort to move the Hollywood taxi franchise from B&W to Regent. He said that effort likely triggered the events that led to George Irving's death.

'Will Mason testify?'

Bosch shrugged.

'I never asked him but he knows the score. He's a cop and he likes his job – enough to end his friendship with George Irving when he realized he was being used. He knows if he's called to testify and he refuses, then his career is over. I think he'll testify. I'm surprised he's not here today. I thought maybe there might be some fireworks.'

Rider scanned the crowd. The service was over and people were starting to drift off amid the tombstones, heading to their cars.

'We don't want fireworks here, Harry. If you see him, you head him off.'

'It's over. He didn't come.'

'So what's your next move?'

'Today's the big day. I'm going to bring McQuillen in for a conversation.'

234

'You don't have enough to charge him.'

'Probably not. I've got a forensics team at the hotel right now with my partner. They're taking a second run at it. If we can put McQuillen in that suite or on the fire escape, it's over.'

'A big "if."'

'There's also his watch and the possibility of matching it to the wounds on the back.'

Rider nodded.

'That might work, but as you mentioned before, it won't be conclusive. We'll have our experts say it's a match. He'll have his experts say it's not.'

'Yeah. Listen, Lieutenant, I think I'm about to have some company. You might want to move out of the way.'

She scanned the remaining crowd.

'Who?'

'Irving's been watching me without really watching me. I think he's going to come over. He's waiting for you to leave, I think.'

'All right, then I'll leave you to it. Good luck, Harry.'

'If that's what it takes. See you, Kiz.'

'Stay in contact.'

'Roger that.'

She walked off and headed toward a clot of people surrounding the chief of police. Almost immediately Irvin Irving took advantage of seeing Bosch alone and headed toward him.

Before Bosch could address him, Irving said what was on his mind.

'It's a devastating thing to put your son in the ground and not even know why he was taken.'

Bosch had to hold himself back. He had decided that

now was not the time to confront Irving. There was still work to be done. McQuillen first, then Irving.

'I understand,' he said. 'I hope to have something for you soon. The next day or two.'

'That's not good enough, Detective. I have not heard from you, and what I hear about you is not comforting. Are you working another case besides the investigation of my son's death?'

'Sir, I have a lot of open cases and things don't come to a standstill because a politician pulled strings and put me on a new one. All you need to know is that I am working the case and will have an update for you before the week is out.'

'I want more than an update, Bosch. I want to know what happened and who did this to my son. Are we clear?'

'Sure, we're clear. And what I would like now is to speak to your grandson for a few minutes. Could you—'

'It's not a good time.'

'It's never going to be a good time, Councilman. But if you are going to demand results, then you can't stop me from throwing the net. I need to talk to the victim's son. He's looking at us right now. Would you please wave him over?'

Irving looked back at the grave site and saw Chad standing by himself. He signaled him over. The young man walked up to them and Irvin Irving made the introduction.

'Do you mind if I speak with Chad alone for a few minutes, Councilman?'

Irving looked like he had been betrayed but didn't want to reveal it in front of his grandson.

'Of course,' he said. 'I'll be at the car. We'll be leaving soon, Chad. And Detective? I want to hear from you.'

'You will, sir.'

Bosch put his hand on Chad Irving's upper arm and steered him away from his grandfather. They walked toward a stand of trees in the center of the cemetery. There was shade there and privacy.

'Chad, I'm sorry about your father's death. I'm looking into it and hope to know what happened very soon.'

'Okay.'

'I hate to bother you at this difficult time but I have a few questions and then I can let you go.'

'Whatever. I don't really know anything.'

'I know but we need to talk to everybody in the family. It's routine. Let's start with, When was the last time you spoke to your father? Do you remember?'

'Yeah, we talked on Sunday night.'

'About anything specific?'

'Not really. He just called and we sort of shot the shit for a few minutes about school and stuff but it was sort of bad timing. I had to go. So that was it.'

'Where did you have to go?'

'I had a study session set up and I had to go.'

'Did he say anything about his work or any sort of pressure he was under, anything that was bothering him?'

'No.'

'What do you think happened to your father, Chad?'

The boy was big and gangly, his face scattershot with acne. He shook his head violently at the question.

'How should I know? I had no idea what was going to happen.'

'Do you know why he would have gone to the Chateau Marmont and rented a room?'

'I don't know.'

'Okay, Chad, that's all. I'm sorry for the questions. But I am sure you want to know what happened.'

'Yes.'

Chad looked down at the ground.

'When do you go back to school?'

'I think I'll stay with my mother for at least the weekend.'

'She'll probably need that.'

Bosch pointed to the cemetery lane where the cars were waiting.

'I think she and your grandfather are waiting for you. Thanks for your time.'

'Okay.'

'Good luck, Chad.'

'Thanks.'

Bosch watched him walk back toward his family. He felt sorry for the kid. He seemed to be walking back to a life of demands and expectations that he had no part in conjuring. But Bosch couldn't think about it too long. He had work to do. As he started walking toward his own car, he pulled his phone and called his partner. It took Chu six rings to answer his phone.

'Yeah, Harry.'

'What've they come up with?'

Bosch had gone through Lieutenant Duvall with a request to have the department's top forensics team go back into the Chateau Marmont and make another sweep of room 79 using all means of evidence detection possible. Bosch wanted the place vacuumed, lasered, black-lighted and superglued. He wanted to try anything that might draw out evidence missed the first time, and possibly link McQuillen to the room.

'We got nothin'. So far, at least.'

'Okay. Were they out on the fire escape yet?'

'They started there. Nothing.'

Bosch couldn't say he was disappointed because he knew it was a long shot in the first place, especially on the fire escape, which had been exposed to the elements for nearly four days.

'Do you need me there?'

'No, I think we're going to wrap soon. How was the funeral?'

'It was a funeral. Not much else to say.'

In order to bring Chu in and oversee the second forensic examination of the crime scene, Bosch had told him in general terms where the investigation was moving.

'Then, what's next?'

Bosch climbed into his car and started the engine.

'I think it's time we spoke to Mark McQuillen.'

'All right, when?'

Bosch had been thinking about that but wanted to consider the how, when and where questions further.

'We'll work it out when you get back to the PAB.'

Bosch disconnected and dropped the phone into his coat pocket. He loosened his tie slightly as he drove out of the cemetery. Almost immediately his phone buzzed and he assumed Chu was calling back with another question. But instead it was Hannah Stone's name on the ID screen.

'Hannah.'

'Hello, Harry. How are you?'

'I just left a funeral.'

'What? Whose?'

'Somebody I never met. It was work. How are things at the center?'

'They're fine. I'm on a break.'

'Good.'

He waited. He knew she wasn't calling just to pass the time.

'I was wondering if you've been thinking about last night.'

The reality was that Bosch had been consumed by the Irving case since he had confronted Robert Mason the night before.

'Of course,' he said. 'That was pretty wonderful for me.'

'It was wonderful for me, too, but I didn't mean that. I meant about what I told you. Before.'

'I'm not sure what you mean.'

'About Shawn. My son.'

This felt jagged and awkward. He wasn't sure what she wanted.

'Well … I don't know, Hannah, what am I supposed to be thinking about?'

'Never mind, Harry. I need to go.'

'Wait, Hannah. Come on, you called me, remember? Don't go and don't get upset. Just tell me, what am I supposed to be thinking about with your son?'

Bosch felt something gripping his insides. He had to consider that for her the night before might have been some sort of means to a hopeful end that was about her son and not them. To Bosch, her son was lost. When Shawn was twenty years old he had drugged a girl and raped her – a sad and terrible story. He pleaded guilty and went to prison. That was five years ago and Hannah had dedicated her life since then to trying to understand where the impulse in him had come from. Was it genetic, was it nature, was it nurture? It was a form of prison in itself for Hannah, and Bosch had felt sympathy as she told him the ugly story.

But now he wasn't sure what she wanted from him besides his sympathy. Was he supposed to say her son's crime was not her fault? Or that her son wasn't evil? Or was she hoping for some sort of concrete help in terms of her son's incarceration? Bosch didn't know because she hadn't said.

'Nothing,' she said. 'I'm sorry. I just don't want it to ruin anything, that's all.'

That eased things for him a small bit.

'Then don't let it, Hannah. Just let things happen. We've only known each other a few days. We like to be with each other but maybe we moved too quickly. Let's just let things happen and don't bring this other stuff into it. Not yet.'

'But I have to. He's my son. Do you have any idea what it's like to live with what he did and to think about him up there?'

The grip inside tightened again and he understood that he had made a mistake with this woman. His loneliness and his own need for connection had led him down the wrong path. He had waited so long and now had chosen so wrong.

'Hannah,' he said. 'I'm in the middle of stuff here. Can we talk about all of this later?'

'Whatever.'

It was said as an invective. She might as well have said *Fuck you, Bosch*. The message was the same. But he acted like he had not received it.

'Okay. I'll call you as soon as I'm clear. Good-bye, Hannah.'

'Good-bye, Harry.'

Bosch disconnected and fought the urge to throw the phone out the car window. His thinking that Hannah Stone could be the one he brought into the life he shared with his daughter had been a fool's dream. He had moved too quickly. He had dreamed too quickly.

He shoved the phone into his coat pocket and buried his thoughts about Hannah Stone and failed romance as deep as George Irving had just been put in the ground.

26

Bosch entered the empty cubicle and immediately saw the stack of large envelopes on Chu's desk. He put his briefcase down on his own desk but then went over to Chu's and spread the envelopes across his blotter. Chu had received the statements and other records from George Irving's credit cards. Going back and checking all credit-card purchases was an important component of a thorough death investigation. Their findings would become part of the victim's financial profile.

The bottom envelope was the thinnest and was from the crime lab. Bosch opened this one, wondering which case it was in regard to.

The envelope contained the report on the analysis of George Irving's shirt. Forensic testing determined that the navy blue dress shirt contained blood and cellular material – skin – on the inside right shoulder panel. This was consistent with the crescent moon – shaped bruises and lacerations found on Irving's shoulder during the autopsy.

Bosch sat down at Chu's desk and studied the report and considered what it meant. He realized it could indicate at least two scenarios. One was that Irving was wearing the shirt when he was choked out and the injury to the skin on his shoulder occurred when the choker's watch pushed the shirt against his skin. The second was that the shirt was put on after the wounds occurred and the blood and skin were transferred.

Two things led Bosch to discount the second scenario. The button found on the floor indicated there might have been a struggle while Irving was still wearing the shirt. And because Irving had plunged naked to his death, it seemed highly unlikely that the shirt was put on over the wound and then removed again.

Bosch zeroed in on the first scenario. It suggested that Irving was surprised from behind and locked into a choke hold. There was a struggle. The button was torn from the right sleeve and the choker moved into the shoulder creep maneuver to control the victim. The bruises and surface abrasions occurred despite the shirt.

Bosch thought about this for a few minutes and no matter which angle he took on it, it still led back to McQuillen. As he had said to Chu, it was time to bring McQuillen in.

Bosch moved over to his desk and started planning the takedown. He decided it would not be a felony arrest. He would seek McQuillen's voluntary agreement to come downtown to the PAB and answer questions. If this effort was unsuccessful, then cuffs would come out and he would be arrested.

McQuillen was a former cop and this made him a dangerous arrest target. Almost all ex-cops owned guns and they all knew how to use them. Bosch would have Chu run a check on the ATF gun registry but he knew that such a check would not be conclusive. Cops picked up and seized guns on the street all the time. Not all of them were turned in to Property. An ATF backgrounding would only tell them what McQuillen legally owned.

Because of these concerns Bosch determined first and foremost that McQuillen would not be approached at home. That would put him too close to whatever known and unknown weapons he had. His car would also be a poor choice for the same reasons.

Bosch had already seen the inside of the B&W garage and dispatch office. This gave him a strategic edge. It would also be the least likely place for McQuillen to be armed. It would be one thing if he was driving a cab on the dark edges of Hollywood, but dispatching cabs there was not as dangerous.

The desk phone rang and the screen simply said LATIMES. Bosch was tempted to let it go to message but then thought better of it.

'Open-Unsolved.'

'Is Detective Bosch there?'

'Speaking.'

'Detective, this is Emily Gomez-Gonzmart across the street at the *Los Angeles Times*. I'm working on a story about the murder investigation of George Irving and I want to ask you a few questions.'

Bosch froze for a long moment. He had a sudden desire for a cigarette. He knew of the reporter. She was nicknamed 'GoGo' because she relentlessly pursued the stories she was following.

'Detective?'

'Yes, sorry, I'm in the middle of something here. You called it a murder. What makes you think it is a murder investigation? It's a death investigation, yes. But we have not called it a murder. We have not made that conclusion.'

Now she paused for a moment before answering.

'Well, my information is that it is a murder investigation and there is a suspect who will be arrested soon, if he has not already been taken into custody. This suspect is a former police officer with an ax to grind against both Councilman Irving and his son. That's why I'm calling you, Detective. Can you confirm this and have you made an arrest in the case?'

Bosch was stunned by the depth of her information.

'Look, I am not confirming anything. There has been no arrest and I am not sure where you are getting your information, but it is not correct.'

Her voice changed now. It became more of a whisper and it carried an intimate *who are you kidding?* quality to it.

'Detective,' she said, 'we both know that my information is correct. We are going with the story and I would like your comments for the record. You are, after all, the lead investigator. But if you can't or won't talk to me, then I'll go without you and I will report just that, that you refused to comment.'

Bosch's mind was scrambling. He knew how it worked. The story would be in the morning's paper, but long before that, it would go out online through the newspaper's website. And when it hit the digital universe it would be read by every assignment editor at every television and radio station in town. Within an hour of the post on the *Times* website, there would be a media frenzy. And whether named in the story or not, McQuillen would know Bosch was coming for him.

Bosch couldn't have that. He couldn't have the media rush him or dictate his moves in any way. He realized that he had to cut a deal here.

'Who is your source?' he asked, just to gain a little time to consider ways of handling this.

GoGo laughed, as Bosch knew she would.

'Detective, please. You know I can't reveal my sources. If you want to become an unnamed source, then I would offer you the same absolute protection. I'd go to jail before revealing sources. But I would prefer to have you on the record.'

Bosch raised his head and looked out of the cubicle. The squad room was mostly deserted. Tim Marcia was at his desk near the lieutenant's office. The L.T.'s door was closed as usual and it was impossible to know if she was holing up in there or out at a meeting.

'I wouldn't mind going on the record,' he said. 'But you know that with a case like this, with the political connections and whatnot, I can't go on the record without permission. It could mean my job. You'll have to hold back until I can get it.'

He hoped that by saying his job was on the line, he'd get some sympathy time. Nobody wants to cause somebody to lose their job. Not even a cold and calculating reporter.

'This sounds like a stall to me, Detective Bosch. With you or without you, I have the story and I am filing it today.'

'Okay, then how long can you give me? I'll get back to you.'

There was a pause and Bosch thought he could hear her typing on a computer keyboard.

'My deadline is five. I need to hear from you before then.'

Bosch checked his watch. He had just gotten three

hours from her. He believed that would give him enough time to take down McQuillen. Once he was in custody it didn't matter what was on the Internet or how many reporters and producers called him or the media relations office.

'Give me your direct number,' he said. 'I'll get back to you before five.'

Bosch had no intention of calling her back but he wrote her name and number down in his notebook anyway.

As soon as he hung up he called Kiz Rider on his cell. She answered right away but sounded like she was in a car.

'Yes, Harry?'

'Are you alone?'

'Yes.'

'The *Times* has the story. It came from either the chief or the councilman. Either way, I'm fucked if it gets out too soon.'

'Hold on, hold on. How do you know?'

'Because the reporter just called me and she knew we're working it as a murder and that we have a suspect who's an ex-cop. She's been told everything.'

'Who's the reporter?'

'Emily Gomez-Gonzmart. I've never talked to her before but I've heard of her. Supposedly they call her GoGo because she doesn't give up on a story.'

'Well, she isn't one of ours.'

Meaning GoGo wasn't on the list of approved and trusted reporters the chief of police dealt with. This meant her source was Irvin Irving or someone on the city councilman's staff.

'But you're saying that she knew you had a suspect?' Rider said.

'That's right. She knows everything but the name. She knew it was either about to go down or it already did.'

'Well, you know reporters often act like they know more than they do as a way of tricking you into confirming things.'

'She knew we had a suspect and he's an ex-cop, Kiz. That wasn't a bluff. I'm telling you, she knows it all. You people up there better get on the phone and jump on Irving's shit for this. It's his own son and he's damaging the case for what? Is there a political advantage to putting this out now?'

'No, there isn't. That's why I'm not convinced it went through him. And the thing is, I was in the room when the chief got him on the phone and updated him. He held back on the suspect because he knew Irving would demand to know the name. So he left that out. He did tell him about the marks on the shoulder and the choke hold connection but he did not say that there was a named suspect. He said we were still working it.'

Bosch was quiet as he contemplated the meaning of all of this. It fell under the heading of high jingo and he knew there was no one to trust other than Kiz Rider.

'Harry, I'm in the car. What I suggest you do is go online and get into the *Times* website. Put in a search with the reporter's name. See what comes up in previous stories. See if she has done stories involving Irving before. Maybe there's a staffer she's connected to and it's obvious from previous stories.'

It was a good and savvy idea.

'Okay, I'll do it but I don't have a lot of time. This is

forcing the issue with McQuillen. As soon as my partner gets in, we're going to go grab him.'

'You sure you're ready?'

'I don't think we have a choice. This story hits the Internet at five o'clock. We need to grab him before that.'

'Let me know the moment it goes down.'

'You got it.'

Bosch disconnected and immediately called Chu, who should have already cleared the Chateau Marmont.

'Where are you?'

'Heading in. We got nothing, Harry.'

'Doesn't matter. We grab McQuillen today.'

'Your call.'

'Yeah, my call and I'm making it. See you back here.'

He disconnected and put his phone down on the desk. He drummed his fingers. He didn't like this. His case actions were being dictated by outside influences. It never felt good. Sure, the plan was to get McQuillen and bring him in for questioning. But before, Bosch was setting the pace. Now it was being set for him and it made him feel like a tiger in a cage. Confined and angry, ready to put a paw out through the bars and take a swipe at the first thing that goes by.

He got up and went over to Tim Marcia's desk.

'Is the L.T. in?'

'Yeah, she's in there.'

'Can I go in? I need to give her an update.'

'She's all yours – if you can get her to open up.'

Bosch knocked on the agoraphobic lieutenant's door. After a pause, he heard Duvall give the okay and he went in. She was at her desk, working on the computer. She glanced up to see who it was but then finished typing something as she spoke.

'What's up, Harry?'

'What's up is that I'm going to be bringing in a body today on the Irving case.'

This made her look up.

'The plan is to get him to come in voluntarily. But if that doesn't work, we'll hook him up.'

'Thanks for keeping me in the loop.'

It was not said as a sincere thanks. Bosch had not updated her in twenty-four hours and a lot had happened in that time. He pulled out the chair in front of her desk and sat down. He gave her the short version, taking ten minutes to lead her up to the phone call from the reporter.

'My bad for not keeping you updated,' he said. 'Things have just been breaking quickly. The chief's office is up to speed – I just spoke to his adjutant today at the funeral – and they'll let the councilman know.'

'Well, I guess I should be glad you kept me in the dark. Now I won't be a suspect in the leak to the *Times*. Any idea about that?'

'I'm assuming it was Irving or someone in his camp.'

'But what does he get out of this? He's not going to end up looking good here.'

It was the first time Bosch had considered this. The lieutenant was right. Why would Irving leak a story that was ultimately going to taint him with, at minimum, the whiff of corruption? That didn't make sense.

'Good question,' Bosch said. 'But I don't have an answer. All I know is that it got across the street somehow.'

Duvall glanced at the blinds that covered the window

looking out at the Times Building. It was as if her paranoia about reporters watching had been confirmed. Bosch stood up. He had said what he needed to say.

'What about backup, Harry?' Duvall asked. 'You and Chu can handle this by yourselves?'

'I think so. McQuillen won't see us coming – and like I said, we want him to come voluntarily.'

She thought about this and then nodded.

'Okay, let me know. In a timely manner this time.'

'Right.'

'That means tonight.'

'You got it.'

Bosch went back to the cubicle. Chu still wasn't back.

Harry was consumed by the idea that the leak hadn't come from the Irving camp. This left the chief's office and the possibility that moves were being made that Kiz Rider didn't know about, or that she was hiding from him. He went to his computer and opened up the *Times* website. In the search box he typed 'Emily Gomez-Gonzmart' and hit return.

Soon he had a page full of citations – the headlines of stories that carried the reporter's byline in reverse chronological order. He started scrolling through, reading the headlines, and quickly came to the conclusion that GoGo did not cover politics or city government. There were no stories in the last year that put her in proximity to Irvin or George Irving. She appeared to be a feature writer who specialized in crime stories. The day-later kind of stories in which she expanded on a crime, reporting on victims and their families. Bosch clicked on a few of these, read the opening paragraphs and then went back to the list.

He scrolled backwards through more than three years of stories, not seeing anything that would connect Gomez-Gonzmart to anyone involved in the George Irving case. And then a headline from early 2008 caught his eye.

Triads Exact Toll on Local Chinese

Bosch opened the story. It was an anecdotal lead about an old woman who owned an apothecary store in Chinatown and who had been paying a monthly protection fee to a Triad boss for more than thirty years. The story then widened into a report on the cultural history of local small-business owners continuing the age-old, Hong Kong-based tradition of paying Triad crime syndicates for protection. The story was spawned by the then-recent murder of a Chinatown landlord that was suspected to have been a Triad hit.

Bosch froze when he got to the ninth paragraph of the story.

'The Triads are alive and well in L.A.,' said Detective David Chu, a member of the LAPD's Asian Gang Unit. 'They prey on people like they've preyed on people in Hong Kong for three hundred years.'

Harry stared at the paragraph for a long moment. Chu had transferred to the Open-Unsolved Unit and to partnering with Bosch two years earlier. Before that he worked in AGU, where he had crossed paths with Emily

Gomez-Gonzmart, and it seemed he had continued the relationship.

Bosch killed the screen and turned in his seat. Still no sign of Chu. He rolled over to his partner's side of the cubicle and opened the laptop Chu had left on his desk. The screen lit up and Bosch clicked on the e-mail icon. He glanced around again to make sure Chu had not entered the squad room. He then opened a new e-mail and typed 'GoGo' in the address box.

Nothing happened. He deleted it and typed 'Emily.' The automatic feature that completed e-mail addresses that had been previously used took over and filled in emilygg@latimes.com.

Bosch felt a rage building. He looked around once more and then went into the e-mail account's sent box and searched for all e-mails to emilygg. There were several. Bosch started reading them one at a time and quickly realized they were innocuous. Chu used e-mail only to set up meetings, often at the *Times* cafeteria across the street. There was no way to determine the kind of relationship he had with the reporter.

Bosch closed out the e-mail screens and shut the laptop. He had seen enough. He knew enough. He rolled in his chair back to his own desk and contemplated what to do. The investigation had been compromised by his own partner. The ramifications of this could extend all the way into court if McQuillen was eventually prosecuted. A defense attorney with knowledge of Chu's impropriety could destroy his credibility as well as the credibility of the case.

That was just part of the case damage. It didn't even speak to the irrevocable harm that Chu had caused their partnership. As far as Bosch was concerned, that relationship had just ended.

'Harry! You ready to rock?'

Bosch turned in his seat. Chu had just entered the cubicle.

'Yeah,' Bosch said. 'I'm ready.'

27

A taxi garage was much like a police station. It operated solely as a hub for the refueling, maintenance and direction of vehicles that continually spread out across a geographic jurisdiction. And, of course, it was the place where those vehicles were replenished with those who drove them. The vehicles were always in play until mechanical failure pulled them out of the lineup. In that there was a rhythm that could be counted on. Cars in, cars out. Drivers in, drivers out. Mechanics in and mechanics out. Dispatchers in and dispatchers out.

Bosch and Chu sat on Gower and watched the front of the Black & White Taxi garage for nearly an hour before they saw the man they believed was Mark McQuillen park a car on the curb and then walk in through the open garage door. He wasn't what Bosch expected. In his mind's eye he was picturing the McQuillen he remembered from twenty-five years earlier. The McQuillen whose photo was splashed across the media as the scapegoat of the choke hold task force. The twenty-eight-year-old stud with the buzz cut and the biceps that looked strong enough to crush a man's skull, let alone his carotid artery.

The man who sauntered into B&W Taxi was thicker in the hips than the shoulders, had straggly hair in an unkempt gray ponytail and walked with the pace of a man going where he didn't really care to go.

'That's him,' Bosch said. 'I think.'

They were his first words in twenty minutes. He had very little to say anymore to Chu.

'You sure?' Chu asked.

Bosch looked down at the copy of the driver's license photo Chu had printed. It was three years old but he was sure he had it right.

'Yeah. Let's go.'

Bosch didn't wait for his partner's response. He got out of the car and headed diagonally across Gower toward the garage. He heard the other door slam behind him and Chu's shoes on the pavement as he scurried to catch up.

'Hey, are we going to do this together or is it one-man-army time?' Chu called out.

'Yeah,' Bosch said. 'Together.'

For the last time, he thought.

It took a moment for their eyes to adjust to the dim lighting of the garage. There was more activity than on their previous visit. Shift change. Drivers and cars coming and going. They headed directly to the dispatch office, not wanting anyone to get the news to McQuillen before they got to him.

Bosch rapped on the door with his knuckles as he opened it. As he stepped in, he saw two men in the room, just as before. But one was McQuillen and the other was a new man as well. McQuillen was standing by his workstation, spraying a disinfectant on the radio headset he was about to put on. He seemed unfazed by the appearance of the two men in suits. He even nodded as if to signal that they were expected.

'Detectives,' he said. 'What can I do for you?'

'Mark McQuillen?' Bosch asked.

'That would be me.'

'Detectives Bosch and Chu, LAPD. We want to ask you a few questions.'

McQuillen nodded again and turned to the other dispatcher.

'Andy, you hold the fort? Hopefully this won't take long.'

The other man nodded and gave the smooth-seas signal with his hand.

'Actually,' Bosch said, 'it might. Maybe you should see if you can get someone in.'

This time McQuillen spoke while looking directly at Bosch.

'Andy, call Jeff, get him out. I'll be back as soon as I can.'

Bosch turned and gestured toward the door. McQuillen started out of the office. He was wearing a baggy shirt that was not tucked in. Bosch stayed behind him and kept his eyes on his hands the whole time. When they got into the garage, he put his hand on McQuillen's back and directed him toward a taxi that was on jacks.

'Do you mind putting your hands on the hood for a minute?'

McQuillen complied, and when he did so his wrists extended past the cuffs of his shirtsleeves. Bosch saw the first thing he was hoping to see. A military-style watch on his right wrist. It had a large steel bezel with grip ridges.

'Not at all,' McQuillen said. 'And I'll tell you right now that in my right-front waistband you will find a little two-shot popper I like to carry. It's not the safest job in the world. I know you have it tougher but we work in there through the night, the garage door always open. We take each driver's bank at the end of shift and sometimes the drivers themselves aren't the nicest guys, if you know what I mean.'

Bosch reached around McQuillen's substantial girth and found the weapon. He pulled it out and held it up to show Chu. It was a Cobra Derringer with a big-bore barrel. Nice and small but hardly a popper. It could fire two .38 caliber rounds and they could do some damage if you used it up close enough. The Cobra had been on the list of guns McQuillen had registered and that Chu had pulled up on the ATF computer. Harry put it into his pocket.

'You have a concealed weapons permit?' Bosch asked.

'Not quite.'

'Yeah, I didn't think so.'

As Bosch finished the pat-down, he felt what he was sure was a phone in McQuillen's right-front pocket. He left it in place, acting as though he had missed it.

'Do you shake down everybody you bring in for questioning?' McQuillen asked.

'Rules,' Bosch said. 'Can't take you in the car without cuffs unless we do the pat-down.'

Bosch wasn't exactly talking about department rules. More his own rules. When he had seen the Cobra on the ATF report, he guessed that it was a weapon McQuillen liked to carry on him – there wasn't really much other reason to have a pocket pistol. Harry's first priority was to separate him from it and anything else that might not have been on the ATF's radar.

'Okay,' he said. 'Let's go.'

They walked out of the garage and into the late afternoon sun. Walking on either side of McQuillen, the detectives led him toward their car.

'Where are we going for this voluntary conversation?' McQuillen asked.

'The PAB,' Bosch replied.

'Haven't seen the new building but if it is all the same, I'd rather go to Hollywood. It's close and I can get back to work sooner.'

This was the start of a cat-and-mouse game. The key thing from Bosch's perspective was to keep McQuillen cooperating. The moment he shut down and said, I want a lawyer, was the moment everything halted. Being a former cop, McQuillen was smart enough to know this. He was playing them.

'We can check if they have the space,' Bosch said. 'Partner, give them a call.'

Bosch had used the code word. As Chu pulled his phone, Bosch opened the back door of their sedan and held it while McQuillen climbed in. He closed it and over the hood of the car gave Chu a hand signal, like a cutoff motion. The meaning was, we are not going to Hollywood.

Once they were all in the car Chu proceeded to fake a phone call with the lieutenant in charge of the detective squad room at Hollywood Division.

'L.T., Detective Chu, RHD, my partner and I are in the vicinity and would like to borrow one of your nine-by-nines for about an hour if we could. We could be there in five. Would that be all right with you?'

There was a long silence followed by 'I see' three times

from Chu. He then thanked the lieutenant and closed his phone.

'No good. They just rolled a DVD counterfeiting warehouse and they got all three rooms stacked. It will be a couple hours.'

Bosch glanced back at McQuillen and shrugged.

'Looks like you get to see the PAB, McQuillen.'

'I guess so.'

Bosch was pretty sure McQuillen had not fallen for the charade. On the rest of the drive Bosch tried to make small talk that would either elicit information or lower McQuillen's guard. But the former cop knew all the tricks of the trade and remained mute almost the entire ride. This told Bosch that the interview at PAB was going to be difficult. Nothing was more difficult than trying to get a former cop to talk.

But that was okay. Bosch was ready for the challenge and had a few things up his sleeve that he was pretty sure McQuillen hadn't seen.

Once they got into the PAB, they walked McQuillen through the vast RHD squad room and then placed him in one of the Open-Unsolved Unit's two interview rooms.

'We just need to check on a few things and we'll get right back to you,' Bosch said.

'I know how it works,' McQuillen said. 'See you in about an hour, right?'

'No, not that long. We'll be right back.'

The door automatically locked when he pulled it closed. Bosch went down the hall to the next door and stepped into the video room. He started the video and audio recorders and then went to the squad room. Chu was at his desk, opening the envelopes containing George

Irving's credit-card records. Bosch took his own seat.

'How long are you going to let him cook?' Chu asked.

'I don't know. Maybe a half hour. I missed his cell phone during the pat-down. Maybe he'll make a call and say the wrong thing and we'll have it on video. Might get lucky.'

'It's happened before. You think he's walking out of here tonight?'

'I kind of doubt it. Even if he gives us nothing. Did you see his watch?'

'No, he's got long sleeves.'

'I saw it. It fits. We book him and take the watch and it goes to forensics. We go for DNA and wound matching. DNA will take a while but maybe they can make the wound match by lunch tomorrow and then we go to the DA.'

'Sounds like a plan. I'm going to get a cup of coffee. You want something?'

Bosch turned and looked at his partner for a long moment. Chu's back was to him. He was putting the credit-card reports into one stack and tapping the edges clean.

'Nah, I'm fine.'

'As long as you're letting him cook awhile, I might sit down and look at all of this stuff. You never know.'

Chu got up, putting the credit-card data into a fresh green file.

'Yeah, you never know.'

Chu walked out and Bosch watched him go. He then got up and went to the lieutenant's office, popping his head in and telling Duvall that they had placed McQuillen in interview room 1 and that he was there voluntarily.

He then went back to his desk and texted his daughter, making sure she had gotten home safely from school. She replied quickly, as her phone was an extension of her right hand and they had a rule that they never delayed responses to each other.

Home safe. Thought you were working last night.

Bosch wasn't sure what she was getting at. He had taken pains that morning to erase any indication that Hannah Stone had been there. He sent back an innocent response and then she nailed him.

Two wineglasses in the Bosch.

They always called the dishwasher after its manufacturer's name. Bosch realized he had left one detail uncovered. He thought for a moment and then typed out a text.

They were getting dusty on the shelf. I just washed them. But I am glad to know you are doing your chores.

He doubted it would get by her but he waited two minutes and there was no reply. He felt bad about not telling her the truth but it wasn't the right time to open up a discussion with his daughter about his romantic life.

Deciding he had given Chu enough of a head start, he took the elevator down to the ground floor. He went out the front entrance of the PAB and over to Spring Street, where he crossed and entered the Los Angeles Times Building.

The *Times* had a full cafeteria on the bottom floor. The PAB had snack machines and that was it. In what was billed as a gesture of neighborliness when the new police headquarters was opened a couple years earlier, the *Times* had offered use of its cafeteria to all PAB officers and workers. Bosch had always thought it was a hollow gesture, primarily motivated by the financially beleaguered newspaper's hope to make at least the cafeteria profitable while no other department in the once powerful institution was.

After badging his way past the security desk, he entered the cafeteria that had been put in the cavernous space where the old printing presses had turned for decades. It was a long room with a buffet line on one side and rows of tables on the other. He quickly scanned the room, hoping to see Chu before his partner saw him.

Chu was sitting on the far side of the room at a table with his back turned to Bosch. He was with a woman who looked like she was of Latin descent. She was writing in a notebook. Bosch walked up to their table, pulled out a chair and sat down. Both Chu and the woman looked like they were being joined at the table by Charles Manson.

'I changed my mind about the coffee,' Bosch said.

'Harry,' Chu blurted out. 'I was just—'

'Telling Emily here about our case.'

Bosch looked directly at Gomez-Gonzmart.

'Isn't that right, Emily?' he said. 'Or can I call you GoGo?'

'Look, Harry, it's not what you think,' Chu said.

'Really? It's not? Because it looks to me like you're laying out our case for the *Times* right here on their home court.'

He quickly reached out and grabbed the notebook off the table.

'Hey!' Gomez-Gonzmart cried. 'That's mine.'

Bosch read the notes on the exposed page. The notes were in some sort of shorthand but he saw repeated notations about *McQ* and the phrase *watch match = key*. It was enough to confirm his suspicions. He handed her the notebook.

'I'm going,' she said as she snatched the notebook out of his hands.

'Not quite yet,' Bosch said. 'Because you two are going to sit here and work out a new arrangement.'

'You don't tell me what to do!' she snapped.

She pushed back her chair so hard it fell over as she stood up.

'You're right, I don't,' Bosch said. 'But I do have your boyfriend's future and career in my hands here. So if any of that means anything to you, then you'll sit down and hear me out.'

He waited and watched her. She pulled her purse strap over her shoulder, ready to walk off.

'Emily?' Chu said.

'Look, I'm sorry,' she said. 'I have a story to write.'

She walked away, leaving Chu's face drained of blood. He stared into the distance until Bosch snapped him out of it.

'Chu, what the fuck did you think you were doing?'

'I thought ...'

'Whatever it was, you got burned. You fucked up and

you better start thinking of a way to back her off. What exactly did you just tell her?'

'I . . . I told her we brought McQuillen in and that we were going to try to turn him in the room. I told her it wouldn't matter if he confessed or not if the watch matched the wound.'

Bosch was so angry, he had to hold back from swinging at Chu and smacking the back of his head.

'When did you start talking to her?'

'The day we got the case. I knew her from before. She did a story a few years ago and we had a few dates. I always liked her.'

'So she calls up this week and starts leading you by the dick right into my case.'

Chu turned and looked at him for the first time.

'Yeah, you got it, Harry. *Your* case. Not our case. *Your* case.'

'But why, David? Why would you do this?'

'You did this. And don't start calling me David. I'm surprised you even know my first name.'

'What? *I* did this? Are you—'

'Yeah, you. You cut me out, Harry. You wouldn't tell me shit and you cut me out, made me chase down the other case while you ran this one. And this wasn't the first time. More like every time. You don't do that to a partner. If you had treated me right, I never would have done it!'

Bosch composed himself and calmed his voice. He sensed they had drawn the attention of people sitting at nearby tables. Newspaper people.

'We're not partners anymore,' Bosch said. 'We finish out these two cases and then you put in for a transfer.

I don't care where you go but you're out of OU. If you don't do it, I'll make it known what you did, how you sold out your own partner and your case for a piece of tail. Then you'll be a pariah and nobody and no unit outside of IAD will take you. You'll be outside looking in.'

Bosch stood up and walked away. He heard Chu call his name weakly but he didn't turn back around.

28

McQuillen was waiting with his arms folded on the table when Bosch reentered interview room 1. He checked his watch – apparently not realizing its importance to the coming conversation – and then looked up at Bosch.

'Thirty-five minutes,' he said. 'I thought you'd go over an hour easy.'

Bosch sat down across from him, putting a thin green file on the table.

'Sorry,' he said. 'I had to bring a few people up-to-date on things.'

'No problem. I called the job. They've got me covered for the whole night if necessary.'

'Good. So I guess you know why you're here. I was hoping we could have a conversation about Sunday night. I think that to protect you and to make this formal, I should let you know your rights. You've come here voluntarily but it's my practice to always let people know where they stand.'

'Are you saying I'm a murder suspect?'

Bosch drummed his fingers on the file.

'That's a hard one to say. I need some answers from you and then I will make a conclusion about that.'

Bosch opened the file and took out the top sheet. It was a rights waiver containing a printout of McQuillen's constitutional protections, among them the right to have an attorney present during questioning. Bosch read it out loud and then asked McQuillen to sign it. He handed him a pen and the ex-cop-turned-cab-dispatcher signed without hesitation.

'Now,' Bosch said, 'are you still willing to cooperate and talk to me about Sunday evening?'

'To a point.'

'What point is that?'

'I don't know yet, but I know how this is done. It's been a while but some things don't change. You're here to talk me into a jail cell. I'm only here because you have some wrong ideas and if I can help you without snagging my nuts on a rusty nail, then I will. That's the point.'

Bosch leaned back.

'Do you remember me?' he asked. 'Remember my name?'

McQuillen nodded.

'Of course. I remember everybody on the task force.'

'Including Irvin Irving.'

'Of course. Man at the top always gets the most attention.'

'Well, I was the man at the bottom, so I didn't have a lot of say. But for what it's worth, I thought you got screwed. They needed to sacrifice somebody and it was you.'

McQuillen clasped his hands together on the table.

'All these years later, that doesn't mean a thing to me, Bosch. So don't bother trying the sympathy angle.'

Bosch nodded and leaned forward. McQuillen wanted to play it hard. He was either smart enough or stupid enough to think he could go one-on-one without calling for a lawyer. Bosch decided to give him just what he wanted.

'Okay, so let's skip the foreplay, McQuillen. Why'd you throw George Irving off the hotel balcony?'

A small smile played on McQuillen's face.

'Before we have this conversation I want some assurances.'

'What assurances?'

'No charges on the weapon. No charges on any of the small stuff I tell you about.'

Bosch shook his head.

'You said you know how it works. Then you know I can't make deals like that. That's the DA. I can tell them you've been cooperative. I can even ask them to give you a break. But I can't make deals and I think you know that.'

'Look, you're here because you want to know what happened to George Irving. I can tell you. And I will, but not without these conditions.'

'That being the gun and the small stuff, whatever the small stuff is.'

'That's right, just some bullshit stuff that happened along the way.'

It didn't make sense to Bosch. If McQuillen was going to admit to killing George Irving, then charges like carrying a concealed firearm were strictly collateral and expendable. That McQuillen was concerned about them told Bosch that he wasn't going to admit to any culpability in Irving's death.

That made it a question of who was playing whom and Bosch had to make sure he came out on top.

'All I can promise is that I'll go to bat for you,' he

said. 'You tell me the story about Sunday night and if it's the truth, I'm not going to be too worried about the small stuff. That's the best I can do right now.'

'I guess I'll just have to take you at your word on that, Bosch.'

'You have my word. Can we start?'

'We already did. And my answer is, I didn't throw George Irving from the balcony at the Chateau Marmont. George Irving threw himself off the balcony.'

Bosch leaned back and drummed his fingers on the tabletop.

'Come on, McQuillen, how do you expect me to believe that? How do you expect anybody to believe that?'

'I don't expect anything from you. I'm just telling you, I didn't do it. You have the whole story wrong. You have a set of preconceived ideas, probably mixed around with a little bit of circumstantial evidence and you put it all together and come up with I killed the guy. But I didn't and you can't prove I did.'

'You hope I can't prove it.'

'No, hope's got nothing to do with it. I *know* you can't prove it because I didn't do it.'

'Let's start at the beginning. You hate Irvin Irving for what he did to you twenty-five years ago. He hung you out to dry, destroyed your career, if not your life.'

'"Hate" is a difficult word. Sure, I've hated him in the past but it's been a long time.'

'What about Sunday night? Did you hate him then?'

'I wasn't thinking about him then.'

'That's right. You were thinking about his son, George.

The guy trying to take away your job this time. Did you hate George on Sunday night?'

McQuillen shook his head.

'I'm not going to answer that. I don't have to. But no matter what I thought about him, I didn't kill him. He killed himself.'

'What makes you so sure of that?'

'Because he told me he was going to.'

Bosch was ready for just about anything he thought McQuillen could parry with. But he wasn't ready for that.

'He told you that.'

'That's right.'

'When did he tell you that?'

'Sunday night. In his room. That's what he was there for. He said he was going to jump. I got out of there before he did.'

Bosch paused again, mindful that McQuillen had had several days to prepare for this moment. He could have concocted an elaborate story that would cover all the facts. But in the file in front of him Bosch still had the photograph of the wound on George Irving's shoulder blade. It was a game changer. McQuillen wouldn't be able to explain it away.

'Why don't you tell me your story and how you came to have this conversation with George Irving. And don't leave anything out. I want the details.'

McQuillen took in a big breath and then slowly exhaled.

'You realize the risk I'm taking here? Talking to you? I don't know what you have or think you have. I could tell you the God's honest truth and you could twist it and use it to fuck me over. And I don't even have a lawyer in the room.'

'It's your call, Mark. You want to talk, then talk. You want a lawyer, we get you a lawyer and all talk ends. Everything ends and we play it that way. You were a cop and you're smart enough to know how this really works. You know there's only one way for you to get out of here and get home tonight. You gotta talk your way out.'

Bosch made a gesture with his hand, as though he was passing the choice to him. McQuillen nodded. He knew it was now or never. A lawyer would tell him to sit tight and keep quiet, let the police put up or shut up in the courtroom. Never give them something they don't already have. And it was good advice but not always. Some things have to be said.

'I was in that room with him,' he said. 'Sunday night. Actually, Monday morning. I went up there to see him. I was angry. I wanted … I'm not sure what I wanted. I didn't want to lose my life again and I wanted to … scare him, I guess. Confront him. But—'

He pointed emphatically at Bosch.

'—he was alive when I left that room.'

Bosch realized that he now had enough on tape to arrest McQuillen and hold him on a murder charge. He had just admitted to being with the victim in the place from which Irving had been dropped. But Bosch showed no excitement. There was more to get here.

'Let's go back,' he said. 'Tell me how you knew George Irving was even in the hotel and where.'

McQuillen shrugged like the question was for a dummy.

'You know that,' he said. 'Hooch Rollins told me. He dropped a fare there Sunday night and happened to see Irving going in. He told me because he'd heard me going on once in the break room about the Irvings. I held a staff meeting after the DUIs and told everybody, "This is what they're doing and this is the guy behind it." Got his photo off Google, the little shit.'

'So Rollins told you he was going into the hotel. How'd you know he had a room and how'd you know which room it was?'

'I called the hotel. I knew they wouldn't tell me his room for security reasons and I couldn't ask to be transferred to the room. What was I going to say, "Dude, do you mind giving me your room number?" No, so I called up and asked for the garage. Hooch had told me he saw him valeting his car, so I called the garage and said I was Irving and wanted them to check and see if I left my phone in the car. I said, You know my room number? Can you bring it up if you find it? And the guy said yes, you're in seventy-nine and if I find the phone I'll send it up. So there, I had his room.'

Bosch nodded. It was a clever plan. But it also showed some of the elements of premeditation. McQuillen was talking himself into a first-degree murder charge. All Bosch seemingly had to do was direct him with general questions and McQuillen provided the rest. It was a downhill path.

'I waited until the end of shift at midnight and went over there,' McQuillen said. 'I didn't want to be seen by anybody or any cameras. So I went around the hotel and found a fire escape ladder that was on the side. It went all the way up to the roof. But on each landing there was a balcony and I could climb off and take a break if I needed it.'

'Were you wearing gloves?'

'Yeah, gloves and coveralls I keep in the trunk. In my business you never know whether you'll be crawling under a car or something. I thought if somebody saw me, I'd look like a maintenance guy.'

'You keep that stuff in the trunk? You're a dispatcher.'

'I'm a partner, man. My name isn't on the franchise with the city because I didn't think we'd get the franchise way back when if they knew I was part of it. But I've got a third of the company.'

Which helped explain why McQuillen would go to such lengths with Irving. Another potential pothole in the case filled in by the suspect himself.

'So you took the fire escape to the seventh floor. What time was this?'

'I went off shift at midnight. So it was like twelve thirty or thereabouts.'

'What happened when you got to the seventh floor?'

'I got lucky. On the seventh floor, there wasn't an exit. No door to the hallway. Just two glass doors on the balcony to two different rooms. One to the left and one to the right. I looked in the one on the right and there he was. Irving was sitting right there on the couch.'

McQuillen stopped. It looked as if he was staring at the memory of that night, at what he had seen through the balcony door. Bosch was mindful of needing to keep the story going but with as little from himself as possible.

'So you found him.'

'Yeah, he was just sitting there, drinking Jack Black

275

straight outta the bottle and looking like he was just waiting for something.'

'Then what happened?'

'He took the last pull out of that bottle and all of a sudden he got up and he started coming right at me. Like he knew I was on the balcony watching him.'

'What did you do?'

'I backed up against the wall next to the door. I figured he couldn't have seen me with the reflection inside on the glass. He was just coming out on the balcony. So I backed up next to the door and he opened it and stepped out. He walked right to the wall and he threw the empty bottle out there as far as he could. Then he leaned over the wall and started looking down, like he was going to puke or something. And I knew when he finished his business and turned around I was going to be standing right in front of him. There was no place to go.'

'Did he vomit?'

'No, he never did. He just—'

A loud and unexpected knock on the door nearly made Bosch jump off his seat.

'Just hold the story right there,' he said.

He got up and used his body to shield the knob from McQuillen. He punched in the combination on the lock and opened the door. Chu was standing there and Bosch almost reached out to strangle him. But he calmly stepped out and closed the door.

'What the fuck are you doing? You know you never barge in on an interview. What are you, a rookie?'

'Look, I wanted to tell you, I killed the story. She's not running it.'

'That's great. You could've told me after the interview was over. This guy's about to give up the whole thing and you knock on the fucking door.'

'I just didn't know if you were making moves with him because you thought the story was going to come out. It won't now, Harry.'

'We'll talk about it later.'

Bosch turned back to the interview room door.

'I'm going to make it up to you, Harry. I promise.'

Bosch turned back to him.

'I don't care about your promises. You want to do something, stop knocking on the door and start working on a search warrant for this guy's watch. When we send it to forensics I want it on a judge's order.'

'You got it, Harry.'

'Good. Go away.'

Bosch punched in the combination, reentered the room and sat across from McQuillen.

'Something important?' McQuillen asked.

'No, just some bullshit. Why don't you keep telling the story? You said Irving was on the balcony and—'

'Yeah, I was standing there behind him against the wall. As soon as he turned to go back in I was going to be like a sitting duck.'

'So what did you do?'

'I don't know. Instinct took over. I made a move. I came up behind him and grabbed him. I started dragging him back into the room. All those houses on the hillside. I thought somebody might see us out there. I just wanted to get him back into the room.'

'You say you grabbed him. How exactly did you grab him?'

'Around the neck. I used the choke hold. Like old times.'

McQuillen looked directly at Bosch as he said it, as if passing on some sort of significance.

'Did he struggle? Did he put up any resistance?'

'Yeah, he was shocked as shit. He started fighting but he was sort of drunk. I backed him in through the door. He flopped around like a fucking marlin but it didn't take long. It never did. He went to sleep.'

Bosch waited to see if he would continue but that was it.

'He was unconscious then,' he said.

'That's right,' McQuillen said.

'What happened next?'

'He started breathing again pretty quick but he was asleep. I told you, he drank that whole bottle of Jack. He was snoring. I had to shake him and wake him up. He finally came to and he was drunk and confused and when he saw me he didn't know me from Adam. I had to tell him who I was and why I was there. He was on the floor, sort of propped up on his elbow. And I was standing over him like God.'

'What did you say to him?'

'I told him he was fucking with the wrong guy and that I wasn't going to let him do what his father had done to me. And that's when things sort of went screwy because I didn't know what he was going to do.'

'Wait a minute, I'm not tracking that. What do you mean by "things going screwy"?'

'He started laughing at me. I had just jumped the fucker and choked him out and he thinks it's funny. I'm trying to scare the shit out of him and he's too drunk. He's on the floor laughing his ass off.'

Bosch thought about this a long moment. He didn't like the way this was going because it was not in any direction he could have expected.

'Is that all he did, laugh? He didn't say anything?'

'Yeah, eventually he got over laughing and that's when he told me I didn't have anything to worry about anymore.'

'What else?'

'That's pretty much it. He said I had nothing to worry about and that I could go on home. He waved me off, like good-bye now.'

'Did you ask him how he was sure there was nothing to worry about?'

'I didn't think I had to.'

'Why not?'

'Because I just sort of got it. He was there to off himself. When he went out on the balcony looking over the wall, he was picking his spot. His plan was to jump and he was drinking the Jack to give him the courage to do it. So I left and that's . . . that's what he did.'

Bosch said nothing at first. McQuillen's story was either an elaborate cover story or just strange enough to be true. There were elements of it that could be checked. The results of the blood-alcohol test were not in yet, but the mention of the bottle of Jack Daniel's was new. There had been no sign of it on the video of Irving checking in. No witness had reported seeing him taking a bottle to his room.

'Tell me about the bottle of Jack,' he said.

'I told you, he drank it and then chucked it.'

'How big was it? Are you talking about a whole fifth?'

'No, no, smaller. It was a six-shooter.'

'I don't know what that means.'

'It's like a smaller flask bottle they put out. Holds a good six shots. I drink Jack myself and I recognized the bottle. We call 'em six-shooters.'

Bosch was thinking that six good-sized shots probably added up to ten or twelve ounces. It was possible Irving could have concealed a flask-shaped bottle that size while he was checking in. Harry also remembered the array of bottles and snacks lined up on the kitchenette counter in the hotel suite. It could have come from there as well.

'Okay, when he threw the bottle, what happened?'

'I heard it shatter out there in the darkness. I think it hit the street or somebody's roof or something.'

'Which direction did he throw it?'

'Straight out.'

Bosch nodded.

'Okay, sit tight, McQuillen. I'll be back.'

Bosch got up, punched in the combo again and left the room. He started down the hall toward Open-Unsolved.

As he passed the video room, the door came open and Kiz Rider stepped out. She had been watching the interview. Bosch wasn't surprised. She knew he was bringing McQuillen in.

'Holy shit, Harry.'

'Yeah.'

'Well, do you believe him?'

Bosch stopped and looked at her.

'The story hangs together and it's got parts we can check. When he went into the interview room he had no idea what we had – the button on the floor, the wounds on the shoulder, the witness who put him on the fire escape three hours too early – and his story hit every marker.'

Rider put her hands on her hips.

'And at the same time, he puts himself in that room. He admits choking the vic out.'

'It was a risky move, putting himself in the dead guy's room.'

'So you believe him?'

'I don't know. There's something else. McQuillen was a cop. He knows—'

Bosch stopped cold and snapped his fingers.

'What?'

'He's covered by an alibi. That's what he hasn't said. Irving didn't go down for another three or four hours. McQuillen's got an alibi and he's waiting to see if we jack him up. Because if we do, he can ride it out, then drop the alibi and walk. It would embarrass the department, maybe give him a little payback for all that happened to him.'

Bosch nodded. That had to be it.

'Look, Harry, we've already primed the pump. Irvin Irving's expecting the announcement of an arrest. You said the *Times* already has it.'

'Fuck Irving. I don't care what he's expecting. And my partner claims we don't have to worry about the *Times*.'

'How's that?'

'I don't know how but he got them to kill the story. Look, I need to put Chu on the Jack Daniel's bottle and then get back in there and get the alibi.'

'All right, I'm going back up to ten. You call me as

soon as you're finished with McQuillen. I need to know where we stand.'

'You got it.'

Bosch went down the hall to Open-Unsolved and found Chu at his computer.

'I need you to check something. Did you release the room at the Chateau?'

'No, you didn't tell me to so I—'

'Good. Call the hotel and see if they put bottles of Jack Daniel's in their suites. I'm not talking about miniatures. Something bigger in a flask-size bottle. If they do, have them see if the bottle is missing from suite seventy-nine.'

'I put a seal on the door.'

'Have them cut it. When you're finished with that, call the ME and see if the blood-alcohol on Irving has come back yet. I'm going back to McQuillen.'

'Harry, you want me to come in when I get this?'

'No, don't come in. Just get it and wait for me.'

Bosch punched in the combo and opened the door. He swiftly moved back to his seat.

'Back so soon?' McQuillen asked.

'Yeah, I forgot something. I didn't get the full story from you, McQuillen.'

'Yes, you did. I told you exactly what happened in that room.'

'Yeah, but you didn't tell me what happened after.'

'He jumped, that's what happened after.'

'I'm not talking about him. I'm talking about you, what you did. You knew what he was going to do and rather than, say, pick up a phone and call somebody to try to stop it, you just shagged your ass on out of there and let him jump. But you were smart, you knew it could come back to you. That someone like me might show up.'

Bosch leaned back in his chair and appraised McQuillen and nodded.

'So you went and got yourself alibied.'

McQuillen kept a straight face.

'You came in here hoping we'd arrest you and then you'd eventually pop the alibi out there and embarrass the department for all the shit you got dragged through before. Maybe get a lawsuit for false arrest going. You were going to use Irving for some payback.'

McQuillen showed nothing. Bosch leaned forward and across the table.

'You might as well tell me because I'm not arresting you, McQuillen. I'm not giving you this play, no matter what I think of what was done to you twenty-five years ago.'

McQuillen finally nodded and flicked a hand as though to say, *What the hell, it was worth a try.*

'I had parked over at the Standard across Sunset. They know me there.'

The Standard was a boutique hotel a few blocks from the Chateau.

'Good customers of ours. Technically, that's West Hollywood, so we can't sit on the place but we've got the doormen wired. When a customer needs a cab, they call us. We always have a car sitting nearby.'

'So you went there after seeing Irving.'

'Yeah, they got a restaurant there called Twenty-four/Seven. It never closes and it's got a camera over the counter. I went there and I never left that counter until the sun came up. You go get the disc and I'll be on it. When Irving jumped, I was drinking hot coffee.'

Bosch shook his head like the story didn't add up.

'How'd you know Irving wouldn't jump before you got there – when you were still in the Chateau or walking over? What was that, fifteen minutes at least. That was risky.'

McQuillen shrugged.

'He was temporarily incapacitated.'

Bosch stared at him for a long moment until understanding came. McQuillen had choked Irving out again.

Bosch leaned across the table and stared hard at McQuillen.

'You put him to sleep again. You choked him out, made sure he was breathing and left him there snoring on the floor.'

Bosch remembered the alarm clock in the room.

'Then you went into the bedroom and brought the clock out. You plugged it in next to him on the floor and set the alarm for four A.M. to make sure he'd wake up. Just so he could jump while you were alibied at the Standard with your hot coffee.'

Another shrug from McQuillen. He was finished talking.

'You're a hell of a guy, McQuillen, and you're free to go.'

McQuillen nodded smugly.

'I appreciate that.'

'Yeah, well, appreciate this. For twenty-five years I thought you got a bad deal. Now I think maybe they got it right. You're a bad guy and that means you were a bad cop.'

'You don't know shit about me, Bosch.'

'I know this. You went up to that room to do something. You don't climb the fire escape just to confront a guy. So I don't care that you got a bad deal before. What I care about is that you knew what Irving was going to do and you didn't try to stop it. Instead, you allowed it to happen. No, actually, you *helped* it happen. To me, that's not small stuff. If it's not a crime, then it should be. And when this is all over I'm going to hit up every prosecutor I know until I find one who will take it to the grand jury. You can walk out of here tonight, but the next time you won't be so lucky.'

McQuillen kept nodding while Bosch spoke, as if he was impatiently allowing Bosch his final say. When Harry was finished, McQuillen was nonchalant in his response.

'Then I guess it's good to know where I stand.'

'Sure. Glad to help with that.'

'How do I get back to B and W? You promised me a ride.'

Bosch got up from the table and headed to the door.

'Call a cab,' he said.

29

Chu was just hanging up the phone as Bosch got back to the cubicle.

'What did you get?' Harry asked.

Chu looked down at the scratch pad on his desk as he answered.

'Yes, the hotel stocks Jack Daniel's in the suites. A flask bottle containing twelve ounces. And yes, the bottle is missing from suite seventy-nine.'

Bosch nodded. It was a further confirmation of McQuillen's story.

'What about the blood-alcohol?'

Chu shook his head.

'Not done yet. The ME's office said next week.'

Bosch shook his head, annoyed that he hadn't used Kiz Rider and the chief's office to push the ME on the blood testing. He went to his desk and started stacking reports on top of the murder book. He spoke to Chu with his back to him.

'How'd you kill the story?'

'I called her. I told her if she ran the story, I would go to her boss and say that she was trading sex for information. I figure even over there that's gotta be an ethical violation. She might not lose her job but she'd be tainted. She knows they'd start looking at her differently.'

'You handled it like a real gentleman, Chu. Where are the credit-card records?'

'Here. What's going on?'

Chu handed over the file containing the purchase records he had received from the credit-card companies.

'I'm taking all of this home.'

'What about McQuillen? Are we booking him?'

'No. He's gone.'

'You kicked him?'

'That's right.'

'What about the warrant on the watch? I'm about to print it out.'

'We won't need it. He admitted he choked Irving out.'

'He admitted it and you cut him *loose*? Are you—'

'Listen, Chu, I don't have time to walk you through it. Go watch the tape if you have an issue with what I'm doing. No, better yet, I want you to go out to the Standard on the Sunset Strip. You know where that is?'

'Yeah, but why am I going there?'

'Go to their twenty-four-hour restaurant and get their disc from the camera over the counter for Sunday night into Monday morning.'

'Okay, what's on it?'

'Should be McQuillen's alibi. Call me when you confirm it.'

Bosch put all the loose reports in his briefcase and then carried the murder book separately because the binder was too thick for the case. He started to walk out of the cubicle.

'What are you going to do?' Chu called after him.

Bosch turned and looked back at him.

'Start over.'

He resumed his movement toward the squad room exit. He stopped at the lieutenant's status board and put his magnet in the out slot. When he turned to the door, Chu was standing there.

'You're not going to do this to me,' he said.

'You did it to yourself. You made a choice. I don't want anything to do with you.'

'I made a mistake. And I told you – no, I promised you – that I would make up for it.'

Bosch reached out and gently moved him by the arm to the side so he could open the door. He went out into the hallway without another word to Chu.

On his way home Bosch drove into East Hollywood and stopped behind the El Matador truck on Western. He remembered Chu's comment about the incongruity of Western Avenue being in East Hollywood. Only in L.A., he thought as he got out.

There was no one in line at the truck because it was still early. The *taquero* was just setting up for the night. Bosch had him put enough carne asada for four tacos into a to-go cup and asked him to roll the flour tortillas up in foil. He added sides of guacamole, rice and salsa and the man put it all in a bag for transport. While Bosch was waiting he sent a text to his daughter telling her he was coming home with dinner because he would be too busy working to cook something. She answered that that was okay because she was starved.

Twenty minutes later he walked through the front door of his home to find his daughter reading a book and playing music in the living room. He stood there frozen in the entranceway, taco bag in one hand, briefcase in the other, murder book under his arm.

'What?' she said.

'You're listening to Art Pepper?'

'Yeah. I think it's good music to read by.'

He smiled and went into the kitchen.

'What do you want to drink?'

'I have water already.'

Bosch made a plate of tacos for her with all the sides and took it out to her. He came back into the kitchen and ate his tacos, fully loaded, while leaning over the sink. When he was finished, he bent down to the faucet and chased it with water right out of the pipe. Wiping his face with a paper towel, he went out to work at the dining room table.

'How was school?' he asked while opening his briefcase. 'Did you skip lunch again?'

'School was a drag like always. I skipped lunch to study for the algebra quiz.'

'How'd you do?'

'I probably flunked.'

He knew she was exaggerating. She was a good student. She hated algebra because she could not perceive a life where it would become useful. Especially when at the moment she wanted to be a cop – or so she said.

'I'm sure you did fine. Are you reading that for IR? What is it?'

She held the book up so he could see it. It was *The Stand* by Stephen King.

'It's my optional choice.'

'Pretty thick for a school read.'

'It's really good. Are you trying to avoid the subject of the two wineglasses by not eating with me and then asking all of these questions?'

She had nailed him.

'I'm not avoiding anything. I do have work to do and I already explained the wineglasses in the dishwasher.'

'But you didn't explain about how one still had lipstick on it.'

Bosch looked at her. He had missed the lipstick.

'So who's the detective in the house now?' he asked.

'Don't try to deflect,' she said. 'The point is, you don't have to lie about your girlfriend with me, Dad.'

'Look, she's not my girlfriend and she is never going to be my girlfriend. It didn't work out. I am sorry I didn't tell you the truth but we can drop it now. When and if I do ever have a girlfriend, I will let you know. Just like I hope you will tell me when you have a boyfriend.'

'Fine.'

'You don't have a boyfriend, do you?'

'No, Dad.'

'Good. I mean, it's good that you aren't keeping a secret. Not good that you don't have a boyfriend. I don't want to be a father who's like that.'

'I get it.'

'Good.'

'Then why are you so mad?'

'I'm—'

He stopped as he realized that her perception was

right on the money. He was mad about one thing and it was showing in something else.

'You know what I said a minute ago about look who the detective in the house is?'

'Yes, I was sitting right here.'

'Well, on Monday night you looked at that video I had of the guy checking in and you called it right there. You said he jumped. Based on what you saw in thirty seconds of video you said he jumped.'

'So?'

'Well, I've been chasing my tail all week, seeing a murder where there wasn't a murder, and you know what? I think you were right. You called it right at the start and I didn't. I must be getting old.'

A look of true sympathy came over her face.

'Dad, you'll get over it and you'll get 'em next time. You're the one who told me you can't solve every case. Well, at least you got this one right in the long run.'

'Thanks, Mads.'

'And I don't want to pile on but ...'

Bosch looked at her. She was proud of something.

'All right, give it to me. But what?'

'There was no lipstick on the glass. I bluffed you.'

Bosch shook his head.

'You know something, kid? Someday you're going to be the one they'll want in the interview room. Your looks, your skills, they'll be confessing to you right and left and lined up in the hall.'

She smiled and went back to her book. Bosch noticed she had left one taco uneaten on her plate and he was tempted to go for it, but instead set to work on the case, opening the murder book and spreading the loose files and reports out on the table.

'You know how a battering ram works?' he asked.

'What?' his daughter replied.

'You know what a battering ram is?'

'Of course. What are you talking about?'

'When I get stuck on a case like this, I go back to the book and all the files.'

He gestured to the murder book on the table.

'I look at it like a battering ram. You pull back and swing it forward. You hit the locked door and you smash through. That's what going through everything again is like. You swing back and then you swing forward with all that momentum.'

She looked puzzled by his decision to share this piece of advice with her.

'Okay, Dad.'

'Sorry. Go back to your book.'

'I thought you just said he jumped. So why are you stuck?'

'Because what I think and what I can prove are two separate things. A case like this, I have to have it all nailed down. Anyway, it's my problem. Go back to your book.'

She did. And he went back to his. He began by carefully rereading all the reports and summaries he had clipped into the binder. He let the information flow over him and he looked for new angles and colors. If George Irving jumped, then Bosch had to do more than simply believe it. He had to be able to prove it not only to the powers that be but, most important, to himself. And he wasn't quite there yet. A suicide was a premeditated killing. Bosch needed to find motive and opportunity and means. He had some of each but not enough.

The CD changer moved to the next disc and Bosch soon recognized Chet Baker's trumpet. The song was 'Night Bird' from a German import. Bosch had seen Baker perform the song in a club on O'Farrell in San Francisco in 1982, the only time he ever saw him play live. By then Baker's cover-boy looks and West Coast cool had been sucked out of him by drugs and life, but he could still make the trumpet sound like a human voice on a dark night. In another six years he would be dead from a fall from a hotel window in Amsterdam.

Bosch looked at his daughter.

'You put this in there?'

She looked up from the book.

'Is this Chet Baker? Yeah, I wanted to hear him because of your case and the poem in the hallway.'

Bosch got up and went into the bedroom hallway, flicking the light on. Framed on the wall was a single-page poem. Almost twenty years earlier Bosch had been in a restaurant on Venice Beach and by happenstance the author of the poem, John Harvey, was giving a reading. It didn't seem to Bosch that anybody in the place knew who Chet Baker was. But Harry did and he loved the resonance of the poem. He got up and asked Harvey if he could buy a copy. Harvey simply gave him the paper he had read from.

Bosch had probably passed by the poem a thousand times since he had last read it.

CHET BAKER

looks out from his hotel room
across the Amstel to the girl
cycling by the canal who lifts
her hand and waves and when
she smiles he is back in times
when every Hollywood producer
wanted to turn his life
into that bittersweet story
where he falls badly, but only
in love with Pier Angeli,
Carol Lynley, Natalie Wood;
that day he strolled into the studio,
fall of fifty-two, and played
those perfect lines across
the chords of My Funny Valentine—
and now when he looks up from
his window and her passing smile
into the blue of a perfect sky
he knows this is one of those
rare days when he can truly fly.

Bosch went back out to the table and sat down.

'I looked him up on Wikipedia,' Maddie said. 'They never knew for sure if he jumped or just fell. Some people said drug dealers pushed him out.'

Bosch nodded.

'Yeah, sometimes you never know.'

He went back to work and continued his review of the accumulated reports. As he read his own summary report on the interview with Officer Robert Mason, Bosch felt he was missing something. The report was complete but he felt he had overlooked something in the conversation with Mason. It was there but he just couldn't reach it. He closed his eyes and tried to hear Mason speaking and responding to the questions.

He saw Mason sitting bolt upright in the chair, gesturing as he spoke, saying that he and George Irving had been close. Best man at the wedding, reserving the honeymoon suite . . .

Harry suddenly had it. When Mason had mentioned reserving the honeymoon suite, he had gestured in the direction of the squad lieutenant's office. He was pointing west. The same direction as the Chateau Marmont.

He got up and quickly went out onto the deck so he could make a call without disturbing his daughter's reading. He slid the door closed behind him and called the LAPD communications center. He asked a dispatcher to radio six-Adam-sixty-five in the field and ask him to call Bosch on his cell. He said it was urgent.

As he was giving his number, he received a call-waiting beep. Once the dispatcher correctly read back the number, he switched over to the waiting call. It was Chu. Bosch didn't bother with any niceties.

'Did you go to the Standard?'

'Yeah, McQuillen checks out. He was there all night, like he knew he needed to sit under that camera. But that's not why I'm calling. I think I found something.'

'What?'

'I've been going through everything and I found something that doesn't make sense. The kid was already coming down.'

'What are you talking about? What kid?'

'Irving's kid. He was already coming down from San Francisco. It's on the AmEx account. I checked it again tonight. The kid – Chad Irving – had an airplane ticket to come home before his father was dead.'

'Hold on a second.'

Bosch went back inside the house and over to the table. He looked through the spread of documents until he found the American Express report. It was a printout of all charges Irving had made on the card going back three years. It was twenty-two pages long and Bosch had looked at every page less than an hour earlier and seen nothing that grabbed his attention.

'Okay, I've got the AmEx here. How are you looking at it?'

'I have it online, Harry. On the search warrant I always ask for printed statements and digital account access. But what I'm looking at is not on your printout. This charge was posted to the account yesterday and by then the printout was already in the mail to us.'

'You have the live account online.'

'Right. The last charge you have on the printout is the hotel room at the Chateau, right?'

'Yeah, right here.'

'Okay, well, American Airlines posted a charge yesterday for three hundred nine dollars.'

'Okay.'

'So I was going back and looking at everything again and I went online to look at AmEx again. I still have digital access. I saw that a new billing had come through yesterday from American.'

'So Chad's using his father's card? Maybe he was given a duplicate card.'

'No, I thought maybe that was the case at first but it's not. I called AmEx security to follow up on the warrant. AmEx just took three days to post the charge on his record but George Irving made the purchase online Sunday afternoon – about twelve hours before he took the high dive. I got the record locator from AmEx and went on American's website. It was a round-trip ticket, SFO to LAX and back. Fly down Monday afternoon at four. Back today at two, except that return got changed to next Sunday.'

It was good work but Bosch wasn't going to compliment Chu just yet.

'But don't they send out e-mail confirmations for online purchases? We looked at Irving's e-mail. There was nothing from American.'

'I fly American and I buy the tickets online. You only get the e-mail confirmation if you click the box. You can also have it sent to someone else. Irving could have had the confirmation and itinerary sent directly to his son since he was the one flying.'

Bosch had to think about this. It was a significant new piece of information. Irving had bought his son a ticket to L.A. before his death. It could have been a simple plan to bring his son home for a visit but it also could have meant Irving knew what he was going to do and wanted to insure that his kid could get home to be with family. It was another piece that fit with McQuillen's story. And with Robert Mason's.

'I think it means he killed himself,' Chu said. 'He knew that he was going to jump that night and he bought his kid a ticket so he could come down to be with his mother. It also explains the call. He called the kid that evening to tell him about the ticket.'

Bosch didn't respond. His phone started beeping. Mason's call was coming in.

'I did good, didn't I, Harry?' Chu said. 'I told you I'd make it up to you.'

'It was good work, but it doesn't make up for anything,' Bosch said.

Bosch noticed his daughter look up from her book. She had heard what he'd said.

'Look, Harry, I like my job,' Chu said. 'I don't want—'

Bosch cut him off.

'I've got another call coming in. I've got to take it.'

He disconnected and switched to the other call. It was Mason responding to the dispatch from the com center.

'The honeymoon suite you rented for the Irvings. It was at the Chateau Marmont, wasn't it?'

Mason was quiet for a long moment before he responded.

'So I guess Deborah and the councilman didn't mention that, did they?'

'No, they didn't. That's why you knew he jumped. The suite. That was the suite.'

'Yeah. I figured things sort of all went wrong for him and he went up there.'

Bosch nodded. More to himself than to Mason.

'Okay, Mason, thanks for the call.'

Bosch hung up. He put the phone down on the table and looked at his daughter on the couch, reading. She seemed to feel his gaze and looked up at him from the words of Stephen King.

'Everything okay?' she asked.

'No,' he said. 'Not really.'

30

It was eight thirty by the time Bosch pulled up in front of the home where George Irving had lived. The lights were still on inside but the garage doors were closed and there were no cars in the driveway. Bosch watched for a few minutes and saw no activity behind any of the lighted windows. If Deborah Irving and her son were inside, they weren't showing it.

Bosch pulled his phone and, as agreed, texted his daughter. He had left her at home alone, telling her he would not be gone more than two hours and that he would check on her upon arrival at and departure from his destination.

She responded quickly.

All good. Finished homework, watching Castle downloads.

Bosch pocketed the phone and got out of the car. He had to knock twice, and when the door opened, it was Deborah Irving by herself.

'Detective Bosch?'

'Sorry to intrude so late, Mrs Irving. I need to speak with you.'

'Can it wait until tomorrow?'

'I'm afraid not, ma'am.'

'Of course. Come in.'

She opened up and led him into the room and to the couch where he had sat before at the start of the case.

'I saw you at the funeral today,' she said. 'Chad said he spoke to you also.'

'Yes. Is Chad still here?'

'He's staying through the weekend but he's not home right now. He went to see an old girlfriend. It's a very difficult time for him, as you can imagine.'

'Yes, I understand.'

'Can I get you a coffee? We have a Nespresso.'

Bosch didn't know what that meant but shook his head.

'I'm fine, Mrs Irving.'

'Please call me Deborah.'

'Deborah.'

'Are you here to tell me you will be making an arrest in the case soon?'

'Uh, no, I'm not. I'm here to tell you there's not going to be an arrest.'

She looked surprised.

'Dad – uh, Councilman Irving – told me there was a suspect. That it had to do with one of the competitors George was dealing with.'

'No, that was how it was looking because I went down the wrong path.'

He checked her reaction. No giveaways. She still looked genuinely surprised.

'You sent me down the wrong path,' he said. 'You and the councilman and even Chad held back on me. I didn't have what I needed and I went stumbling off after a murderer when there never was a murderer.'

Now she was beginning to look indignant.

'What do you mean? Dad told me there was evidence of assault and that George was choked. He said it was most likely a cop. Don't tell me you are covering up for the cop who did this.'

'That's not the case, Deborah, and I think you know it. That day I came here, the councilman told you what to say, what to leave in and what to leave out.'

'I don't know what you're talking about.'

'Like that the room your husband rented was the room you two shared on the night you got married. Like that your son was already scheduled to come home Monday – before your husband even went out that night.'

He let that sink in for a long moment, letting her come to realize what he had and what he knew.

'Chad was coming home because you two had something to tell him, right?'

'This is ridiculous!'

'Is it? Maybe I should talk to Chad first, ask him what he was told when he was sent the airline ticket Sunday afternoon.'

'You leave Chad alone. He's going through a lot.'

'Then talk to me, Deborah. Why'd you hide it? Can't be money. We checked the insurance policies. They're all mature, no suicide clauses. You get the money whether he jumped or not.'

'He didn't jump! I'm going to call Irvin. I'm going to tell him what you're saying.'

She started to stand up.

'Did you tell George you were leaving him? Is that it? Is that why he put your anniversary date into the combination on the room safe? Is that why he jumped? His son was gone and now you were going, too. He had already lost his friend Bobby Mason and all he had left was a job working as a bagman for his father.'

She tried what Bosch always viewed as the last best defense of a woman. She started crying.

'You bastard! You'll destroy a good man's reputation. Is that what you want? Will that make you happy?'

Bosch didn't answer for a long time.

'No, Mrs Irving, not really.'

'I want you to leave now. I buried my husband today and I want you out of my house!'

Bosch nodded but made no move to get up.

'I'll leave when you give me the story.'

'I don't have the story!'

'Then Chad does. I'll wait for him.'

'All right, look, Chad doesn't know a thing. He's nineteen years old. He's a boy. If you talk to him you'll destroy him.'

Bosch realized that it was all about the son, about protecting him from knowing that his father had killed himself.

'Then you have to talk to me first. Last chance, Mrs Irving.'

She gripped her chair's armrests and bowed her head.

'I told him our marriage was over.'

'And how did he take it?'

'Not well. He didn't see it coming because he didn't see what he had become. An opportunist, a taker, a bagman, like you said. Chad had gotten away and I decided I would, too. There was no one else. There was just no reason to stay. I wasn't running to something. I was just running away from him.'

Bosch leaned forward, elbows on his knees, making the conversation more intimate.

'When did this conversation take place?' he asked.

'A week before. We talked about it for a week but I wasn't changing my mind. I told him to bring Chad down or I would go up there to tell him. He made the arrangements Sunday.'

Bosch nodded. All the details were fitting together.

'What about the councilman? Was he told?'

'I don't think so. I didn't tell him and it never came up after – when he was here that day and told me that George was dead. He didn't mention anything about it then and he didn't at the funeral today either.'

Bosch knew that this didn't mean anything. Irving could have been keeping his knowledge to himself as he waited to see which way the investigation would go. In the long run it didn't matter what Irving knew or when he knew it.

'On Sunday night, when George went out, what did he say to you?'

'As I told you before, he said he was going out for a drive. That's all. He didn't tell me where.'

'Did he threaten to kill himself during any of your discussions in the week prior to his death?'

'No, he didn't.'

'Are you sure?'

'Of course, I'm sure. I'm not lying to you.'

'You said you talked about it for several nights. He did not accept your decision?'

'Of course not. He said he wouldn't let me go. I told

him he didn't have a choice. I was leaving. I was pre-pared. It wasn't a rash decision. I've been in a loveless marriage for quite a long time, Detective. The day Chad got the acceptance letter from USF, that was the day I started planning.'

'Did you have a place you were going to go?'

'A place, a car, a job – everything.'

'Where?'

'San Francisco. Close to Chad.'

'Why didn't you tell me all of this from the start? What's the point of hiding it?'

'My son. His father was dead and it wasn't clear how. He didn't need to know that his parents' marriage had been coming to an end. I didn't want to put that on him.'

Bosch shook his head. She apparently didn't care that her deception had almost resulted in McQuillen's being accused of murder.

There was a noise from somewhere in the house and Deborah became alert.

'That's the back door. Chad is home. Do not tell him this. I beg you.'

'He's going to find out. I should talk to him. His father must've told him something when he told him he needed to fly home.'

'No, he didn't. I was in the room when he called. He just told him we needed him to come home for a few days because of a family emergency. George assured him that everybody was fine healthwise but that he needed to come home. Do not tell him about this. *I* will tell him.'

'Mom?'

It was Chad calling from somewhere in the house.

305

'In the living room, Chad,' his mother called back.

Then she looked at Bosch with beseeching eyes.

'*Please,*' she whispered.

Chad Irving entered the living room. He was dressed in blue jeans and a golf shirt. His hair was unkempt and it looked startlingly different from the carefully combed look he'd had at the funeral.

'Chad,' Bosch said. 'How are you doing?'

The boy nodded.

'Fine. What are you doing here? Did you arrest someone for killing my father?'

'No, Chad,' his mother said quickly. 'Detective Bosch was just doing some follow-up on your father. I had to answer a few questions about the business. That's all and, in fact, Detective Bosch was just about to leave.'

The time was rare that Bosch would allow someone to speak for him and lie and even push him out the door. But Bosch played along. He even stood up.

'Yes, I think I have what I need for now. I do want to talk a little more with you, Chad, but that can wait until tomorrow. You are still around tomorrow, right?'

Bosch looked at Deborah the whole time he spoke. The message was clear. If you want to be the one who tells him, then tell him tonight. Otherwise, Bosch would be back in the morning.

'Yes, I'm staying until Sunday.'

Bosch nodded. He moved out of the seating area.

'Mrs Irving, you have my number. Call me if anything else comes up. I'll show myself out.'

With that, Bosch headed through the living room and then out of the house. He went off the front walkway and crossed the lawn diagonally to his car.

He received a text as he walked. It was from his daughter, of course. No one else ever texted him.

Going to read in bed. Night, Dad.

He stood next to his car and answered her right away.

On my way home now . . . O?

Her response was quick.

Ocean.

It was a game they played, though a game with a higher purpose. He had taught her the LAPD's phonetic alphabet and often tested her in texts. Or while out driving together, he'd point out a license plate and have her call it out in phonetic code.

He texted her back.

TMG

That's my girl.

Once he was in the car, he lowered the window and looked up at the Irving house. The lights had been turned off now in the downstairs rooms. But the family – what was left of it – was still awake upstairs, dealing with the debris George Irving had left behind.

Bosch started his car and headed toward Ventura Boulevard. He opened his phone and called Chu's cell. He checked the dash clock and saw it was only nine thirty-eight. There was plenty of time. The *Times* deadline for the morning print edition was eleven.

'Harry? Everything all right?'

'Chu, I want you to call your girlfriend at the *Times*. Give—'

'She's not my girlfriend, Harry. I made a mistake and I resent how you keep sticking the knife in and turning it.'

'Well, I resent you, Chu. But I need you to do this. Call her and give her the story. No names, it's got to come from "informed sources." The LAPD—'

'Harry, she won't trust me. I killed the story before by threatening to ruin her. She won't even talk to me anymore.'

'Yes, she will. If she wants the story. Send her an e-mail first that says you want to make it up to her and give her a story. Then call her. Just no names. Informed sources. The LAPD will announce tomorrow that the George Irving case has been closed. His death has been ruled a suicide. Make sure you say to her that a week's investigation has determined that Irving was facing marital issues and tremendous job pressures and difficulties. You got that? I want it said that way.'

'Then why don't you call her?'

Bosch turned onto Ventura and headed toward the Cahuenga Pass.

'Because she's yours, Chu. Now call her or text her or send her an e-mail and give it to her exactly the way I said.'

'She'll want more. This is generic. She'll want what she calls the telling details.'

Bosch thought for a moment.

'Tell her that the room Irving jumped from had been his honeymoon suite twenty years ago.'

'Okay, that's good. She'll like that. What else?'

'Nothing else. That's enough.'

'Why now? Why not in the morning?'

'Because if it's in tomorrow's print edition, it's going to be hard to change. And that's what I'm guarding against. High jingo, Chu. This isn't the conclusion that's going to make the city councilman happy. That in turn won't make the chief happy.'

'But it's the truth?'

'Yeah, it's the truth. And the truth gets out. Tell GoGo that if she does this right, there's going to be a follow-up she'll want to get a piece of.'

'What follow-up?'

'I'll tell you about it later. Just get this going. She has a deadline.'

'Is this how it's always going to be, Harry? You just tell me what to do and when to do it. I never get a say?'

'You'll have a say, Chu. With your next partner.'

Bosch closed the phone. As he drove the rest of the way home, he thought about the things he was setting in motion. With the newspaper, with Irving and with Chu.

He was making risky moves and he couldn't help but wonder if this was because he had been led so far astray on the investigation. Was he punishing himself or those who had led him astray?

Just as he started climbing Woodrow Wilson toward his home he got another call. He expected it to be Chu, confirming that he had made the call and that the story would be in the morning print edition of the *Times*. But it wasn't Chu.

'Hannah, I'm working.'

'Oh, I thought maybe we could talk.'

'Well, I'm alone now and have a few minutes but like I said, I'm working.'

'Is it a crime scene?'

'No, an interview, you could call it. What's up, Hannah?'

'Well, two things. Is there any update on the case involving Clayton Pell? Clayton asks me about it every time I see him. I wish there was something to tell him.'

'Well, there really isn't. It kind of got back-burnered while I work on this other thing. But that is ending now and I'll be back on the Pell case pretty quick. You can tell Clayton that. We'll find Chilton Hardy. I guarantee it.'

'Okay, that's good, Harry.'

'What's the other thing you wanted to talk about?'

He knew what it was but it was her call. She had to ask it.

'Us ... Harry, I know I messed things up with my issues about my son. I am sorry about that and I hope it didn't completely spoil things. I like you a lot and I hope we can see each other again.'

Bosch pulled to a stop in front of his house. His daughter had left the porch light on. He stayed in the car.

'Hannah ... the truth is, all I've been doing is working. I've got two cases here and I'm trying to work them both. Why don't we see how we feel over the weekend or early next week? I'll call you then or you can call me if you want.'

'Okay, Harry. We'll talk next week.'

'Yes, Hannah. Good night and have a good weekend.'

Bosch opened the car door and practically had to roll out of the car. He was tired. The burden of knowledge was heavy. And all he wanted was to crash into a black dream where nothing could find him.

31

Bosch got in to the squad room late Friday morning because his daughter had been late in getting ready for school. By the time he entered and headed toward his cubicle, the rest of the Open-Unsolved Unit was in place. He could tell they were watching him without watching him and this told him that the story he had told David Chu to feed to Emily Gomez-Gonzmart had been published that morning in the *Times*. As he entered his cubicle, Harry threw a casual glance toward the lieutenant's office and noted that the door was closed and the blinds were down. She was either late herself or hiding.

A copy of the *Times* was waiting for Bosch on his desk, courtesy of his partner.

'You see it yet?' Chu asked from his seat.

'No, I don't get the *Times*.'

Bosch sat down, putting his briefcase on the floor next to his chair. He didn't have to hunt through the newspaper for the story. It was on the bottom left corner of the front page. The headline was all he needed to read.

LAPD: Councilman's Son's Death Ruled Suicide

He noted that the byline was shared by Emily Gomez-

Gonzmart and another reporter, Tad Hemmings, whom Bosch had never heard of. He was about to read the story when his desk phone buzzed. It was Tim Marcia, the squad whip.

'Harry, you and Chu have a forthwith from the chief's office. The lieutenant's already up there and they're waiting for you.'

'I was hoping to get a cup of coffee but I guess we'd better go up.'

'Yeah, I would. Good luck up there. I heard the councilman was in the building.'

'Thanks for the heads-up.'

Bosch stood and turned to Chu, who was on the phone. Bosch pointed toward the ceiling, meaning they were going upstairs. Chu got off his call and stood up, grabbing his sport coat off the back of his chair.

'The chief's office?' he asked.

'Yeah. They're waiting for us.'

'How do we play this?'

'You talk as little as possible. Let me answer the questions. If you don't agree with something I say, don't show it or say it. Just agree with it.'

'Whatever you say, Harry.'

Bosch noted his partner's sarcasm.

'Yeah. Whatever I say.'

There was no need for further discussion. They took the elevator up in silence and when they entered the OCP, they were immediately whisked into a meeting room where the chief of police waited. It was the fastest Bosch had ever been able to gain an audience with a member of the department's command staff, let alone the chief himself.

The boardroom looked like it belonged in a downtown law firm. Long polished table, glass wall of views across the civic center. Seated at the head of the table was the chief of police and to his right was Kiz Rider. The three seats going down one side of the table were taken by Councilman Irvin Irving and two members of his staff.

Across from them sat Lieutenant Duvall, with her back to the city view, and she signaled Bosch and Chu to the seats next to her. Eight people in a meeting about one suicide, Bosch noted. And nobody in the entire building who gave a shit about Lily Price being dead for twenty years or Chilton Hardy being free for just as long.

The chief did the talking first.

'All right, everybody's here. I'm sure everybody's seen the *Times* today or read it online. I think everybody is a bit surprised by the public turn this case has taken and—'

'More than surprised,' Irving cut in. 'I want to know why the *L.A. goddamn Times* had this information before I did. Before my son's family did.'

He stabbed a finger down on the table to hammer home his outrage. Luckily Bosch was seated on a swivel chair. This allowed him to calmly pivot and look at the faces across from him and at the head of the table. He said nothing in response, waiting for the power in the room to tell him to speak. That power was not Irvin Irving, no matter how hard he hit the table with his stubby finger.

'Detective Bosch,' the chief finally said. 'Tell us what you know about this.'

Bosch nodded and swiveled back so that he was directly facing Irving.

'First of all, I don't know anything about the story in the paper. It didn't come from me but it doesn't surprise me. This investigation has been leaking like a sieve since day one. Whether it was coming out of the OCP or the city council staff or RHD doesn't matter, the story is out there and it's accurate. And I want to correct one thing the city councilman said. The victim's immediate family was informed of our conclusions. The victim's wife, in fact, provided the information that was most important to my partner and me in calling the death a suicide.'

'Deborah?' Irving said. 'She told you nothing.'

'On the first day she told us nothing. That is correct. It was during a subsequent interview that she was more forthcoming about the details of her marriage and her husband's life and work.'

Irving leaned back, dragging a balled fist on the table.

'I was informed by this office just yesterday that this was a homicide investigation, that there was evidence of assault on my son's body prior to the fatal impact and that it was likely that there was a former or current police officer involved. Now today I pick up the paper and read something completely different. I read that it's a suicide. You know what this is? This is a payback. And it's a cover-up and I will formally petition the council for an independent review of your so-called investigation and I will ask the district attorney – whoever that may be after next month's election – to also review the case and its handling.'

'Irv,' the chief said. 'You asked for Detective Bosch to be put on the case. You said let the chips fall and now you don't like how they have fallen. So you want to investigate how it was investigated?'

The chief went back long enough in the department to call the councilman by his first name. No one else in the room would even dare.

'I chose him because I thought he had the integrity not to be swayed from the truth but what obviously has—'

'Harry Bosch has more integrity than anybody I've ever met. Anybody in this room.'

It was Chu and the whole room looked at him, shocked by his outburst. Even Bosch was taken aback.

'We're not going to get into personal attacks here,' the chief said. 'We first want to—'

'If there is an investigation of the investigation,' Bosch said, daring to cut the chief off, 'it will most likely lead to your indictment, Councilman.'

That stunned the group. But Irving recovered quickly.

'How dare you!' he said, his eyes full of growing rage. 'How dare you say such a thing about me in front of other people. I will have your badge for this! I have served this city for nearly fifty years and not once has anyone accused me of any impropriety. I am less than a month from being reelected to my seat for the fourth time and you won't stop me or the will of the people who want me to represent them.'

A silence followed, during which one of Irving's aides opened a leather folder with a legal pad inside. He wrote something down on the pad and Bosch half-imagined it was *Take Bosch's badge*.

'Detective Bosch,' Rider said. 'Why don't you explain your statement?'

It was said with a tone of shock and maybe even outrage, as if she were joining the defense of Irving's reputation. But Bosch knew that she was giving him the entrée he needed to say what he wanted.

'George Irving billed himself as a lobbyist, but he wasn't really much more than a fixer and a bagman. He sold influence. He used his own connections as a former cop and assistant city attorney but his most notable connection was to his father, the city councilman. You wanted something? He could get it to his father. You wanted a concrete supply contract or a taxi franchise, George was the man to see because he could get it done.'

Bosch looked directly at Irving when he mentioned the taxi franchise. He saw a slight tremor in one eyelid and took it as a tell. He wasn't saying anything the old man didn't already know.

'This is outrageous!' Irving bellowed. 'I want this stopped! This man is using a long-held grudge to tarnish what I have worked for all my life.'

Bosch stopped and waited. He knew this was the moment when the police chief would choose sides. It was going to be him or Irving.

'I think we need to hear what Detective Bosch has to say,' the chief said.

He shared his own hard stare with Irving, and Bosch knew that the chief was taking a major gamble. He was positioning himself against a powerful force in city government. He was banking on Bosch, and Harry knew he had Kiz Rider to thank for that.

'Go ahead, Detective,' the chief said.

Bosch leaned forward so he could look directly down the table at the chief.

'A couple months ago George Irving parted ways with his closest friend. A cop he had known since the police academy. The friendship ended when the cop realized George and his father had been using him without his knowledge to help swing a lucrative taxi franchise toward one of George's clients. The cop was asked directly by the councilman to start hitting the existing franchise holder with DUI spot checks, knowing that a file full of such stops or arrests would damage their efforts to retain the franchise.'

Irving leaned across the table and pointed a finger at Bosch.

'This is where you are way off base,' he said. 'I know who you are talking about and that was a request made in response to a complaint to my office. It was a request passed on in a social setting, nothing more. In fact, it was my grandson's graduation party.'

Bosch nodded.

'Yes, a party that occurred two weeks after your son signed a one-hundred-thousand-dollar service contract with Regent Taxi, which would later announce plans to seek the city franchise currently being held by the company you complained about. I'm just guessing but I think a grand jury would find the coincidence of that hard to believe. I am sure your office would be able to provide the name of the citizen who made the complaint and she and her story would be vetted.'

Bosch pointedly looked at the aide with the legal pad.

'You might want to write that down.'

He turned his attention back to the head of the table.

'The officer in question learned that he was being used by the Irvings and confronted George Irving. Their friendship ended there. In the course of four weeks George lost three of the most important people in his life. His friend exposed him as a user if not a criminal, his only child left his home for college and life after, and last week his wife of twenty years told him she was leaving. She had stayed in the marriage until their son was gone, and now she, too, was finished.'

Irving reacted as if slapped in the face. He clearly knew nothing about the implosion of the marriage.

'George tried for a week to talk Deborah out of her decision and to hang on to the one person he had left,' Bosch continued. 'To no avail. On Sunday – twelve hours before his death – he bought his son an airplane ticket to come home the next day. The plan was to tell the boy of the split. But instead, that night George checked into the Chateau Marmont with no luggage. When he was told suite seventy-nine was available he took it because that was the suite he and Deborah shared on their honeymoon.

'He spent about five hours in that room. Our information is that he was drinking heavily – an entire twelve-ounce bottle of whiskey. He was visited by a former cop named Mark McQuillen who knew by happenstance that he was in the hotel. McQuillen had been run out of the police department in a political witch hunt headed by Deputy Chief Irving twenty-five years ago. Now he was part owner of the taxi franchise George Irving was trying to destroy. He confronted George in the room and, yes, assaulted him. But he didn't throw him from that balcony. He was in an all-night restaurant three blocks away when George jumped. We have confirmed the alibi and I have come to no other conclusion about this case. George Irving jumped.'

Bosch leaned back in his chair, finished with his report.

There was no immediate response from anyone at the table. It took Irving a few moments to look at all the angles in the story and come up with something.

'McQuillen should be placed under arrest. This was obviously a carefully planned crime. I was correct when I said it was a payback. McQuillen perceived that I took his career. He took my son's life.'

'McQuillen is on video in that restaurant from two till six,' Bosch said. 'His alibi holds up. He was with your son at least two hours before his death. But he was not in the hotel when your son jumped.'

'And there's the airline ticket,' Chu added. 'Chad Irving was already flying down Monday. It wasn't because his father had died, as the family suggested to us Monday. He had the ticket before, and there is no way McQuillen could have made that play.'

Bosch glanced at his partner. Chu had disobeyed Bosch's order to maintain silence twice now. But both times it had been to great effect.

'Councilman Irving, I think we've heard enough for now,' the chief said. 'Detectives Bosch and Chu, I want the full summary of the investigation on my desk before two o'clock today. I'll review it and then I'll hold a press conference. I plan to keep it brief and keep the details of the investigation brief. Councilman, you are invited to join me if you like, but I know that this is a very personal matter and you may want it to close up and simply go away. I'll expect to hear from your office if you are coming.'

The chief nodded once and waited a split second for any reply. There was none, so he stood up. The meeting was over and so was the case. Irving knew he could press it and call for reviews and re-investigations but that path would be fraught with political peril.

Bosch had him pegged as a pragmatist who would let this one go. The question was, Would the police chief? Bosch had delivered the elements of a crime of political corruption. It would be difficult to pursue, particularly with a key player dead. And it was unknown whether they could get anything by leaning on the people at Regent Taxi. Would the chief follow up or would he hold it as an ace in a card game played on a level Bosch knew nothing about?

Either way, Bosch was pretty sure he had just delivered to the chief the means of turning a powerful anti-police voice in city government toward the positive. If he worked it right, he might even be able to get the overtime budget funded again. Meantime, Bosch was satisfied that he had completed his job. An old nemesis now had renewed enmity toward him but that was of no consequence. Bosch would never be able to live in a world without enemies. It came with the turf.

Everyone stood to leave the meeting, which was going to present an awkward situation when Irving and Bosch went out and waited for the elevator together. Rider saved Harry from it by inviting him into her office, along with Chu.

As the Irving entourage left the suite of offices, Bosch and Chu followed Rider into her space.

'Can I get you men something?' she asked. 'I guess the time to have asked was at the start of the meeting.'

'I'm good,' Bosch said.

'Same here,' Chu said.

Rider appraised Chu. She had no idea about Chu's traitorous activities.

'That was good work, gentlemen,' she said. 'And Detective Chu, I admire your willingness to stand up in there for your partner and your case. Well done.'

'Thank you, Lieutenant.'

'Now, do you mind stepping out into the waiting area? I have some things to discuss with Detective Bosch relating to his DROP date.'

'No problem. Harry, I'll be out here.'

Chu left and Rider closed the door. She and Bosch were left looking at each other for a long moment. She then slowly broke into a smile and shook her head.

'You must've been lovin' that in there,' she said. 'Seeing Irving have to shut down or be put down like the dog he is.'

Bosch shook his head.

'Not really. I don't care about him anymore. I still don't get it, though. Why did he really want me on the case?'

'I think it was exactly what he said. He knew you would be relentless and he needed to know if somebody went through his son to get to him. The only thing is, he didn't think you'd get to the place you got to.'

Bosch nodded.

'Maybe.'

'Now, the chief didn't show it in front of Irving, but you just gave him the golden ticket. And the good news is, he is going to be happy to reward you. I was thinking I'd start by getting your DROP moved up to the whole five years. How would that be, Harry?'

She smiled, anticipating that Bosch would be delighted

by the additional twenty-one months on the job.

'Let me think about that,' he said.

'You sure? You might want to strike while the iron's hot.'

'Tell you what. See if you can get Chu moved out of OU, but keep him in RHD. Get him a good gig over there.'

She narrowed her eyes and he continued before she could speak.

'And do it no questions asked.'

'You sure you don't want to talk to me about this?'

'No, Kiz, I don't.'

'Okay. I'll see what I can do. Irving's probably down the elevator by now. You should get back down to OU to work on your report. By two o'clock, remember?'

'See you at two.'

Bosch stepped out of the office and closed the door behind him. Chu was waiting there, smiling with pride over the stand he had made and completely unaware that his career path had just been set without a word of input or preference from him.

32

Saturday started early for Bosch and his daughter. While still in darkness they drove down out of the hills, took the 101 freeway into downtown and then pivoted south on the 110 toward Long Beach. They caught the first ferry over to Catalina, Bosch never letting go of the locked gun case as they rode into a cold gray dawn. Once on the island, they ate breakfast at the Pancake Cottage in Avalon, the only place Harry had ever thought compared favorably to Du-par's back in L.A.

Bosch wanted his daughter to eat a full breakfast because the plan was to eat lunch late in the day, after the pistol competition. He knew that the little tickle of hunger she'd get in the early afternoon would help her stay focused and keep her aim tight.

A year earlier when she had announced to him that her plan was to become a police officer, she had begun learning about guns and their safe use and storage. There was no philosophical debate about it. Bosch was a cop and there were guns in the house. It was simply a given and he considered it good parenting to teach his daughter how to use and safeguard the weapons. He supplemented his mentoring by enrolling her in courses at a firing range up in Newhall.

But Maddie had taken it far past a rudimentary knowledge of practice and safety. She took to shooting at paper targets with a passion and developed a steady hand and cold eye. Within six months her marksmanship put her father's to shame. They ended each training lesson with a one-on-one match and she soon became unbeatable. She owned the ten ring at ten yards and could keep her aim steady through a sixteen-round clip.

Soon beating her old man with his own guns was not enough. And that brought them to Catalina. Maddie's first competition was a junior match at the gun club on the back side of the island. It was a single-elimination pistol match that would pit her against all teenage entrants. Each face-off involved shooting six rounds at paper targets from ten, fifteen and twenty-five yards.

They had chosen Catalina for her first foray into competitive shooting because it was a small tournament and they knew they could make a fun day of it no matter how she performed. Maddie had never been to Catalina, and Harry had not been out to the barrier island in years.

As it turned out, she was the only girl in the competition. It was Maddie and seven boys, randomly bracketed into one-on-one matches. She won her first match going away, overcoming a weak grouping on the ten-yard target to hit seven of eight rings in the fifteen- and twenty-five-yard distances. Bosch was so proud and happy for her that he wanted to rush to the line and hug her. But he held back, knowing it would only underline that she was the only girl. Instead, he was the lone spectator applauding from the picnic tables behind the shooting line. He then put on his sunglasses so no stranger would see the look in his eyes.

His daughter was eliminated in the next round by a single-ring shot but took the disappointment well. The fact that she had competed and won her first match had made the journey worth it. She and Bosch stuck around to watch the final round and then the start of the adult competition. Maddie tried to goad Harry into entering the adult round but he demurred. His eyes were not what they once were and he knew he didn't stand a chance.

They ate a late lunch at the Busy Bee and window-shopped along Crescent before catching the four-o'clock ferry back to the mainland. They sat inside because the sea air was cold, and along the way, Bosch put his arm around his daughter's shoulders. He knew that other girls her age weren't learning about guns and shooting. They weren't watching their fathers at night poring over murder books and autopsies and crime scene photos. They weren't left alone in the house while their fathers went out with their guns to chase bad guys. Most parents were raising citizens of the future. Doctors, teachers, mothers, keepers of family businesses. Bosch was raising a warrior.

A momentary thought of Hannah Stone and her son shot through him and he squeezed his daughter's shoulder again. He had been thinking about something and it was now time to discuss it.

'You know,' he said, 'you don't have to do any of this if you don't want to. Don't do it for me, Mads. The gun stuff. The being a cop thing, too. You do what you want to do. You make your own choices.'

'I know, Dad. I do make my own choices and it's what I want. We talked about this a long time ago.'

It was Bosch's hope that she would be able to leave her past behind and forge something new. He had been unable to do it himself and it haunted him that she might be the same way.

'Okay, baby. There's a lot of time between now and then anyway.'

A few minutes went by while he thought of things. He could see the disguised oil derricks in the harbor just coming into view. A call came in on his cell and he saw it was from David Chu. He let it go to message. He wasn't going to spoil this moment with work or, more likely, Chu groveling for a second chance. He put the phone away and kissed the top of his daughter's head.

'I guess I'll always have to worry about you,' he said. 'It's not like you could want to be a teacher or something safe like that.'

'I hate school, Dad. Why would I want to be a teacher?'

'I don't know. To change the system, make it better so the next kids don't hate it.'

'One teacher? Forget it.'

'It just takes one. It always starts with one. Anyway, like I said, you do what you want. You've got time. I guess I'll worry about you no matter what you do.'

'Not if you teach me all you know. Then you won't have to worry because I'll be like you out there.'

Bosch laughed.

'If you're like me out there, then I'll have to walk around all day with rosary beads in one hand, a rabbit's foot in the other and maybe a four-leaf clover tattooed on my arm.'

She drove an elbow into his side.

Bosch let another few minutes go by. He pulled his phone and checked to see if Chu had left a message.

There was nothing and Bosch figured his partner had been calling to once again plead his case. It was not the kind of thing you would put into a voice-mail.

He put the phone away and turned the father–daughter conversation more serious.

'Look, Mads, I've been wanting to tell you something else, too.'

'I know, you're marrying the lady with the lipstick?'

'No, serious now, and there was no lipstick.'

'I know. What is it?'

'Well, I'm thinking about turning in my badge. Retiring. It might be time.'

She didn't respond for a long time. He had expected an immediate and urgent demand that he trash such thoughts but to her credit she seemed to be running it through her processes and not kicking out a first and possibly wrong response.

'But why?' she finally asked.

'Well, I am thinking that I'm tailing off, you know? Like anything – athletics, shooting, playing music, even creative thinking – there's a drop-off of skills at a certain point. And, I don't know, but maybe I'm getting there and I should get out. I've seen people lose their edge and it increases the danger. I don't want to miss the chance to see you grow up and shine at whatever you decide you want to do.'

She nodded as if in agreement but then the keen perception and disagreement came out.

'You're thinking all of this because of one case?'

'Not just the one case but that's a good example. I totally went the wrong way with it. I have to think that wouldn't have happened five years ago. Even two years ago. I might be losing the edge you need to do this.'

'But sometimes you have to go the wrong way to find the right way.'

She turned in her seat to look directly at him.

'Like you told me, you make your own choices. But if I were you, I wouldn't do anything real quick.'

'I'm not. There's a guy out there that I have to find first. I was thinking that would be a good one to go out on.'

'But what would you do if you quit?'

'I'm not sure but I know one thing. I think I would be able to be a better father. You know, be around more.'

'That doesn't necessarily make you a better father. Remember that.'

Bosch nodded. He sometimes had a hard time believing he was talking to a fifteen-year-old. This was one of those times.

33

On Sunday morning, Bosch dropped his daughter off at the mall in Century City. The day had been reserved a week earlier for her and her friends Ashlyn and Konner to meet at the mall at eleven and then spend the day shopping, eating and gossiping. The girls scheduled mall days once a month and targeted a different shopping center each time. This time Bosch felt the most comfortable leaving them on their own. No mall was safe from predators but he knew that security would be at its maximum on a Sunday and the Century City mall had a good record of vigilance. They had undercover officers posing as shoppers all through the place and much of the weekend security force was composed of moonlighting cops.

On most mall Sundays, Bosch would head downtown after the daughter drop and work in the deserted OU squad room. He liked the stillness of the place on the weekends and it usually brought a strong focus to his case work. But this time he wanted to stay away from the PAB. He had picked up the *Times* early that morning when he went down the hill to buy milk and coffee at the convenience store. Standing in line, he had noticed that there was another front-page story related to George Irving's death. He bought the paper and read the story in the car. Reported by Emily Gomez-Gonzmart, it focused on George Irving's work for Regent Taxi and raised questions about the seeming coincidence of his representation of the company and the rise of legal issues that befell Black & White, its competitor for the Hollywood area franchise. The story made the leap to Irvin Irving. Arrest records led them to Officer Robert Mason, who told the same tale of being directly asked by the councilman to crack down on B&W.

Bosch guessed that the story was going to cause a stir at the PAB as well as City Hall. He would steer clear of the place until he had to go in to work the next morning.

As he drove away from the mall, Bosch pulled his phone to make sure it was on. He was surprised he had not heard from Chu, if only to deny that he was the source who had steered GoGo toward the story. He was also surprised not to have received a call from Kiz Rider. The fact that it was closing in on noon and she had not called him about the story told him one thing. That she was the story's source and was lying low herself.

Either on her own or more likely in concert with the chief's tacit direction, the play had been to out Irvin Irving rather than coerce his cooperation through silence. It was hard not to agree with the choice. Dangling him out there in the media, tainting him with the brush of corruption, could serve to eliminate him as a threat to the department. A lot could happen in the final month of an election campaign. Maybe the chief had decided to take his best shot now and see if the story might gather steam and affect the outcome of the election. Maybe he wanted to take the chance that Irving's opponent would be a friend to the department rather than a compromised and coerced enemy.

It didn't really matter to Bosch either way. It was all high jingo. But what did matter to him was that Kiz Rider, his friend and former partner, was now fully ensconced on the tenth floor as a political operative. He knew he had to keep that in mind as he had further dealings with her and that realization hit him like a deep loss.

He knew his best move at this point was to keep his own head down. He was sure now that he was marking his last days in the department. The thirty-nine months he had been so happy to receive a week ago now seemed almost like a sentence to be served. He'd take the afternoon off and steer clear of the PAB and everything else about the job.

While he had the phone out he took a flier and called Hannah Stone's cell. She answered right away.

'Hannah, are you at home or work?'

'Home. No therapy on Sundays. What's up? Did you find Chilton Hardy?'

There was an excited tone of anticipation in her voice.

'Uh, no, not yet. But he'll be the priority starting tomorrow. Actually, I was calling because I sort of have the afternoon free. Until I pick my daughter up around five at the mall. I thought if you were off and had the day free, we could have lunch or something. I want to talk about things. You know, see if we can't find a way to try this.'

The truth was, Bosch couldn't quite dismiss her. He had always been drawn to women hiding tragedy behind their eyes. He had been thinking about Hannah and believed that if they just set certain boundaries in regard to her son, then they might be able to carve out a chance for themselves.

'That would be great, Harry. I want to talk, too. Do you want to come here?'

Bosch checked the dash clock.

'I'm in Century City. I think I can be there by about twelve to pick you up. Maybe you can think of a place to go on Ventura Boulevard. Hell, I'm even willing to try sushi.'

She laughed and Bosch liked the sound of it.

'No, I meant come here,' she said. 'For lunch and to talk. We can just stay here and be private and I can just make something. Nothing fancy.'

'Uh . . .'

'And then we'll just see what happens.'

'You sure?'

'Of course.'

Bosch nodded to himself.

'Okay, then I'm on my way.'

34

David Chu was already in the cubicle when Bosch arrived for work Monday morning. When he saw Harry he swiveled in his chair and raised his hands in a *hands-off* manner as Bosch entered.

'Harry, all I can say is that it wasn't me.'

Bosch put his briefcase down and checked his desk for messages and delivered reports. There was nothing.

'What are you talking about?'

'The *Times* story. Did you see it?'

'Don't worry. I know it wasn't you.'

'Then who was it?'

Bosch pointed toward the ceiling as he sat down, meaning the story had come from the tenth floor.

'High jingo,' he said. 'Somebody up there decided this is the play.'

'To control Irving?'

'To move him out. Change the election. Anyway, it's not our business anymore. We turned in the report and that one's done. Today it's Chilton Hardy. I want to find him. He's been running free for twenty-two years. I want him in a cell by the end of the day.'

'Yeah, you know, I called you Saturday. I came in to do some stuff and I was wondering if you wanted to take a ride down to see the father. But I guess you had daughter stuff. You didn't answer.'

'Yeah, I had "daughter stuff" and you didn't leave a message. What did you come in to do?'

Chu turned back to his desk and pointed to his computer screen.

'Just backgrounding Hardy as much as I can,' he said. 'Not a lot there on him. More on his father buying and selling properties. Chilton Aaron Hardy Senior. He's lived down there in Los Alamitos for fifteen years. It's a condo and he owns it outright.'

Bosch nodded. It was good intel.

'I also tried to find a Mrs Hardy. You know, in case there was a divorce and she's living somewhere and could be a lead to Junior.'

'And?'

'And no go. Came up with an obituary from 'ninety-seven for Hilda Ames Hardy, wife of Chilton Senior and mother of Chilton Junior. Breast cancer. It listed no other children.'

'So it looks like we go down to Los Alamitos.'

'Yeah.'

'Then let's get out of here before the shit hits the fan on that story. Bring the file with the DMV photo of Pell.'

'Why Pell?'

'Because Senior may be predisposed not to give up Junior. I think we run a play on him and that's where Pell comes in.'

Bosch stood up.

'I'll go move the magnets.'

* * *

It was a forty-minute drive south. Los Alamitos was at the northern tip of Orange County and one of a dozen or so small, contiguous bedroom communities between Anaheim on the east and Seal Beach to the west.

On the way down Bosch and Chu worked out how they would handle the interview with Chilton Hardy Sr. They then cruised through his neighborhood off Katella Avenue and near the Los Alamitos Medical Center before stopping at the curb in front of a complex of town houses. They were built in sets of six with deep front lawns and double garages off rear alleys.

'Bring the file,' Bosch said. 'Let's go.'

There was a main sidewalk that led past a bank of mailboxes to a network of individual walkways to the front doors of the residences. Hardy Sr.'s home was the second one in. There was a screen door in front of a closed front door. Without hesitation Bosch pushed a doorbell button and then rapped his knuckles on the aluminum frame of the screen.

They waited fifteen seconds and there was no response.

Bosch hit the button again and raised his fist to hit the frame when he heard a muffled voice call out from inside.

'Someone's in there,' he said.

Another fifteen seconds went by and then the voice came again, this time clearly from right on the other side of the door.

'Yeah?'

'Mr Hardy?'

'Yeah, what?'

'It's the police. Open your door.'

'What happened?'

'We need to ask you some questions. Open the door, please.'

There was no reply.

'Mr Hardy?'

They heard the sound of the deadbolt lock turning. Slowly the door opened and a man with Coke-bottle-thick glasses peered out at them through a six-inch opening. He was disheveled, his gray hair unkempt and matted, with two weeks of white whiskers sprouted on his face. A clear plastic tube was looped over both ears and then under his nose, delivering oxygen to his nostrils. He wore what looked like a pale blue hospital smock over striped pajama pants and black plastic sandals.

Bosch tried to open the screen door but it was locked.

'Mr Hardy. We need to talk with you, sir. Can we come in?'

'What is it?'

'We're down from the LAPD and we are looking for someone. We think you might be able to help us. Can we come in, sir?'

'Who?'

'Sir, we can't do this out on the street. Can we come in to discuss this?'

The man's eyes lowered a moment as he considered things. They were cold and distant. Bosch saw where his son's eyes had come from.

Slowly, the old man reached through the opening and unlocked the screen door. Bosch opened it and then waited for Hardy to back away from the front door before pushing through.

Hardy moved slowly, leaning on a cane as he walked into the living room. Over one bony shoulder he had a strap that supported a small oxygen canister attached to the network of tubes that led to his nose.

'The place isn't clean,' he said as he moved toward a chair. 'I don't have visitors.'

'That's all right, Mr Hardy,' Bosch said.

Hardy slowly lowered himself into a well-used cushioned chair. On the table next to it was an overloaded ashtray. The house smelled of cigarettes and old age and was as unkempt as Hardy's person. Bosch started to breathe through his mouth. Hardy saw him looking at the ashtray.

'You're not going to tell the hospital on me, are you?'

'No, Mr Hardy, that's not why we're here. My name is Bosch and this is Detective Chu. We are trying to locate your son, Chilton Hardy Junior.'

Hardy nodded, as if expecting this.

'I don't know where he's at these days. What do you want with him?'

Bosch sat down on a couch with frayed cushion covers so he would be at Hardy's eye level.

'All right if I sit here, Mr Hardy?'

'Suit yourself. What's my boy gone and done that brings you here?'

Bosch shook his head.

'As far as we know, nothing. We want to talk to him about somebody else. We are doing a background investigation on a man we believe lived with your son a number of years ago.'

'Who?'

'His name is Clayton Pell. Did you ever meet him?'

'Clayton Powell?'

'No, sir. Pell. Clayton Pell. Do you know that name?'

'I don't think so.'

Hardy leaned forward and started coughing into his hand. His body jerked with spasms.

'Goddamn cigarettes. What's this Pell character done, then?'

'We can't really reveal the details of our investigation. Suffice it to say we think he's done some bad things and it would help us in dealing with him if we knew his background. We have a photo we'd like to show you.'

Chu produced the mug shot of Pell. Hardy studied it for a long time before shaking his head.

'Don't recognize him.'

'Well, that's him now. He lived with your son about twenty years ago.'

Hardy now seemed surprised.

'Twenty years ago? He'd be just a – oh, I know, you're talking about that boy who lived with Chilton with his mother up there in Hollywood.'

'Close to Hollywood. Yes, he would've been about eight years old back then. You remember him now?'

Hardy nodded and that made him start to cough again.

'Do you need some water, Mr Hardy?'

Hardy waved the offer away but continued a wheezing cough that left spittle on his lips.

'Chill came around here with him a couple times. That's all.'

'Did he ever talk to you about the boy?'

'He just said he was a handful. His mother would go off and leave him with Chill and he wasn't the fatherly type.'

Bosch nodded as though it was important information.

339

'Where's Chilton now?'

'I told you. I don't know. He doesn't visit me anymore.'

'When was the last time you saw him?'

Hardy scratched the stubble on his chin and then coughed into his hand once more. Bosch looked up at Chu, who was still standing.

'Partner, can you go get him some water?'

'No, I'm fine,' Hardy protested.

But Chu had gotten the partner message and went down the hallway next to the staircase to a kitchen or bathroom. Bosch knew it would give him the chance to take a quick look around the first floor of the town house.

'Do you remember when you last saw your son?' Bosch asked again.

'I ... no, actually. The years ... I don't know.'

Bosch nodded as though he knew how families and parents and children could drift apart over time.

Chu came back with a glass of water from a sink. The glass didn't look very clean. There were smears of fingerprints on it. As he handed it to Hardy, he gave Bosch a furtive shake of his head. He had not seen anything useful in his quick foray into the house.

Hardy drank from the glass, and Bosch tried once again to get a line on his son.

'Do you have a phone number or an address for your son, Mr Hardy? We would really like to talk to him.'

Hardy put the glass down next to the ashtray. He reached a hand up to where the breast pocket of a shirt would have been but he had no pocket on the smock he was wearing. It was a subconscious move to a pack of cigarettes that weren't there. Bosch remembered doing that himself back when he was addicted.

'I don't have a phone number,' he said.

'What about an address?' Bosch asked.

'Nope.'

Hardy cast his eyes down as it seemed to register that his answers were a testament to his failings as a father, or his namesake's failings as a son. As Bosch often did in interviews, he jumped nonsequentially in his questions. He also dropped the ruse of the visit. He no longer cared whether the old man thought they were investigating Clayton Pell or his son.

'Did your son live with you while he was growing up?'

Hardy's thick glasses magnified his eye movements. The question got a reaction. Rapid-eye movement as an answer was formulated was a tell.

'His mother and I got divorced. That was early on. I didn't see much of Chilton. We lived far apart. His mother – she's dead now – she raised him. I sent her money . . .'

Said as if the money were his only duty. Bosch nodded, continuing the pose of understanding and sympathy.

'Did she ever tell you about him being in trouble or anything like that?'

'I thought . . . you told me you were looking for that boy. Powell. Why are you asking about my son growing up?'

'Pell, Mr Hardy. Clayton Pell.'

'You're not here about him, are you?'

That was it. The play was over. Bosch started to stand.

'Your son isn't here, is he?'

'I told you. I don't know where he is.'

'Then you wouldn't mind if we took a look around for him, right?'

Hardy wiped his mouth and shook his head.

'You need a warrant for that,' he said.

'Not if there is a safety issue involved,' Bosch said. 'Why don't you just sit right there, Mr Hardy, and I'll take a quick look around. Detective Chu will stay with you.'

'No, I don't need—'

'I'm just going to make sure you're safe here, that's all.'

Bosch left them there, with Chu attempting to calm Hardy's agitation. He moved down the hallway. The town house followed a typical plan with the dining room and kitchen stacked behind the living room. There was a closet beneath the staircase and a powder room as well. Bosch glanced quickly into these rooms, assuming that Chu had already searched them when he went to get water, and opened the door at the end of the hall. There was no car in the garage. The space was crowded with stacks of boxes and old mattresses leaning against one wall.

He turned and headed back to the living room.

'You don't have a car, Mr Hardy?' he said as he approached the staircase.

'I get the taxi when I need to. Don't go up there.'

Bosch stopped four steps up and looked at him.

'Why not?'

'You got no warrant and you got no right.'

'Is your son upstairs?'

'No, nobody's up there. But you're not allowed.'

'Mr Hardy, I need to make sure we're all going to be

safe in here and that you're going to be safe after we leave.'

Bosch continued up. Hardy's demand that he not go up gave him caution. As soon as he reached the second level, he drew his gun.

Again the town house followed a familiar design. Two bedrooms and a full bath between them. The front bedroom was apparently where Hardy slept. There was an unmade bed and laundry on the floor. A side table had a dirty ashtray and a bureau had extra oxygen canisters. The walls were yellowed with nicotine and there was a patina of dust and cigarette ash on everything.

Bosch picked up one of the canisters. There was a label that said it contained liquid oxygen and was to be used by prescription only. There was a phone number for pickup and delivery from a company called ReadyAire. Bosch hefted the canister. It felt empty but he wasn't sure. He put it back down and turned to the closet door.

It was a walk-in closet with both sides lined with musty clothes on hangers. The shelves above were stacked with boxes that said U-Haul on the sides. The floor was littered with shoes and what looked like previously worn clothes in a laundry pile. He backed out and left the bedroom, proceeding down the hall.

The second bedroom was the cleanest room in the home because it appeared to be unused. There was a bureau and a side table but no mattress on the bed frame. Bosch recalled the mattress and box spring he had seen earlier in the garage and realized that the set had probably been moved down from here. He checked the closet and found it crowded but more orderly. The clothes were hung neatly in plastic bags for long-term storage.

He went back into the hall to check the bathroom.

'Harry, everything okay up there?' Chu called from downstairs.

'Everything's cool. Be right down.'

He re-holstered his weapon and leaned his head into the bathroom. Dingy towels hung on a rack and one more ashtray was on top of the toilet tank. A plastic air freshener sat next to it. Bosch almost laughed at the sight of it.

The bathtub enclosure had a plastic curtain with mold on it and the tub completed the motif with a ring of grime that looked years in the making. Disgusted, Bosch turned to go back down the stairs. But then he thought better of it and returned to the bathroom. He opened the medicine cabinet and found the three glass shelves fully racked with prescription bottles and inhalers. He randomly took one off its shelf and read the label. It was a four-year-old prescription for Hardy for something called generic theophylline. He replaced it and took down one of the inhalers. It was another generic prescription, this time for something called albuterol. It was three years old.

Bosch studied another inhaler. Then another. And then he checked every inhaler and bottle in the cabinet. There were many different generic drugs and some of the bottles were full while most of them were almost empty. But there wasn't a prescription in the cabinet that was more recent than three years old.

Bosch closed the cabinet, coming to his own face in the mirror. He looked at his dark eyes for a long moment.

And suddenly he knew.

He left the bathroom and walked quickly back to Hardy's bedroom. He closed the door so he would not be heard from the living room. Pulling his phone as he picked up one of the oxygen canisters, he called the number for ReadyAire and asked to speak to the delivery and pickup coordinator. He was connected to someone named Manuel.

'Manuel, my name is Detective Bosch. I work for the Los Angeles Police Department and I am conducting an investigation. I need to know very quickly when you last delivered prescription oxygen to one of your customers. Can you help me?'

Manuel at first thought the call was a joke, a prank perpetrated by a friend.

'Listen to me,' Bosch said sternly. 'This is no joke. This is an urgent investigation and I need this information right now. I need you to help me or put me on with someone who can.'

There was a silence and Bosch heard Chu call his name out again. Bosch put down the canister and covered his phone with his hand. He opened the bedroom door.

'I'll be right down,' he called out.

He then closed the door and went back to the phone.

'Manuel, are you there?'

'Yes. I can put the name into the computer and see what we have.'

'Okay, do it. The name is Chilton Aaron Hardy.'

Bosch waited and heard typing.

'Uh, he's here,' Manuel said. 'But he doesn't get his oh-two from us anymore.'

'What do you mean?'

'It shows our last delivery to him was July of oh-eight. He either died or started getting it from somewhere else. Probably somewhere cheaper. We lose a lot of business that way.'

'Are you sure?'

'I'm looking at it right here.'

'Thank you, Manuel.'

Bosch disconnected the call. He put his phone away and pulled his gun back out.

35

As Bosch descended the stairs his adrenaline level rose. He saw that Hardy had not moved from his chair but he was now smoking a cigarette. Chu was sitting on the arm of the couch, keeping watch.

'I made him turn off the tank,' he said. 'So he wouldn't blow us all up.'

'There's nothing in the tank,' Bosch said.

'What?'

Bosch didn't answer. He moved across the room until he was standing directly in front of Hardy.

'Stand up.'

Hardy looked up, confusion on his face.

'I said stand up.'

'What's going on?'

Bosch reached down with both hands, grabbed him by the shirt and yanked him up out of the chair. He spun him around and pushed him face-first against the wall.

'Harry, what are you doing?' Chu asked. 'He's an old—'

'It's him,' Bosch said.

'What?'

'It's the *son*, not the father.'

Bosch pulled his handcuffs off his belt and bound Hardy's arms behind his back.

'Chilton Hardy, you're under arrest for the murder of Lily Price.'

Hardy said nothing as Bosch recited his Constitutional rights. He turned his cheek to the wall and even had a small smile on his face.

'Harry, is the father upstairs?' Chu asked from behind him.

'No.'

'Then, where is he?'

'I think he's dead. Junior's been living here as him, collecting his pension and social security and all that stuff. Open the file. Where's the DL photo?'

Chu stepped forward with the blowup shot of Chilton Aaron Hardy Jr. Bosch turned Hardy around and then held him against the wall with one hand on his chest. He held the photo up next to his face. He then flicked the thick eyeglasses off him and they fell to the floor.

'It's him. He shaved his head for the DL photo. Changed his appearance. We never pulled up his father's photo. I guess we should have.'

Bosch handed the photo back to Chu. Hardy's smile grew broader.

'You think this is funny?' Bosch asked.

Hardy nodded.

'I think it's pretty fucking funny that you don't have any evidence and you don't have a case.'

His voice was different now. A deeper timbre. Not the fragile old man's voice from before.

'And I think it's pretty fucking funny that you searched this place illegally. No judge is going to believe I gave you permission. Too bad you didn't find anything. I'd love watching the judge throw it all out.'

348

Bosch grabbed a handful of Hardy's shirt and pulled him off the wall, then slammed him back against it. He felt his rage building.

'Hey, partner?' he said. 'Go out to the car and get your computer. I want to write up a search warrant right now.'

'Harry, I already checked on my phone, there's no Wi-Fi here. How're we going to send it in?'

'*Partner,* just go get the computer. We'll worry about Wi-Fi after you write it up. And close the door when you leave.'

'Okay, partner. I'll go get the laptop.'

Message received.

Bosch never took his eyes off Hardy's. He saw them register the situation, that he was about to be left alone with Bosch, and the beginning of fear entered their shiny coldness. As soon as he heard the front door close, Bosch pulled his Glock and pushed the muzzle into the flesh under Hardy's chin.

'Guess what, asshole, we're going to end this right here. Because you're right, we don't have enough. And I'm not letting you run free another fucking day.'

He violently yanked Hardy off the wall and spun him to the floor. Hardy crashed into the side table, knocking the ashtray and water glass onto the rug, and landed on his back. Bosch dropped down on him, straddling his torso.

'The way this will work is, we didn't know it was you, you see? We thought it was your father all along and when my partner went out to the car you jumped me. There was a struggle for the gun and – guess what? – you didn't win.'

Bosch held the gun up sideways, displaying it in front of Hardy's face.

'There will be two shots. The one I'm about to put through your black fucking heart, and then after I take off the cuffs, I'll wrap your dead hands around my Glock and cap one into the wall. That way we both get gunshot residue and everybody's cool with it.'

Bosch leaned down and positioned the gun with the barrel at an upward angle to Hardy's chest.

'Yeah, I think like this,' he said.

'Wait!' Hardy yelled. 'You can't do this!'

In his eyes Bosch saw true terror.

'This is for Lily Price and Clayton Pell and everybody else you killed and hurt and destroyed.'

'Please.'

'Please? Is that what Lily said to you? Did she say please?'

Bosch changed the angle of the gun slightly and leaned farther down, his chest now only six inches from Hardy's.

'Okay, I admit it. Venice Beach, nineteen eighty-nine. I'll tell you everything. Just take me in and set it up. I'll tell you about my father, too. I drowned him in the bathtub.'

Bosch shook his head.

'You'll tell me what I want to hear just to get out of here alive. But it's no good, Hardy. It's too late. We're past that. Even if you truly confessed, it wouldn't hold up. Coerced confession. You know that.'

Bosch pulled back the slide on the Glock to chamber a round.

'I don't want a bullshit confession. I want evidence. I want your stash.'

'What stash?'

'You keep stuff. All you guys keep stuff. Pictures, souvenirs. You want to save yourself, Hardy, tell me where the stash is.'

He waited. Hardy said nothing. Bosch put the muzzle down against his chest and angled the gun again.

'All right, all right,' Hardy said desperately. 'Next door. Everything's next door. My father owned both places. I have it set up with a phony name on the deed. You go look. You'll find everything you need.'

Bosch stared down at him for a long moment.

'If you're lying, you're dying.'

He withdrew the gun and holstered it. He started to get up.

'How do I get in?'

'The keys are on the counter in the kitchen.'

The odd smile returned to Hardy's face. A moment ago he was desperate to save his own life, now he was smiling. Bosch realized it was a look of pride.

'Go check it out,' Hardy urged. 'You're going to be famous, Bosch. You caught the goddamn record holder.'

'Yeah? How many?'

'Thirty-seven. I planted thirty-seven crosses.'

Bosch had guessed that there were going to be numbers, but not that high. He wondered if Hardy was inflating his kills as part of one last manipulation. Say anything, give anything, just to get out the door alive. All he had to do was survive this moment and he could slip into the next transformation, from unknown and uncharted killer to figure of public fascination and fear. A name that would inspire dread. Bosch knew it was part of the fulfillment process with their kind. Hardy had probably lived in anticipation of the time he would become known. Men like him fantasized about it.

In one smooth and swift move, Bosch pulled the Glock from his holster again and brought its aim down on Hardy.

'*No!*' Hardy yelled. 'We have a deal!'

'We don't have shit.'

Bosch pulled the trigger. The metal snap of the firing mechanism sounded and Hardy's body jerked as if shot, but there was no bullet in the chamber. The gun was empty. Bosch had unloaded it up in the bedroom.

Bosch nodded. Hardy had missed the tell. No cop would've had to chamber a round, because no cop would've left the chamber empty. Not in L.A., where the two seconds it takes to chamber a round could cost you your life. That had been just part of the play. In case Bosch had had to string it out.

He reached down and rolled Hardy over. He put the gun down on his back and from his suit pocket took out two snap ties. He cinched one around Hardy's ankles, binding them tightly together, and then used the other on his wrists so he could remove his handcuffs. Bosch had a feeling he would not be the one escorting Hardy to jail and he didn't want to lose his cuffs.

Bosch stood up and hooked his cuffs back on his belt. He then reached back into his coat pocket and took out a handful of bullets. He ejected the empty magazine from his gun and started reloading it. When he was finished, he slid the magazine back into place and racked one bullet into the chamber before returning the weapon to its holster.

'Always keep one in the chamber,' he said to Hardy.

The door opened and Chu stepped back in, carrying his laptop. He looked at Hardy lying prone on the floor. He had no idea what Bosch's play had been.

'Is he alive?'

'Yes. Watch him. Make sure he doesn't do the kangaroo.'

Bosch walked down the hallway to the kitchen and found a set of keys on the counter where Hardy had said they would be. When he came back to the living room, he looked around, trying to figure out a way of securing Hardy while he and Chu conferred privately outside about how to proceed. An embarrassing story had gone around the PAB a few months earlier about a robbery suspect dubbed the Kangaroo. He had been bound at the ankles and wrists and left on the floor of a bank while the arresting officers looked for another suspect they believed was hiding in the building. Fifteen minutes later officers in another responding car saw a man hopping down the street, three blocks from the bank.

Finally, Bosch got an idea.

'Get the end of the couch,' he said.

'What are we doing?' Chu asked.

Bosch pointed him to the end.

'Tip it.'

They tipped the couch forward on its front legs and then down over Hardy. It tented him and made it almost impossible for him to try to stand up with his arms and legs bound.

'What is this?' Hardy protested. 'What are you doing?'

'Just sit tight, Hardy,' Bosch replied. 'We won't leave you too long.'

Bosch signaled Chu toward the front door. As they were going out, Hardy called out.

'Be careful, Bosch!'

Bosch looked back at him.

'Of what?'

'Of what you'll see. You won't be the same after today.'

Bosch stood with his hand on the knob for a long moment. Only Hardy's feet were visible, extending from under the overturned couch.

'We'll see,' he said.

He stepped out and closed the door.

36

It was like being at the end of a maze and having to work their way back to the starting point. They had the location they wanted to search – the town house next door, where Hardy claimed he kept his stash of keepsakes from his kills. They just had to figure out the chain of events and legal steps taking them to it that could be put in a search warrant and that would be accepted and approved by a superior court judge.

Bosch did not reveal to Chu what had occurred in Hardy's living room while Chu was back at the car. Not only was there the trust issue that had exploded on the Irving case, but Bosch had no doubt coerced a confession from Hardy, and he would not share that transgression with anyone. If and, more likely, when Hardy claimed coercion as part of his defense, Bosch would simply deny it and dismiss it as an outrageous defense tactic. There would be no possibility of anyone other than Hardy – the accused – being able to attack Bosch's story.

So Bosch told Chu what they needed to do and they worked out how to get there.

'Chilton Hardy Senior, who is most likely dead, is supposed to be the owner of these two town houses. We need to search them both and we need to do it now. How do we get there?'

They were standing on the grass in front of the town

house complex. Chu looked at the facades of units 6A and 6B as if the answer to the question might be painted on them like graffiti.

'Well, probable cause on six B is not going to be a problem,' he said. 'We found him there living as his father. We're entitled to search for any indication of what happened to the old man. Exigent circumstances, Harry. We're in.'

'And what about six A? That's the place we really want.'

'So we ... we just ... Okay, I think I got it. We came down to interview Chilton Hardy Senior but halfway through we realize that the guy in front of us is actually Chilton Hardy Junior. There is no sign of Hardy Senior and we're thinking he might be tied up somewhere, being held captive, who knows what. Maybe he's alive and maybe he's dead. So we run a history search on the property appraiser's database, and lo and behold, he used to own the place right next door and the transfer of title looks phony. We have an obligation to go in there to see if he is alive or in some kind of peril. Exigent circumstances again.'

Bosch nodded but frowned at the same time. He didn't like it. It sounded to him like exactly what it was. A story made up to get them in the door. A judge might sign the search warrant but they'd have to find a friendly one. He wanted something bulletproof. Something that any judge would approve and that would hold up upon subsequent legal challenges.

Suddenly he realized he had their access right in his hand. In more ways than one. He held up the key ring. There were six keys on it. One carried the Dodge logo and was obviously to a vehicle. There were two full-size Schlage keys that he assumed were the keys to the front doors of the two apartments, and then three smaller keys. Two of these were the small keys used to open private mailboxes like the kind they had seen out at the curb.

'The keys,' he said. 'He's got two mailbox keys. Come on.'

They headed to the bank of mailboxes. When they got there Bosch tried the keys in the boxes assigned to complex 6. He was able to open the boxes for units 6A and 6B. He noted that the name on 6A was Drew, which Bosch took to be an attempt at humor on Hardy's part. Hardy and Drew living side by side in Los Alamitos.

'Okay, we found two mailbox keys in Hardy's possession,' he said. 'That led us here and we learned that he had access to two boxes. Units six A and B. We noted also that he had two Schlage deadbolt keys and this led us to believe he had access to both six A and B. We checked the ownership records and saw the transfer from the father on six B. It doesn't look right because it took place after we think the son started playing the father. So we need to check out A to see if the old man is being held there. We knocked, got no answer, and now we want permission to go in.'

Chu nodded. He liked it.

'I think it works. You want me to write it up that way?'

'Yeah. Do it. Go write it up inside so you can keep an eye on Hardy.'

Bosch hefted the key ring in his hand.

'I'm going in six A to see if this is worth our while.'

It was called jumping the warrant. Checking a place out before a search has officially been approved by a judge. If it was ever acknowledged as a police practice, people could lose their badges, even end up in jail. But the truth was, many were the times that search warrants were authored with full knowledge of what would be found in the targeted structure or vehicle. This was because the police had already been inside.

'You sure you need to, Harry?' Chu asked.

'Yeah. If Hardy made a play on me while I was playing him, then I want to know sooner rather than later so we aren't spinning our wheels.'

'Then just wait till I'm inside so I don't know about it.'

Bosch gestured toward the door of 6B like a maître d', with his arm out and his body slightly bent at the waist. Chu headed back to the town house but then stopped and came back.

'When are we going to tell the other LAPD that we're here and what we're doing?'

'What other LAPD?'

'Los Alamitos Police Department.'

'Not quite yet,' Bosch said. 'When we get an approval on the warrant, we can call them in.'

'They're not going to like that.'

'Tough shit. Our case, our arrest.'

Bosch knew that a department the size of Los Alamitos could easily be bigfooted by the 'real' LAPD.

Chu started toward the door to 6B again and Bosch headed back to the car. He popped the trunk and from the equipment box took several pairs of latex gloves and put them into his coat pocket. He grabbed a flashlight in case it was needed and closed the trunk.

Bosch walked back to 6A but was distracted by the sound of yelling coming from 6B as he approached. It was Hardy.

Bosch went through the door of 6B. Hardy was still lying prone under the couch. Chu was sitting on a chair he had brought out from the kitchen and was working on his laptop. Hardy went silent as Bosch entered.

'What's he yelling about?'

'First he wanted a cigarette. Now he wants his attorney.'

Bosch looked down at the overturned couch.

'As soon as you're booked you get your phone call.'

'Then book me!'

'We are securing the scene first. And if you keep yelling, then we are going to further secure you with a gag.'

'I'm entitled to an attorney. You said so yourself.'

'You'll get the phone call when everyone else gets the phone call. When you're booked.'

Bosch turned back toward the door.

'Hey, Bosch?'

He turned back.

'Did you go in yet?'

Bosch didn't answer. Hardy continued.

'They're going to make movies about us.'

Chu glanced up and exchanged a look with Bosch. There were killers who got off on their infamy and the fear their legends created. Real-life bogeymen, urban myth becoming urban reality. Hardy had stayed hidden for so many years. Now it would be his turn in the spotlight.

'Sure,' Bosch said. 'You're going to be the most famous asshole on death row.'

'Please. You know I'll be able to beat the needle for twenty years. At least. Who do you think will play me in the movie?'

Bosch didn't answer. He stepped out onto the stoop and casually glanced around to see if there were any nearby pedestrians or motorists. It was clear. He quickly walked to the door of 6A and pulled Hardy's key ring out of his pocket. He tried one of the Schlage keys on the deadbolt and got lucky with his first try. The key also fit the knob lock. He pushed the door open and entered, then closed it behind him.

Standing still in the entry, Bosch pulled on a set of latex gloves. The place was as dark as night. He swept the wall with his freshly gloved hand until he found a switch.

A dim ceiling light exposed 6A as a house of horrors. A jerry-built wall had been constructed across the front windows, ensuring darkness and privacy as well as a layer of soundproofing. All four walls of the front room had been used as a gallery for photo collages and newspaper stories of murder and rape and torture. Newspapers from as far as San Diego, Phoenix and Las Vegas. Stories about unexplained abductions, body dumps, missing people. It was clear that if these cases were the work of Hardy, then he was a traveler. His hunting territory was immense.

Bosch studied the photos. Hardy's victims included both young men and women. Some were children. Bosch moved slowly, studying the horrible images. He stopped when he came to a full front page of the *Los Angeles Times,* yellowed and cracked now, with the smiling face of a young girl in a photo next to a story about her disappearance from a West Valley mall. He leaned closer to read the story until it said her name. He knew the name and the case and he now remembered why the address on Hardy's driver's license had sounded familiar to him.

Eventually he had to break away from the ghastly images. This was a pre-search sweep. He had to keep moving. When he came to the door to the garage, Bosch knew what he would find before he opened it. There in the bay sat a white work van. Hardy's most important abduction tool.

It was a late-model Dodge. Bosch used the key to unlock it and look inside. It was empty except for a mattress and a hanging tool rack with two rolls of duct tape on it. Bosch put the key in the ignition and started the engine so he could check the mileage. The van had over 140,000 miles on it, another indication of the killer's territory. He cut the engine and relocked the van.

Bosch had seen enough to know what they had, but he was drawn upstairs, anyway. He checked the front bedroom first and found it empty of furniture. All that was here were several small piles of clothing. There were T-shirts with pop stars' faces on them, several pairs of blue jeans, separate piles just for bras and underwear and belts. The clothing of the victims.

The walk-in closet had a hasp and padlock on it. Bosch pulled the key ring again and fitted the smallest key into the padlock. He opened the closet door and flicked the switch on the outside wall. The small room was empty. The walls, ceiling and floor had been painted black. Two thick steel eyebolts protruded from the back wall, three feet off the ground. It was clearly a storage room for Hardy's victims. Bosch thought about all of the people who had spent their last hours in this room, gagged, secured to the bolts, waiting for Hardy to end their agony.

In the back bedroom, there was a bed with a bare mattress on it. In the corner was a camera tripod without a camera. Bosch opened the closet doors and found it to be the electronics center. There were video cameras, archaic still and Polaroid cameras and a laptop computer, and the upper shelves were lined with DVD cases and VHS tapes. On one of the shelves were three old shoe-boxes. Bosch pulled one down and opened it. It was filled with old Polaroids, mostly bleached out now, depicting many different young women and men engaged in oral sex with a man whose face was never seen.

Bosch put the box back in its place and closed the closet doors. He went back into the hallway. The bath-room was just as dirty as the bathroom in 6B but the tub ring was brownish-red and Bosch knew that this was where Hardy washed the blood off. He backed out of the room and checked the hallway closet. It was empty except for a black plastic case that stood about four and a half feet high and was roughly the shape of a bowling pin. There was a handle on the top of it. Bosch grabbed it and tipped it forward. There were two wheels on the bottom and he rolled it out into the hallway. The case felt empty and Bosch wondered if it had contained a musical instrument.

But then he saw a manufacturer's plate on the side of the container. It said Golf+Go Systems and Bosch realized it was a case for transporting golf clubs on planes. He laid it down on the carpet and opened it, noting that the two latches could be locked with a key. It was empty but Bosch saw that there were three rough-edged holes the size of dimes cut into the top facing of the container.

Bosch closed it, righted it and put it back in the closet to be found later during the official search. He shut the door and headed back downstairs.

When he was halfway down the stairs, Bosch suddenly stopped and gripped the banister. He knew the dime-sized holes in the golf clubs carrier were to allow air into the case. And he knew a child or small person could fit inside. The inhumanity and depravity suddenly seized him. He could smell the blood. He could hear the muffled pleas. He knew the misery of this place.

He put his shoulder against the wall for a moment and then slid down to a seated position on the steps. He leaned forward with his elbows on his knees. He was hyperventilating and tried to slow down his breathing cycle. He ran a hand back through his hair and then held the hand across his mouth.

He closed his eyes and remembered another time when he was in a place of death, huddled in a tunnel and far from home. He was really just a boy then and he was scared and trying to control his breathing. That was the key. Control your breathing and you control the fear.

He sat there for no more than two minutes but it seemed like an entire night went by. Finally his breathing returned to normal and the memory of the tunnels faded.

His phone buzzed and it brought him out of the dark

moment. He pulled it and looked at the screen. It was Chu.

'Yeah?'

'Harry, you okay over there? You're taking a long time.'

'I'm cool. I'll be over in a minute.'

'Are we good?'

Meaning did Bosch find what they needed in 6A.

'Yeah, we're good.'

He disconnected and then called Tim Marcia's direct number. He obliquely explained to the squad whip what was going on.

'We're going to need people down here,' Bosch said. 'I think there's going to be a lot of work to do. We are also going to need media relations and a liaison with the locals. We should set up a command post because we're going to be here all week.'

'Okay, I'm on it,' Marcia said. 'I'll talk to the lieutenant and we'll start mobilizing. It sounds like we're going to need to send everybody.'

'That would be good.'

'Are you all right, Harry? You sound weird.'

'I'm all right.'

Bosch gave him the address and hung up. He sat still for another two minutes and then made the next call, to Kizmin Rider's cell.

'Harry, I know why you're calling and all I can tell you is that it was thought out very carefully. A decision was made that was best for the department and we're never going to talk about it. It's best that way for you, too.'

She was talking about the *Times* story on Irving and

the taxi franchise. The case seemed so distant to Bosch now. And so meaningless.

'That's not why I'm calling.'

'Oh. Then, what's up? You don't sound right.'

'I'm fine. We just took down a big one that I'm sure the chief's going to want to get in on. You remember the Mandy Phillips case up in the West Valley about nine, ten years ago?'

'No, refresh me.'

'Thirteen years old, she got grabbed at a mall out there. Never found, nobody ever arrested.'

'You got the guy?'

'Yeah, and get this. When he got a driver's license three years ago? He gave the girl's address as his own.'

Rider was silent as she registered Hardy's audacity.

'I'm glad you got him,' she finally said.

'She's not the only one. We're down in Orange County putting it together. But it's going to get big. The guy claims his number is thirty-seven.'

'Oh, my god!'

'He's got a closet full of cameras and photos and tapes. There are VHS tapes, Kiz. This guy's been at this a very long time.'

Bosch knew he was taking a risk in revealing to Rider what he had found while jumping the warrant. They had been partners once but the bulletproof bond they shared then was now rusting through. Still, he risked it. Politics and high jingo aside, if he couldn't trust her, then he could trust no one.

'You told Lieutenant Duvall all of this?'

'I told the whip. Not everything, but enough. I think they're coming down with everybody.'

'Okay, I'll check in and monitor things. I don't know if the chief will go down there. But he'll want to get involved. They may want to use the theater here for something like this.'

The PAB complex had a ground-level theater that was used for award programs, special events and major press conferences. This would be one of those.

'Okay, but that wasn't the main reason I called.'

'Well, what was the main reason?'

'Did you do anything yet about moving my partner out of the unit?'

'Uh, no. I've been a little busy this morning.'

'Good. Then don't. Never mind that.'

'You sure?'

'Yes.'

'Okay, then.'

'And that other thing you mentioned. About me getting the whole five years on the DROP. Is that something you still think you can do?'

'I was pretty sure I could get it done when I made the offer. After this case, I think it's a cinch. They're going to want to keep you around, Harry. You're about to get famous.'

'I don't want to be famous. I just want to work cases.'

'I understand that. I'll go for the full five.'

'Thanks, Kiz. And I guess I should get back to it now. A lot going on here.'

'Good luck, Harry. Keep it between the lines.'

Meaning don't break the rules. The case is too big, too important.

'Got it.'

'And Harry?'

'Yeah.'

'This is why we do this. Because of people like this guy. Monsters like him, they don't stop until we stop them. It's noble work. Remember that. Just think how many people you just saved.'

Bosch nodded and thought about the golf clubs carrier. He knew it was going to be something that stayed with him forever. Hardy had been right when he warned that going into 6A would change Bosch.

'Not enough,' he said.

He disconnected and thought about things. Two days ago he didn't think he could leg out the last thirty-nine months of his career. Now he wanted the full five years. Whatever his failings were on the Irving case, he now understood that the mission didn't end. There was always the mission and always work to be done. His kind of work.

This is why we do this.

Bosch nodded. Kiz got that right.

He used the banister to pull himself up to a standing position and then started down the stairs again. He needed to get out of the town house and into the sunlight.

37

By noon a search warrant had been signed by superior court judge George Companioni and the horrors contained inside town house 6A were officially and legally confirmed by Bosch, Chu and other members of the Open-Unsolved Unit. Chilton Hardy was then moved to one of the squad's cars and transported to the Metropolitan Detention Center for booking by detectives Baker and Kehoe. Bosch and Chu, as the lead investigators, remained behind to work the crime scene.

Soon the street outside the side-by-side town houses where Hardy had lived as his father and carried out his ghastly desires took on a circus atmosphere as reports of the horrific findings drew more investigators and law enforcement officers as well as forensic technicians and the media from two counties. It would not be long before tiny Los Alamitos attracted the attention of the entire world as the story was catapulted onto every news site on the Internet as well as the cable and broadcast television networks.

A jurisdictional squabble between the two LAPDs was quickly settled in favor of Los Angeles handling all of the investigative aspects of the case, while Los Alamitos was given site security as well as crowd and media control. The latter included a traffic shutdown on the block and an evacuation of all other residents in the six-unit town house complex where Hardy lived and operated. Both sides dug in for what was expected to be a minimum weeklong crime scene investigation. Both sides brought in onsite media spokesmen to handle the expected crush of reporters, cameras and satellite trucks that would descend on the once quiet neighborhood.

The chief of police and the commander of the Robbery-Homicide Division put their heads together and created an investigative battle plan that had at least one immediate surprise attached. Lieutenant Duvall, supervisor of the Open-Unsolved Unit, was aced out of running the show. What would be arguably her unit's finest hour and most important investigation was placed in the hands of Lieutenant Larry Gandle, another RHD squad leader who had more experience than Duvall and was considered far more media savvy. Gandle would direct the ongoing investigation.

Bosch couldn't complain about the move. He had been on Gandle's homicide team previous to his assignment in OU and they had worked well together. Gandle was a roll-up-his-sleeves kind of guy who trusted his investigators. He was not the kind of supervisor who hid behind closed doors and shuttered blinds.

One of the first moves Gandle made after conferring with Bosch and Chu was to call for a meeting of all the investigators on the scene. They stood together in the dark front room of unit 6A after Gandle temporarily shooed a team of forensic photographers and technicians out.

'Okay, people, listen up,' he said. 'I didn't think we should meet together outside in the sunshine and fresh air. I thought it would be better for us to be in here, where it's dark and it stinks of death. The indications are that many people died in this place and that they died horribly. They were tortured and murdered and we must respect them and honor them by doing our very best work here. We cut no corners, we bend no rules. We do it right. I don't care if this guy Hardy is riding in that car right now with Baker and Kehoe and confessing his ass off. We are going to put together a case that is absolutely fucking bulletproof. We all make the vow right now that this guy never sees the light of day again. Destination: death row. Nothing else. Everybody got that?'

There were a few nods across the room. It was the first time Bosch had ever seen the lieutenant giving a pep talk like a football coach. Harry liked it and thought it was a good move to remind everyone in the room how high the stakes were with the investigation.

After the preamble Gandle proceeded to divide responsibilities among the teams. While much of the investigation inside the two town houses would involve the gathering of forensic evidence, the heart of the case would undoubtedly be the videos found in the second bedroom closet and the photos taped to the walls throughout the town house. The OU investigators would be charged with documenting who the victims were, where they came from and what exactly happened to them. It would be a terribly grim task. Earlier, Chu had put one of the DVDs from the bedroom closet into his computer so that he and Bosch could get a sense of what was on the vast collection of tapes and discs. The video showed Hardy raping and torturing a woman to the point that she began begging him – after he pulled down her gag – to kill her and simply put her out of her misery. The video ended with the woman choked unconscious but clearly still breathing and Hardy turning to his camera and smiling. He had gotten what he wanted from her.

In all of his years as a cop, Bosch had seen nothing so gut-wrenching and horrible. There were images on that one disc that he knew were indelible and that he would have to try to push into the recesses of his mind. But there were dozens more discs and tapes and hundreds of photographs. Each would need to be viewed, described, catalogued and placed into evidence. It was going to be painful, soul-searing work, guaranteed to leave the kind of internal scars only homicide cops carry. Gandle said that he wanted everyone in the unit to be open to discussing the harrowing duty with therapists in the department's Behavioral Sciences Unit. Every cop knew that quietly carrying the horrors of the job inside could be like carrying untreated cancer. Still, seeking help for dealing with the burden was seen by many as a weakness. No cop wanted to be weak, whether it was in the view of the bad guys or their fellow good guys.

Gandle next turned the meeting over to Bosch and Chu, the lead investigators, and they quickly summarized the steps that led them to Hardy and the side-by-side town houses.

They also discussed the dichotomy in the investigation that they now faced. There was a need for speed on one level but also a necessity to move deliberately and carefully to ensure that they conducted the most thorough investigation possible.

The department was under the legal obligation to file

charges against Hardy within forty-eight hours of his arrest. He would be brought into court for his first appearance before a judge on Wednesday morning. If by then he was not charged with a crime, he would be released.

'What we're going to do is file one case against him,' Bosch said. 'One murder now and then we add on later when we're ready with the rest. So on Wednesday we go with Lily Price. Right now, it's a wobbler but it's still our best bet. We have a DNA hit, and while it's not Hardy's, we think we can prove it puts him at the scene. What we're hoping is that between now and Wednesday morning we find an image of Lily somewhere in this place.'

Chu held up a 5 × 7 photo of Lily Price taken from the original murder book. It was her yearbook photo. She was smiling and innocent and beautiful. If they found her image anywhere among Hardy's souvenirs, it wouldn't look the same.

'We're talking nineteen eighty-nine so she won't be on any of the DVDs unless we find out that Hardy was transferring VHS to DVD,' Chu said. 'But this is unlikely as there is no transfer machine here and this isn't the kind of thing you send out to have done.'

'We're going to take a quick run at the still photos,' Bosch said. 'Those of you working the VHS, keep an eye out for her. If we find her on one of this guy's tapes or photos, then we're gold on Wednesday.'

When Bosch and Chu were finished, Gandle took back the lead to wrap things up with a final rally cry.

'Okay, people,' he said. 'That's it. We all know what we have to do. So let's do it. Make it count.'

The group started to break up. Bosch could feel an air of urgency among the detectives. Gandle's charge had worked.

'Oh, one other thing,' Gandle said. 'No time limitations on the work on this. We have full overtime authorization and that comes directly from the chief's office.'

If the lieutenant was expecting a cheer or even a round of applause, he was disappointed. There was little reaction to the good news that money would flow unabated into the investigation. OT was a good thing and it had been in short supply all year. But there was a reluctance to consider financial remuneration for the work this case would entail. Bosch knew that everyone in the room would work whatever hours were needed whether paid or not.

This is why we do this.

Bosch thought about what Kiz Rider had said to him earlier. It was all part of the mission and this case told that tale better than most.

38

It took the three teams of detectives assigned to the photographic and video evidence two hours to package all the materials from the second bedroom closet into evidence boxes. As if in a solemn funeral procession three unmarked cars then transported the boxes north to Los Angeles and the PAB. Bosch and Chu were in the last car, three boxes of still photos on the rear seat. There was little to talk about as they drove. They had a grim duty ahead of them and thoughts of preparing for it were all-consuming.

The media relations office had tipped the media to the arrival of the procession and as the detectives carried their boxes into the police headquarters, they were documented by photographers and videographers lined up outside the building's entrance. This was not done simply to appease the media. Rather, it was part of what would be an ongoing effort to use the media to hammer home with the public – and the local jury pool – that Chilton Hardy was guilty of ghastly deeds. It was part of the subtle complicity that would always exist between the police and the media.

All three of the meeting rooms had been assigned to what was being known as the Hardy Task Force. Bosch and Chu took the smallest room because it did not have video equipment. They were going to sort through still photographs and didn't need it.

Hardy had shown no apparent rhyme or reason in his cataloguing of the photos. Old and new, the photographs were tossed into several shoeboxes and placed on the shelves of the closet. There was no writing on the front or back of any of them. Several photos were taken of the same individuals but these might be spread across two or three different shoe boxes.

As Bosch and Chu began to go through them, they attempted to group the photos in a variety of ways. First and foremost they tried to put all photos of the same individual together. They then tried to estimate the age of the photos and organize them chronologically. Some of the photos had date stamps on them and these were helpful, though there was no way of knowing if the camera used had been set with the proper date.

In most of the photos the individual who was depicted alone or with Hardy or with a man's body assumed to be Hardy's was clearly alive in the photograph. He or she was either engaged in a sex act or in some cases smiling directly at the camera. In other cases the depiction was of a person looking in fear and sometimes pain at the camera.

Photos that had individual identifiers were placed in a priority category. These were victims who wore distinctive jewelry or had tattoos or facial moles. These markers would help the investigators seek identities later in the investigation.

Bosch could feel his insides being hollowed by the process. The eyes of the victims were the most difficult.

So many of them looked at the camera with eyes showing that they knew they were not going to live. It tapped into a deep well of helpless rage in Bosch. For years Hardy had cut a bloody trail across the landscape and no one had seen it. Now they were left to make piles out of photographs.

At one point there was a knock on the door and Teddy Baker came in, holding a file.

'I thought you might want to see this,' she said. 'They took it at MDC during booking.'

She opened the file and put an 8 × 10 photo down on the table. It depicted a man's back. Spread from shoulder blade to shoulder blade was a depiction of a cemetery with black crosses across the landscape. Some of the crosses were old and faded, the ink having spread with the skin. Some of the crosses were sharply drawn and looked new. In a black script beneath the image were the words *Bene Decessit*.

Bosch had seen RIP tattoos before, but usually they were on gangbangers trying to keep track of the body counts of their own homies. This was new and yet not surprising. It also didn't come as a surprise that Hardy had found a tattoo artist who apparently didn't think the cemetery image was suspicious enough to contact authorities.

'That's your boy,' Baker said.

'And did you count the crosses?' Bosch asked.

'Yeah. There's thirty-seven of them.'

Bosch had not told her or the others that Hardy had said his number was thirty-seven. He had only told Kiz Rider that. He ran his finger below the words on Hardy's back.

'Yeah,' Baker said. 'We Googled it. It's Latin. Means "died well." Like they all died well.'

Bosch nodded.

'Sweet,' Chu said. 'The guy's fucked up.'

'Can we put the photo in the package?' Bosch asked.

'It's all yours.'

Bosch put the photo to the side of the table. He would include it in the charging package he would take to the DA.

'Okay. Thanks, Teddy,' he said.

He was dismissing her. He wanted to get back to the photo work. He needed to find Lily.

'Do you guys need some help?' Baker said. 'Gandle didn't give us a piece of anything. Out of sight, out of mind, I guess.'

She and Kehoe had been driving Hardy to the MDC for booking when Gandle had given out assignments. It was quickly becoming the kind of case everyone wanted a part of.

'I think we got this, Teddy,' Bosch said quickly before his partner could tell her to join them. 'Maybe the others could use a hand with the videos.'

'Okay, thanks. I'll check with them.'

Bosch interpreted her tone to mean that she thought he was being a selfish prick. She went to the door but then turned back to them.

'You know what's weird so far?' she asked.

'What's weird?' Bosch responded.

'No bodies. There's DNA in that town house. But where are all the bodies? Where did he hide them?'

'Some were found,' Bosch said. 'Like Lily Price. Others he hid. That's his last chit. By the time we're finished

377

with this, that's all Hardy will have left to trade. He gives up the bodies, we give up the death penalty.'

'Think the DA will go for it?'

'I hope not.'

She left the room then and Bosch got back to work with the photos.

'Harry, what's up?' Chu said. 'We've got about a thousand photos still to look through.'

'I know that,' Bosch said.

'So, why couldn't we use her? She and Kehoe are part of OU. They're just looking for something to do.'

'I don't know. I just think that if Lily Price is in here somewhere, then we should find her. Know what I mean?'

'I guess so.'

Bosch relented.

'Go get her. Bring her back.'

'No, that's okay. I understand.'

They went back to work, silently looking and sorting and stacking. Such a grim duty and so many victims. If not of murder or rape, then of Hardy's manipulations and inhumanity. Bosch had to admit to himself that it was another reason he didn't want to bring Teddy Baker in. It didn't matter that she was a veteran investigator who had seen everything there was to see on the underside of life. And it didn't matter that Hardy was a predator who targeted weakness, whether the victim be male or female. Bosch would never be comfortable viewing the photos in the company of a woman. It was just the way he was.

Only twenty minutes later Bosch saw Chu stop his routine motion of checking a photo and then holding it up over his head while considering the stack he would place it on. He looked over. Chu was studying a Polaroid.

'Harry, I think . . .'

Bosch took the photo from him and looked at it. It was a shot of a young girl lying naked on a dirty blanket. Her eyes were closed and it was impossible to determine if she was alive or dead. The photo had faded over time. Bosch held it next to the yearbook photo of the smiling face of Lily Price, taken eighteen months before her death.

'You think?' Chu asked.

Bosch didn't answer. He kept shifting his eyes from photo to photo, studying them and making minute comparisons. Chu handed him a magnifying glass he had brought from the cubicle but neither had used. Bosch put both photos down on the table and compared them under magnification. Finally he nodded and answered.

'I think you found her. We take this over to photo for digital analysis and see what they say.'

Chu pounded his fist on the table.

'We got this guy, Harry. We got him!'

Bosch put the magnifier down on the table and leaned back in his chair.

'Yeah,' he said. 'I think we do.'

He then leaned forward and pointed to the stacks of photos that still had not been checked.

'Let's keep going,' he said.

'You think there's more?' Chu asked.

'Who knows? Maybe. But there's also another one we should try to find.'

'Who?'

'Clayton Pell. He said Hardy took his picture, too. If he saved it, then it should be in here.'

39

Bosch gathered himself, took a final breath and punched in the number. He wasn't even sure if the phone number would still be good after so many years. He checked one of the overhead clocks and did the math again. Three hours ahead in Ohio. It would be well after dinner but they would still be awake.

A woman picked up after three rings.

'Mrs Price?' Bosch asked.

'Yes, who am I speaking to?'

There was an urgent tone in her voice and Bosch guessed that she had caller ID on her phone. She knew it was the police calling. Reaching across time and distance.

'Mrs Price, this is Detective Bosch with the Los Angeles Police Department. I'm calling because there have been some developments in the investigation of your daughter's death. I need to talk with you.'

Bosch heard the catch in her breath. Then she covered the receiver and spoke to someone else. He could not tell what she was saying.

'Mrs Price?'

'Yes, I'm sorry. I told my husband. Lily's father. He went upstairs to get on the other line.'

'Okay, we can wait for—'

'Is this about what they're showing on TV? We were watching the Fox channel and I had to wonder if that man they said is known as Chill was the one who took Lily.'

She was crying before she finished the question.

'Mrs Price, can we—'

There was a click and they were joined on the line by her husband.

'This is Bill Price.'

'Mr Price, I was telling your wife, my name is Harry Bosch. I'm a detective with the LAPD. I need to inform you about developments in the investigation of your daughter's death.'

'Lily,' Mr Price said.

'Yes, sir, your daughter Lily. I work in the Open-Unsolved Unit, which handles cold case homicide investigations. Last week we got a good break in the case. DNA from blood found on Lily's body was connected to a man named Chilton Hardy. It was not his blood but it was blood that belonged to someone who knew Hardy and could connect him to the crime. I'm calling to tell you that we arrested Chilton Hardy today and we will be charging him with your daughter's murder.'

There was only the sound of Mrs Price weeping.

'I don't know if there is any more to say at this point,' Bosch finally said. 'The investigation is still unfolding and I will keep you posted on developments as we go forward with the prosecution. Once it is revealed that this man has been charged with your daughter's murder, you may be contacted by the news media. It is up to you whether you want to talk to them or not. Do you have any questions for me?'

Bosch tried to imagine them in their home in Dayton. On different floors, connected by an open phone line to a man they had never met. Twenty-two years ago they had sent their daughter to Los Angeles to go to college. She never came home.

'I have a question,' Mrs Price said. 'Hold on, please.'

Bosch heard the phone being put down and then her weeping in the background. Her husband finally spoke.

'Detective, thank you for not forgetting about our daughter. I'm going to hang up now so I can go downstairs and be with my wife.'

'I understand, sir. I am sure we will be talking soon. Good-bye.'

When Mrs Price came back on the line, she had composed herself.

'On the cable news they said that the police were looking at pictures and videos of the victims. They're not going to show those on TV, are they? They're not going to show Lily, are they?'

Bosch closed his eyes and pressed the phone hard against his ear.

'No, ma'am, that won't happen. The photos are evidence and they won't be released. There may come a time when they will be used in the trial. But if that happens, the prosecutor assigned to the case will discuss it with you. Or I will. You will be kept informed about everything involved in the prosecution. I'm sure of that.'

'Okay, Detective. Thank you. I never thought this day would come, you know.'

'Yes, ma'am, I know it's been a long time.'

'Do you have children, Detective?'

'I have a daughter.'

'Keep her close.'

'Yes, ma'am. I will. I'll get back to you soon.'

383

Bosch hung up the phone.

'How'd that go?'

Bosch swiveled in his seat. Chu had come back into the cubicle without his noticing.

'About how they all go,' he said. 'Just two more victims . . .'

'Yeah. Where are they?'

'Dayton. What's happening with the others?'

'Everybody's about to head out. I think they've seen enough for one day. It's truly horrible stuff.'

Bosch nodded. He checked the clock on the wall again. It had been a long day, almost twelve hours for him. Chu was talking about the other detective teams that were assigned to the investigation and had been sifting through videos of torture and murder for the past six hours.

'I was going to head out with them, Harry, if that's okay.'

'Sure. I gotta go home, too.'

'I think we're in good shape for tomorrow, don't you?'

They had a 9 A.M. appointment at the District Attorney's Office to present their case and seek murder charges against Hardy in the Lily Price case. Bosch turned sideways to his desk and put his hand on the thick pocket file that contained the reports they would give to the DA. The package.

'Yeah,' Bosch said. 'I think we're set.'

'Okay, then, I'm out of here. I'll see you in the A.M. We meet here and walk over?'

'Yeah.'

Chu was a backpack guy. He swung his bag over his shoulder and headed out of the cubicle.

'Hey, David,' Bosch said. 'Before you go ...'

Chu turned back and leaned on one of the cubicle's four-foot walls.

'Yeah?'

'I just wanted to say you did good today. We did good as partners.'

Chu nodded.

'Thanks, Harry.'

'So never mind all that stuff from before, okay? We'll just start from here.'

'I told you I'd make it up.'

'Yeah, so go home ... and I'll see you tomorrow.'

'See ya, Harry.'

Chu went off, a happy man. Bosch saw there had been a moment of expectancy in his face. Maybe a makeup beer or a bite of food would have solidified the partnership further, but Harry needed to get home. He needed to do exactly what Mrs Price had told him to do.

The new PAB cost nearly half a billion dollars and had half a million square feet of space in its ten floors of limestone and glass, but it didn't have a snack bar, and parking was available for only a privileged few of high rank. As a detective three Bosch barely made the grade, but taking advantage of parking in the PAB's sub-terranean garage was a costly perk. A fee would've been deducted from his paycheck each month. He opted out because he could still park for free in the old 'erector set,' the rusting steel parking structure located three blocks away and behind the old police headquarters, Parker Center.

He didn't mind the three-block walk to and from

work. It was right through the heart of the civic center and a good length for prepping for the day ahead or decompressing after it.

Bosch was on Main Street, crossing behind City Hall, when he noticed the black Town Car cruise quietly up in the bus lane and stop at the curb twenty feet in front of him.

Even as he saw the rear window glide down, he acted like he had not noticed and kept walking, his eyes on the sidewalk in front of him.

'Detective Bosch.'

Bosch turned to see Irvin Irving's face framed in the open rear window of the Lincoln.

'I don't think we have anything to say to each other, Councilman.'

He kept walking and soon enough the Town Car pulled forward and started moving next to him, matching his speed. Bosch might not have wanted to talk to Irving but Irving certainly wanted to talk to him.

'You think you're bulletproof, Bosch?'

Bosch waved him off.

'You think this big case you just scored makes you bulletproof? You're not bulletproof. Nobody is.'

Bosch had had enough. He suddenly veered toward the car. Irving pulled back from the window as Bosch put his hands on the sill and leaned in. The car came to a slow stop. Irving was alone in the backseat.

'I had nothing to do with that story in the paper yesterday, okay? I don't think I'm bulletproof. I don't think I'm anything. I was doing my job, that's all.'

'You blew it, that's what you did.'

'I didn't blow anything. I told you I had nothing to do

with it. You have a problem, go talk to the chief.'

'I'm not talking about a newspaper article. I don't give a good goddamn about the *L.A. Times*. Fuck them. I'm talking about you. You blew it, Bosch. I counted on you and you blew it.'

Bosch nodded and dropped down to his haunches, still holding on to the car's windowsill.

'Actually, I got the case right and you and I both know it. Your son jumped, and more than anybody, you know why. The only mystery left is why you asked for me. You know my history. I don't lie down on cases.'

'You fool. I wanted you for exactly that reason. Because I knew that if they got even the slimmest chance, they would turn this into a play on me, and I thought you would have enough integrity to stand up against it. I didn't realize you had your nose so far up your former partner's ass that you couldn't see the setup she was running.'

Bosch laughed and shook his head as he stood up.

'You're good, Councilman. The right outrage, judicious use of off-color language, the planting of seeds of distrust and paranoia. You might be able to convince somebody with all of that. But not me. Your son jumped and that's all there is to it. I feel bad for you and his wife. But the one I feel most sorry for is his son. He didn't deserve this.'

Bosch stared down at Irving and watched the old man attempt to modulate his rage.

'I have something here for you, Bosch.'

He turned away to reach across the seat and Bosch had a fleeting thought of Irving turning back and pointing a gun at him. He thought Irving's ego and arrogance were such that he could actually bring himself to do it and believe he could get away with it.

But when Irving turned back, he proffered a piece of paper through the window.

'What is it?' Bosch asked.

'It's the truth,' Irving said. 'Take it.'

Bosch snapped the document out of his hand and looked at it. It was a photocopy of a phone message form dated May 24 and addressed at the top to someone named Tony. There was a return number with a 323 area code and a handwritten message that read, *Gloria Waldron complained that she got into a B&W cab at Musso-Frank last night and driver was obviously drunk. She had him pull over so she could get out. Could smell alcohol in the cab, etc. Please call for follow up.*

Bosch looked from the photocopy back to Irving.

'What am I supposed to do with this? You could've written it up this morning.

'I could have but I didn't.'

'So what happens if I call this number? This Gloria Waldron swears to me she called in this complaint and then you happened to mention it to Bobby Mason at Chad Irving's party? It doesn't wash, Councilman.'

'I know it doesn't. It's a dead line. Now. My community outreach officer Tony Esperante remembers calling her and getting the details. And I passed them on to Mason. But the line is disconnected now and look at the date, Detective.'

'I did. May twenty-fourth. What's it mean?'

'May twenty-fourth was a Tuesday. She said she got into the cab at Musso's the night before.'

Bosch nodded.

'Musso's is closed Mondays,' he said. 'The call – if there was a call – was bogus.'

'That's right.'

'Are you trying to tell me you were set up, Councilman? By your own son? That you innocently passed information on to Mason without knowing you were doing your son's bidding?'

'Not by my son, but by someone.'

Bosch held up the photocopy.

'And this, this is your proof?'

'I don't need proof. I know. Now you do, too. I was used by someone I trusted. I admit that. But so were you. Up there on the tenth floor. You gave them the means to take the shot at me. They used you to get to me.'

'Well, that's an opinion.'

'No, it's the truth. And someday you'll know it. You watch, they'll come to you at some point and you'll see it. You'll know.'

Bosch handed the photocopy back but Irving didn't take it.

'You keep it. You're the detective.'

Irving turned and said something to his driver and the Town Car started to pull away from the curb. Bosch watched the smoked window glide up into place as the car moved back into the traffic lane. He stood there for a long moment, considering what had been said. He folded the photocopy and put it in his pocket.

40

It was almost 11:30 by the time Bosch and Chu got to the Buena Vista apartments on Tuesday morning. Bosch had called ahead and talked to Hannah Stone. She told him Clayton Pell was scheduled to report to work at the market at noon but she agreed to hold him at the facility until the detectives arrived.

At the front gate they were buzzed through without delay. Stone came to greet them in the entranceway. It was awkward because Bosch was with his partner and it was all business. He extended his hand and they shook. Chu did the same.

'Okay, we have you set up in one of the interview rooms, if that's all right.'

'That's perfect,' Bosch said.

He had talked to her on the phone for more than an hour the evening before. It was late, after his daughter had gone to bed. Bosch had been too keyed up from the day's events to sleep. He had called Hannah and sat on the deck with the phone until close to midnight. They talked about many things but mostly the Hardy case. She was now more informed than anyone who had watched the news or read the *Los Angeles Times*.

Stone led Bosch and Chu into a small room with two stuffed chairs and a couch.

'I'll go get him,' she said. 'Should I sit in again?'

Bosch nodded.

'If it will make him more comfortable and get him to sign the document.'

'I'll ask him.'

She left them there and Chu looked at Bosch with raised eyebrows.

'When I interviewed him last week, he would only talk to me if she was in the room,' Bosch said. 'He trusts her. He doesn't trust cops.'

'Got it. And by the way, Harry, I think she digs you.'

'What are you talking about?'

'The way she was looking at you with that smile. I'm just saying. I think it's there if you want it.'

Bosch nodded.

'I'll keep it in mind.'

Bosch sat down on the couch and Chu took one of the chairs. They said nothing else as they waited. They had spent two hours that morning delivering the charging package to a filing deputy in the DA's Office. His name was Oscar Benitez and Bosch had taken cases to him before. He was a good, smart and cautious deputy assigned to major crimes. His job was to make sure the police had a case before filing charges against a suspect. He wasn't a pushover and that was one of the things Bosch liked about him.

Their package had been received well by Benitez. He just wanted a few things cleaned up or formalized. One of them was Clayton Pell's contribution to the prosecution of Chilton Hardy. Bosch and Chu were here to make sure that this part of the case was on solid ground. When Benitez was told of Pell's pedigree, he became concerned about his role as a key witness and whether he might try to work the prosecution for some sort of payoff, or might work the other side and be willing to change his story. Benitez made a strategic decision to put Pell on paper, meaning they should get him to sign a statement. This was rarely done because a statement not only locks the details of a story into place but also must be turned over to the defense in discovery.

A few minutes later Stone came in with Clayton Pell. Bosch pointed him to the remaining chair.

'Clayton, how are you? Why don't you sit there? You remember my partner, Detective Chu.'

Chu and Pell exchanged nods. Bosch looked at Stone as if to ask if she was staying or leaving.

'Clayton would like me to sit in again,' she said.

'That's fine. We can share the couch.'

Once everyone was seated Bosch opened his briefcase on his lap and started talking as he removed a file.

'Clayton, have you been watching the news since last night?'

'Sure have. Looks like you got your man.'

He folded his legs up under himself. He was so small he looked like a child seated in the big stuffed chair.

'Yesterday we arrested Chilton Hardy for the murder I spoke to you about last week.'

'Yeah, that's cool. Did you arrest him for what he did to me?'

Bosch was anticipating that Pell would ask him exactly that question.

'Well, we are hoping to bring a number of charges against him. That's why we're here, Clayton. We need your help.'

'And like I said last week, what do I get out of it?'

'Well, just like I said last week, you get to help us put this man away for good. Your tormentor. You may even get to face him in court if the DA needs you as a witness against him.'

Bosch opened the file on his briefcase.

'My partner and I spent the morning at the DA's Office presenting our case against Hardy in the murder of Lily Price. We have a good, solid case and it's only going to get better as the investigation continues. The DA plans to file a murder charge before the end of the day. We told him about your role and how it was actually your blood found on the victim and—'

'*What role?*' Pell shrieked. 'I told you I wasn't even there and now you're telling the DA I had a role in it?'

Bosch dropped the file on his briefcase and held both hands up in a calming gesture.

'Hold on, Clayton, that's not what we did at all. That was a poor choice of words but you have to let me finish. What we did was walk him through the case. What we knew, what the evidence is and how we see it all hanging together, all right? We told him your blood was on the victim but you weren't even there. And not only that but you were just a kid at the time and there's no way you were involved. So he gets all of that, okay? He knows you were a victim of this guy as well.'

Pell didn't respond. He turned sideways on the chair as he had done the week before.

'Clayton,' Stone said. 'Please pay attention. This is important.'

'I gotta go to work.'

'You won't be late if you listen and don't interrupt.

393

This is very important. Not only for this case but for you, too. Please turn around and listen.'

Pell reluctantly turned back in his seat so that he was facing Bosch.

'Okay, okay, I'm listening.'

'All right, Clayton, I'll give it to you straight. There is only one crime that doesn't have a statute of limitations on it. Do you know what that means?'

'It means they can't charge you after a certain amount of time's gone by. Like for sex crimes it's usually three years.'

Bosch realized that Pell had more than a passing familiarity with the statute of limitations. While he was in prison he probably gained an understanding of the California statute because of his own crimes. It was a grim reminder that the petulant little man who sat across from him was a dangerous predator and predators always knew the lay of the land they walked.

The statute of limitations for most sex crimes was three years. But Pell was wrong. There were various exceptions to the statute on the basis of the type of crime committed and the age of the victim. The DA's Office would need to render an opinion as to whether Hardy could be prosecuted for the crimes against Pell. Bosch thought that it was probably too late. Pell had been telling this story to prison evaluators for years but nobody ever bothered to push for an investigation. Bosch was sure Hardy's run as a predator was over and he would pay for at least some of his crimes. But he would likely never pay for what he did to Clayton Pell.

'That's generally right,' Bosch said. 'It's usually three years. So then you probably know the answer to your own question. I don't think Hardy will ever be prosecuted for what he did to you, Clayton. But that doesn't matter because you can play an instrumental part in his prosecution for murder. We told the DA that it's your blood on Lily Price and you will be able to tell a jury how it got there. You will be able to testify about what he did to you – the sexual *and* physical abuse. You will provide what is called bridge testimony, Clayton. You will help us build a bridge from the DNA found on that girl to Chilton Hardy's doorstep.'

Bosch picked up the document again.

'One of the things the DA needs right now is a signed statement from you that sets forth the facts of your relationship with Hardy. This morning my partner and I wrote this up based on my notes from last week. I want you to read it, and if it is accurate, then sign it and you will be helping make sure Hardy spends the rest of his life on death row.'

Bosch offered him the document but Pell waved it away.

'Why don't you just read it to me out loud?'

Bosch realized that Pell probably couldn't read. There was no indication in his record that he had ever attended school with any regularity and he certainly wasn't encouraged to read or educate himself at home.

Bosch proceeded to read the one-and-a-half-page document. It purposely followed the adage that less is more. It briefly outlined Pell's acknowledgment that he lived in Hardy's home at the time of the Lily Price murder and was abused during the period both sexually and physically. It described the physical abuse in regard to the use of Hardy's belt and stated that Pell often sustained beatings that led to his bleeding from wounds on his back.

The statement also described Pell's recent identification of Hardy in a photographic lineup as well as his accurate recognition of the home he lived in with Hardy in the late 1980s.

'The undersigned agrees with these facts and believes them to be a true and accurate accounting of his involvement with Chilton Aaron Hardy Junior in nineteen eighty-nine,' Bosch read. 'And that's it.'

He looked at Pell, who was nodding his head as if in agreement.

'Is that good?' Bosch prompted.

'Yeah, it's good,' Pell said. 'But it mentions that Chill took a picture of me copping his joint.'

'Well, not in those words, but—'

'Does that part need to be in there?'

'I think it does, Clayton. Because we found the photo you told us Hardy took. We found the shoebox. So we want it in your statement because the photo corroborates what you say.'

'I don't know what that means.'

'You mean "corroborate"? It means like it confirms your story. It verifies it. You say this is what the guy made you do and then here's the picture that proves it.'

'So people are going to see the picture?'

'Very few people. It will not be released to the media. It's just an element that helps build the case.'

'Besides that,' Stone interjected, 'there is nothing to be ashamed about, Clay. You were a child. He was an adult. You were under his command and control. He victimized you and there was nothing you could do about it.'

Pell nodded, more to himself than Stone.

'Are you willing to sign the statement?' Bosch asked. It was put-up or shut-up time.

'I'll sign it but what happens next?'

'We take it back to the DA and it goes in the file and is backup on the charges he'll file this afternoon.'

'No, I mean to him. To Chill. What happens next with him?'

Bosch nodded. Now he understood.

'He's being held right now without bail in the Metropolitan Detention Center. If the DA's Office files the charges today, he'll be arraigned tomorrow morning in superior court. He'll probably get a bail hearing, too.'

'They're *giving* him bail?'

'No, I didn't say that. He's entitled to a bail hearing. Everybody is. But you don't have to worry, this guy's not going anywhere. Hardy will never breathe free air again.'

'Could I go to that and talk to the judge?'

Bosch looked at Pell. He immediately understood the request but was surprised by it, anyway.

'Uh, I don't think that would be smart, Clayton. You being a potential witness. I'll check with the DA's Office if you want but I think they'll say no. I think they want to hold you back and spring you at the trial. Not have you sitting in court, especially when Hardy is there.'

'All right. I just thought I'd ask, is all.'

'Sure.'

Bosch motioned with the witness statement toward his briefcase.

'You want to sign it on top of this? Might be the best way to do it. Only flat surface we've got.'

'Yeah.'

The small man hopped out of his chair and came over to Bosch. Harry reached in his pocket for a pen and handed it to him. He bent down, his face very close to Bosch's and poised with the pen over the document. When he spoke, Bosch could feel his hot breath on his face.

'You know what should be done to this guy, don't you?'

'Who? Hardy?'

'Yeah, Hardy.'

'What should be done?'

'They should hang him by his balls for what he did to that girl and to me and all the others. I saw the TV last night. I know what he's done. They should bury him ass up and ten feet deep. Instead they'll put him on *Sixty Minutes* and make him a star.'

Bosch shook his head once. Pell was making some big leaps.

'I'm not so sure what you mean about making him a star but my guess is that they'll go for the death penalty and they'll get it.'

Pell laughed derisively.

'That's a fucking joke. If you're going to have the death penalty, then you've got to use it. Not dance around it for twenty years.'

This time Bosch nodded in agreement but said nothing further. Pell scratched his name on the document and proffered the pen toward Bosch. When Harry took it, Pell held on to it. They looked at each other for a moment.

'You don't like it any more than I do,' Pell whispered. 'Do you, Detective Bosch?'

Pell finally released the pen and Bosch put it into one of his inside coat pockets.

'No,' he said. 'I don't.'

Pell backed away then and they were finished.

Five minutes later Bosch and Chu were heading out through the iron gate when Bosch suddenly stopped. Chu turned and looked back at him and Bosch tossed him the keys to the car.

'Get it started,' he said. 'I forgot my pen.'

Bosch went back to Hannah Stone's office. She seemed to be expecting him. She was standing in the reception area, waiting.

'Come on back, Detective.'

They went back into the interview room and she closed the door. When she turned around, the first thing she did was kiss him. Bosch got embarrassed.

'What?' she asked.

'I don't know,' he said. 'I don't think we should be mixing things like this.'

'Okay, I'm sorry. But you did come back – just like I guessed you would.'

'Yeah, well . . .'

He smiled at being caught in the inconsistency.

'Look, how about tomorrow night?' he asked. 'After Hardy's arraigned. It sounds odd to say I want to celebrate but it's like, when you put another one down . . . it feels good, you know?'

'I think so. And I'll see you tomorrow night.'

Bosch left her then. Chu had pulled the car up directly out front and Harry jumped into the passenger seat.

'So,' Chu said. 'Did you get her number?'

'Just drive,' Bosch said.

41

On Wednesday morning Bosch and Chu decided they would go to court to witness the first step of the judicial process involving Chilton Hardy. Though they were not needed for the proceedings involving Hardy's first appearance on the murder charge, Bosch and his partner wanted to be there. It was rare in homicide work that an investigator brought to ground one of the true monsters in the world, and Hardy was one of them. They wanted to see him shackled and displayed, brought before the People.

Bosch had checked with the MDC and knew that Hardy was on the bus that transported white inmates. It was the second bus scheduled for departure. This would put off his appearance in court until at least ten. It gave Harry time to drink a coffee and glance at the stories the investigation had generated in the morning papers.

The phones in the cubicle kept ringing unanswered as journalists and producers left a series of messages seeking comment or inside access to the ongoing investigation. Bosch decided to get away from the noise and head over to the courthouse. As he and Chu stood and put their jackets on – without conferring they had both come dressed in their A suits – Harry could feel the eyes of the squad room on them. He went over to Tim Marcia's desk and told him where they were going. He said that they would be back directly after Hardy's appearance unless the prosecutor assigned to the case wanted to talk to them.

'Who got the case?' Marcia asked.

'Maggie McPherson,' Bosch said.

'Maggie McFierce? I thought she was up in the Valley.'

'She was. But now she's in major crimes. It's a good break for us.'

Marcia agreed.

They took the elevator down and there were reporters waiting outside the PAB. A few of them recognized Bosch and that started the stampede. Bosch brushed them off with no comment and he and Chu headed to the sidewalk. They crossed First and Bosch pointed to the monolithic Times Building.

'Tell your girlfriend she did a good job with the story in today's paper.'

'I told you, she's not my girlfriend,' Chu protested. 'I made a mistake with her and it's been corrected. I didn't read the story but whatever she got, she got without my help.'

Bosch nodded and decided he would finally let up on Chu about it. It was behind them now.

'So how's your girlfriend?' Chu asked, jabbing back at Bosch.

'My girlfriend? Uh, as soon as I meet her I'll ask how she's doing and let you know.'

'Come on, Harry. You gotta go for that. I saw the look, man.'

'Didn't you just fall in and out of the shit by allowing a work relationship to become something more than a work relationship?'

'Your situation is something totally different.'

Bosch's cell buzzed and he pulled it and looked at the screen. Speak of the devil, it was Hannah Stone. Bosch pointed to the phone as he answered it so Chu would know not to say anything in background.

'Dr Stone?'

'I guess that means you're not alone.'

There was stress in her voice.

'No, but what's up?'

'Um, I don't know if it means anything but Clayton Pell didn't come back to the facility last night, and it turns out that he didn't go to work when he left here after signing the statement for you.'

Bosch stopped on the sidewalk and took a moment to compute this.

'And he's still not back?'

'No, I just found out when I came in.'

'Did you call his work?'

'Yes, I talked to his boss. He said Clayton called in sick yesterday and never showed. But he left here right after you left. He said he was going to work.'

'Okay, what about his PO? Was he informed last night?'

'Not last night. I just called him before calling you. He said he hadn't heard anything but would do some checking. Then I called you.'

'Why did you wait until this morning? He's gone almost twenty-four hours now.'

'I told you; I just found out. Remember, this is a voluntary program. We have rules and everyone must abide by them when they're here, but when someone takes off like that, there's really very little you can do about it. You wait and see if they come back and you inform Probation and Parole that he's left the program. But because of what happened this week and him being a witness in the case, I thought you should know.'

'Okay, I get it. So any idea where he would have gone? Does he have friends or family around?'

'No, he's got nobody.'

'Okay, I'll make some calls. Let me know if you hear anything.'

Bosch closed the phone and looked at Chu. An uneasy feeling was rising in his chest. He thought he might know where Pell was.

'Clayton Pell is in the wind. He apparently took off right after we talked to him yesterday.'

'He's probably . . .'

But Chu didn't finish because he didn't have a good answer.

Bosch thought he did. He called the communications center and asked an operator to run the name Clayton Pell through the computer to see if he'd had any recent interaction with the justice system.

'Okay,' the operator said. 'We have a Clayton Pell arrested yesterday on a two-forty-three felony class.'

Bosch didn't need a translation on California Penal Code 243. Every cop knew it. Battery on a peace officer.

'What agency?' he asked.

'It was us. But I don't have the details other than that he was taken into custody at the PAB.'

Bosch had been out of the PAB for most of Tuesday running down the final details for the prosecutor, but when he'd gotten back at the end of the day he'd heard some squad room chatter about a cop having been attacked in the plaza right out front. It was completely unprovoked. The cop suffered a broken nose when the attacker stopped him to ask a question and then inexplicably head-butted him in the face. But the attacker was dismissed in the banter as a crazy and his name was never mentioned.

Bosch now knew what had happened. Pell had made his way downtown and to the PAB with the purpose of getting arrested. This would ensure that he would be booked into the nearby Metropolitan Detention Center, where he knew Hardy was being held. Anyone arrested in downtown by the LAPD would be booked into the MDC, as opposed to any of the other city and county jails that served as regional booking locations.

Bosch disconnected the call, then went to the recent call list on his phone and picked the number of the MDC watch office. It was the number he had called earlier to check on Hardy's schedule.

'What is it, Harry?' Chu asked.

'Trouble,' Bosch said.

His call was answered.

'Metro Detention, Sergeant Carlyle, can I put you on—'

'No, don't put me on hold. This is Bosch, LAPD, we spoke a little while ago.'

'Bosch, we're kind of busy at the moment. I need—'

'Listen, I think there is going to be an attempt on Chilton Hardy's life. The guy I called about.'

'He's already gone, Bosch.'

'What do you mean "gone"?'

'We put him on the sheriff's bus. He's headed to the courthouse for arraignment.'

'Who else is on the bus? Can you check a name? Clayton Pell. That's Paul-Edward-Lincoln-Lincoln.'

'Hold on.'

Bosch looked at Chu and was about to update him when the watch sergeant came back on the line, unmistakable urgency in his voice.

'Pell is on the bus with Hardy. Who is this guy, and why weren't we informed that these two had an issue?'

'We can talk about all of that later. Where's the bus?'

'How would we know? It just left.'

'Do you know the route? Which way does it go?'

'Uh ... I think it's San Pedro to First and then up to Spring. The garage is on the south side of the courthouse.'

'Okay, get on the phone to the sheriff's office, tell them what they've got and stop the bus. Keep Pell away from Hardy.'

'If it's not too late.'

Bosch disconnected without reply. He turned and started back toward the PAB.

'Harry, what's happening?' Chu called out as he followed.

'Pell and Hardy are on the jail bus. We have to stop it.'

Bosch pulled his badge off his belt and held it up as he stepped into the intersection of Spring and First. He raised his hands to stop traffic and moved diagonally across the intersection. Chu followed.

Once they were safely across, Bosch ran to a row of three black-and-whites parked in front of the PAB plaza. A uniformed cop was leaning against the front fender of the first car and busy looking at his phone. Bosch slapped his hand on the roof as he ran up. He was still holding his badge out.

'Hey! Need your car. We've got an emergency.'

Bosch opened the front passenger door and jumped in. Chu got in the back.

The uniform jumped off the fender but didn't go toward the driver's side door.

'Can't, man, we're waiting on the chief. He's got a homeowner's mee—'

'Fuck the chief,' Bosch said.

He saw that the officer had left the keys in the ignition and the car running. He raised his legs out of the foot well and slid into the driver's seat, moving around the shotgun rack and the mobile computer terminal.

'Hey, wait a minute!' the cop yelled.

Bosch dropped the car into drive and bolted away from the curb. He reached up to hit the siren and lights and then sped down First. He went three blocks in ten seconds and then took a wide left turn onto San Pedro, keeping as much speed as he could hold on the curve.

'There!' Chu yelled.

A sheriff's bus was lumbering down the street and coming toward them. Bosch realized the driver hadn't gotten the message relayed from Carlyle at MDC. He pinned the accelerator and moved on a direct line toward the bus.

'Harry?' Chu called out from the back. 'What are you doing? That's a bus!'

At the last moment, Bosch hit the brakes and yanked the wheel left, bringing the car into a sideways skid and stopping it in the direct path of the bus. The bus lurched into a skid as well and came to a stop four feet from Chu's door.

Bosch jumped out and moved toward the front door of the bus, holding his badge high. He hammered the heel of his palm hard on the steel door.

'LAPD! Open up. This is an emergency.'

The door was cranked open and Bosch was looking at the business end of a shotgun held by a uniformed sheriff's deputy. Behind him, the driver – also a uniformed deputy – held his sidearm aimed at Bosch as well.

'Let's see some ID to go with that badge.'

'Call your dispatch. MDC put through a stop order.'

He threw his ID case up to the driver.

'You got a guy on there who's going to try to take out another.'

Bosch had no sooner said it than he heard sounds of a commotion erupt from the back of the bus, followed by shouts of encouragement.

'Do it! Do it! Kill that motherfucker!'

Both deputies turned back to look but froze.

'Let me on!' Bosch yelled.

The driver finally yelled, *'Go! Go! Get in there!'*

He slapped his hand down on a red button that unlocked the cage door leading to the rear of the bus. The deputy with the shotgun went through and Bosch ran up the steps into the bus to follow.

'Get backup!' he yelled as he passed the driver and followed the other deputy into the back.

Almost immediately the deputy went down as he was tripped somehow by a prisoner able to extend his shackled feet into the aisle. Bosch didn't stop. He jumped over the deputy's back and moved farther toward the rear of the bus. The attention of every prisoner on the bus was directed to the rear right side, where Bosch saw Clayton Pell standing and leaning over the seat in front of him. He had wrapped a chain around Chilton Hardy's neck and was strangling him from behind. Hardy's face was purple and his eyes bugged. He could do nothing to defend himself because his wrists were shackled at his waist.

'Pell!' Bosch yelled. 'Let him go!'

His shout was lost in the chorus of men shouting for Pell to do the opposite. Bosch took two more steps and launched his body into Pell, knocking him back from Hardy but not away. Bosch realized that Pell was cuffed to the chain that was around Hardy's neck. It was the chain that was supposed to be around Pell's waist.

Bosch moved his hands toward the chain, shouting at Pell to let it go. The deputy soon recovered but couldn't take his hands off the shotgun to help. Chu moved past him and tried to grab the chain pulled tightly against Hardy's throat.

'No, pull his hand,' Bosch yelled.

Chu worked one of Pell's hands while Bosch worked the other and they soon overpowered the smaller man. Bosch pulled the chain off Hardy's neck and he collapsed forward, his face hitting the back of the seat in front of him before his body fell into the aisle at Chu's feet.

'Let him die!' Pell yelled. 'Let that fucker die!'

Bosch shoved Pell back into his seat and then leaned his whole weight on top of him.

'You stupid fool, Clayton,' Bosch said. 'You'll go back in for this.'

'I don't care. I got nothing outside, anyway.'

His body shuddered and he seemed to give up strength. He started moaning and crying, repeating, 'I want him dead, I want him dead.'

Bosch turned to look into the aisle. Chu and the deputy were tending to Hardy. He was either unconscious or dead and the deputy was checking his neck for a pulse. Chu had his head down and his ear turned toward Hardy's mouth.

'We need paramedics,' the deputy yelled to the driver. 'Fast! I'm not finding a pulse.'

'On the way,' the driver yelled back.

The report regarding the lack of a pulse brought cheering and renewed energy from the other prisoners on the bus. They shook their chains and stomped their feet on the floor. It was unclear to Bosch whether they knew who Hardy was or if it was simply blood lust that had them calling for murder.

Through it all Bosch heard coughing and looked down to see Hardy coming to. His face was still a deep shade of red and his eyes were glassy. But they focused for a moment on Bosch until the deputy's shoulder moved between them.

'Okay, we got him back,' the deputy reported. 'He's breathing.'

This report was greeted with a chorus of boos from the men on the bus. Pell let out a high-pitched keening sound. His whole body shook beneath Bosch. The sound seemed to sum up a lifetime of anguish and despair.

42

That night, Bosch stood on the back deck, looking down at the ribbon of lights on the freeway. He was still wearing his best suit, though the left shoulder had been scuffed with dirt during the struggle with Pell on the bus. He wanted a drink but wasn't drinking. He'd left the sliding door open so he could hear the music. He'd gone back to the music he always went to in the solemn moments. Frank Morgan on the tenor sax. Nothing better to sculpt the mood.

He had canceled his date with Hannah Stone. The events of the day eliminated any desire to celebrate, any desire to even talk.

Chilton Hardy had survived the attack on the sheriff's bus largely unscathed. He was transported to the jail ward at County-USC Medical Center and would remain there until doctors discharged him. His arraignment would be postponed until then.

Clayton Pell was rearrested and additional charges stemming from the attack were added. A parole violation was also added and it was clear that Pell was heading back to prison.

Normally, Bosch would be pleased to learn that a serial sex offender was going back into lockup. But he couldn't help but be wistful about Pell's situation and to feel somewhat responsible. And guilty.

Guilty about intervening.

When Bosch had put it all together while standing on First Street, he could have let things run their course, and the world would now be rid of a monster, a man as depraved as any Bosch had ever encountered. But Bosch had intervened. He had acted to save the monster and now his thoughts were clouded with regret. Hardy deserved death but would likely never get it, or would get it only when it was so far distant in time from his crimes as to be almost meaningless. Until then he would hold forth in court and in prison and would enter the halls of the criminal zeitgeist, where men like him were talked about, written about and in some dark corners even revered.

Bosch could have stopped all of that but didn't. Adhering to a code of *everybody counts or nobody counts* hardly seemed to cover it. Or excuse it. He knew he would carry the guilt for his actions of the day for a long time.

Bosch had spent most of the day writing reports and being interviewed by fellow investigators about the events on the sheriff's bus. It was determined that Pell knew how to get to Hardy because he knew the system. He knew the methods and routines. He knew that whites were segregated and transported separately and that he had a good chance of getting on the bus with the man he wanted to kill. He knew that he would be shackled at the hands and feet and that his hands would be locked to a waist chain. He knew that he could slip that waist chain down over his small hips and beneath his feet and that it would become his murder weapon.

It had been a grand plan and Bosch had ruined it. The

incident was being investigated by the sheriff's department because it had taken place on their jail bus. The deputy who interviewed Bosch had asked him point blank why he had intervened. Bosch simply said he didn't know. He had acted on instinct and impulse, without thinking that the world would be a better place without Hardy in it.

As Bosch stared down at the unending river of metal and glass, Pell's anguish clawed at him. He had robbed Pell of his one chance at redemption, the moment when he would make up for all the damage inflicted on him and, to his way of thinking, the damage he had inflicted on others. Bosch didn't necessarily agree with it but he understood it. Everybody is looking for redemption. For something.

Bosch had snatched it all away from Pell and that was why he listened to Frank Morgan's mournful music and wanted to drown himself in drink. He felt sorry for the predator.

The doorbell sounded above the tone of the saxophone. Bosch went in but as he moved through the living room, his daughter bolted out from the bedroom hallway and beat him to the door. She put her hand on the knob and then her eye against the peephole before opening up, just as he had taught her. She paused and then pushed off the door, taking little robot steps backwards and right past Harry.

'It's Kiz,' she whispered.

She turned and went into the hallway so she would have cover.

'Okay, well, no need to panic,' Bosch said. 'I think we can handle Kiz.'

Bosch opened the door.

'Hello, Harry. How are you?'

'I'm good, Kiz. What brings you out?'

'Oh, I guess I was hoping to maybe sit out on the deck with you for a little bit.'

Bosch didn't respond at first. He just looked at her until the moment became embarrassingly long.

'Harry? Knock, knock. Anyone home?'

'Uh, yeah, sorry. I was just – uh, come on in.'

He opened the door wide and let her in. She knew her way to the deck.

'Um, I don't have anything alcoholic in the house. I've got water and some sodas.'

'Water's fine. I'm going back downtown after.'

As she passed by the bedroom hallway Maddie was still standing there.

'Hi, Kiz.'

'Oh, hey there, Maddie. How're you doing, girl?'

'I'm good.'

'Glad to hear it. You let me know if you ever need anything, okay?'

'Thank you.'

Bosch turned into the kitchen and grabbed two bottles of water out of the refrigerator. He was only a few seconds behind Rider but she was already at the rail, taking in the view and the sounds. He slid the door closed behind him so Maddie wouldn't hear whatever it was Kiz had come to say.

'Always amazes me how no matter where you go in this city, you can't get away from the traffic,' she said. 'Even up here.'

Bosch handed her a bottle.

'So if you're going back downtown and working tonight, this must be an official visit. Let me guess, I'm getting written up for stealing one of the chief's motorcade cars.'

Rider waved that away like it was a fly.

'That was nothing, Harry. But I am here to warn you.'

'About what?'

'It's starting. With Irving. This next month is going to be all-out war and there are going to be casualties. Just be ready.'

'It's me, Kiz. Be specific. What's Irving doing? Am I already a casualty?'

'No you're not, but for starters he's gone to the police commission and he wants them to review the whole Chilton Hardy case. From bust to bus. And they'll do it. Most of them have their seats because of his patronage. They'll do what he says.'

Bosch thought of his relationship with Hannah Stone and what Irving could do with it. And jumping the Hardy warrant. If Irving could get to that, he'd be holding press conferences every day till the election.

'Fine, let them come,' he said. 'I'm clean on it.'

'I hope so, Harry. But I'm not as worried about your part in the investigation as I am about the twenty years before that. When Hardy was running below the radar and there was *no* investigation. We're going to look very bad when all of that comes out.'

Now Bosch understood why she was there and had come in person. This was how high jingo worked. And this was what Irving had told him would happen.

Bosch knew that the more the Open-Unsolved squad documented the crimes and victims of Chilton Hardy, the greater the public outrage would be over his seeming freedom to act with impunity for more than twenty years. The guy was never concerned enough about the police even to move out of the area.

'So what do you want, Kiz? You want us to stop at Lily Price? Is that it? Tie it all up in one case and go for the death penalty? After all, we can only kill him once, right? Never mind the other victims, like Mandy Phillips with her photo hanging in Hardy's fucking dungeon. I guess she's one of the casualties you're talking about.'

'No, Harry, I don't want you to stop. We can't stop. First of all, the story's gone international. And we want justice for *all* of the victims. You know that.'

'Then what are you telling me, Kiz? What do you want?'

She paused, looking for a way to avoid saying it out loud.

But there was no way. Bosch waited.

'Just slow things down a bit,' she finally said.

Bosch nodded. He understood.

'The election. We slow things down until the election and hope Irving gets dumped. That's what you want?'

He knew that once she said it, their relationship would never be the same.

'Yes, it's what I want,' she said. 'It's what we all want for the good of the department.'

Those five words ... 'the good of the department.' They never added up to anything but high jingo. Bosch nodded and then turned and looked off at the view. He didn't want to look at Kiz Rider anymore.

'Come on, Harry,' Rider said. 'We have Irving on the ground. Don't give him what he needs to get back up and hurt us, to continue to damage the department.'

He leaned over the wood railing and looked directly down into the brush below the deck.

'It's funny,' he said. 'I think in all of this, Irvin Irving turns out to be the one who had things right, who was probably even telling the truth.'

'I don't know what you're talking about.'

'It didn't make sense to me: why would he press the case if he knew it could come back to his own complicity in a pay-for-play scam?'

'Harry, there's no need to go there. The case is closed.'

'The answer was that he pressed the case because he wasn't complicit. He was clean.'

He reached into his soiled suit coat and pulled out the folded photocopy of the phone message Irving had given him. He had been carrying it with him since then. Without looking at Rider, he handed it to her and waited as she unfolded the page and scanned it.

'What's this?' she said.

'It's Irving's proof of innocence.'

'It's a piece of paper, Harry. This could have been slapped together at any time. It's not proof of anything.'

'Except you and I and the chief, we all know it's real. It's true.'

'Speak for yourself. This is worthless.'

She refolded it and handed it back. Bosch put it back in his pocket.

'You used me, Kiz. To get to Irving. You used his son's death. You used the things I found out. All to get a bullshit story in the newspaper you hoped would knock him to the mat.'

She didn't respond for a long time and when she did,

it was just the company line. Not an acknowledgment of anything.

'Thirty days, Harry. Irving is a thorn in the department's side. If we can get rid of him, we can build a bigger and better department. And that makes it a safer and better city.'

Bosch stood up straight and cast his eyes back out at the view. The reds were turning purple. It was getting dark.

'Sure, why not?' he said. 'But if you have to become him to get rid of him, what's the difference?'

Rider banged her palms lightly on the railing, a signal that she had said enough and was finished with this conversation.

'I'm going to go, Harry. I have to get back.'

'Sure.'

'Thanks for the water.'

'Yeah.'

He heard her steps on the wood planking as she moved toward the sliding door.

'So was what you said to me the other day bullshit, Kiz?' he asked, his back still turned to her. 'Was that just part of the play?'

The steps stopped, but she didn't say anything.

'When I called you and told you about Hardy. You talked about the noble work we do. You said, "This is why we do this." Was that just a line, Kiz?'

It was a while before she spoke. Bosch knew she was looking at him and waiting for him to turn and look at her. But he couldn't do it.

'No,' she finally said. 'It wasn't just a line. It was the truth. And someday you may appreciate that I do what

I need to do so that you can do what you need to do.'

She waited for his response but he said nothing.

He heard the door slide open and then close. She was gone. Bosch looked out at the fading light and waited a moment before speaking.

'I don't think so,' he said.

Acknowledgments

This story was in part suggested by Robert McDonald. For that the author is very grateful.

Many others contributed to this work and they are also gratefully acknowledged. They include Asya Muchnick, Bill Massey, Michael Pietsch, Pamela Marshall, Dennis Wojciechowski, Jay Stein, Rick Jackson, Tim Marcia, John Houghton, Terrill Lee Lankford, Jane Davis, Heather Rizzo and Linda Connelly. Many thanks to all.

Twenty years later, Harry Bosch is still fighting for justice every day on the streets of LA. Discover how he has survived.

Read on for a special early extract from the new novel from
MICHAEL CONNELLY
THE BLACK BOX

Snow White, 1992

By the third night the death count was rising so high and so quickly that many of the divisional homicide teams were pulled off the front lines of riot control and put into emergency rotations in South-Central. Detective Harry Bosch and his partner Jerry Edgar were pulled from Hollywood Division and assigned to a roving B-watch team that also included two patrol gunners for protection. They were dispatched to any place they were needed – wherever a body turned up. The four-man team moved in a black and white patrol car, jumping from crime scene to crime scene and never staying still for long. It wasn't the proper way to carry out homicide work, not even close, but it was the best that could be done under the surreal circumstances of a city that had come apart at the seams.

South-Central was a war zone. Fires burned everywhere. Looters moved in packs from storefront to storefront, all semblance of dignity and moral code gone in the smoke that rose over the city. The gangs of south L.A. stepped up to control the darkness, even calling for a truce to their internecine battles to create a united front against the police.

More than fifty had died already. Store owners had shot looters, National Guardsmen had shot looters, looters had shot looters and then there were the others – killers who used the camouflage of chaos and civil unrest to settle long held scores that had nothing to do with the frustrations of the moment and the emotions displayed in the streets.

Two days before, the racial, social and economic fractures that ran under the city broke the surface with seismic intensity. The trial of four LAPD officers accused of excessively beating a black motorist at the end of a high-speed chase had resulted in the delivery of not-guilty verdicts across the board. The reading of the all-white jury's decision in a courtroom thirty miles away had an almost immediate impact on south Los Angeles. Small crowds of angry people gathered on street corners to decry the injustice. And things soon turned violent. The ever-vigilant media went high and live from the air, broadcasting the images into every home in the city, and then the world. The department was caught flat-footed. Most of the command staff were out of town at a leadership retreat. No one took charge and, more importantly, no one went to the rescue. The whole department retreated and the images of unchecked violence spread like wildfire in the media. Soon the city was out of control and in flames.

Two nights later the acrid smell of burning rubber and smouldering dreams was still everywhere. Flames from a thousand fires reflected like the devil dancing in the dark sky. Gunshots and shouts of anger echoed non-stop in the wake of the patrol car. But the four men in 6-adam-16 did not stop for any of these. They stopped only for murder.

It was Friday, May 1st. B Watch was the emergency mobilization designation for night watch, a 6 P.M. to 6 A.M. shift. Bosch and Edgar had the back seat while Officers Robleto and Delwyn had the front.

They were rolling to a dead body found in an alley off Crenshaw Boulevard. The call had been relayed to the emergency communications center by the National Guard, which had been deployed in the city during the state of emergency. It was only ten-thirty and the calls were stacking up. Adam-16 had already handled a homicide call since coming on shift – a looter shot dead in the doorway of a discount-shoe store. The shooter had been the store's owner.

That crime scene was contained within the premises of the business. That allowed Bosch and Edgar to work with relative safety, Robleto and Delwyn posted with shotguns and full riot gear on the sidewalk out front. And that also gave them time to collect evidence, sketch the crime scene and take their own photos. They recorded the statement of the store owner and watched the videotape from the business's surveillance camera. It showed the looter using an aluminum softball bat to smash through the glass door of the store. The man then ducked in through the jagged opening he had created and was promptly shot twice by the store owner, who was hiding behind the cash counter and waiting.

Because the coroner's office was overrun with more death calls than the office could handle, the body was removed from the store by paramedics and transported to County-USC Medical Center. It would be held there until things calmed down – if they ever did – and the coroner caught up to the work.

As far as the shooter went, Bosch and Edgar made no arrest. Self defense or murder while lying in wait, the DA's office would make the call later.

It was not the right way to do it but it would have to do. In the chaos of the moment the mission was simple: preserve evidence, document the scene as best and as fast as possible, and collect the dead.

Get in and get out. And do it safely. The real investigation would come later. Maybe.

As they drove south on Crenshaw they passed occasional crowds of people, mostly young men, gathered on corners, roving in packs. At Crenshaw and Slauson a group flying Crips colors jeered as the patrol car moved by at high speed without siren or flashing lights. Bottles and rocks were thrown but the car moved too fast and the missiles fell harmlessly in its wake.

"We'll be back, muthafuckers! Don't you worry."

It was Robleto who had called out and Bosch had to assume he was speaking metaphorically. The patrol car's windows were up. The young patrolman's threat was as hollow as the department's response had been once the verdicts were read on live TV, Wednesday afternoon.

Robleto, behind the wheel, only began to slow as they approached a blockade of National Guard vehicles and soldiers. The strategy drawn up the day before with the arrival of the Guard was to take back control of the major intersections in south L.A. and then spread containment from there. They were less than a mile from one of those key intersections, Crenshaw and Florence, and the Guard troops and vehicles were already spread up and down Crenshaw for blocks. Only as he pulled up to the barricade at 62nd Street did Robleto lower his window.

A guardsman with sergeant stripes came to the door. As he leaned in to look at the car's occupants, Bosch read the name on his uniform. Burstin.

"Homicide," Robleto said.

He hooked a thumb toward Bosch and Edgar in the back. Burstin made an arm motion so that a path could be cleared and they could be let through.

"Okay," he said. "She's in the alley on the east side between Sixty-sixth Place and Sixty-seventh Street. Go on through and my guys will show you. We'll form a tight perimeter and watch the rooflines. We've had unconfirmed reports of sniper fire in the neighborhood."

Robleto put the window back up as he drove through.

"'My guys,'" he said, mimicking Burstin's voice. "That guy's probably an accountant back in Modesto or some place. I heard that none of these guys they brought in are even from L.A. They couldn't find Liemert Park with a map."

"Two years ago, neither could you, dude," Delwyn said.

"Whatever. The guy doesn't know shit about this place and now he's all like take charge? Fucking weekend warrior. All I'm saying is we didn't need these guys. Makes us look bad. Like we couldn't handle it and had to bring in the pros from Modesto and Fresno and San Luis O-fucking-Bispo."

Edgar cleared his voice and spoke from the back seat.

"I got news for you," he said. "We *couldn't* handle it and we couldn't look any worse than we already did Wednesday night. We sat back and let the city burn, man. You see all that shit on TV? The thing you didn't see was any of us on the ground kicking ass. So don't be blaming the accountants from Modesto. It's on us."

"Whatever," Robleto said.

Bosch remained silent. Not that he disagreed with his partner. The department had embarrassed itself with its feeble response to the initial break-out of violence. But Harry wasn't thinking about that. He had been struck by what the sergeant had said about the victim being a she. It was the first mention of that and as far as Bosch knew, there hadn't been any female murder victims so far. This wasn't to say that women weren't involved in the violence that had raked across the city. Looting and burning were equal opportunity endeavors. Bosch had seen women engaged in both. The night before he'd been on riot control on Hollywood Boulevard and had witnessed the looting of Frederic's, the famous lingerie store. Half the looters had been women.

But the sergeant's report had given him pause nonetheless. A woman had been out here in the chaos and it had cost her her life.

Robleto drove through the opening in the barricade and

continued south. Four blocks ahead a soldier was waving a flashlight, swinging its beam toward an opening between two of the retail shops that lined the east side of the street.

Aside from soldiers posted every twenty-five yards, Crenshaw was abandoned. There was an eerie and dark stillness. All of the businesses on both sides of the street were dark. Several had been hit by looters and arsonists. Others had been miraculously left untouched. Still others had boarded up fronts that announced with spray paint that they were "Black Owned," a meager defense against the mob.

The alley opening was between a looted wheel and tire shop called Dream Rims and a completely burned out appliance store called Used, Not Abused. The burned building was wrapped with yellow tape and had been red-tagged as uninhabitable by city inspectors. Bosch guessed that this area had been hit early in the riots. They were only twenty blocks or so from the spot where the violence had initially touched off at the intersection of Florence and Normandy, the place where people were pulled from cars and trucks and beaten while the world watched from above.

The guardsman with the flashlight started walking ahead of 6-Adam-16, leading the car into the alley. Thirty feet in the guardsman stopped and held up his hand in a fist, as if they were on recon behind enemy lines. It was time to get out. Edgar hit Bosch on the arm with the back of his hand.

"Remember, Harry, keep your distance. A nice six-foot separation at all times."

It was a joke meant to lighten the situation. Of the four men in the car, only Bosch was white. He'd be the likely first target of a sniper. Any shooter for that matter.

"Got it," Bosch said.

He and Edgar had to wait until Robleto and Delwyn got out and opened the rear doors of the cruiser for them.

Bosch then finally stepped out into the night. He wanted to smoke a cigarette but time was of the essence, and he also knew he was down to a final smoke in the package he carried in his shirt pocket. He had to conserve it for he had no idea when or where he would get the chance to replenish.

Bosch looked around. He didn't see a body. The alley was clotted with debris, old and new. Old appliances, apparently not worthy of resale, had been stacked in places against the side wall of Used, Not Abused. Trash was everywhere and part of the roof eave had collapsed to the ground during the fire.

"Where is she?" he asked.

"Over here," the guardsman said. "Against the wall."

The alley was lit only by the patrol car's lights. The appliances and other debris threw shadows against the wall and the ground. Bosch put on his Maglite and aimed its beam in the direction the guardsman had pointed. The wall of the appliance shop was covered with gang graffiti. Names, RIPs, threats – the wall was a message board for the local Crips set, the Rolling 60s.

He walked three steps behind the guardsman and soon he saw her. A small woman lying on her side at the bottom of the wall. She had been obscured by the shadow cast by a rusting out washing machine.

Before approaching any further, Bosch played his light across the ground. At one point in time the alley was paved but now it was broken concrete, gravel and dirt. He saw no footprints or evidence of blood. He slowly moved forward and squatted down. He rested the heavy barrel of the long, steel flashlight on his shoulder as he moved its beam over the body. From his long experience at looking at dead people, he guessed she had been deceased at least twenty-four hours. The legs were bent sharply at the knees and he knew this could be the result of rigor mortis or an indication she had been on her knees in the moments before her death. The skin that was visible on the arms and neck was ashen and dark where blood had coagulated. Her hands were almost black and the odor of putrefaction was strong in the air.

The woman's face was largely obscured by the long blonde hair that had fallen across it. Dried blood was visible in the hair at the back of the head and was matted in the thick wave that obscured her face. Bosch moved the light up the wall above the body and saw a blood spatter and drip pattern that indicated she had been killed here, not just dumped.

Bosch took a pen out of his pocket and reached forward, using it to lift the hair back from the victim's face as he played the light on it. There was gunshot stippling around the right eye socket and a penetration wound that had exploded the eyeball. She had been shot from only inches away. Point-blank range. He put the pen back in his pocket and leaned in further, pointing the light down behind her head. The exit wound, large and jagged, was visible. Death had no doubt been instantaneous.

"Holy shit, is she white?"

It was Edgar. He had come up behind and was looking over Bosch's shoulder like an umpire hovering over a baseball catcher.

"Looks like it," Bosch said.

He moved the light over the victim's body now.

"What the hell's a white girl doing down here?"

Bosch didn't answer. He had noticed something hidden under the right arm. He put his light down so he could pull on a set of gloves.

"Put your light on her chest," he instructed Edgar.

Gloves on, Bosch leaned back in toward the body. The victim was on her left side, her right arm extending across her chest and hiding something that was on a cord around her neck. Bosch gently pulled it free.

It was a bright orange LAPD press pass. Bosch had seen many of them over the years. This one looked new. Its lamination sleeve still clear and unscratched. It had a mug-shot-style photo of a woman with blonde hair on it. Beneath it was her name and the media entity she worked for.

Anneke Hjejle
Berlingske Tidende

"She's foreign press," Bosch said. "First name Anneke. I can't pronounce the rest."

"From where?" Edgar asked.

"I don't know. Germany, maybe."

"Why would they send somebody all the way over from Germany for this? Can't they mind their own business over there?"

"I don't know for sure if she's from Germany. I can't tell."

Bosch tuned out Edgar's banter and studied the photograph on the press pass. The woman depicted was plain but attractive even in a mugshot. No smile, all business, her hair hooked behind her ears, her skin so pale as to almost be translucent.

Bosch turned the press pass over. It looked legit to him. He knew press passes were updated yearly and a validation sticker was needed for any member of the media to enter department news briefings or pass through media check-points at crime scenes. This pass had a 1992 sticker on it. It meant that the victim would have received it sometime in the last 120 days, but noting the pristine condition of the pass, Bosch believed it had been recent.

Harry went back to studying the body. The victim was wearing blue jeans and a vest over a white shirt. It was an equipment vest with bulging pockets. This told Bosch that it was likely that the woman had been a photographer. But there were no cameras on her body or nearby. They had

II

been taken, and possibly had even been the motive for the murder. Most news photographers he had seen carried multiple, high-quality cameras and related equipment.

Harry reached to the vest and opened one of the breast pockets. It held three black film canisters. He didn't know if this was film that had been shot or was unused. He re-buttoned the pocket and in doing so felt a hard surface beneath it. He knew rigor mortis comes and goes in a day, leaving the body soft and moveable. He pulled back the equipment vest and knocked a fist on the chest. It was a hard surface and the sound confirmed this. The victim was wearing a bulletproof vest.

"Hey, check out the hit list," Edgar said.

Bosch looked up from the body. Edgar's flashlight was now aimed at the wall above. The graffiti directly over the victim was a 187 count or hit list with the names of several bangers who had gone down in street battles. Ken Dog, G-Dog, OG Nasty, Neckbone and so on. The crime scene was in the Rolling 60s territory. The 60s were a subset of the massive Crips gang. They were at endless war with the nearby 7-Treys, another Crips subset. The general public was largely under the impression that the gang wars that gripped most of south L.A. and claimed victims every night of the week came down to a Bloods versus Crips battle for supremacy and control of the streets. But the reality was that the rivalries between subsets of the same gang were some of the most violent in the city and largely responsible for the weekly body counts. The Rolling 60s and 7-Treys were at the top of that list. Both Crips sets operated under kill on sight protocols and the score was routinely noted in the neighborhood graffiti. A RIP list was used to memorialize homies lost in the endless battle while a line-up of names under a 187 heading was a hit list, a record of kills.

"Looks like what we've got here is Snow White and the Seven-Trey Crips," Edgar added.

Bosch shook his head, annoyed. The city had come off its hinges and here in front of them was the result – a woman put up against a wall and executed – and his partner didn't seem to be able to take it seriously.

Edgar must have read Bosch's body language.

"It's just a joke, Harry," he said quickly. "Lighten up. We need some gallows humor around here."

"Okay," Bosch said. "I'll lighten up while you go get on the radio. Tell them what we've got here, make sure they know it's a member of the out-of-town media and see if they'll give us a full team. If not that, at least a photographer and some lights. Tell them we really could use some time and some help on this one."

"Why, cause she's white?"

Bosch took a moment before responding. It was a careless thing for Edgar to have said. He was hitting back because Bosch had not responded well to the Snow White quip.

"No, not because she's white," Bosch said evenly. "Because she's not a looter and because she's not a gangbanger and because they better believe that the media is going to jump all over a case involving one of their own. Okay? Is that good enough?"

"Got it."

"Good."

Edgar went back to the car to use the radio and Bosch went back to working the crime scene. The first thing he did was delineate the perimeter. He backed several of the guardsmen down the alley so he could create a zone that extended twenty feet on either side of the body. The third and fourth sides of the box were the wall of the appliance shop on one side and the wall of the rim store on the other.

As he marked it off, Bosch noted that the alley cut through a residential block that was directly behind the row of retail businesses that fronted Crenshaw. There was no uniformity in the containment of the backyards that lined the alley. Some of the homes had concrete walls while others had wood-slat or chain-link fences running the perimeter.

Bosch knew that in a perfect world he would search all those yards and knock on all those doors, but that would have to come later, if at all. His attention at the moment had to be focused on the immediate crime scene. If he got the chance to canvas the neighborhood he would consider himself lucky.

Bosch noticed that Robleto and Delwyn had taken positions with their shotguns at the mouth of the alley. They were standing next to each other and talking, probably sharing a complaint about something. Back in Bosch's Vietnam days that would have been called a sniper's two-for-one sale.

There were eight guardsmen posted inside the alley on the interior perimeter. Bosch noticed that a group of people were beginning to congregate and watch from the far end. He waved over the guardsman who had led them into the alley.

"What's your name, soldier?"

"People call me Drummer."

"Why?"

"I guess because my name's Drummond."

"Okay, Drummer, tell me who found her?"

"The body? That was Dowler. He came back here to take a leak and he found her. He said he could smell her first. He knew the smell."

"Where's Dowler now?"

"I think he's out at the southern barricade."

"I need to talk to him. Will you get him for me?"

"Yes, sir. I'll radio down there."

Drummond started to move toward the entrance of the alley.

"Hold on, Drummer, I'm not done."

Drummond turned around.

"When did you deploy to this location?"

"We've been here since eighteen hundred yesterday, sir."

"So you've had control of this area since then? This alley?"

"Not exactly, sir. We started at Crenshaw and Florence last night and we've worked east on Florence and north on Crenshaw. It's been block by block."

"So when did you get to this alley?"

"Maybe six hours ago. Maybe longer."

"And all the looting and burning in this immediate area, that was already over?"

"Yes, sir, happened first night from what I've been told."

"Okay, Drummer, one last thing. We need more light back here. Can you bring one of those trucks you have out there with all the lights on top back here?"

"It's called a Humvee, sir. We used them in Desert Storm."

"Yeah, well, bring one back here from that end of the alley. Come in past those people and point the lights right at my crime scene. You got it?"

"Got it, sir."

Bosch pointed to the end opposite the patrol car.

"Good. I want to create a cross-hatching of light here, okay? It's probably going to be the best we can do."

"Yes, sir."

He started to trot away.

"Hey, Drummer."

Drummond turned around once more and came back.

"Yes, sir."

Bosch whispered now.

"All your guys are watching me. Shouldn't they be turned around, eyes out?"

Drummond stepped back and twirled his finger over his

head.

"Hey! Turn it around, eyes out. We've got a job here. Keep the watch."

He pointed down the alley toward the gathering of on-lookers.

"And make sure we keep those people back."

The guardsmen did as they were told and Drummond headed out of the alley to radio Dowling and get the light truck.

Bosch's pager buzzed on his hip. He reached to his belt and snapped the device out of its holder. The number on the screen was the command post and he knew he and Edgar were about to be given another call. They hadn't even started here and they were going to be yanked. He didn't want that. He put the pager back on his belt.

Bosch walked over to the first fence that started off the back corner of the appliance shop. It was a wood-slat barrier that was too tall for him to look over. But he noticed it had been freshly painted. There was no graffiti, even on the alley side of it. He noted it because it indicated that there was a home owner on the other side who cared enough to whitewash the graffiti. Maybe it was the kind of person who kept their own watch and might have heard or even seen something.

From there he crossed the alley and dropped to a squatting position at the far corner of the crime scene. Like a fighter in his corner, waiting to come out. He started playing the beam of his flashlight across the broken concrete and dirt surface of the alley. At the oblique angle, the light refracted off the myriad surface planes, giving him a unique look. Soon enough he saw the glint of something shiny and held the beam on it. He moved in on the spot and found a brass bullet casing lying in the gravel.

He still had his gloves on. He picked up the casing and held the light on it. It was a 9mm copper jacket with the familiar Federal brand mark stamped into the cap. There was an indentation from the firing pin. This had been part of a bullet that had been fired. He held the open end up to his nose. He could smell the burnt gunpowder and imagined the shell had been fired recently but he knew there was no scientific proof in that. It was just instinct.

Bosch pulled a plastic baggy from his pocket and was bagging the shell when Edgar stepped back into the crime scene. He was carrying a toolbox and that told Bosch that they weren't going to get any help.

"Harry, what'd you find?"

Bosch held up the baggy.

"Nine millimeter Federal."

"Well, at least we found something useful."

"Maybe. You get the CP?"

Edgar put down the toolbox. It was heavy. It contained the equipment they had quickly gathered in the kit room at Hollywood Division once they heard they could not count on any forensic backup in the field.

"Yeah, I got through but it's no-can-do from the command post. Everybody's otherwise engaged. We're on our own out here, brother."

"No coroner, either?"

"No coroner. The National Guard's coming with a truck for her. A flatbed troop transporter."

"You gotta be kidding me."

"Not only that, we got our next call already. A crispy critter. Fire Department found him in a burned-out taco shop on MLK."

"Goddamnit, we just got here."

"Yeah, well, we're up again and we're closest to MLK. So they want us to clear and steer."

"Yeah, well, we're not done here. Not by a long shot."

"Nothing we can do about it, Harry."

Bosch was obstinate.

"I'm not leaving yet. There's too much to do here and if we leave it till next week or whenever, then we've lost the crime scene. We can't do that."

"We don't have a choice, partner. We don't make the rules."

"Bullshit."

"Okay, tell you what. We give it fifteen minutes. We take a few pictures, bag the body and then shuffle on down the road. Come Monday, or whenever this is over, it isn't even going to be our case anymore. We go back to Hollywood after everything calms down and this thing stays right here. Somebody else's case then. This is Seventy-seventh's turf. It'll be their problem then."

It didn't matter to Bosch what came later, whether the case went to detectives at 77th Street Division or not. What mattered was what was in front of him. A woman named Anneke from someplace far away lay dead in front of him and he wanted to know who did it and why.

"Doesn't matter that it's not going to be our case," he said. "That's not the point."

"Harry, there is no point," Edgar said. "Not now, not with complete chaos all around us. Nothing matters right now, man. The city is out of control. You can't expect —"

The sudden rip of automatic gunfire split the air. Edgar dove to the ground and Bosch instinctively threw himself toward the wall of the appliance shop. Bursts of gunfire from several of the guardsman followed until finally it was quelled by shouting.

"Hold your fire! Hold your fire! Hold your fire!"

The gunshots ended and Burstin, the sergeant from the barricade, came running up the alley. Bosch saw Edgar slowly getting up. He looked like he was unharmed but his partner was looking at Bosch with an odd expression.

"Who opened first?" the sergeant yelled. "Who fired?"

"Me," said one of the men in the alley. "I thought I saw

a weapon on the roofline."

"Cosgrove? Where? What roofline? Where was the sniper?"

"Over there."

The shooter pointed to the roofline of the rim store.

"Goddamnit!" the sergeant yelled. "Hold your fucking fire. We cleared that roof. There's nobody up there but us! Our people, Cosgrove!"

"Sorry, sir. I saw the —"

"I don't give a flying fuck what you saw. You get any of my people killed and I will personally frag your ass myself."

"Yes, sir. Sorry, sir."

Bosch stood up. His ears were ringing and his nerves jangling. The sudden spit of automatic fire wasn't new to him. But it had been almost twenty-five years since it was a routine part of his life.

Sergeant Burstin walked up to him.

"Continue your work, detectives. If you need me I'll be on the north perimeter. We have a truck coming in for the remains. I then understand that we are to provide a team to escort your car to another location and another body."

He then charged out of the alley.

"Jesus Christ, you believe that?" Edgar asked. "Like Vietnam or something. What the hell are we doing here, man?"

"Let's just go to work," Bosch said. "You draw the crime scene, I'll work the body, take pictures. Let's move."

Bosch squatted down and opened up the toolbox. Edgar kept talking. The adrenaline rush from the shooting was not dissipating. He talked a lot when he was hyper. Sometimes, too much.

"Harry, did you see what you did when that yahoo opened up with the gun?"

"Yeah, I ducked like everybody else."

"No, Harry, you covered the body. I saw it. You shielded Snow White over there like she was still alive or something."

Bosch didn't respond. He lifted the top tray out of the toolbox and reached in for the Polaroid camera. He noted that they only had two more packs of film left. Sixteen shots plus whatever was left in the camera. Maybe twenty shots total, and they had this scene and the one waiting on MLK. It was not enough. His frustration was peaking.

"What was that about, Harry?" Edgar persisted.

Bosch finally lost it and barked at his partner.

"I don't know! Okay? I don't know. So let's just go to work now and try to do something for her so maybe, just maybe, somebody sometime will be able to make a case."

His outburst had drawn the attention of most the guardsmen in the alley. Cosgrove, the one who had started the shooting earlier, stared hard at him, happy to pass the mantle of unwanted attention.

"Okay, Harry," Edgar said quietly. "Let's go to work. We do what we can. Fifteen minutes and then we're on to the next one."

Bosch nodded as he looked down at the dead woman. Fifteen minutes, he thought. He was resigned. He knew the case was lost before it had even started.

"I'm sorry," he whispered.